ONE CHANCE

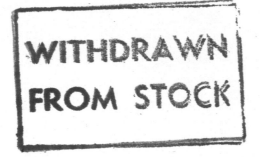
www.**transworldbooks**.co.uk

www.transworldireland.ie

Also by Emily Gillmor Murphy

YOU AND I

ONE CHANCE

Emily Gillmor Murphy

TRANSWORLD IRELAND

TRANSWORLD IRELAND
an imprint of The Random House Group Limited
20 Vauxhall Bridge Road, London SW1V 2SA
www.transworldbooks.co.uk

First published in 2014 by Transworld Ireland,
a division of Transworld Publishers

A CIP catalogue record for this book
is available from the British Library.

ISBN 9781848271449

Addresses for Random House Group Ltd companies outside the UK
can be found at: www.randomhouse.co.uk
The Random House Group Ltd Reg. No. 954009

The Random House Group Limited supports the Forest Stewardship Council® (FSC®), the
leading international forest-certification organisation. Our books carrying the FSC label are
printed on FSC®-certified paper. FSC is the only forest-certification scheme supported by the
leading environmental organisations, including Greenpeace. Our paper procurement policy can be
found at www.randomhouse.co.uk/environment

Typeset in 12.5/15pt Bembo by Falcon Oast Graphic Art Ltd.
Printed and bound in Great Britain by
CPI Group (UK) Ltd, Croydon, CR0 4YY

2 4 6 8 10 9 7 5 3 1

For the ones who have experienced all the excitement, thrills, spills and heartbreak.

For the ones who live and breathe the sport.

For the winners and risk takers.

For the riders, this one is for you.

1

Introducing Matthew

SOME PEOPLE CALL IT AN ADDICTION, OTHERS AN ADRENALINE rush – the feeling of absolute terror when you approach that first fence. Pure concentration: every movement, every decision, it all matters. It seems so simple, doesn't it? Just clear the fence. But there is so much more to it than that: pace, stride, scope, height, length and, most importantly, luck. There is one way to do it right and a million ways to do it wrong. So why do I do it? Because there are those times you do it right, those times you make those turns, when you get the perfect stride, and you win. Once you've experienced that feeling, even if it's only once, you'll spend the rest of your life trying to achieve it again.

The bangs, the bruises, the hits, the falls . . . if you think about it logically, it's madness. The sport is full of cheaters – dogs – people who would walk all over you just to get what they want. Money? Money doesn't exist in showjumping. You work your whole life just to fund this insanity, and by the end of it you have no profit to show. Innocence will only get you in trouble, and that's what I was, innocent. How stupid I was, thinking I had a clue when I got into this world! For months I've been battered about, and with no reward. So why do I keep doing it? Pride? Stubbornness? Fear? Probably a little of each, but there's more to it than that. I've never felt anything like the exhilaration I feel when I'm on a horse. It's powerful and terrifying: nothing can compare to it. Well, nothing until I met her.

'There's no way, Matt! There is absolutely no way you're leaving school. You're seventeen, for God's sake!' I'd expected him to be angry, stubborn even. But I hadn't expected such an explosion. I never argue with my father; his manner and broad build have always intimidated me. My whole life, there's been no doubt who's in charge in this house. My dad is a kind person, but no one crosses him, no one dares argue with him, not even my mother – until now. A huge part of me wants to back down, to stay silent and do as my father tells me, as I have always done. But I can't. I can't forget this; I can't go back to school and work for something that I know I don't want. I want to leave the only home I have ever known; I want to be a showjumper. I've never wanted anything more. And I'm going to fight for it with every breath I've got.

'Dad?' I plead, but his face stays stern and unemotional. I look to my mum for help, but she lowers her head, avoiding my gaze. She doesn't want me to go either, and even if she did she would never disagree with Dad.

'Do you not understand that this is pure madness?' He says it slowly, as if I'm stupid. 'You'll end up shovelling shit for the rest of your life . . . You know that?'

'I won't!' I argue, but my voice is quiet and full of doubt. I'm terrified to leave. Terrified that I'll fail. Dad buries his face in his hands.

'Explain to me once more what you would be doing?' He mumbles this through his hands. I've explained it to him several times, but he doesn't seem able to process anything I'm saying.

'Shane Walker, the professional showjumper, has offered me a job as a working rider and groom. I would live on his yard and work full time.' I try not to sound patronizing, but I'm frustrated that he just won't understand.

'And what would you be doing as a *working rider*?' His sarcasm stings more than I expect it to.

'Well, I'll start off working as Shane's groom, and then he said I may be able to start competing with some of his young horses after a while . . .' Dad scoffs before I've even finished talking.

'And you would live at the yard?'

'Yes, with the other grooms . . .' I've never lived away from home before, but I think it's about time that I learn to take care of myself.

'So you're giving up school to maybe do a job that you think you want to do?'

I feel the anger building up in me. He's not taking me seriously. I know I'm only seventeen, I know it's a big risk, but this is what I want to do. It's all I've ever wanted to do, right since I sat on my first pony six years ago.

The world of competitive showjumping isn't where I expected to end up. I'd never thought much of horses as a kid, I always believed that horse riders were little girls who liked to prance around on their pretty little ponies and that no boy with any self-respect would be seen dead on a horse. I grew up on a farm in Wicklow so I always knew how to handle animals. Mostly cows and sheep, but I enjoyed working outside alongside my dad. My first experience of showjumping wasn't until I was eleven. My dad and I were attending the local agricultural show; we'd brought some of the better-looking cattle in the hopes of selling them for a decent profit.

It was obvious that this particular year something was happening – for years we'd attended this agricultural show, and

I'd never seen such large crowds or such excitement among the locals. It was a sunny day, which always attracted people, but not this many.

'What's going on, Dad? Where have all these people come from?' He was tying the cows to the posts. They would be examined and scored by the officials later on in the day. The higher the score, the more they were worth.

'It's the first time they've got permission to hold a Grand Prix.'

'What's a Grand Prix?' I asked. What was so great about it that it'd cause such an increase in the crowd?

'It's a showjumping competition,' he answered, attaching the last of the cattle. They were very tame creatures, and it didn't take much to keep them from getting free.

'All that for a showjumping competition?' I was shocked; I'd always found showjumping very dull. At least with racing or cross-country there was a bit of excitement, a bit of danger. In showjumping, as far as I could see, all the rider did was sit there trying to look good.

'These are serious riders, Matt,' Dad said, smiling at me. 'We'll go watch it later. Trust me, it's a lot more exciting than you'd think.' I wasn't convinced.

Dad sold four out of the five cows he'd brought with him that day. He had an offer for the fifth but thought the buyer would offer more if he held out. This had been by far Dad's best year; the Grand Prix and the big crowd seemed to have encouraged people to dig deeper into their pockets.

'She's still young yet, that cow. Even if that man doesn't get back to me, she will make a nice sell next year.' I nodded in agreement as I loaded her back into the empty trailer.

'Your mum and sister will be thrilled, Matt. We've made a nice little profit today.'

At that moment a loud voice broke out across the speakers that were scattered across the various fields.

'Announcement to all riders: the Grand Prix will begin in ten minutes!'

'Ah, perfect timing.' Dad cheered, clapping his hands together. 'Come on, we'll make our way over. I think they're holding it in the far field.'

'But it's not even starting for another ten minutes,' I moan. My stomach was grumbling, and the thought of Mum's stew was making me want to go home.

'We'll watch the warm-up. Some of these horses are amazing!'

Annoyed and hungry, I followed him.

The far field was a lot flatter than the field we'd been in. It was usually used for parking but, today, there were white posts and rails cordoning off two arenas. The one on my left was filled with brightly coloured fences; the poles and wings looked freshly painted and varnished. There must have been at least twenty fences. The poles were built to nearly the top of the wings. They must put the fences down when the competition starts, I think to myself. To my right there was a smaller arena, only two fences in the middle, and at least a dozen horses cantering in circles.

There are lots of people surrounding both arenas. Dad and I make our way to the warm-up, which is in the arena on my right. I've never seen horses like these before. First of all, they're a lot larger than any of the ponies the girls in my class ride, and secondly, I've never seen animals so perfectly groomed. Their coats gleam in the sun, their tails and legs are beautifully trimmed and their manes tied in plaits so small I don't know how the grooms managed it. The horses canter at a slow, bouncy pace, their heads curved towards their chests, nose in, froth gathering at their mouths.

'What are those people in the middle doing, Dad?'

'They're the grooms, they're helping the riders warm up.'

'Why?'

'See those two fences in the warm-up? Well, that's all they get to practise on, and the grooms have to build the fences up to whatever the rider needs. Also, they help with adjusting the tack on the horse and give the rider anything they might want.'

'Do the grooms give the riders advice?' I ask, watching one build a parallel that looks impossibly high to me.

'I doubt it. The grooms tend to work for the riders. It would be like telling your boss how to do his job.'

'Why on earth would you want to be a groom then?'

'When you really love something, you'll do anything to be a part of it,' he replies.

I didn't understand what Dad meant back then. To me, it looked like being a groom was basically being someone's servant.

That was the turning point, though. I remember I saw a grey horse circling towards the huge parallel the groom had just built. He came into the fence at the same pace all the other riders were doing at the sides. There's no way the horse can jump from such a slow speed, I think, and, to make things worse, his head is still down. How is he supposed to see this gigantic fence? He's only a couple of strides away from it! Why is he not pulling up? Surely that fence is way too high to clear?

I get ready for the crash that is undoubtedly coming. I know I should probably look away, but I can't help staring. But there is no crash, no last-minute pulling up by the rider. The horse lifts its head on the last stride and balloons over the fence, clearing it by what seems like miles. He lands at the same speed he approached the fence and canters away, horse and rider unfazed.

'Dad! Oh my God! Dad! Did you see that?' I'm pulling at his sleeve, praying that he hasn't missed it. 'That horse was unreal!'

'Told you it's pretty cool.' After that, I can't take my eyes away from the horses. One after another, they approach the humongous fences and clear them with ease.

The warm-up is over. 'Come on, Matt,' says Dad. 'The competition is starting.'

Those ten minutes feel like seconds. I've been so transfixed by the horses that I haven't even noticed that all the crowds have moved to the other arena. Dad and I make our way over. It's packed. I manage to push myself into a small gap between two older men, who don't look happy about being shoved to the side. My dad is a tall man, so he stays behind the crowd and watches from there. The grey horse I saw jump earlier canters into the ring.

'We now have our first competitor, Michael O'Doherty, riding the ten-year-old Irish-bred mare Rosa. Michael is fifteen, making him our youngest competitor today.' I haven't looked at the rider until now, but as soon as I see his young, boyish face, there's no doubt about his age.

Michael canters into the first fence at the same mesmerizingly slow pace as in the warm-up, and clears easily. Second fence – clear; third, fourth, fifth, sixth, seventh, eighth, ninth, tenth, eleventh, twelfth, thirteenth – all clear; parallels, straights, doubles, trebles – all clear. Nothing seems to faze this pair; the rider turns his horse towards the last fence, a red brick wall that is larger than any other fence in the arena. His approach looks like perfection. He may have the face of a young boy, but the look of determination and concentration on it makes him seem far older. He reaches his final stride and for half a second the horse looks as if it's going to hesitate. Then it's so quick I don't quite believe it's happening. The horse clears the last fence, and across the PA system a clear round is announced. Michael's face relaxes and he drops the reins to give the horse a pat on the neck.

'He was very lucky, that young lad was, on that last fence,' says one of the older men standing next to me.

'Very lucky indeed. That horse definitely had second thoughts about that wall,' replies the other. I watch the rest of the competition with utter fascination. I'm amazed at how important every little action is and how easily it can cause you a stop or a knock. And I can't get over the horses.

For the next few weeks I talk of nothing but showjumping, to the point where my whole family is sick of listening to me. I research it on the Internet, in books, newspapers. I begin following the international circuit. I know all the top showjumpers in the world and what horses they ride, where they compete and what they've won. I keep my new obsession quiet at school. I was afraid I'd be teased if they knew I was into horses, but, with my family, I could talk of nothing else. My twelfth birthday began to loom, and I begged and begged for a horse of my own.

'It's a huge responsibility, Matt,' Mum would say, 'and your father and I would end up taking care of it. Which neither of us has the time to do.'

'I swear, Mum! I swear I'd take care of it myself. You and Dad won't have to do anything.'

'What about when you're in school?'

'I'll make time, I promise.'

'I don't know,' she'd reply, unconvinced. Luckily, my dad was not as negative and, on my twelfth birthday I woke up to my little sister screaming in my ear, 'Come outside! Come outside! You have to see!'

In front of us stands a small, bay, hairy pony. It can't be

bigger than thirteen hands and it has a mane and tail that look completely unmanageable. I don't care. I finally have what I've wanted for months now. My parents bought him at the local horse sales; he's only four and has been sat on just a couple of times. Mum has an old bridle and saddle from when she was young and she gives it to me. The leather is old and hard and needs a good oiling – my hands are stained black for the next few weeks. The following day, I attempt to sit on the pony for the first time. My sister has named him Bowie. I have only ridden ponies at riding schools, under strict supervision and instruction: doing this on my own is a mystery to me. Mum helps me fit the tack to the small pony and then gives me a leg-up.

'Sit still and get your balance.'

I do as she tells me, adjusting my stirrups until they feel comfortable. 'Now squeeze your legs gently against his sides.' Mum was the only one in the family with riding experience, and she'd decided that I needed to be taught the basics before anything else. I'd rather have been left to my own doing, but I wasn't going to argue with her now that I'd got what I wanted.

Bowie doesn't even react, he merely flicks an ear at me as if to say, Go away!

'Try again,' says Mum.

This time I squeeze as hard as I can. Bowie takes a couple of steps forward, but as soon as I relax my legs he comes to a halt.

'You need to have constant pressure on his sides. Your legs are too loose.'

I try again, gripping with all my strength. Bowie begins to trot and I feel myself bouncing around on the saddle.

'Rise with him!' Mum calls, but I have no idea what she means. I just keep bouncing around uncomfortably with no balance.

Bowie comes to a sudden halt; he has seen a cow in the opposite field and starts to snort loudly in fear. I lose my seat and it takes me a minute to get myself together.

'Make him walk forward!' I squeeze as hard as I can, but it's no good: Bowie is having none of it.

'Just give him a kick!' my sister shouts. She's sitting on the fence, a spectator to my humiliation.

I dig my heels into the pony's belly, but still he doesn't move.

'Ask again.'

'I am!' I shout back at Mum, getting frustrated. I take my legs away from the side of the pony and kick him as hard as I can. Bowie shoots forward at a full canter. My body is leaning backwards and my legs are swaying uncontrollably from side to side. I try to pull him up but I've lost my reins and I'm not able to gather them up again. Mum is shouting something, but I can't make out what she is saying. Bowie is charging at full pace towards the iron gate. I panic that he's going to try to jump it.

We're only one stride away from it now, and I lean back, preparing myself for the sudden leap. When Bowie reaches the base of the gate he comes to an abrupt halt and I feel myself being flung forward. I fall to the ground as he drops his head in front of me. I flip over and land on my bum, the grass beneath feeling like concrete.

Bowie has trotted a couple of feet away and has his head down, eating away at grass happily, as if the last few seconds didn't happen. I can hear my little sister laughing as I stand up, rubbing my sore bum.

Mum looks at me sympathetically. She's already caught Bowie and is holding him still for me.

'Are you OK?' she asks. I can tell she is trying not to laugh too.

'Fine,' I mumble, trying to ignore my sister's chuckles.

'Shall we try again?' she says, gesturing towards Bowie. I could swear the pony looks almost proud of itself.

'Yeah,' I say. 'Let's try again.'

Looking back, Bowie was the best pony I could have had for my first horse. He was cheeky and clever, and he threw me off constantly. He'd stop at fences all the time and take off with me down the fields. He was a nightmare to handle as well; it was months before I was able to tack him up without my mother's help. He was also difficult to catch in the field – sometimes I would be out there until it was pitch black before I could get him to come in. It took weeks for us to figure out it was him that was opening all the cow stalls at night and setting the animals free across the farm. My parents had blamed me, saying I must have not been closing them properly at the end of the day. It wasn't until Dad saw Bowie do it with his own eyes that he realized the pony was the true culprit. We triple-bolted Bowie's door after that, and it seemed to keep him from escaping.

But even with all his flaws and cheeky tricks, Bowie was a brilliant pony. Yes, he was wilder and cheekier than your average first-time pony, but he was also braver and bolder. My weekends soon became packed with local jumping competitions; Mum would take us to them. There would be days when Bowie was the star of the show, winning every competition by miles, and then there were others when he would dump me at the first fence. That was just the way he was.

After three years of thrills and spills my legs became so long my feet went way past Bowie's stomach and I unwillingly handed him down to my eager little sister. I spent the next few months riding various different ponies; I had established a name for myself as being tough and strong. Women asked my mother would I be willing to ride their daughters' ponies, ones who had started to behave badly. I was more than happy to oblige. I often found these ponies had just been spoilt rotten, and after a couple of firm words and hard kicks they would behave perfectly.

My parents didn't offer to buy me another horse. I knew why. Now, two years later, summer was wrapping up and, even though I had another year of school left, I really didn't want to go back, and they could tell.

'You can't force me to go back to school,' I say, finally taking a stand. My dad just stares at me; I can see surprise emerging on his face. I never disagree with him.

'I'm still your legal guardian, Matt. I *can* force you if I have to,' he replies, with menace in his voice.

'Fine, force me then!' I say, raising my voice at my father for the first time ever. 'I'll skip school, purposely fail exams, try to get myself expelled. I'll fight you every day until the second I turn eighteen, when I can finally leave and do what I want. And I swear to you, another year of school and arguing with you is not going to change my mind. It's only going to make me more determined.' I know if I show any sort of weakness, any sort of doubt, he'll never let me go.

Dad seems to weigh up what I'm saying. He's clearly torn and unable to handle anyone arguing with him. I know he doesn't want another year of this. I don't know if I could stick to my threat, but I need him to believe that I will. He groans.

'How did you even get in contact with Shane in the first place?' he asks, changing tack.

'Mum gave me his number,' I say cautiously. I hate involving Mum – she can't handle conflict, especially with my father – but I have to tell him the truth if he's ever going to trust me on this. He jerks his head towards her; she's been sitting in the corner quietly the whole time. Her eyes widen. I wish I hadn't said anything now.

'I knew him when I jumped ponies as a kid.' She scrambles over her words, trying to explain herself. 'I never thought Shane would actually offer Matt a job . . .' She practically whispers the last bit. In truth, it's pure luck that Shane has hired me. In my interview, he admitted that three people have quit on him in the last few months and he's desperate for someone to work for him full-time. He told me from the beginning that he doesn't want part-time workers. He only wants people who are fully committed. I know my mum feels guilty; she feels as if this whole argument is her fault. Dad's face relaxes as he looks at her. He has a soft spot when it comes to my mother and my sister. He can never stay mad at either of them for long. It's different with me. He never holds back with me.

'Do you really want this job that much?' he asks, turning towards me. There's a hint of sadness in his voice.

'Yes!' He's going to agree, I think. He's going to let me do it. He stays silent for a long time and the tension between us builds and builds until I feel I can't bear it any more.

'Fine,' he finally mumbles. I nearly don't believe he's said it.

'Thank you,' I whisper, too shocked to say anything else.

I leave the room quickly, before Dad can change his mind. My heart is going a million miles a minute. I took on Dad and I won! I never believed I'd be able to do that. Then the reality hits me like a ton of bricks. I'm not going back to school. I'm moving and I'm going to work. I'm going to work for the thing I want most in the world.

I don't go up to my room straight away. Instead I stay outside the kitchen door and listen to what my parents are saying.

'What are you doing?' I hear Mum say. 'I thought you wanted him to finish school.'

'Of course I do,' Dad replies. He sounds exhausted. 'But

there's no point in forcing him. Let him shovel shit for a couple of months – he'll realize what hard work it is, and, I guarantee you, he'll go back to school willingly.' He's trying to comfort her, but even I can hear the uncertainty in his voice.

After a moment or two she replies. Her voice sounds scared. She simply says, 'I hope you're right.'

I call Shane the next morning to tell him that I want the job. He explains to me what I'll be doing – and it's a lot! I'm to get up at seven every day, feed the thirty horses stabled on the grounds, some his own and some liveries. Then they need throwing out in specific fields. When we had Bowie we just threw him out with anything – sheep, cattle, other horses – and he was always fine. Shane explains that the horses on his grounds are so valuable, he can't afford to have them fighting or injuring each other. If I don't stick to his 'throwing-out schedule' absolutely, I'll be out myself.

It was obvious that, from the moment I started working for Shane, the horses would always be much more valuable to him than I was. And, I hate to admit it, but my father would be right about the shovelling-shit part. Those thirty stables would need to be cleaned every day, and Shane makes it very clear that that responsibility will fall to me. On the phone he explains that cleaning stables will take me till about lunchtime. My afternoons will vary from day to day: some days I'll be cleaning tack and horses and preparing for upcoming shows; others it'll be hard labour, repairing fences and painting poles. On the odd afternoon I have free Shane's promised to school me on some of his horses. I can't wait for that. I've watched his career for so long, to get the opportunity to learn from him is like gold.

Shane started off a simple country boy like myself. At fifteen he quit school and started working for international showjumper Tony Mullins. Slowly he made his way up the grades, buying young, untalented horses for pennies and getting the most he could physically get out of them. By the time he hit his mid-twenties he had a name for being tough and unbelievably determined. He was often handed difficult and troublesome horses, which had been given up on by other riders. It was one of those difficult horses that made his name – FireCracker.

FireCracker was a horse that had been handed around end-lessly; numerous professionals had given up on him, saying that he was unmanageable and that the horse had no future. FireCracker's owners were desperate when they went to Shane. Nobody knew what a perfect partnership it would become. Shane moved up the international rankings quickly with the horse, surprising everyone by eventually winning International Horse of the Year with him.

After three years of unblemished success FireCracker was sold to someone in America. Rumour is that Shane sold him for a million, but no one knows for sure. FireCracker made Shane's career and, after he was sold, Shane had a long list of owners who wanted him to ride their horses, and he's stayed in the top-ten world rankings ever since.

I don't admire Shane just for his success, but also for how he achieved it. Most of the international riders have a lot of money behind them; some of them belong to some of the richest families in the world. Shane never had that: he worked his way to the top through blood, sweat and tears. He showed everyone that it *can* be done.

He's so cool and collected on the phone – unlike me: I can't hide the glee in my voice.

'Can you start the day after tomorrow?' he says abruptly.

'OK . . .' I answer, surprised at how quickly it's all happening.

'Great,' he says, and hangs up.

Mum begins to cry when I tell her I'm leaving the next day. Dad doesn't say anything, just leaves the room silently. I can't handle Mum crying. I never know what I should say or do. I pat her on the back awkwardly, hoping that I'm providing some sort of comfort. It doesn't help that Ann is crying too, but I think that has more to do with the fact that Mum is upset. Ann is eleven at this stage and, even though she understands that I'm leaving school and moving out, she doesn't get why it's such a big deal.

'You will still come home for dinner sometimes?' Mum hiccups, tears still falling from her eyes.

'Of course.' I try to reassure her, but it doesn't seem to work. Then I get frustrated. 'For God's sake, Mum, it's not like I'm dying . . .' I blurt out. After that I leave the room pretty quickly, before Dad comes back inside and yells at me for upsetting her.

The next day, I take the bus to Shane's yard. It's not far at all, just outside of Dublin – less than an hour from my family home in Wicklow. I didn't dare ask Dad for a lift, and I can't handle sitting in the car with my mum when she's all emotional. I don't want either of them dampening my excitement.

It's late afternoon by the time I arrive at Shane's. He'd advised me to come the night before I began work if I could, since I'd be starting so early. My bag isn't very heavy: I don't own many clothes and I only brought things I could work in. I know I'll be doing a lot of dirty, physical work here. There are loads of people about, but no one bothers to stop and say hello, no one even gives me a second glance. Some are young like me, and are carrying buckets and forks, so they must work here. The other people are slightly older and dressed a bit more smartly. I try not to stare, but I'm curious who they are. Friends of Shane? Did they get lessons off him? Or perhaps these are the people who keep their horses in livery here.

I walk slowly towards the office; I know where it is, because it's where he interviewed me. I take my time, wanting to absorb everything around me. Most of the sheds are either a dark green or grey; there's not much colour at all, except for the numerous green paddocks. There are horses everywhere I look – in the stables, out in the fields, being led or ridden directly in front of me. My father is a farmer, so I'm used to the smell of animals, but the smell here is not the same – the cows and sheep at our farm stink. There's no bad smell here. It's difficult to describe, but there's a sense of warmth and fun to this yard. When I finally reach Shane's door, I knock on it gingerly.

'Come in!' he shouts from inside. 'Matt!' he exclaims as soon as he sees me. There's someone standing next to him and, when I walk in, he gives me a cheeky grin.

'So this is the new meat?' the stranger says eagerly.

'Stop teasing him,' Shane says sternly and the stranger goes quiet. He's still grinning at me, though, and I feel a bit self-conscious. 'This is Nick, Matt. You'll learn to ignore his silly comments. I know I have.'

Nick is tall and strongly built, though when you look at his face properly you can see that he's still young. I would guess he's in his late teens, early twenties. It reassures me a bit to know that he can't be that much older than me. 'Nick is your room-mate, and he'll be the one to step you through everything tomorrow. He'll also be the one guiding you for the first few weeks, but I suggest you learn quickly. I don't like slackers in my yard. There's a lot to be done here and I don't need someone who can't keep up.'

Shane stares at me, waiting for an answer. I nod, letting him know that I understand.

'Good,' he continues, his face softening a little. 'Nick will show you where you'll be living.' He strides out of the office and I realize this is his way of saying that the conversation is over.

I turn back towards Nick and smile. 'Hi!' I say, to break the silence.

'Hello there.' Nick exudes confidence, and I sense he's enjoying trying to make me feel awkward.

'Have you worked here long?' I try.

'Nearly four years . . .'

'Wow! You must like it here then?' He's done it: that *was* awkward. He shrugs his shoulders, unwilling to give anything away. 'So . . . can you show me where I'll be staying?'

'Of course,' he replies brightly. He walks quickly towards the door and I grab my bag smartly and follow him. Nick is much taller than me and I nearly need to do two steps to match one of his big strides. We're both silent, and I don't stop until a flash of grey catches my eye. I look to my left and see a beautiful grey mare sticking her head out of a stable door. I don't know if Nick has seen me pause, but I make my way over to the stable anyway.

'Hello there,' I whisper as the mare gently nips at my pockets, looking for treats. It's a warm evening and the horse has no rug on. I inspect her carefully. I can't get over how strong and beautiful she is. Nothing I've ever ridden even compares to her. Her body is like a sculpture, and her mane, tail and face are trimmed and groomed perfectly. I realize now that every horse I've ridden in the past was like a van or a pickup truck. This mare standing in front of me is a Ferrari – beautiful, powerful and fast.

'Good eye . . .' Nick's voice makes me jump slightly, but I smile.

'She's stunning,' I say, patting the mare's grey face.

'She is indeed. She's Shane's main Grand Prix horse. He even did a few Nation Cups on her . . . She's a bit of a favourite in this yard.' I don't take my eyes off the mare and Nick lets me admire her in silence for a while.

After a while he taps me hard on the back, breaking my trance. 'You won't find your average country cob here,' he says when I turn to look at him. 'These horses' – he gestures to the stables around us – 'they're the real deal.'

I can't read Nick at all. I don't know whether he's boasting to intimidate me, or whether he loves the horses as much as I do. I feel a rush of adrenaline and excitement. All that matters is that I'm finally where I'm supposed to be.

2

Introducing Elizabeth

I SHUT MY EYES, FEELING MY BODY LIFT OFF THE GROUND. MY ears pop and the knots in my stomach tighten, to the point where I'm worried I'm going to be sick. I hear voices around me, but I can't ignore the sound of my heart beating louder and louder every second. I grip my hand with my other one, and it almost hurts I'm squeezing so hard, but I'm too afraid to let go.

I don't hear her at first. I think she's just another passenger chattering away calmly, not knowing the fear I'm feeling at the moment. But then she speaks again, louder and clearer, and I'm forced to open my eyes.

'I was just wondering, are you all right, miss?' An air hostess stands in front of me. Her bleached-blonde hair is tied back in a tight bun and, though her make-up is harsh and heavy, there's a certain kindness to her face.

'Oh . . . I'm fine,' I choke out, but she doesn't seem convinced.

'Are you a nervous flyer?'

'A bit,' I admit, trying to relax my grip on my hand. The air hostess smiles before leaning in a little closer.

'What's your name?' she asks, giving my shoulder a gentle squeeze.

'Elizabeth,' I reply.

'Would you like a drink, darling? Just to help you relax.' I'm dying to say yes – I know nothing would cure me better than a double vodka and tonic right now – but I can't, not today. Today, I need to be alert and prepared.

'I'm fine, thank you,' I reassure her, and force myself to smile. She gives me a polite nod before going to check on the other passengers.

As soon as she's out of sight I reach into my handbag and take out a bottle of Rescue Remedy. I spray it into my mouth numerous times before slipping it into my pocket. I almost wish I could down the whole bottle, but I would never forgive myself if it slowed my reactions. I take a few deep breaths as the plane continues its ascent, constantly telling myself to relax. I know my fear of flying is all in my head, and the unusual part of it is that I'm not afraid of the flying part, I'm not scared of plummeting to the earth and my death, like any normal person who is afraid of flying would be. I'm afraid of the anxiety I know I'll feel as soon as I step on a plane. My heart begins to hammer and sometimes I make myself ill. I tell myself it's mind over matter. If I believe the Rescue Remedy will calm me down, then it will. Some days this method works; others it doesn't, and I live in fear of those days. Today is one of those lucky days, and I feel those knots in my stomach loosen as the plane levels out. I could practically giggle with happiness, feeling my whole body relax a little more. The anxiety is still there, but it's manageable, it won't engulf me completely like it has done before.

I take out my iPhone and reread the email I've already looked at hundred times:

Mrs O'Brien,

I have just discovered that the chestnut mare, Wildfire, is for sale. This news is not public knowledge yet and we would want to get in there first if possible.

Have Elizabeth meet me at Hickstead showground, UK, tomorrow midday. I will be there to meet her.

Best,

Edward Dawson

My mother received this email at ten o'clock last night, much to her disgust. I can still hear her shrill voice as I think back on it now.

'Who dares contact someone so late and then demand that we meet him the next day *in a different country*! I don't know why you are so desperate to have him find you a horse, Elizabeth. The man *clearly* has no manners.'

I'd ignored my mother's rants, though, and booked the earliest flight out of Dublin. I'd tried to explain to her on numerous occasions who Edward Dawson was, but her lack of interest in the international showjumping world always prevails. I gave up caring about my mother's opinion of my dreams long ago. I want to be a world-class showjumper and, though she may not approve of it, she continues to pay the bills and, though I know I should be grateful for that, it's hard to be grateful to someone who disapproves of everything you do.

My mother has always found it strange that we've never met Edward before. They have talked over the phone and been in contact by email, but I know that Edward's life is full of travelling and competing and for him to turn up today must mean that this horse is really something special. Since I started jumping ponies as a kid I've always wondered what it would be like to meet Edward Dawson. He won a gold medal back in the 2000 Olympics, and I've been obsessively following his career ever since. Ireland has always punched above its weight when it comes to the showjumping circuit, and a lot of that is due to Edward. He personifies ambition, drive and success. I want his talent, I want his ability, I want to jump alongside him – but, most importantly, one day I want to beat him. If nothing else, I know I have the competitive side I need to be a great show-jumper. When I watch the best competitors in the world on TV, I don't imagine that I'm as good as them, I imagine that I'm better. It may sound overly confident, but if I'm going to make it in this sport, I need that confidence.

The sound of the pilot's voice across the intercom wakes me from my fantasies and I'm thrilled but nervous to realize that we're beginning our descent. When we land in the UK, I push and shove a little to get out of the plane. The air hostess from earlier gives me another nod. She must think I'm dashing out because I can't wait to get off the plane but, in reality, it's because I can't wait to meet Edward. I can feel the groupie coming out in me, and I'm worried I'll embarrass myself by collapsing into a fit of giggles when I finally do see him.

Hickstead showground is only a thirty-minute drive from Gatwick Airport. It's one of the things that convinced me to fly rather than taking the ferry; the port is hours away. Even though Hickstead is so close, I soon discover that no car-rental office is willing to consider renting a car out to an 18-year-old girl. After at least six pointless and frustrating conversations, I give up on the idea and go outside and take a taxi.

As it approaches Hickstead I wonder how I should act with Edward. Should I be quiet and passive and let him do all the talking? Or should I be outspoken and assertive? Try to convince him that I'm not just some silly girl whose parents have a lot of money? But what if I get it wrong? I'd feel humiliated, and it would look as if I don't belong in this world, and if I don't belong here, then I don't think I belong anywhere.

All too soon and not soon enough I'm there. I nearly gasp with shock when I see the taxi meter, and I root in my pockets and give the driver pretty much all the sterling I have. He barely looks at me.

I'm cursing myself for not bringing more cash, and then I see him. He's leaning casually against a wall in front of me, cigarette in one hand, phone in the other. He's even stronger- and fitter-looking than I expected. On TV, he always looks lean and fit, but seeing him in the flesh, muscular and tanned, it's clear TV does him no justice at all. He's not much taller than me, but I don't find this surprising, as I tower over most boys, with my long legs. He's wearing a blue polo shirt and black jodhpurs. I step closer, and he lifts his head.

'Elizabeth, I assume?' He'd been on his phone but puts it away and hits me with a boyish grin. His teeth are so white and his face so youthful I have to remind myself that this man is in his late thirties.

'Hi,' I say sheepishly. His eyes are so blue they match his shirt.

'I'm Edward Dawson,' he says, gripping my hand and looking me straight in the eye. I have to stop myself from exclaiming, *I know!* and remind myself to act like an adult and not a star-struck teenager with a massive crush.

'Nice to meet you,' I respond.

'Shall we go in? They're waiting for us.' He gets straight to the point. I nod, hoping that I'm not blushing, and follow him.

Hickstead is massive, and as we cross its perfectly manicured green fields, Edward tells me everything he knows about Wildfire.

'She's a ten-year-old American mare bred out of Wild Card and FireStarter. She's a small horse with a big attitude, definitely more suited to a female rider. Up until now, she's been ridden and owned by a woman named Maddie Orwell, and in the last year the combination managed to crack the top-fifty-riders world rankings. Maddie is an American but, luckily for us, she married an Englishman, so that's why she and the horse are based here . . .'

I nod along. Edward needs no encouragement from me; he's focused on this horse and nothing else. I'd researched Wildfire quickly myself last night, but nearly all of what Edward is saying is new to me.

'Maddie and Wildfire were seriously making a name for themselves this season, and it even looked as though she may be picked for the American Nations Cup team—'

'Why's she for sale then?' I ask.

'Well, she's not . . . officially,' Edward answers with a mischievous smile. He looks at me properly for the first time since we started walking.

'Maddie is not selling Wildfire by choice . . .' He stops walking and speaks in a much quieter voice. 'Maddie comes from the family who own the Anem Arms hotel chain . . . I don't suppose you watched the RTÉ news last night?'

'I did actually,' I answer, thrilled with myself for having turned it on while I was making dinner. 'They said it had announced bankruptcy.' Edward smiles at me and I want to squeal with delight.

'That they have, my girl . . . and that means Maddie no longer has the finance to keep Wildfire. In fact, Maddie can't even pay for her livery any more. The owner here is letting Wildfire be kept here out of kindness.' What Edward is saying hits me and I no longer feel the same excitement. I think of Maddie and how upsetting it must be for her to be forced to sell such an amazing horse. All this must be heartbreaking for her.

'Poor girl!' I exclaim, without really thinking. Edward loses his grin and frowns.

'You won't pity Maddie once you meet her. She's a right cow,' he says, and with that he starts walking again.

We've walked right across the equestrian centre to the far end, where there's a sand arena. There are two people in it, a young lad in dark jodhpurs and a tall, dark, stern-looking woman who can only be Maddie. The lad is adjusting tack on a bright chestnut horse – Wildfire. Her red coat shines in the spring sun and her muscular body looks toned and defined. Maddie has her arms crossed and her face in a scowl as Edward and I approach. She looks unfriendly and intimidating, but I remind myself that no one would be in a good mood if they were in her situation.

'Maddie, darling. How are you?' Edward exclaims as we reach her.

'Oh, shut up, Edward. I'm not in the mood for your crap today.'

I'm so taken aback by Maddie's reaction that I only just notice Edward giving me a knowing wink, as if to say, Told you!

'This is Elizabeth,' he continues, as if Maddie's outburst hasn't happened. 'She's the one interested in purchasing Wildfire.' I hold out my hand for Maddie to shake, but she doesn't even look at it.

'Let's get this over with,' she mutters, turning her back on me. I look at Edward for help and he gestures towards Wildfire.

'Go ahead, hop on up,' he says casually.

'Are you not riding her first?' I ask, practically in one breath.

'Why would I? She's not for me.' I stare at Wildfire nervously; I've never sat on a horse like her before. What if she throws me off? Edward said she has a 'big personality', and everyone in the horsey world knows that is code for 'difficult'.

'Oh, for God's sake, Edward. Why did you bother bringing this girl if she's too afraid to sit on the bloody horse? She's wasting all our fucking time.' I look at Maddie. She's practically sneering at me.

Silently, I put on my riding hat and walk over to Wildfire. She looks alert but not unsettled. The young lad holds out his hands and gives me a leg-up. Wildfire feels slight underneath me, and I like the fact that she's a little smaller; suddenly, I don't feel so intimidated by her. I take my time riding Wildfire on the flat; I walk, trot and canter her slowly, getting used to her movement and attitude. She's a sensitive horse and incredibly quick to react to anything I ask her.

'Are you going to jump a fence at all?' Maddie asks rudely, but instead of shying away from her, this time I hold her gaze, and that seems to keep her quiet, at least for a little while. The young groom puts out a small straight for me and Wildfire and I jump it with ease. He puts the fence up a small bit but Edward speaks up.

'Put that fence to a decent height, please.' I turn around, surprised at Edward's request. He smiles at me encouragingly and I decide it's best not to say anything. The fence is put up to near the top of the wings, and I stare at it, terrified. I pick up the pace of my canter and approach, but Wildfire spots the large fence as I round the corner and she begins to canter sideways, out of excitement. I can hear my old instructor shouting in my head: *Tighten your reins and kick her on!* But I don't do that; instead I loosen my hands and lean forward a little. I'm taken aback when Wildfire straightens and soars over the fence easily. I pat her encouragingly on the neck and the mare relaxes under me once again.

'That girl has good instincts, but she's still a very sloppy rider.'

I smile to myself, knowing it's as close to a compliment that I will get from Maddie.

'Good girl. I'll work with you if you work with me,' I whisper to Wildfire. I realize then that Wildfire is not a horse you can bully but she's a horse that will try her heart out for you if you help her.

Edward and Maddie are talking. Maddie looks even grumpier

than she did before, but Edward is beaming. Once more he gives me a wink, and this time I catch it full on. I ride over on Wildfire.

'So what do you think?' Edward asks.

'She's nice,' I say, knowing I can't show how excited I am.

'Nice?' Maddie scoffs. 'She's the best bloody horse *you'll* ever sit on, I can tell you that.' Her face mellows slightly as Wildfire sniffs in her pockets. She takes out a packet of Polo mints and gives her about four. The mare eats them up keenly, then Maddie's face returns to its scowl as Edward speaks again.

'I think Elizabeth and Wildfire are a good fit. What do you think?'

'The girl needs a lot of fucking training. My groom is more secure in the saddle than her, but . . . she could be a lot worse.' I can't help but feel a little smug at Maddie's words. 'What age are you, girl?' she asks, out of the blue.

'Twenty-two,' I lie, not wanting her to think that she can push me around, but it doesn't work.

'Fucking child!' is all she mutters.

'I'm glad you agree,' Edward continues, ignoring Maddie's rudeness. 'What kind of money were you hoping to get for her?'

'What kind of money are you offering?' I can see the determined business side come out in both Maddie and Edward, and I know a battle is coming.

'Elizabeth's family is prepared to pay 60,000 euro, which I think is a very fair price for this horse.'

'Fair, my arse!' Maddie bursts out. 'This is one of the best horses on the circuit.'

'She is, in your opinion. Personally, I think Wildfire is a very good horse with a lot of potential but she hasn't quite proven herself yet,' Edward explains calmly.

Maddie looks ready to explode.

'Hasn't proven herself? Bull! This horse has beaten everyone, including yourself, on numerous occasions.' Maddie's voice is getting shriller; she's almost screaming at Edward. Wildfire stands there, relaxed. Maybe she's used to these outbursts from her owner.

'She's never jumped on a Nations Cup team.'

Maddie flinches. It's obvious he's hit a sore spot.

'You know I would have been selected for the American team this year if . . . if I were in the position to keep her . . .' Her voice has gone quiet, but she looks so angry I wouldn't be surprised if she took a swing at Edward.

'I don't know that. Nobody could know that.' He shrugs, as if the two of them were just having a mild chat. They go silent for a moment. I have no idea what's going through Maddie's mind.

'I'd sell her for 100,000.' My heart sinks. My parents may be wealthy, but there's no way I could convince them to spend that much money on a horse.

'That's stupid money!' Edward exclaims. For the first time, he seems to lose his cool a little.

'That's what the Arabs will pay once they hear she's for sale.'

'And you'd sell that horse to them?' Edward asks judgementally. There are always horrible rumours about what happens to horses that are sold to the Middle East. It usually goes along the lines of: some wealthy sheikh purchases an expensive horse for his son, who, more than likely, has no riding ability. The son will either fall off or lose interest in the horse and then the sheikh will want the horse gone. He won't care where it goes, so long as it's no longer his problem. I don't know if these rumours are true, but so many of them circulate I have to believe some of them must be.

'The money is all I care about. After that, the horse is no longer my problem,' Maddie says and, with that, any sympathy I might have had left for her is gone. I'd attributed her rudeness to heartbreak up until that point, but now I can see her for the money-hungry monster she is. Even Edward seems a little startled by her answer. In that moment, I realize what I can do to get this horse.

'Seventy thousand,' I announce, knowing that I can convince my parents to buy Wildfire for that amount. Edward looks at me, confused, and Maddie scoffs at me.

'Don't be stupid, girl. I told you I'll get 100,000 off the Arabs.'

'Yeah? And how long will that take? A few weeks? Months, maybe?' She looks at me seriously for the first time and I know I have her hooked. 'You need money, and my family can have that 70,000 in your bank account by this afternoon. I guarantee no one else can offer you that.' I hold her stare for what feels like a lifetime. I try my best to keep my face calm, but my heart is going like the clappers. I can't read Maddie's facial expression, and when she does open her mouth I have no idea what she is going to say.

'Fine, you have that money to me this afternoon, and Wildfire is yours.' I almost can't make sense of the words coming out of her mouth. It's not until Edward claps his hands together that I realize I'm buying this horse.

'Sounds like a deal,' he says brightly. Maddie grunts and stomps off.

Edward looks up at me from the ground and, once more, he's beaming.

'Well, Elizabeth, I must say that was some impressive negotiating.'

I blush. 'Thanks,' I mumble, unable to meet his striking blue eyes.

'When are you flying home?'

'Tomorrow morning,' I reply.

'Let me take you out to dinner to celebrate. Don't tell

Maddie I said this, but, my girl, you have just purchased one of the best horses in the world. Champagne needs to be popped!'

I let out a giggle when he says this, and it only seems to make him smile more. A moment ago I felt like a strong, independent woman but, now, with Edward beaming up at me, his boyish features alight, I feel heady, like a schoolgirl with a giant crush.

Edward deals with Maddie and my mother after that and, though I am surprised he doesn't include me at all in the logistics, I'm grateful I'm not the one who has to explain to my parents that they have to transfer 70,000 euro that evening. Instead, I go with Wildfire to her stable and get the groom to explain her daily routine to me. I'm surprised to find out that she is in no way a high-maintenance animal. She likes to be well fed and thrown out every day if possible; other than that, I was thrilled to be told, the horse has no vices.

Even though by this afternoon I would officially own Wildfire, it would be a few days before she could be transported to Ireland, by ferry. I didn't mind, because I knew I had a lot to sort out before her arrival. It seems that Edward and Maddie have been in the office for hours, but now they emerge. Maddie looks ready to kill someone while Edward looks as calm as ever.

'You ready for some champagne?' he asks as he guides me back to the entrance of the equestrian centre.

'Oh, I have nothing to wear to a restaurant!' The only things I packed in my rucksack were pyjamas and a pair of jeans I'd planned to travel home in.

'Screw it! We'll go to a fancy restaurant in our jodhpurs. We'll upset all the old fogeys. Come on, it'll be a laugh.' Edward's good mood is contagious, and I find I can't hold back the giggles now.

Edward strolls into the restaurant as if he owns it. Now that we're here, I find myself mortified to be in my jodhpurs, but Edward is rushing me to a table and I don't have a chance to say that I feel uncomfortable. The waiter arrives with the menus, but Edward doesn't even look at them.

'We'll have two lobsters and an extra large portion of fries for the middle of the table. And I would like a bottle of champagne, please. Whichever one is your best is fine, and when the first one is empty just open another one; there is no need to check with me. Thank you.' I'm a little irritated by the fact that he's ordered for me, but his phone buzzes before I get a chance to say anything. He picks it up immediately.

'Hello . . . yes . . . that's fine . . . Bye.' He hangs up. It's the fifth phone call he's received since we parted company with Maddie.

'Terribly sorry about that, Elizabeth, but my life never stops. I'm going to turn this damn phone off, though, because this is your night. And I want to enjoy this moment with you.' I watch him flick it off, and my irritation disappears. Anyway, I've always loved lobster and champagne.

'Thank you,' I say, genuinely delighted to be here with him.

Our champagne arrives quickly and, within two glasses, I find myself a little bit giddy and loose-lipped. My shyness from earlier is gone and Edward has me in hysterics, telling me scandalous stories about the showjumping community.

'Have you ever met Dan Copain, who jumped on the UK Nations Cup team in Dublin last year?' he asks.

'Briefly,' I admit. 'His marriage just broke up, didn't it?' I feel sorry for him even though I don't know him personally. It must have come over in my voice.

'Ah, don't be too sad about Dan's divorce. He isn't.' Edward fills his glass and then mine, and I find myself hoping that our lobster arrives soon.

'Didn't his wife run off with some groom?'

Edward nods. 'She did, but so did he. Their families pretty much forced them to get married. Neither of them wanted it really.' Edward shrugged, as if things like this happened every day.

'He ran off with some girl too?' I ask, surprised.

Edward begins to laugh. 'Well . . . he ran off with someone . . . It wasn't a girl . . .'

I can tell that he's enjoying my shock. My jaw has dropped. 'No!'

'Yep.'

'So he's gay?'

'As Christmas.' And, with that, the two of us break into hysterics.

I practically inhale my lobster when it arrives, and Edward is not too far behind me.

'This is delicious,' I say.

'It sure is.' There's a slight lull in the conversation. I see Edward frown ever so slightly before he speaks again.

'May I ask you something, Elizabeth?' His tone of voice has changed, and I'm worried for a second what he's going to ask. 'Why did you lie about your age today?'

'Who says I did?' I say, instantly going on the defensive.

Edward gives me a knowing smile. 'Elizabeth, do you really think I agreed to find you a horse without doing some research on you? Not only do I know what age you are, but I also know what competitions you have won, what horses and ponies you have competed on and every single instructor who has taught you up until now.'

I find myself blushing again and, for the first time all evening, I feel the age gap between us. 'Eighteen just sounds so young,' I reply, feeling humiliated.

'That's because it *is* young. But don't be wishing away your youth – you don't know how much money I'd give, just to be eighteen again.' I smile, appreciating Edward's kindness. 'At eighteen you can do anything.'

'I already know what I want to do,' I say – before I think. Edward looks at me quizzically. 'My dream is to be a professional showjumper,' I add, a little embarrassed that I'm talking about my dreams to somebody who's living his own, similar dream. I expect a patronizing smile but instead he looks at me properly for the first time.

'Elizabeth, you may be young, but you're ambitious, clever and talented, and now you have one serious horse to compete on. Your dream is incredibly close to becoming a reality and don't let anyone else tell you otherwise.' His eyes don't flicker for a moment, and I realize he's being honest. It's the first time someone has taken my dreams seriously, and I couldn't appreciate it more.

'Thank you,' I say, really meaning it. Edward smiles warmly at me and butterflies start in my stomach.

The evening flies by in a blur of food and champagne, and I'm surprised how disappointed I am when the bill arrives. Edward doesn't even acknowledge me when I say I'll pay half; he just shakes his head at me as if it was stupid to suggest it. He offers to walk me back to my hotel and I'm delighted to prolong my evening with him. As we get near, I try desperately to think of ways to keep the evening going. When we pass a pub, I try to convince him to come in with me.

'One drink on me? Come on, you have to let me thank you for the gorgeous dinner.' He laughs as I try to push him towards the bar.

'I'd love to, but I'd better not,' he says. 'An old married man like me needs his sleep.' His words sober me up instantly.

Married? But of course I *know* he's married. Everyone does. I saw it on television when he proposed to her at Olympia Horse Show four years ago; I looked at the pictures from their wedding in the *Irish Field* and thought what a beautiful bride she was. I've known all day and all night that he's married and yet, when he says it, it feels like a slap in the face. I've been flirting with a married man all evening. I got excited when he squeezed my arm; I had even let myself fantasize about what it would be like to kiss him. Did I forget he was married? Or did I just not care?

'You're right,' I say slowly. 'I'm pretty tired.'

Edward and I walk the rest of the way in silence.

'Thank you for dinner,' I say politely as I'm about to go in the door, but as I turn to leave he grips my arm and stops me.

'It was lovely to meet you, Elizabeth,' he whispers, and he leans in and kisses me on the cheek.

That night I dream of the international showjumping competitor Edward Dawson but, this time, it has nothing to do with showjumping.

The next few days are beyond hectic, what with organizing travel arrangements for Wildfire and dealing with my erratic mother. I had prayed that she wouldn't be around when I walked into the family home the following day. My head was pounding after all the champagne from the night with Edward, and I knew she would be in a bad mood the second I saw her after all the craziness yesterday. The one thing my mother despises most is being rushed.

'Hello?' I call out as I step into the white maze that is my home. My mother values cleanliness over everything else so the house looks like a showroom – beautiful, but not particularly friendly. My father is more a man of comfort, but he travels a lot and is rarely here, so he lets my mother do what she pleases with the house. There's silence as I walk through the door and, for a moment, I think I'll have some peace. But my hopes are dashed.

'Elizabeth, is that you?' I don't answer but instead make my way to her bedroom, where I know she will be, getting ready for another one of her 'do's'.

'Hi, Mum, how are you?' I ask, making myself comfortable on her king-sized bed as she sits at her mirror adjusting her already perfect make-up. She's a beautiful woman, there's no denying that. I remember when I was little I would watch her get ready every day, doing her face and putting on her beautiful clothes. I used to think that I couldn't wait to grow up and look like her. But I didn't grow up to look like her; I got her blonde hair and fair skin, but that's where the similarities end. My mother is petite and curvy with a sweet button nose; I'm tall and thin and my body shape is more similar to a boy's.

'I'm *hectic*, as always. I'm getting ready for a charity lunch as we speak, and then I'll be running to Bethany's dinner party at the Four Seasons this evening. Darling Bethany has gone to *such* effort, so you know I just *have* to attend.' My mother continues to inspect her face as she speaks, scrutinizing every detail of her flawless work.

'Sounds like fun . . . Will Dad be going with you?'

'Oh, who *knows*? You know that *father* of yours. He works on his own time. Too rude to tell anyone where he is or where he's going.'

I hate to admit it, but my mother's right. He's a diplomat, so he spends his time travelling everywhere and anywhere, but contacting him is near impossible. I often send him texts and emails, but it's a rarity to get a reply, and when I do it's always something like, 'Manic at the moment, call soon.' Which of course he never does. I learnt long ago to not be hurt by it. It's just the way things are. If I see him, it's by complete fluke – he never seems to tell my mother or me when he's returning home.

When I was younger, she always made excuses for him, saying that he was working so hard to provide for us. But I've noticed a certain bitterness form between the two of them in the last few years, and I know something has drastically changed. At this point I'm just waiting for one of them to announce that they want a divorce. Not that that much would change with a divorce; I'm used to being isolated from my parents' lives, and now that I have Wildfire I can learn to be completely independent from them.

'You and Edward Dawson seemed to get in some trouble yesterday,' my mother announces, out of nowhere. My stomach does flips, and I can feel myself going red. How can she know how I feel about Edward? *I'm* not even sure how I feel about him.

'What do you mean?' I ask, trying not to let my voice shake. My mother frowns at me.

'Getting me to transfer money like that in a matter of *hours*. I thought Edward must be *joking* when he called me.' Her eyes drill into me, but I still find myself relaxing, reassured by the fact that she doesn't know what's going on in my head.

'It's what we had to do to get the horse and, Mum, you have no idea how amazing Wildfire is. She's just perfect. I know I'm going to do so well on her.' I can feel the excitement building up in me at the thought of competing with Wildfire, but my mother doesn't look the least interested.

'I don't *care* what this horse is like, it was a *ridiculous* request, and, frankly, I'm shocked at your *rashness*, Elizabeth.' Since I was a child, my mother has had this amazing skill for making me feel small and insignificant.

'Well, thank you for doing it anyway,' I say, as quiet as a mouse.

'I didn't do anything,' she announces, standing up to put on her coat.

'What do you mean?' I ask, puzzled.

'Well, I told Edward that I couldn't *possibly* transfer that sort of money without contacting your father and I simply didn't have time to contact him right away. You know how *busy* I am, Elizabeth. Next thing I know, Edward contacts your father directly, without even consulting me first. The *rudeness* of it all appalled me. I don't even know how Edward managed to get *through* to your father — you know how *difficult* that man is to contact . . . Anyway, I don't know *what* Edward said to him, but within *hours* he had the money transferred. And it was all done without my permission . . . It's bloody *ridiculous*.'

I stare at my mother, shocked. It's obvious now why Edward was in Maddie's office so long.

'I'd better email Dad and say thanks,' I mumble, more to myself than to her.

'Do what you like . . . I'm washing my hands of the whole thing,' she scoffs.

She picks up her handbag and I think she's about to leave when she looks at me again.

'Have you looked at any of those college brochures I left on your bed?' she asks. My mother has always been more beautiful than me, but when it comes to business and intelligence, I inherited my father's brain. I've always found school easy but boring and maybe one of the reasons my mother and I just don't connect is because she resents the fact that I've always excelled there. She has relied on her looks her whole life, and perhaps she's realizing now that it's not quite enough. I think it's why she's pushing so hard for me to go to college. If I were closer to her, maybe I'd appreciate that she's just thinking of my future, she's worried about me putting all my eggs in one basket. But I'm not interested in the life she wants for me. I know what I want to do, who I want to be and that's it. I wish she'd understand but she doesn't, she never understands.

'A bit,' I lie. I have no interest in college. I sat my leaving cert only a few months ago and I have no intention of sitting another exam. If I'm going to be an international showjumper, I need to start now, and there's no way I'm letting college get in the way.

'Your headmaster told me that they expect high results from you and that you could pretty much do any course you want.' My mother is speaking more softly now, but I'm still getting annoyed. This is a conversation we have had a hundred times, and she knows how I feel about it.

'I've missed the CAO deadline. I couldn't start college this year even if I wanted to,' I say, looking at my feet.

'There's always *next* year . . .'

'I don't want to go to college,' I say sternly, but she just stares at me.

'Yes, well . . . We'll see about that.' I can tell by the tone of her voice that she doesn't want to talk about this any more – and neither do I. She leans in to give me a kiss on the cheek before she leaves.

'You should wear blush, Elizabeth. Then your face wouldn't look as flat,' she says as she walks out the door. I lower my head and stay silent. I wish I could say that her little comments don't annoy me any more, but every time she criticizes my appearance like that, I feel as if she's punching me in the stomach.

I'm ashamed to admit that my mind is filled with nothing but Edward the day Wildfire arrives in Ireland. I decide to keep her in Edward's yard. It seems like the obvious choice, since he helped me find the horse and his yard is based in Dublin. Also I want a reason to see him and talk to him again. Every time I catch myself fantasizing about him, I scold myself: he's married and, even if he weren't, he wouldn't be interested in a silly girl like me. I tell myself that it's nothing but a stupid crush; I only like him because of who he is and how successful he is. It will eventually go away, like every other celebrity crush I've had. Even so, I can't stop myself being a little hurt when he replies to my emails with curt responses. I only contact him to ask about the details of Wildfire's sale, but I still wish he would act the way he had in the UK. I keep reliving the look he gave me when I jumped that massive fence on Wildfire: he had looked so impressed. I *impressed* Edward Dawson!

Edward's yard can only be described as being like a factory. People come and go all the time, and everybody seems to be busy with something; nobody stops even for a moment. It's massive, with people absolutely everywhere, and as soon as I walk in the gates everyone seems to know my name. One of Edward's grooms, Patrick, shows me Wildfire's new stable, and it's only at that moment that the full extent of what is happening hits me and I really start to believe that my dream is coming true. Wildfire arrives exhausted and hungry. Some horses find travelling stressful but she seems to step out of the lorry fairly unfazed. Patrick helps me rug her and get her settled in. As we feed her and sort out her bed, I realize how gentle and sweet a horse she really is.

'Where's Edward?' I ask Patrick, trying not to sound too interested. I know he's a busy man but I had hoped he would be here when Wildfire arrived and that I'd get an opportunity to spend more time with him.

'In his office,' Patrick replies casually.

I go and knock on the door gingerly, afraid that I might be disturbing him.

'Come in,' he says, rather harshly, but then he sees it's me and gives me a dazzling smile that makes my knees shake.

'Hello, Elizabeth, how are you?'

'Hi,' I practically whisper back at him. 'I'm good – and you?' I can't believe I've forgotten how good-looking he is.

'I'm great, thank you. I trust that Wildfire has arrived safely?'

'Oh, yeah . . . she's perfect . . . Patrick helped me,' I stutter.

'Good.' An awkward silence follows and I realize that Edward is waiting for me to explain why I'm here.

'I wanted to ask you something . . .' I blurt out.

'Shoot away.'

'I was wondering . . . well, I was hoping that you might consider being my trainer?' Edward's smile flickers for a moment and he breaks his eye contact with me. I decide to keep going. 'I mean . . . I was just thinking it because you were the one to find Wildfire and . . . I'm keeping her here and everything, and you know . . . you know what I want to achieve . . .'

He looks back up at me at the last bit and I see a smile form for an instant in the corner of his mouth.

'I would love to train you, Elizabeth, but I don't think it would be the best idea . . . for either of us . . .' His words hurt more than I thought they would, and I feel suddenly very embarrassed.

'Oh, OK—' I start, wanting to leave, but Edward interrupts me.

'It's not because I don't think you're talented enough . . . I think you have so much potential . . . it's just . . .' He seems to be struggling to get his words out, and stands up abruptly as if frustrated.

'God, this is hard . . . Elizabeth, can I be frank with you?' He sounds a little vulnerable. I nod, all of a sudden incredibly nervous.

'I like you . . . I like you a lot more than I should. I think you are so brave and strong and, well . . . beautiful . . . I think you are wonderful and you're probably the most amazing woman I have ever met, and that's wrong because . . . well, you know why that's wrong . . .'

I freeze to the spot. I hear him speaking, but I can't seem to take in anything he's saying. This is Edward Dawson telling me that he likes me, that he thinks I'm beautiful. I can't remember anyone ever telling me I was beautiful. *But he's married*, the voice whispers in my ear; *But he wants me!* another screams back.

Edward stands there, looking younger and terrified, and my heart reaches out for him.

'I . . . I don't know what to say . . .'

Edward takes a step towards me. We're only inches apart. He smells of cologne and cigarettes and my heart is pumping so hard he has to hear it.

'Tell me you don't feel the same way. Tell me that you could never see me that way because I'm older and . . . married . . . Tell me that you don't want me and I promise I will lock away my feelings for you and I will never bring this up again . . .' His voice is strong, but shaking. I can see his chest rise slightly. His blue eyes dig into me and I'm convinced he can see the turmoil inside my head. I can't do this . . . but I really want to. His desire for me is exciting and terrifying. I don't know if I can handle it, and yet the last thing I want is for him to walk away.

'I can't!' I choke out. 'I can't say any of that, because . . . it wouldn't be true . . .' Edward's facial expression changes from vulnerability to excitement. He puts his hands on the back of my neck and kisses me roughly. It's so intense that my knees begin to wobble. When he pulls away and stares at me once again with those striking blue eyes, I realize I will never be able to walk away from him.

3

Lost

'MATT, MATT! GET UP, YOU FUCKER! SHANE IS GOING TO KILL US!' Nick is hitting me with a magazine. I want to tell him to stop but my head hurts too much, so instead I just groan loudly.

'It's nearly seven o'clock! We haven't fed the horses and we still have to clean the tack.'

'Fuck!' I mumble from under my cocoon of duvets. Nick and I are staying at a show in Cavan. We had planned to be up at 6 a.m. We have a lot of work to do, and now it is going to be a serious rush.

Shane doesn't stay at the shows at night with the horses. That's our job. It's been over four years since I started working for him and it's still always a push to get everything done in time. The shows where we stay the night, or a few nights, are always the best. Everyone parks their lorry in the same area and the partying begins as soon as the competition ends for the day. It's great fun, and we run on adrenaline, food, alcohol and absolutely no sleep. In fact, I don't think I've had a proper night's sleep in four years.

I force myself into a sitting position and look around. The

truck is a state, empty bottles and pizza boxes scattered across the counters. The floor is covered in muck and shavings.

'Fuck!' I say again, louder this time. 'This place is a tip. We need to clean it before Shane gets here.' We may stay in the lorry during away shows, but it was bought by and belongs to Shane and we can't abuse it.

'Yeah, yeah.' Nick is pulling on his jeans, which are covered in numerous stains. 'We have to get those horses ready first, and then we'll worry about the lorry. Seriously, Matt, get the fuck out of bed!'

The stables are already busy; most of the grooms have fed as Nick and I throw the buckets into the horses' stables, praying that Shane doesn't arrive early. I hadn't meant for last night to be a late one. I'd had great intentions of having an early meal, one drink in the bar and then going straight back to the lorry for some much needed sleep. But that's not what happened. That's never what happens. The bar is in the equestrian centre, just 30 yards from the lorry, so it's all too easy to stay out and forget about everything else. One quiet drink turns into ten, then Nick and I find ourselves stumbling back to the lorry at some ungodly hour.

As I'm scrubbing the tack, which I know I should have done last night, I wonder why I keep doing this. Every damn show is the same thing: binge drinking and sleep deprivation followed by a day of suffering where I have to pretend I'm not severely hung over. Shane is no fool, he knows what we get up to at these things, but he also has no problem in telling us to cop on to ourselves when he thinks we've taken it too far. At least Nick didn't bring anyone back with him this time. He's a serious charmer, and on more than one occasion I've woken up to see him cuddling up next to some guy. I'm a heavy sleeper and I've never heard or seen anything, but I still feel uncomfortable waking up to the bare bum of a guy I don't know.

Nick is twenty-three now and he has worked for Shane the longest of all the grooms. When I first started he was the one who taught me how to ride 'correctly'. This involved endless hours of sweat and pain, but after six months I was finally considered good enough to ride at shows. Nick and I only ride the young horses; any horse that is jumping at a decent height is handed over to Shane. He's the one with the money and the reputation. There are four other grooms who work with us at the yard in Dublin, but Nick and I are the only ones who live on site. At the very big shows Shane might put a third groom with us, but it's nearly always just Nick and me. I'm not as close to the other grooms as I am to Nick, mostly because they're only temporary.

There are other riders at Shane's, who keep their horses there on livery, and they often come to the shows with their own horses. It's nice to have lots of people around back at the yard. There's always someone to have a quick chat with, or to have a moan to. Probably the best thing about the yard is that it's impossible to feel alone. The one time it's empty is those early mornings, when a gentle silence engulfs the place and the only noise is the quiet whinnying of hungry horses. I love those mornings. They're a perfect calm moment before a hectic day.

I didn't get to go to competitions with Nick straight away, and I hated those first six months stuck in the yard week after week. Most days I didn't even get to go out of the front gates. I was stuck in the same repetitive routine. A lot of times, I felt like leaving. I even packed my bags once, but I couldn't bear the thought of returning home and going back to school. And I couldn't stand the thought of my parents discovering that they had been right all along, that I wasn't cut out for this life; I wasn't tough enough, talented enough, strong enough. I had begged for this opportunity and I was going to prove to people I could do it. I was desperate to go to the shows with Shane, to witness the competitions and take part.

The standard of the shows we attend varies a lot. At the international shows there are hundreds upon hundreds of competitors. The classes begin at 1.10 metres and go all the way up to Grand Prix height, which is 1.60 metres. These shows tend to go on for a few days or a week, at least. Then there are training shows, which is where I started. These are one-day shows with limited classes and limited competitors and no prizes or places. Training shows are where you make all your mistakes. They're where you find out the horse's ability and your own.

The day Shane decided I could start jumping at shows was one of the scariest moments in my life. Nick and I had been exercising in Shane's indoor arena, newly built, with the perfect surface, and spotless. Nick had been under strict instructions not to allow me to jump any of the horses without Shane's permission; I was only to work on the flat. Nick didn't enforce this rule for too long, though. Shane was rarely around and Nick was next in charge after him, so we didn't have to worry about being caught by anyone else. I also think Nick wanted a bit of healthy competition. If he was the only one jumping then he had no one to beat, and Nick loves to win.

I was on Harvey, an up-and-coming four-year-old gelding. The woman who owned him had given him to Shane to see if he had any talent. Shane and the rest of us knew that this four-year-old had more talent than most of the horses out there, and Shane wanted to be the one to take advantage of it. Nick was sitting on the fence smoking a cigarette, and the smell was making me crave one myself.

'He's a good horse and everything, but I bet he couldn't jump that.' Nick was gesturing towards a grid that was at least 1.30 metres high, and wide with it.

'He definitely could,' I say confidently, not knowing Harvey's limit at all. 'This horse is something special,' I go on, patting his dark-brown neck. Harvey is definitely my favourite horse in Shane's yard. Not only is he extremely talented, but he has a brilliant attitude, always eager to please. He's also one of the easiest horses to handle; he doesn't kick or bite, like most of the others. Harvey's owner is one of those people who doesn't compete or ride very much but has money and uses that money to be part of the success. To these owners, it doesn't matter if they don't take part in the training or the competition – as long as they own the horse, they feel like a winner. Often that is all these owners want.

'Give it a go then, if you're so sure.' Nick is smiling. He knows I'm bluffing; I ride Harvey a lot on the flat but I've never jumped him. Nick only ever lets me jump the experienced horses, the horses it would be pretty impossible for me to do anything wrong with. But I'm tempted to do it anyway, because I know I can, because I know I'm good enough. I'm about to reply to Nick when I hear another voice.

'I wouldn't mind seeing you give it a go either.' Nick's face goes ice-white. He drops the cigarette on the ground and quickly puts it out. We aren't supposed to smoke around the horses.

I know who it is before I even turn around. Shane is standing there, his arms crossed. His sandy hair is cut short and he's wearing a white V-necked polo top with light-blue jeans. He's frowning, and looking straight at me.

'We were only messing, Shane – of course we wouldn't jump Harvey over that.' Nick forces a laugh, but Shane doesn't smile, he just carries on staring at me. I stumble over my words.

'Honestly . . . I wouldn't . . . Not without your permission . . .'

'Really?' he says, raising his eyebrows sceptically. 'Well . . . you have my permission now, so give it a go.'

I'm not sure what to do. I look at Nick, but he has the same helpless look I know has to be on my face. Whatever I do, I'm in deep trouble. There's no way out: I'm going to lose the job I fought so hard for. Shane slowly makes his way over to the grid, standing directly next to the fence so he has a perfect view.

'Go on,' he says, still not taking his eyes off me.

Fuck it, I think, there's nothing else I can do now. I pick up the reins and ask Harvey to pop up into a canter. He obeys without hesitation. I do a couple of circles first, to make sure he isn't too relaxed, before I turn into the grid. The first part of the three-fenced grid is a small cross-pole. Harvey pops this without effort. I barely move over the top, knowing that I need to keep his balance for the next two fences. The second fence is a much taller straight; here I can feel his ability as he kicks out his back legs in enjoyment. Next is the 1.30-metre parallel. How desperately do I want to forget all my training and just kick on hard at the fence? – but I force myself to sit quiet and only release when I feel Harvey's front legs lift off from the ground. An overwhelming feeling of relief hits me as I feel all four legs hit the ground safely and smoothly. I let Harvey canter on for a couple of strides before pulling him up and trotting back towards Shane.

My relief is short-lived. As soon as I see Shane's glare I know the danger's not over yet. This is a test, and I have no idea whether I've passed or not. I imagine the humiliation of telling my parents I've been fired, that I've worked harder than I've ever worked before and I have absolutely nothing to show for it. Shane rubs his chin with his hand, lost in thought. The silence seems to last an eternity.

'Not bad,' he mumbles eventually. He says it so quietly I'm not even sure if he's talking to me. 'Not bad at all. Your balance was a little off the whole way through, and your approach was not straight enough, but it wasn't a bad attempt.' He's still rubbing his chin.

'Thanks,' I reply, surprised by what he's saying and not sure what to expect next.

'I have a couple of four-year-olds I'd like to get some show experience on . . . just metre tracks. You think you would be up for that, Matt?'

'Oh . . . yeah . . . yeah . . . of course.' I trip over my words, I'm so excited. Not only have I not been fired but I'm going to get to jump at competitions.

'Good, you can help Nick at the shows as well. I know the work was getting a bit heavy for him.' He turns towards Nick, who looks like someone has slapped him in the face.

'Nick, walk him through the preparations for the show, OK?' Nick just nods, too shocked to speak.

As Shane walks towards the exit, Nick and I stare at each other, knowing we are the luckiest men on the planet. I feel a smile forming on my face, when I hear Shane call back from the opposite end of the indoor arena.

'By the way, guys, don't ever do something I told you not to do again . . . or you'll both be out of here so fast. Trust me, I'll have no bother replacing you.'

Since then, my days have been filled with endless jumping lessons and preparations for the shows. At first I adored it. The horses were young and inexperienced but I was finally doing what I'd wanted to do all along, and I got great pleasure school- ing these young horses and bringing them up the grades.

But it wasn't long before I realized that the horses might evolve but I stayed at the same level. As soon as a horse gained enough experience they'd be handed over to Shane, Nick or the owners – I never got to ride them longer than a couple of months.

Four years of this, and I'm beginning to wonder why I'm still here. Jumping horses I don't care about, getting drunk because there's nothing better to do. I want something exciting, something that scares me, and I don't know if that is horses any more.

Now, I can't stop yawning as I scrub the saddle. Nick and I have managed to get everything done before Shane arrived, but he can tell that the two of us are suffering.

'Late one?' he asks, patting me on the shoulder. I nod. Talking takes too much energy.

'You can put that away, Matt,' he says, gesturing towards the saddle. 'I want you to come and see this horse.' He sounds excited, which makes me curious; he only gets excited about a horse if it's something really special.

'So, who is this horse then?' I ask as we walk towards the jumping ring.

'Wildfire,' he replies.

'Wildfire? As in the American horse that's a sure thing for Nations Cup team this year? What's she doing here?' We're at a big show, but a horse like Wildfire usually jumps abroad. It's amazing that she's in Ireland. Shane smiles to hear the excitement in my voice.

'New owner for the new season. And she's only just turned nineteen, I hear.' The showjumping season, technically, peaks in the summer, but it only really stops for Christmas. It's January now, and we are all back ready to compete until next winter.

'Wow!' I whistle. 'Lucky girl. Who is she?'

'Her name's Elizabeth O'Brien.'

4

In Over Your Head

I SLIP OUT OF BED AS QUIETLY AS I CAN. EDWARD LIES THERE heavily, face down and dead to the world. Half his body is covered by the bedsheets, so only his back is visible. It's perfectly sculpted but criss-crossed with the scars he's acquired over the years. I'm sure by now I know the story behind each one. It's strange to think back to the first time we slept together six months ago. My sexual experience at that point had pretty much been seventeen-year-old, pale, skinny schoolboys who didn't really know what they were doing. Edward changed all that. He changed everything, really. Our first time was so nerve-racking. His strong, experienced body intimidated me and his intense desire to have me was like nothing I'd ever experienced before. It excited me.

I hear Edward stir, and I freeze. He grumbles a little then falls back asleep. Over the last few months I've learnt that Edward is a terrible sleeper, especially when he gets stressed. When things are going well he sleeps more than a baby, but when a good horse is lame or when he has a bad day jumping he can stay awake for days. This time, I know I'm the source of his stress, so there's no way I'm going to be the one to wake him. I look around his beautiful Georgian home and I can't help but feel I'm not welcome. Katherine, Edward's wife, seems to spend a lot of time with her family in Spain, so I nearly always stay here with him. When Katherine's home, he'll book a room in a hotel. We spend nearly every second or third night together, more if possible. Edward seems desperate to have me by his side, and I get anxious when we spend more than a few days apart, afraid that his desire for me will wilt, but I don't know why.

I don't have much to compare my relationship with Edward to. I soon find out that his moods are more unpredictable than a chestnut mare's. One day he can be boyish and affectionate, the next he'll scream at anyone who crosses his path. After that day in his office I felt so bad and so guilty I locked myself away at home for days, but I knew I had to face him some time. I had to ride Wildfire; I had to keep at my dream: it's all I have. I hadn't been at his yard five minutes when he found me. He practically dragged me into his office.

'Where have you been? I called, I emailed, I even thought about driving to your house.' Edward looked frantic, angry even.

'I'm sorry . . . I just—' I started, but he interrupted me.

'I wanted to see you again. Didn't you want that too?' He was forcing his voice to stay calm.

'I do,' I said, trying to get some control over the situation. 'But I just feel so . . . guilty . . . What about your wife?'

Edward ran his hands through his thin blond hair before answering me. 'I need to tell you something. My wife, Katherine, and I are separated . . . and we've been separated for quite some time now . . . Katherine and I realized our marriage wasn't working about a year after our wedding, but she comes from a seriously Catholic family. If I divorced her, she would be humiliated and her family would probably never speak to her again. I may not love Katherine any more, but I could never do such a thing to her . . . You have to understand that.' Edward was pleading with me, but it was so much to take in.

'But you guys still live together?' I asked, perplexed.

'Only for show . . . No one can know we're separated, but we haven't shared a bed for years now. You must believe me, Elizabeth. I don't love Katherine, she doesn't love me, but I think . . . I think I could fall for someone like you . . .'

His words made me shiver from head to toe. I didn't say anything; instead, I stepped forward and lunged at him. He responded immediately, kissing me back. His kiss deepened and I melted. He pulled away first, and looked at me seriously.

'Don't cut me out like that again. I can't handle it, Elizabeth.' He had one hand on either side of my face, and I realized that no one had ever felt so intensely about me, before him.

'I won't, I promise,' I said.

Since then, we've seen each other practically every day. He trains me on Wildfire during the day and every two or three nights he takes me out to lavish restaurants and parties in Dublin, and when he's competing around Europe he'll sometimes fly me out, just so I can be with him. I almost feel as if I hadn't been really living until I met Edward, my relationship with him is *so* exciting. But it's also exhausting. I'm nervous when I'm with him, so desperate to please him.

I'm disturbed from my thoughts by more groaning. I look over at Edward. His eyes are open.

'Morning, beautiful,' he says sleepily. 'Big day today.'

'Don't remind me!' He looks up at me with those sleepy blue eyes and I smile. He opens his arms and I know he wants me to get back into bed. I'm worried about my day, but I can't resist him, so I crawl back in and he begins to spoon me gently and kiss my neck.

'Today is going to go great,' he whispers in my ear.

'Just concentrate and ride with purpose. This is your season.'

I know he's trying to be kind, but I feel the pressure grow heavier and heavier on my shoulders. This is my first full season with Wildfire and I know there will be so many people watching to see how we perform together. I only got Wildfire in the spring of last year, and between getting used to each other and starting so late in the season, we didn't make much impact on the competition circuit. But, by the end of last season, everything had clicked. Wildfire trusts me and I trust her; she jumps her heart out for me and I do everything I can to help and encourage her. I know the two of us could be real contenders this season, especially with Edward's advice and support.

'Who are you riding today?' I ask Edward, trying to move the subject away from me.

'Minnie,' Edward says casually. A Grand Prix is nothing for him; it's merely a stepping stone to what he really wants: yet another spot on the Irish Aga Khan team in Dublin Horse Show. He's already been on the team four times. It's what all the top Irish riders want — it's also what I want — but that dream seems so far out of reach at the moment, especially if I can't get through today. But I know Edward's dreams go beyond even that. Not only does he want a spot on the team, he wants to lead the team to victory.

'She seems to be going well,' I add.

'Ah, she's not a bad horse. A bit bulging and strong, but once she realizes who's in charge . . . She'll do just fine.' Over the months I've spent here with Edward I've realized just how different our approaches to riding are. He is aggressive and dominating and often forces his horses into submission. I, on the other hand, like to work *with* Wildfire, help her so that she'll help me. I want always to be in sync with her. Edward is a great coach, full of wisdom and with years of experience, but it's this vital difference in our riding styles that often causes us to have mighty rows during our schooling sessions. Edward hates people disagreeing with him, especially when it comes to showjumping, but sometimes, when he tells me to punish Wildfire or push her harder, I have to stand up for her. This is usually followed by a fight and maybe a day of not speaking to each other. Edward never apologizes, and neither do I; we just agree to disagree and drop the topic. I know I'm talented, and I know Wildfire and I are getting closer to my dream of jumping for Ireland every day, but I also know I need Edward's help if I'm ever going to get there.

'Your mother called me again last night,' Edward groans from behind me. I tense. This is what's making him lose so much sleep.

'What did she say this time?'

'Same as always. She wants you to go to college . . . She sees Wildfire as a distraction from the real world . . . It's time to give up on this dead-end sport . . . Blah, blah, blah . . .' Edward pulls away from me, crawls out of bed and makes his way to the bathroom.

'I know she's your mother, but that woman is a fucking whack job,' he announces just before closing the door. I know when it comes to my mother Edward has a point; I just wish he wouldn't be so blunt about it.

Only a few months after we purchased Wildfire my parents announced that they were getting a divorce. I wasn't that surprised – I can't remember the last time I saw them enjoy each other's company. The worst thing about this divorce is that my mother has made it her personal mission to get rid of Wildfire and get me to go to college. Luckily, my father is the one who officially owns Wildfire, since he paid for her, but it hasn't stopped her trying every other angle. She rings Edward constantly, begging him to stop training me, but he just informs her that I'm over eighteen and that he will only stop training me if I request it myself. She attacks me every time I go home, tells me that I'm wasting the best years of my life on a career that will never go anywhere.

At first, she was quite logical about it, asking me just to consider going to college and perhaps do showjumping as a hobby. But once I told her that showjumping would never be a hobby for me, that it would always be a career, she flipped. Whatever our relationship was before, now that I'm standing my ground, she really is on the warpath. Every time I leave for a training session or a show, she rants on and on. Last week she even left a pile of printed-out news articles on my bed about riders who had seriously injured themselves, or even died, on horses. Sometimes I think she only wants to sell Wildfire because Dad bought her without her permission, and that this argument isn't about me or my life decisions but her pride. Either way, it has become practically unbearable to live with her, and I'm happy to spend as many nights as I can away from her.

Of course, my mother has figured out that I'm seeing someone – I've never been good at lying and sneaking around, I'm pretty honest. But I tell her that I'm not ready to introduce him to people yet and, for now, that seems to be keeping her at bay. I don't know what my mother would do if she found out that I'm dating Edward.

He emerges from the bathroom looking slightly more awake. He has slicked back his hair with water, and I begin to worry what my own must look like.

'She called your father yesterday too,' he declares, sitting on the edge of the bed.

'She what?' I ask, sitting upright, shocked. I'd thought that my parents hadn't spoken for months.

'Don't worry. I got the impression from both your father and mother that the conversation didn't go well.' Ever since we bought Wildfire, my father and Edward have been in regular contact. It makes sense really: they are two incredibly driven men who are very successful in their fields. But any time I hear Edward mention my father I can't help but feel a sting of sadness that my father has a better relationship with Edward, a man who is essentially a stranger to him, than he does with me.

'You don't think my father will sell Wildfire, do you?' I ask, trying to push away my feelings of jealousy.

'I don't think so. Your father sees Wildfire as seventy grand your mother can't get her greedy hands on.' I hate the way Edward speaks about my mother, but it's hard to defend her when she's been acting so irrationally lately. He places his hand on my cheek.

'What's wrong?' he asks.

'I'm . . . I'm just nervous about today,' I lie.

He pulls me in for a kiss, and any irritation thaws as I fill up with excitement. 'How about you join me in the shower and I wash away all your worries?' he says. He picks me up like a rag doll and I break out into giggles as he carries me into the bathroom.

Edward and I arrive at the show separately. It hasn't got anything to do with appearances – in fact, I sometimes think Edward is far too affectionate with me in public – it's just I like to drive my own lorry to the show. I jumped ponies when I was younger and did really well, so as a 'well done' present, Dad very generously purchased me a lorry for my seventeenth birthday. The second I was able to drive a car, I learnt how to drive a lorry. It gave me my independence, and it also meant that I had somewhere to sleep at the overnight shows. It used to be fun going in the lorries with the grooms, but now I like to be in control of how I and the horse get to the shows – there's nothing worse than turning up with a stressed horse because you're running late and have had to speed along and then slam on the brakes.

The showground is packed. It's the first main show of the season, and everyone is here to make their mark and establish their status. I park up and make my way into the ring. Edward's lorry isn't here yet; his groom driver must have got lost. I watch as the humongous course I'll have to face in a matter of hours is built. Now, I wish I weren't alone here. I wish Edward were here with me looking at the course, reassuring me that I'm more than ready for this, or even Orla, my closest friend, who would make me relax with a few silly jokes.

I hear two boys close by shouting at each other as they make their way to the stables.

'Grab that saddle, Matt. Shane will expect that to be clean by now.' It's the taller one speaking, who has reddish-brown hair that has grown to the point where it looks rather scruffy. The boy he's shouting at looks younger, about my age. He's thin but fit, and his hair is dark brown and cut very short, showing off his striking features. He has a piercing on his left eyebrow and his showjumping shirt is hiding what looks like a tattoo on his right upper arm. I find myself staring at the darker guy, trying to figure out have I ever seen him before. I decide that I haven't, because I would've remembered a face like his, and yet I don't want to look away.

'What are you staring at?' I jump with fright when I hear Edward's voice.

'Nothing,' I mutter, guiltily – but I'm not quite sure why. 'I just thought I recognized someone.' But I can tell that Edward no longer cares; he's staring at the course.

'Have you walked it yet?'

I shake my head. 'I was waiting for you.'

'Well, let's go then.'

Edward's skill and experience really show when we are at

competitions. He knows exactly how a horse will react to each fence and what will catch riders out. I listen carefully as he talks on, reassured by the fact that what he says reflects exactly what I'm thinking. The only time I speak up is when we finish walking the speed round.

'I think you should take the long turn into this last fence,' he announces, as we stare at it.

'Really?' I ask, surprised. There're two options on the last fence, the safer one being to go around another fence so as to be straight for the final parallel. The drawback with that is that it takes longer, and the object of the speed round is to be clear and fast. The other option is to slip inside the fence and jump the final parallel at an angle. This increases your chance of knocking the fence, but it will shave seconds off your time. I think I can pull off the tighter turn and I'm hurt that Edward doesn't agree.

'That turn is harder than you think. It will lure people in and, I guarantee you, nearly everyone who tries it will have that parallel down. Go around and you'll have a beautiful clear. Trust me.' He sounds so certain I feel myself being swayed by him. I look at the final turn again. I have to trust him.

5

And Then She Came Along

SHANE TALKS NON-STOP AS WE HEAD TOWARDS THE RING. HE tells me about Wildfire's history, her breeding, where she has competed and who has been lucky enough to ride her. When we reach the ringside I see her for the first time. She's a small mare, and her chestnut coat is an unusual bright orange.

'There she is.' Shane is virtually drooling. 'Gorgeous, isn't she?'

'Yeah,' I say, smiling, but I'm not talking about the horse. Holding Wildfire is a tall, blonde girl who is possibly the most stunning person I have ever seen.

The mare has her head low towards the blonde girl, resting against her hand. The girl looks as if she's saying something to the horse, but I'm too far off to hear what.

'Who's the girl holding Wildfire? A groom?' I ask, trying to not sound too eager.

He laughs. 'That's definitely not a groom, Matt, that's Elizabeth.'

'Oh,' I say, surprised, and a little disappointed.

Shane realizes what I'm thinking. 'Why are you asking, Matt?

You like the look of her?' He's elbowing me in the ribs and I can feel the heat rising to my face.

'No, no, I'm just curious,' I say, trying to dig myself out of the hole I've just created.

'Ah, Matt, I'm only teasing you . . . I wouldn't blame you anyway. She's very pretty. The family is loaded too. Something to do with being diplomats . . . I wouldn't bother trying anything, though; apparently, Edward has his eye on her. He's instructing her.'

'Edward Dawson?' I blurt, shocked. 'But he's, like, forty? And married!'

Shane shrugs his shoulders. 'Never stopped Edward before. Anyway, it might just be a rumour.' I look back over in Elizabeth's direction. She's adjusting the straps on the horse's bridle, her perfect face frowning in concentration. Edward is there too. He's a short but strong-looking man; he can't be any taller than her. His hair is hidden under his hat, and he's more tanned than your average Irish person, probably a result of all his travelling. His skin is well weathered but you can tell he was very good-looking in his day. Him and her? I think. Can't be true. *Must* be a silly rumour; those get around a lot at these shows.

Edward has his hand on Elizabeth's shoulder and seems to be whispering something into her ear. Her cheeks go red as he helps to lift her on to the petite mare.

'Is she jumping in the Grand Prix?' I ask, impressed and slightly jealous.

'She sure is, and she has a pretty good chance of winning it too. She and that horse are expected to have a very good season.' The two of us stand there for a while in silence, lost in our own thoughts. I know Shane is thinking about Wildfire. He's a brilliant rider, probably the best one in the country. I know he dreams of being able to ride a horse like her. I'm in my own fantasy as well, but it has nothing to do with horses. How come

I've never seen this girl before? I'm shaken out of myself when Shane hits me hard on the back.

'Come on, lover boy. I need you to get my horse ready.'

I sigh and follow him. 'For fuck's sake, Shane! I only asked you what her name was . . .'

The Grand Prix ends up being an incredibly exciting class. Out of ninety riders, only ten manage to get through to the speed round, Shane, Elizabeth and Edward among them. The speed round is tricky, and the last turn seems to be catching everyone out. The crowd breathes in with excitement every time each rider takes that risky turn to the last fence, and so far it has been followed by a groan of disappointment as each horse kicks it out. Finally, Shane comes in, riding with a grace and composure that only a man like him can pull off. The crowd feels let down when he cleverly takes the long way into the last fence, giving himself a clear. He's slow, but he goes straight into the lead, as every rider before him has had at least one fence on the ground.

Elizabeth is next. She looks as pale as a ghost as she canters into the ring. Her hands are shaking violently as she gives Wildfire a gentle pat on the neck. Despite her nerves, however, she jumps a beautiful clear, taking the same turn into the last fence as Shane but, because Wildfire's pace is naturally faster, she slips into the lead. Her smile is massive when she canters out and she's practically hugging Wildfire's neck.

'Surprised she didn't try that last turn,' I hear Nick comment next to me as we both watch her leave the ring. 'Wildfire was jumping so well, I'd say the two of them would have pulled it off.'

'Yeah, you're right,' I say, agreeing with him. I start to think, is she just too afraid to take the risk?

Edward canters into the ring, the final rider in the class. His

horse is hot and buzzing, and it's clear that Edward has excited
her up in the warm-up so that he will go faster. Edward jumps
with perfect accuracy and control. While everyone before has
struggled with the course, he jumps it with complete ease. He
turns sharply for the last fence and takes the turn which has
caught everyone out. Minnie rubs the last fence slightly, but the
pole stays in its cups, giving Edward the winning round by
miles.

'That was class!' Nick cheers, watching Edward canter around
the ring to the crowd's applause. But I'm not looking at
Edward; instead I'm looking at Elizabeth, who's standing at the
far side of the ring, her mouth open in shock.

Later on that night, we go to the pub. Nick goes up to the bar
and returns to our table laden with drinks.

'Celebrations, Matt! We made it through the day without
getting fired.' It's getting dark now, and Shane has headed back
to his hotel to meet his fiancée, Justine, for dinner. Only on rare
occasions did the two ever join us at the bar in the evening.

'Fuck's sake, Nick, I'm still hung over . . . and I have two
horses to jump tomorrow and you have three!'

'Ah, lighten up.' Nick is already shoving a vodka and coke in
my face. 'I ride better after a few drinks. So do you . . . more
relaxed.' Nick gives me a wink, and I laugh.

'Bullshit,' I mumble, taking a sip. There's no point in arguing
with him.

Both at the same time, Nick and I look up at the bar TV
screen. The majority of people in the room are staring at it and
after a few seconds I realize why. Todd Watermen, showjumping's world number one, is being interviewed after
winning yet another Nations Cup. He is English and in his
fifties. Years of hardship are evident in his scarred face. His body
must be battered too. The woman interviewing him is young,

and she's clearly done her research, as her questions are detailed and accurate. I listen carefully. Nick's silence tells me he's doing the same.

'Todd, is it true that you broke your back off a horse three years ago?' the blonde interviewer asks, knowing full well it's true.

Todd nods politely before answering, 'Oh, yes, it's true . . . and it couldn't have happened at a worse time for me either. I had the ride on the most talented horse I had ever had up to that point and I was quickly making my way up the world rankings until I had a nasty fall at home . . .'Todd speaks with a posh English accent, but his voice is deep and harsh.

'And what exactly happened, if you don't mind me asking?'

'Not at all. Sure, most people on the showjumping circuit know already . . . I was schooling a young stallion at home when he spooked at a loud noise. He reared up and fell on top of me. I don't remember much after that . . . I woke up in hospital a few days later and was told that I had a broken back and that I would need to learn how to walk again.' The interviewer shakes her head gravely as Todd speaks. 'I was in a wheelchair for six months after that. But I was determined to get back to showjumping as soon as I could. The first six doctors I saw told me I would never ride a horse again and that I should be thankful I could still walk. I just kept changing doctors until I found one that told me I could showjump again. It took a lot of work, but I'm thrilled to get back to where I want to be . . .' Todd tells the story with ease and grace. He has talked about it in hundreds of interviews, and I have heard it many times before. But it's still a great story.

'That's amazing!' says the interviewer. 'Were you at all afraid to get back on a horse?'

'No.' Todd answers without hesitation. 'Showjumping, like all horse sports, is high risk. The danger of injuries is all part of it.

Anyone who wants to be successful at it has to accept that from the start. My only fear was that I wouldn't be *able* to get back on a horse again.'

'One more question, Todd. Through all the hard work, injuries, doctors and disappointments . . . what has kept you going?' The interviewer leans in towards Todd, eager to hear his answer. A grin grows on his face and he shrugs playfully.

'It's addictive . . . I don't think I could ever give it up, even if I wanted to . . .'

The interview ends, and the screen flicks to an ad with a meerkat talking about car insurance.

'Wow!' I say it under my breath.

Nick is shaking his head. 'The fucker is crazy! But, God, would I love to be him!'

Three drinks later, and Nick is chatting to some guy I vaguely know. That is kind of the way the showjumping world works. You don't really know anyone, but you recognize everyone. The three of us had been chatting, but Nick had given me the signal to disappear, so I have made up some excuse about wanting a smoke. Once I'm out of sight I find myself a table in the corner of the bar, enjoying the time to myself. Tomorrow is the last day of the show, and people are out drinking, either celebrating their success or drowning their sorrows. Either way, alcohol is the main form of entertainment for the evening.

I flinch as someone with soft, warm hands covers my eyes with them. I lower my drink and place it on the table in front of me so that I won't spill it.

'Guess who?' Her voice is soft and has a south Dublin accent. I smile, knowing straight away.

'Hi, Linda,' I say warmly. She pulls her hands away and jumps into a seat next to mine.

'Damn it, how'd you know it was me?' She giggles as she

struggles to get her small frame on to the stool, and I can tell she's a little tipsy.

'You're the only person here that doesn't have a boggar accent.'

Linda slaps my arm and laughs again. She keeps her horse in livery at Shane's yard. She's in her mid-thirties and has a full-time job as a real-estate agent. Showjumping to her is a hobby; she never worries about being the best or winning classes. She just comes to these shows to have a bit of fun. I envy her sometimes.

'How did you get on today?' I ask. Her face lights up.

'I won the amateur class.'

'That's brilliant,' I say, delighted for her. The amateurs might be a class for non-professionals but it's as competitive as any you'll watch. Winning it is not easy. 'Let me buy you a drink to say well done.' I get up to go to the bar, but Linda stops me.

'You're very kind, Matt, but no thank you. I'm already tipsy enough, and I don't want Roger to have to carry me back to the lorry.' She gestures towards her husband, who is standing at the far side of the bar, talking to a small group of men.

'Did Roger jump today?' I ask. Linda shakes her head.

'His horse had a stone bruise this morning. Nothing serious – he should be fine by next week – but, obviously, he couldn't jump . . . Anyway, with him out of the competition, it gave me a better chance,' she says jokingly, and I have to laugh. 'Did you watch the big class today?' she asks, changing the subject.

'Yeah, I did. It was great. Dawson did a cracker of a round. Did you see it?'

'I did. It was really exciting to watch . . . Those fences are *huge*. To be honest, I have no desire to jump that big. I'll happily stick to my small but fun classes.'

'That horse Wildfire is great, isn't she? Elizabeth is a lucky girl.' Linda takes a mouthful of her drink, and I realize she has moved on to the water.

'Do you know her?' I ask.

'Not really . . . I sold her mother, Barbara, the house that she and Elizabeth live in now . . . Her mother is an . . . interesting character.' Linda raises her eyebrows at the last two words.

'Really? How so?' I say, no longer able to hide my interest.

'Ah, she was very highly strung about everything . . . At first I thought she was just a controlling cow, but then I heard about the divorce, and it all made a bit more sense . . .'

'Divorce?'

'Oh, yes. Elizabeth's parents are going through a very messy divorce. Loads of fighting over money and property . . . It's all over the newspapers too. Rumour is that Barbara sneaks the stories to the press herself, just to humiliate her soon to be ex-husband.' Linda talks as if all this is common knowledge, and I'm almost surprised I haven't heard any of it before.

'Poor thing . . . Where are her parents now?'

'Not sure . . .'

'Do you know who she hangs out with?' As I ask the question, I know I've taken it a step too far. Linda smiles at me.

'Oh, Matt, do you have a bit of a crush?' she says in a cutesy voice.

'No,' I say, too defensively.

'Why not? She's your age, and she's very pretty . . .'

'Yes . . . No . . . I guess . . .' I stumble over my words, wondering how I'm going to get out of this. The last thing I want is any story going around that I have a crush on Elizabeth; I don't even know the girl. Linda laughs.

'It's all right, Matt. I won't tell.'

'There's nothing *to* tell,' I say, frustrated. Linda looks as if she's about to say something when Roger appears at her side.

'I think it's time for bed,' he announces, kindly but firmly. He smiles at me. 'How are you, Matt?'

'Just fine,' I say, hoping that Linda doesn't say a word.

'I think you're right,' Linda says to her husband. 'Goodnight, Matt, and enjoy your night!' She winks at me in an obvious way and I feel like I'm going to die of humiliation. Roger looks from one of us to the other, and I know that as soon as they're out of earshot he's going to ask what that was about, and so the rumours will begin. As they walk away, I debate going to bed myself, but for some reason I feel more awake than I have all night.

I look around, wondering if Elizabeth is here. I'm trying to be subtle, but I'm really hoping I spot her. The bar is busy and familiar faces keep passing by, but then I see her. I stare at her as she fiddles with her perfect blonde curls. Her shirt looks freshly ironed and her jodhpurs would nearly blind you they're so white. Another spoilt rich girl, you might say, to look at her. And most do. I've caught up with all the gossip now. It seems she's been the main focus of everyone's conversation for a while. But she seems so timid sitting there in front of me that I choose not to believe any of it. She's even more beautiful now that I see her up close. She's thin and very tall; her skin looks soft, and is fair. Most people are looking at her, and she seems to know it too. She's virtually hiding behind her drink.

She's sitting alone, with a glass of wine in her hand. She keeps her head down, embarrassed, her hands shaking slightly. I want to stay sitting where I am. I want to finish my drink and then leave. The thought of having to get up at 5 a.m. and get eight horses cleaned, plaited and tacked is making me feel exhausted. But I don't want to walk away from her, especially since, for the first time all day, she's alone. It's weird – even though I had hoped to see her out, I don't want to speak to her now. I'm a bit hesitant when it comes to making the first move; Nick is normally so ballsy with new people that I just have to follow his lead. But strangely, this time, I want to be the brave one. I get up from my seat and make my way over to her. She looks up at me when she hears the chair I pull out scrape against the floor.

'Hi,' I say, offering my hand. She takes it.

'Hi.'

'I'm Matt.'

'Elizabeth,' she says, giving me a knowing smile. I laugh.

'It's actually Matthew,' I say, offering my hand again.

'Liz,' she replies, giggling. 'So, *Matthew*,' she asks, 'were you riding today?'

I'm suddenly very conscious of all the people in the bar watching us. I normally like to stay in the background; I've never been the guy who likes to be the centre of attention.

'Um . . . yeah, I was, had a couple of horses in the four-year-old classes. They went well.' Before I can stop myself, I say, 'How about you?'

'Well, I came second in the Grand Prix . . .'

I nod, pretending this information is new to me, but she knows I'm bullshitting.

'That's brilliant!' I say enthusiastically, and she gives me a little smile.

There's silence. When I talk to girls I usually make jokes and whip out my country accent, but I have nothing to say to a girl like this. I'm trying to think of excuses to get away without looking stupid when she speaks.

'I like your piercing,' she says.

I raise my hand to my eyebrow. 'Oh, thanks . . . it was a dare on a drunken night . . . I don't even like it that much. But I thought it would be a waste of money to take it out.'

Liz smiles at my awkwardness. 'I like it. It's . . . kind of sexy.'

I smile back, a little chuffed with myself. 'Now, Liz, we have only just met. You'd better not be flirting with me,' I say.

'I certainly am not,' she replies, pretending to be horrified. 'I want to get my tongue pierced,' she goes on, sticking it out like a five-year-old. I shake my head.

'Don't! A pierced tongue would not suit a girl like you!'

'What do you mean, "a girl like me"?'

'I didn't mean it in a bad way,' I reply. What's the matter with me? I'm stumbling over my words. 'I just mean . . . piercing your tongue is a way to stand out . . . and I think you already stand out . . .' I regret it as soon as I say it, but it's too late to take it back now.

'That's kind of sweet,' she says, a confused look on her face. I'm thrilled, though, that my pathetic attempt at a compliment seems to have worked.

The two of us end up being among the last few people in the bar. The conversation has relaxed into a nice flow and, oddly enough, jumping and horses have not been brought up once.

'I'm serious . . . More than likely, Nick has brought this lad back to the lorry, and that means I have nowhere to sleep.'

Liz is doubled over laughing. 'Aw, you poor thing.' She pats my shoulder and I feel the hairs stand up on the back of my neck. 'I would offer you a place in my lorry, but I don't think Marshall would be too happy.'

'Who's Marshall?' I ask.

'My dog. He keeps me company at these things.'

'You come to the shows on your own?'

'Not really. There are always friends around during the day – but I stay in the truck on my own at night.'

I don't know whether it's the drink, but I suddenly see an opportunity. 'The bar is closing up . . . do you want to head back to your lorry? We can have another drink or something?' I know as soon as I say it that there's no hope.

Liz looks down at her feet before replying. 'Look, Matt . . . I'm flattered, honestly. But I'm kind of seeing someone . . .' My heart sinks as soon as the words come out.

I've made the wrong move, but try to pull back. 'No bother . . . Sorry – I have a habit of being a bit forward.'

'It's fine,' she says, smiling kindly.

'I'll walk you back to your lorry. It's late,' I say. I just want the evening to end now.

'Thanks.' She grabs her jacket and the two of us head out into the freezing-cold night air.

It's buzzing out here. Music is blaring from various lorries, all parked up tightly together. Liz's is only two trucks down from ours. It's gun-metal grey, sparkling clean and brand-new. It makes Shane's lorry look like a down-and-out's camper van.

'Thanks for walking me back; Marshall will take care of me from here,' she says.

'No problem. See you tomorrow.'

'See you tomorrow.'

But I haven't quite given up. 'We should hang out some time . . . you know, as friends . . .'

She stares at me for what feels like an age. I can see she's trying to work me out. 'Yeah,' she finally replies. 'Yeah, we should.'

I go to bed that night feeling like a fool. Why do I get it so wrong sometimes? Nick is in the bed above me, snoring loudly. Thankfully, he's alone. I look at my watch: 3 a.m. The thought of getting up in two hours makes me feel ill. I close my eyes and try to fall asleep. As I drift off, I try to plan out my day's work for tomorrow, but it's hopeless. I can't focus. My mind keeps going back to her.

6

Betrayed

I FEEL HOT AND STICKY. MY EYES ARE SHUT TIGHTLY BUT I CAN feel the sun glaring down on me through the lorry window. Marshall is curled up next to me, making me feel even hotter. I gently push him away, but he growls at me as I wake him. My head is sore and my mouth unpleasantly dry. When I open my eyes I realize that I had one too many glasses of wine last night. I stare at my phone and decide that I can't avoid it any longer. It was so nice to turn it off last night and forget about what happened earlier, but I know I have to face it now. It starts to buzz immediately and I know I have a long day ahead of me. Six missed calls: three from Edward, one from Orla and two from my mother. I groan when I recall my conversation with Edward yesterday. It comes rushing back to me.

'What was *that*?' I'd asked him as soon as I had him alone after the Grand Prix. We were in his lorry, the prize-giving seemed a long time ago, our horses had been put away and we were completely alone.

'What do you mean?' he asks innocently.

'You know exactly what I mean. You told me not to do that turn, you said it was undoable, and then you stab me in the back!' I know I'm being a tad irrational, but I can't help but feel completely betrayed. Edward's face hardens.

'You're acting like a child, Elizabeth,' he says spitefully.

'You purposely gave me the wrong advice,' I shout, throwing my hands in the air. He swoops towards me and stares down at me. I go silent. I realize that, right now, I'm a little afraid of him.

'Elizabeth, I've spent the last six months training you and preparing you. I've put in hours upon hours of work to help you achieve your dream, and today you came second, beating numerous people who have been competing at this level a whole lot longer than you. How dare you imply I tried to sabotage you?' Edward's voice is full of anger, and I suddenly feel so ashamed for saying what I did. I move my mouth, about to speak, but he is far from finished.

'I told you to take the longer turn because I knew it would give you a clear and a high placing. You're still new to this competition circuit, Elizabeth, and you need to prove yourself as a contender. You did that today because of my advice. You should be thanking me, not accusing me . . . When you have more experience and a better head for competition, *then* you can take the risks necessary to win a Grand Prix.' He stares at me with those fierce blue eyes and I wish I hadn't said anything. He grabs his jacket and goes to leave.

'I think we both need some space tonight,' he says. 'I'll talk to you tomorrow.' And, with that, he's gone.

Underneath, though, I was still angry with him, so I turned off my phone so he couldn't contact me – and also so that I wouldn't cave in and call him. But lying here now, I feel like such an immature idiot. I was second in my first Grand Prix of the season, and I owe it all to Edward and his training. Last night started out as torture: I should've been happy but instead I felt scolded. I thought a few drinks in the bar would relax me, but I found myself getting more depressed, not wanting to talk to anybody and worrying that, this time, I had pushed Edward too far. It feels like our relationship is always teetering on the rocks: one wrong step and I could lose him.

I was about to give in and call Edward to apologize when I heard Matthew pull out the chair next to me. I nearly died with embarrassment when I saw it was him. I was convinced he must have seen me staring at him earlier and was now going to ask me why. But instead he was so kind and sweet and I found myself relaxing and enjoying his company. It didn't take me long to figure out that he was flirting with me, and I'm ashamed to admit to myself how much I enjoyed and even encouraged it. It wasn't that I wanted to sleep with Matthew; it was just that I was having so much fun and I was afraid that if I didn't flirt back he would lose interest in me and just walk away.

Matthew isn't like anyone I've met before, especially in the showjumping world. He's in no way cocky or self-centred, yet he seems focused and intelligent. His jokes were light-hearted and fun and in no way cruel or harsh. The biggest thing that stood out about him was that he seemed to be in no way a gossip. He didn't once talk about other people in a negative way, and when I did try to engage him in talking about scandals, he just nodded politely and moved on to another subject. I know Edward and I are the subject of whispers in the showjumping world. As much as I deny it, I'm almost convinced that most people know what is going on, and it makes me nervous and anxious nearly all the time. Matthew's disdain for gossip and rumour spreading is refreshing and, in a strange way, alluring. I can be anyone I want to be with him – an opportunity that few people, in this world, ever get.

★

I jump with fright when Marshall leaps off the bed and runs to the door of the lorry. Only then do I realize someone is knocking.

'Who is it?' I shout, not wanting to open my door in my pyjamas.

'It's the cookie monster wanting to know who took all the cookies from the cookie jar.' I jump out of bed and run to the door. As soon as I open it Orla grabs me in a bear hug. I don't think I've ever been so happy to see my best friend.

'I thought you were only coming up this afternoon,' I say, surprised but delighted.

'I swapped some shifts around at work so I could have the full day off.' Orla competes as well, but only at an amateur level. She works full-time as a nurse, so showjumping is just a fun hobby for her, something she does when she has some time. She also keeps her horse at Edward's yard, but she doesn't train with him like I do. Orla is a few years older than me, and I think of her as my sister. I honestly believe I could tell her anything. She's the only person in my life who knows the truth about the relationship between Edward and me.

'How are you, darling?' she asks, pulling away from me and jumping on to my fold-out bed.

'Not so bad,' I reply, my spirits instantly lifted now that she's here. 'I'm suffering a bit after last night.'

'I'd say so,' she says cheerfully. 'I heard you came second in the Grand Prix. You and Edward must have done some serious celebrating last night.'

'Actually, I stayed here, Edward went back to his hotel . . . But I still had a good night.'

Orla cocks her head to the side and looks at me sympathetically. 'What happened?'

'We had a fight . . . But it was my fault. Thinking back, I completely overreacted.'

Orla frowns, and I know what she's thinking. 'Are you sure it was your fault?' she asks. 'Or did Edward just make it sound like your fault?' Orla has never hidden the fact that she dislikes Edward and the type of relationship we have. She would never be rude to him or ever make me feel that I should leave him, but I know she thinks that he takes advantage of my being so much younger. I just have to remind myself that she doesn't know Edward as well as I do.

'No, it really was,' I assure her.

Orla doesn't look convinced, but I know, as my friend, she will accept it. 'Well, if you really feel it was your fault, then all you can do is apologize,' she says encouragingly.

'Yeah, I guess . . .' I'm worried, though, about what I'm going to have to face later, when I see him.

'So what did you get up to last night then?' Orla asks, knowing that I want to change the subject.

'I think I made a new friend,' I say, a little shyly, which makes Orla laugh. 'His name is Matthew and he works for Shane Walker.'

'Oh, I've seen him about. He's really hot!'

'Yeah . . . I guess he is,' I say, almost afraid to agree with her, for some reason.

'You'll have to introduce me to him . . . Do some match-making for me?'

'Oh . . . OK . . . No bother . . .'

Orla seems to notice my hesitation. 'Do you mind?'

'No, of course not,' I reply, quickly this time. 'You're right – he's really cute and nice.'

'I'll find myself a man yet!'

'And a lucky man he will be!'

Orla and I turn around, hearing a noise. Edward is at the door.

'I'm sorry to interrupt, girls,' he says politely, giving Orla a kiss on the cheek.

'No bother at all,' Orla says, chirpy as ever. 'I have to go walk my course anyway. I'll talk to you later, Liz.' She gives me a quick wink as she leaves, which I hope Edward doesn't see.

He sits silently on the edge of my bed. He no longer looks aggressive and forceful, like he did yesterday; instead, he is calm and composed. We both sit there in silence for a moment, neither one of us knowing what exactly we want to say. After a while, I look at Edward properly. I'm surprised to see that he's smiling.

'I like your T-shirt,' he says. I look down at my Powerpuff Girls T-shirt, which I bought when I was ten and regularly use as a pyjama top. I giggle, he laughs, and instantly the tension melts.

'I'm sorry,' I announce. 'I overreacted . . . I just got a shock when I saw you doing the thing you told me not to do.'

'Elizabeth, if you had asked what *I* had planned to do at that turn, I would have told you the truth . . . But I don't see how my plan should affect yours.' Edward holds my hand gently, and I know I'll say anything to end this fight. I just want him to want me again.

'I'm sorry,' I repeat.

'I only want the best for you,' he says, smiling again.

'I know.' I feel even guiltier than I did before. Edward leans into me and kisses me gently. But soon the gentle kisses become more eager and I know what direction we're heading in.

'I think I'd prefer this T-shirt on the floor,' he groans in between kisses. Part of me wants to pull away. His advances excite me — they always do — but my headache is only getting worse the longer I'm awake without food, and my stomach feels bloated. It's hard to enjoy sex when you don't feel at all sexy. But I don't say anything, because I'm just so happy we're not arguing any more and I don't want to do anything to ruin our truce.

Afterwards I lie on Edward's chest. I feel safe wrapped inside his strong arms. I nuzzle into his neck, and he pats my hair gently. This is where we work best together, when we're alone, when the rest of the world doesn't interfere. When it's just him and me, it works.

'I'm sorry I left you alone last night. As soon as I woke up this morning I knew I shouldn't have done it. I tried to call, but your phone was off?' I can tell that Edward means the last part of that sentence as a question.

'My battery died,' I lie, knowing it will only annoy him if I tell him that I needed space. It seems to satisfy him.

'I still should've taken you out to celebrate your achievement. Second in your first Grand Prix, Elizabeth. That's amazing.' He kisses me again, and I can tell that he's truly sorry.

'It's OK,' I say reassuringly. 'Actually, I had a lot of fun here.'

'Oh, really?'

'Yeah, I hung out with some people . . . had a few drinks . . . it was fun,' I say, trying to sound nonchalant.

'Anyone I know?' he asks. His voice is measured and relaxed, but I can't see his face.

'I don't think so,' I answer honestly. 'His name was Matthew. He works for Shane Walker.'

'A groom?' he asks – a bit snobbishly, I think. I don't like his question, so I don't answer it, but he's obviously taken my silence to mean something else. 'Do you *like* this groom?'

I turn round to face him for the first time since we started talking. 'Of course not.' It comes out more defensively than I intended it to.

Edward cocks his head to one side, looking at me. 'Is there something going on here?'

'No,' I say quickly. 'He's just a friend . . . It's kind of nice to meet different people. I'm still new to this community.' I pull myself out of bed and get dressed. I can feel Edward's eyes burning into the back of my head.

'Well – I'm glad you're making some friends,' he says, rather hesitantly. Then he jumps up and grabs me around the waist, making me jump with fright.

'I have an idea,' he announces, his voice suddenly much more upbeat. 'Enda Brown is having her sixty-fifth birthday party next week. Why don't you come with me and I can introduce you to all the important people in the showjumping world?'

I turn around and look at Edward, my mouth open in excitement.

'Are you serious?' I ask. Enda Brown was an international showjumper, now retired, but in her day she was considered one of the best. Her career spanned over twenty years. She was world number one for three full seasons. But my excitement starts to diminish when I think about it properly.

'Wait – will people not find it strange if you bring me?'

'I don't think so . . . Katherine never comes to these things anyway. People will just think I'm introducing you to the showjumping world, which is what I *am* doing.'

I still feel a pang of guilt every time I hear Katherine's name. In all the time I've been seeing Edward I've never once met her. She never comes to shows any more, or even to Edward's yard. This makes me believe that their marriage really is nothing but a front, like Edward says.

'So what do you think?' he asks.

'I'd love to go,' I reply, feeling excited again.

He smiles at me broadly and I rack my brain about what I'm going to wear.

'I love you,' he says, tenderly pushing a stray hair away from my face.

'I love you too.'

★

When I finally emerge from my lorry, showered and dressed, I find Orla sitting at the show canteen with a large cup of coffee in her hand. As soon as I sit down, a waitress appears and I order a full Irish breakfast, as my stomach is about ready to eat itself. I'm still smiling from earlier and Orla can tell I'm in a good mood.

'I'm guessing from your massive grin that you and Edward sorted everything out?' she asks, taking a sip of her coffee.

'We certainly did,' I answer, practically giddy. I tell her all about Enda Brown's birthday party, and she almost drools with jealousy.

'That sounds incredible. I can't believe you get to go. Is it a fancy affair?'

'Black tie,' I answer. My full Irish arrives and I dig in.

'Oh my God! We have to go shopping for a dress!' she squeals.

'I think I'll just borrow one of my mum's. She'll be delighted that I'm doing something girly for once.' I laugh, but Orla doesn't say anything. 'What?' I ask.

'Your mum's been calling me a lot the last few days.'

I moan in frustration. Orla is one of the few friends I have that my mother approves of, and it's not a rarity for the two of them to be speaking, but I can tell by Orla's tone of voice that something is up.

'She's not on at you about selling Wildfire as well, is she?'

'No . . . She was asking me if I knew anything about the guy you were dating.'

I don't say anything for a moment. I wish we were talking about something else. 'What did you say?' I ask nervously.

'I just said I hadn't met him yet . . . but I reckon she thinks something might be up.' Orla has put on her 'I'm worried about you' voice. I stare down at my food.

'I'm sorry she's been annoying you,' is all I manage to say.

'It's OK,' Orla says, placing a hand on mine. 'I'm just curious to know if you and Edward have talked about where your relationship is going?' She knows she's on dangerous ground. I can feel myself starting to get irritated by her nosiness.

'We haven't been together that long,' I mutter under my breath.

'I know, but . . . you guys must have some sort of plan? Is he going to move out? Is he going to divorce Katherine and marry you?'

I know Orla's questions are justified, and I've found myself asking them before, but I don't understand why she is trying to ruin my good mood.

'I'm nineteen, Orla! And we've only been together for six months. Would you ask a guy about marriage and commitment after six months?' I say, rather rudely.

'No, I wouldn't,' Orla says softly, aware she has pushed me too far. 'I'm sorry, Liz. I know it's none of my business. I just . . . I just want to make sure you're happy.'

'I am,' I reassure her, no longer wanting to talk about this.

Orla gets the message. We talk about horses, dresses and boys. I soon forget that I'm angry with her, and I'm sad to see her go when she dashes off to get her horse ready for the next class. I relax with my coffee, watching people come in and out. I'm not competing today – Wildfire needs a day's rest after her brilliant performance yesterday. I'm just staying to support Orla and Edward in their classes.

I spot Matthew through the window, making his way up to the stables. I watch him: he moves quickly and with purpose. Should I say hi? Surely there's nothing wrong with just saying hello? It's not inappropriate in any way. Loads of people in relationships have close male friends. Anyway, I reason with myself, if I get to know him better, I can introduce him to Orla.

Matthew is well out of my sight by the time I've debated all this in my head, but I know where Shane's horses are stabled, and Matthew is bound to be there. I take one final mouthful of coffee and walk up to the stables. I'm just saying hello, I tell myself, but before I leave the canteen I pull out a napkin and scribble down my number. I put it in my pocket before I can over-analyse anything. I'm just saying hello.

7

The Competition Begins

LACK OF SLEEP ONLY MAKES ME FEEL MORE HUMILIATED. I KEEP reliving the moment over and over again, the look of confusion and pity on her face. She'll probably ignore me today, and maybe it's better that way. She was the only one to witness my desperation; if she doesn't say anything, then I can at least pretend that none of it happened. It doesn't help that Nick is in a particularly cheery mood. He told me that he scored the lad he had been talking to at the bar last night; luckily, he spared me the gory details.

'No offence, Matt, but you look like shit this morning. What time did you get in?' I had quickly looked at myself in the mirror before leaving the lorry, and it wasn't a pretty sight. I have huge bags under my eyes, my skin looks unnaturally pale and my greasy hair is in serious need of a wash.

'Late enough,' I mumble, scrubbing the same saddle I scrubbed yesterday.

'You meet a girl?'

I don't even speak this time; I just shake my head.

'I'm going to say this in the nicest way possible . . .' Nick turns me around so I am facing him '. . . you need to get *laid*.'

'Fuck off!' I try to push him away, but I'm laughing at the same time.

'Like, seriously, Matt, when was the last time you had sex?'

'Shut up, Nick!' I try to ignore him, but he's on a roll now, and nothing I say will stop him.

'Come on, you can tell me. It is nothing to be ashamed of . . . Well, unless it's more than a few months – then you *should* be ashamed . . .'

'Do you think about anything but sex?'

'Not really,' he says. 'But that's perfectly healthy. A lad who doesn't think about sex most of the time, gay or straight, is weird. Sex is a natural thing that should be celebrated.'

'Would you stop talking about sex?' I'm starting to get embarrassed. The equestrian centre is getting busy and it feels like Nick is shouting at the top of his voice.

'Now, Matt, that is an unhealthy attitude. We should be able to talk about sex openly . . . maybe you need to be educated . . .'

I look down and pretend that I'm not listening; if I say anything, it will only make things worse.

'When a man and a woman love each other very much, or when they're drunk or just really, really *horny* . . .'

I turn around and throw the sponge in my hand as hard as I can at Nick, who is now doubled over, laughing. It flies past his head and hits the back of the person standing behind him. I freeze when I see who it is. Liz picks it up, and walks towards us.

'This belong to you?' she asks, smiling.

'Yeah,' I murmur. 'Thanks.' I try desperately to think of something funny to say, but Nick starts talking before I get a chance.

'Hi, I'm Nick,' he says, wiping his hand on his jeans before offering it to her.

'Elizabeth,' she replies, giving me a sly wink, then takes his hand.

'Well, Elizabeth, it's nice to meet you. This is my friend Matt,' Nick says, gesturing towards me. I smile at her, praying she doesn't say anything.

'Yeah. I know, we met last night.'

'You did?' Nick gives me a look, and I know I need to get Liz away from him as quickly as possible.

'Umm . . . Liz, I need to get one of the horses ready. Do you mind helping me?'

'OK,' she says, a little puzzled. 'It was nice to meet you, Nick.'

'Yes, you too.'

I can see that he's ready to explode; I know I'll be interrogated severely when I get back. I grab the grooming kit and make my way to the far end of the stables, and Liz follows me in silence.

'I'm sorry about Nick . . . he's a bit of a jackass,' I say, once I know we're out of earshot.

'It's fine,' she replies, curling her blonde hair in her fingers. 'You guys seemed to be having an interesting conversation anyway.'

'Oh shit, you didn't hear all that rubbish, did you?'

She nods, giggling. 'It was rather funny – he seems to care more about your love life than you do.'

I laugh as well. 'Nick doesn't care about my love life – sex is all he really cares about.' I take a brush from the grooming kit and start to groom one of the four-year-olds I have to jump later; he's a grey stallion that has had very little experience. He started to misbehave with his owner and he's been handed over to me to school. He's been with us for nearly three months now, and only recently has he started to jump clear. I know it's only a matter of weeks before he'll go back to his real owner. Even though I'm used to this by now, horses coming and going, I'm a little saddened by the thought of this stallion leaving. He's an affectionate horse, and I'm the one who's put the most work into him.

'Yeah, I guess sex and love are two very different things,' Liz mumbles after a little while. It's almost like she's talking to herself, not me.

'Are you riding today?' I ask, keen to change the subject.

'No . . . but my friend Orla is,' she replies, her voice perking up. 'She's jumping in the 1.20 metres.'

'Oh, cool,' I say, not really knowing how to reply. I hate that I'm so awkward around her.

'What about you?' she asks.

'Just the four-year-old classes again. I'd love to be jumping Grand Prix, but I don't have the money to buy a good horse.' Liz nods politely but I see her go slightly red and I scold myself for bringing up money.

She stands there silently for a while, staring at the stallion, a frown on her face. I keep working, trying to keep myself busy, but as the silence continues my nerves only get worse. I try to think of something to say but my mind has gone blank. I let out a sigh of relief when I hear her speak.

'So who's this then?' she asks, stroking the grey stallion's neck.

'We call him Hughie. He loves attention. He's jumping the one metre today.'

'Well, hello, Hughie.' The stallion starts to nibble Liz's hands and pockets, looking for treats. She laughs.

'He's so cute – is he yours?'

'No, I'm just riding him for a while to give him experience. He'll be going back to his owners soon.' There's a hint of sadness in my own voice: I really have grown to like this horse.

'I would hate that,' Liz says suddenly.

'Hate what?' I ask.

'Getting used to a horse, riding it, bonding with it, putting

hard work into it, and then you just have to give them back.'
I shrug, unsure of what to say.

'I'm used to it,' I reply honestly. I finish grooming Hughie
and put the brush back in the box. 'And, anyway, not all the
horses I ride are as nice as this guy.' I pat Hughie on the neck.
'Some of them are complete assholes.'

Liz smiles at me and I can't help but smile back. 'I'd better go;
the 1.20 metres is starting soon,' she says, still smiling, her voice
warm and friendly.

'Oh, yeah . . . no bother . . . Does your friend need a hand
warming up or anything?'

'No, it's OK, I can do it.'

I nod, feeling the nerves building up again. 'Well, tell your
friend good luck.'

'Thanks. Good luck to you too,' she says. I expect her to walk
away, but instead she stands there, biting her lip. I'm starting to
wonder if she wants something from me when she hands me a
white napkin with a number on it.

'If you fancy seeing a film or something next week, give me
a call.' Then she turns around and jogs off before I can reply.

I stare down at the napkin. I can't believe she's given it to me.
I'm still smiling when Nick comes back.

'Would you like to tell me what is going on between you and
that hot blonde girl?' he asks bluntly.

'Nothing,' I say, trying to get past him. I'm carrying Hughie's
tack and it's getting heavy.

'Matt, you had me thinking that you're some poor little lad
that couldn't get a girl's attention even if you stripped down
naked . . . Now I see that is clearly not the case.' I know he's
dying for details – he's the biggest gossip in the world – but
there's no way I'm going to give in to him.

'She's just a friend . . . that's it.'

'A friend?' Nick raises his eyebrows.

Shane walks over to us. His face is freshly shaven and his clothes are spotless. 'What are you guys gossiping about?' he says. I'm filthy and unwashed, and I feel a flash of jealousy.

'Nothing,' I say, praying that Nick keeps his mouth shut.

'Yeah, nothing,' Nick answers, with a mischievous smirk. 'We were just talking about Matt's new *friend*.' I feel my face going red and turn away from the both of them. I don't say anything and tack up the horse to keep myself busy.

'What new friend?' Shane asks, mildly interested.

'Elizabeth,' Nick says, attempting a posh accent.

'Elizabeth O'Brien?' I can hear the surprise in Shane's voice.

'The one and only. I have to say, little Matt here has impressed me.' I feel Nick pat me on the back, but I don't turn around. I know I must be the colour of a beetroot by now.

'Cop on, Nick, stop giving the kid such a hard time and do some work.'

Nick may treat Shane like a friend but there is no doubt that Shane is Nick's superior, and if Shane tells Nick to do something then he is to do it without question or hesitation. By the time I've finished tacking Hughie, Nick's already gone.

'You ready to head down to the warm-up?' Shane asks, handing me my crop and helmet. I nod, hoping that my face has returned to a more normal colour.

Shane and I walk the course together, and he gives me advice and instructions on how to handle Hughie and how to approach each fence. I'm thankful that he seems to have no interest in what Nick was saying earlier.

'He's being a bit difficult today — make sure to ride him strong into each fence,' Shane says to me as I begin jumping my warm-up fences. He nearly always warms me up, unless he's too busy with his own horses. We're always under his strict scrutiny and this means that I always have to be on top of my game, even if I feel awful. I pull Hughie up and walk over to Shane, who's standing in the middle of the warm-up ring. He gives the stallion a pat on the neck.

'Well done, Matt, you're riding well today,' he says. The praise is unexpected.

'Thanks,' I mutter, and then I'm distracted.

Liz looks relaxed and confident as she leans against the post and rails at the side of the warm-up. She smiles at me when I catch her eye. Shane's voice breaks my trance.

'Matt!' I jump slightly, before turning towards him, hoping he has no idea what's going on in my head. 'Take my advice: be careful with Elizabeth . . . I've heard things, and I don't think she's as sweet and innocent as she looks.' He speaks so quietly I can barely hear him, but one look at his face tells me he's serious. I don't say anything. I don't think he expects or wants me to. Then his expression softens and he speaks aloud.

'Careful with him today — I think he's getting a bit too big for his boots.' I wonder if he thinks the same thing about me.

It's a hectic day, as always: Nick and I don't stop. When it's all over, I'm relieved to pack away. We have an endless amount of gear and everything needs to be put away carefully and in the right space, otherwise there's no chance it will all fit. The only place for our leftover hay is the roof of the lorry. I hate putting it up there: the lorry is nearly 20 feet high, and there's nothing to hold on to for support. Nick knows I don't like doing it and therefore always makes me — another element of his cruel sense of humour. I climb down the ladder on the side of the lorry after one load. It doesn't matter how many times I do this, I still don't like it. The ladder only reaches halfway to the ground, so I put a plastic box out to climb down on. I let go of the ladder, expecting my feet to land on the box, but I don't find it. The drop is longer than I expect, and I crumble as I hit hard concrete.

'Fuck!' I look at my hands. They're grazed, and are now

starting to sting and bleed. I push myself up and feel a dull pain in my ankle when I put my weight on it.

'Oh God, I'm so sorry.' I turn around to see the dark and intimidating figure of Edward Dawson. 'I asked my groom to move that box so I could reverse my lorry. I didn't realize it was being used for something.' He looks relaxed, even though he's apologizing. I don't know the man well, but I take a dislike to him. He has a strong sense of superiority about him.

'It's fine,' I mumble, knowing that I can't say anything against him. I lean on the side of the lorry and try again to put some weight on my ankle. Edward eyes me up.

'Can I do anything for you? I feel terrible,' he says. His concern seems to be genuine, but I find I don't trust him.

'No, I'm fine, thank you.' I look him up and down. Do I only dislike him because of the rumours about him and Liz, which may not even be true? Am I jealous?

'Do I know you?' he asks with a sudden grin.

'I don't think so,' I say, trying my hardest to be civil.

'No, no, I definitely do. Are you a friend of Elizabeth?'

I say nothing. I just stare back, wondering where this conversation is going. Is it possible that Edward is jealous of *me*? After a while, I nod.

'I knew it. Well, I'm glad she's starting to meet some new people. That girl is really something.' I give him a quick smile, unable to tell what he means by this.

'Yes, she is,' I reply, trying to ignore the pain in my ankle and hands.

Edward walks over to me. The two of us are less than a foot apart now.

'She's a very attractive girl too, isn't she?' He winks and I now know that I'm *not* jealous of him. I dislike him because he's arrogant. I don't say anything, because I'm afraid of what will come out of my mouth if I open it. 'Nice to meet you, Matt.

Take care of that ankle now.' He pats me hard on the back as he walks away, nearly making me lose my balance. It's only after he has left that I realize his lorry is nowhere to be seen.

8

Broken

I HEAR WILDFIRE WHINNY IN DISTRESS. I LOOK AROUND frantically, but I can't see her.

'Wildfire!' I scream. She wails back, and it sounds like she's in pain but, still, I can't see her.

'Wildfire!' I'm starting to get hysterical. I can't see anything; everything is foggy; even the ground underneath me feels unsteady. I run forward, and Wildfire's cries become more distant. I try to run back to where I was, but I'm so lost and confused.

'Where are you?' I shout. I feel the tears falling down my face. Her cries grow quieter and quieter, and I know I'm losing her. I fall to my knees in desperation and bury my head in my hands. But as my legs hit the ground, green grass tickles my limbs. I look up, and I'm no longer in the grey mess I was in before but in a beautiful green paddock, and the sun is blazing down on my face. It takes my eyes a few minutes to adjust to the striking sunlight. I no longer hear Wildfire's wails.

I turn around and there she is, calm and relaxed in the beautiful sun. She whickers to me encouragingly and I make my way over to her. As I get closer I see a boy sitting next to her.

'Hi,' Matthew says as I approach him.

'Hi,' I reply, puzzled as to why he is here. Silently, I sit down next to him on the grass and we both watch Wildfire as she grazes.

'She got lost. But she's OK now,' Matthew says gently.

'Did you find her?' I ask.

'No. She found her own way back.' Matthew reaches out for my hand and squeezes it affectionately. I don't pull away; holding his hand feels natural. 'We all get lost sometimes . . . and that's OK – as long we keep trying to find our way back.'

'Am I lost?' I ask, no longer able to take my eyes off him.

'Are you?' he says, turning the question on me. I don't quite know what he means.

'What are you doing here?' I say, but as I do so I realize I don't want him to go.

'You tell me.'

'I want to kiss you,' I announce, my heart racing.

'Then kiss me.'

I place my hand nervously on his cheek. Matthew doesn't move but lets me decide the pace. His facial expression is so calm, but there is a hint of a cheeky smile, as if he had planned this all along. I lean in and peck his lips; they're warmer than I expect them to be. I don't think about anything I'm doing but let my instincts take over. I'm not sure where his hands are or where mine are either, but I don't care, because everything just feels so good and comfortable. Our bodies move in sync together and I find myself getting excited, really excited. It builds and builds until I let out a moan of relief. I open my eyes and realize I'm no longer in the field and that I am alone.

My bedroom is bright in the morning, sun seeping in through my window. I shift in my bed and feel an aftershock from my dream.

'Well, that was different,' I whisper to myself, shocked at what my own mind has just created. I have never had an orgasm in my sleep before; I hear that it happens to some girls, but it never has to me – till now. I'm surprised at how intense it was, that I could achieve such pleasure from my own imagination, without even being touched. But what surprises me most is not the power of my imagination but the subject of it. I've only just met Matthew and yet I feel as if he's got into my head. It's pointless trying to tell myself I'm not attracted to him after the dream I've just had. But I don't want to be with him, I want to be with Edward, I'm sure of that. I push the dream to the back of my mind as I get up. Everyone has sex dreams about strange people, I tell myself. I have nothing to feel guilty about. But as I shower and get dressed I find myself in a surprisingly good mood.

I skip down the stairs of my mother's house two steps at a time, humming away to myself. It's a fairly sunny day for late January and I have an early schooling session with Edward, so I'm glad I'm feeling perky, no matter what the cause. As I stroll into the kitchen, I'm taken aback to see my mother sitting there, a cup of coffee in her hand.

'Hi,' I say. Looking down at my watch, I see that it's before eight o'clock. 'You're up early.' My mother rarely gets up before nine, which means I'm nearly always out of the house before she even wakes up.

'Well, I've a *lot* to do today,' she says quietly, taking a sip of her coffee. Her hair and make-up are perfectly done, as always, but she looks more tired than she normally does. I grab a banana out of the fruit bowl and make a dive for the door before she can lecture me about something, but she calls me back.

'Can I show you something, Elizabeth?'

I take a few deep breaths before I turn back to face her. I'm determined not to let her ruin my good mood. 'Of course,' I say, as respectfully as possible, hoping that if I don't argue with her maybe she won't argue with me. She hands me a brown envelope that has already been opened. I look at her. She's smiling and, surprisingly, it looks genuine.

'It's actually quite exciting,' she says cheerfully. 'Go on, look at it.' I pull the letter out of the envelope and read it as quickly as possible, now conscious of the fact that I'm running late for my schooling session with Edward.

Dear Elizabeth O'Brien,

Thank you for your application to the University of Oxford. We are delighted to inform you that you have been accepted to our business programme in Economics and Management . . .

I stop reading and look up at my mother. She's still smiling, but I'm bubbling over with anger.

'What is this?' I ask, trying to control myself.

'Your old business teacher told me it's one of the *best* qualifications you can get, and Oxford is such a beautiful place—'

'I didn't apply to Oxford,' I interrupt.

'I did it for you. I know how easily distracted you get, so I thought I would save you the hassle. I've already told your father. He's thrilled.' As my mother finishes her sentence, I tear the letter up. Her smile fades.

'I'm not going,' I say curtly.

'Oh, don't be so *ridiculous*, Elizabeth. Do you know how *lucky* you are to get into a place like Oxford? You *can't* turn something like that down.' She's talking to me as if I were a six-year-old who doesn't want to eat her dinner, and it's driving me insane.

'How many times have we had this conversation?' I plead with her. 'I don't want to go to college. I don't want to be a businesswoman. I want to be a showjumper. Why don't you understand that?'

'I *do* understand that,' she says, now standing up. 'I understand that you like horses and that it's a fun hobby, but you're wasting your time on a silly dream that *won't* happen. You're an intelligent girl who's acting stupid.'

'You have no idea what I'm capable of,' I say, the sting of her words biting into me.

'Don't you want to go to college and pursue a dream that is *achievable*, not this stupid horse fantasy? Do you not realize, lots of people would *kill* to be as smart as you are?' She grabs both my hands as she speaks, but I pull away.

'Stop trying to live your life through me!' I'm virtually screaming at her. 'Just because you were too thick to go to college doesn't mean you have the right to force me to go.' I know I've gone too far, but I don't regret what I said. She has said so many hurtful things to me in the past I think it's only fair she knows what it feels like to be on the receiving end.

My mother stands there frozen, and for one awful moment I think she's going to hit me. She doesn't, but what she says instead hurts so much more.

'We're selling Wildfire.'

'No, you're not. Dad won't let you,' I reply, wishing I could get out of here and pretend none of this is happening.

'He agreed last night . . . when he heard you'd been accepted to Oxford.'

I stare at her for a moment and I know she's telling the truth. 'You can't,' I blurt, the tears starting in my eyes.

'You'll thank me for this in the long run.' She doesn't even try to make eye contact with me.

'Please! Don't! That horse means everything to me.' But I know this is exactly what she has wanted all along.

'I don't want to discuss this *any more*,' she says calmly, sitting back down. At this moment, I think I hate her.

'You *can't* sell Wildfire . . . Edward won't let you . . .'

'Why would Edward care?' my mother scoffs.

'Because he—' I want to say 'Because he loves me,' but I can't, because it will only make things worse — but then again, how can things *get* any worse? 'Because he cares about me . . .' It's as if a light bulb has blinked on over my mother's head. She stares at me in shock.

'The man you're seeing — don't tell me it's Edward?'

I don't reply. I run upstairs to my bedroom, but she follows me.

'Don't you *dare* walk away from me, Elizabeth!' She storms into my room as I grab a large bag from under my bed.

'I'm leaving,' I mutter, grabbing as many clothes as I can from my drawers.

'And where the hell are you going to go? To move in with Edward and *his wife*?' She's almost hysterical. I've never seen her lose her cool like this. I stop packing and turn towards her.

'You don't understand, because you're too selfish and stuck-up to understand anything. Your life is nothing but boring lunches and dinner parties. I want excitement, I want to live. Your life is my idea of a nightmare, and I hate everything about you!' She doesn't say anything after that, she just leaves. I'm shaking with anger as I finish packing and walk out the door. When I get into my car, I collapse into tears.

Over the next thirty minutes, I do my best to pull myself together, but then I think about losing Wildfire and I fall to pieces again. I hear my phone ring and look down to see Edward's name. I pick up and tell him everything as best I can, but I know it's an out-of-control rant.

'Come to my house *now*, Elizabeth. I'll fix this,' he insists. I take my time driving; having to concentrate on the road seems to calm me down. When I reach the house, I feel a bit more together. I have to believe that Edward can fix this.

He hands me a gin and tonic as soon as I walk in the door.

'I don't want a drink, thank you,' I say, making my way into the kitchen.

'Take it. It'll calm you down,' he says, rather forcefully. I only realize how much my whole body is shaking when I lift the glass up to my mouth. The gin is strong and burns my throat, but I force myself to take three large mouthfuls before sitting at the kitchen table.

'Where's Katherine?' I ask, praying she isn't going to walk in on us.

'She's in Dublin city centre. She's got an interview with *Gloss* magazine to be a fashion consultant or something.' His tone is sarcastic, and I know he's not happy about her being in Ireland.

'So, if she gets this job . . . she's going to be around a lot more,' I say.

For the second time today I feel the panic take hold in my stomach. It's so easy to disregard Katherine and her relationship with Edward, because she's never here, but now everything could change. I want to collapse into tears, but instead I take another large sip of my drink.

'Let's not worry about that now . . . Tell me exactly what your mother said.'

I explain everything. I tell him that she applied to Oxford for me; that she has convinced my father to sell Wildfire; that she knows we are together. I tell him the last bit cautiously, afraid that he might be mad at me, but he's not. His blue eyes are gentle and he squeezes my hand affectionately.

'I'm sorry . . .'

'Why are you sorry?'

'I shouldn't have told her about us . . .'

'Elizabeth, that is the least of my worries. People are bound to find out eventually, anyway . . .' My heart lifts a little at this. *People are bound to find out eventually* – he thinks about the future. He thinks about us being together, without it being a secret. 'What we really need to figure out is how we are going to stop her from selling Wildfire . . .'

'She's determined,' I say, feeling defeated. 'And she's not going to listen to anyone, especially us. Not now that she knows we're together . . .'

Edward stands up and starts pacing. 'That mother of yours, she's an absolute bitch . . . Does she not realize you are *this* close to really making a name for yourself? Every week and every show, you're winning more attention. It won't be long before the Irish Horse Board selection committee spots you – with a bit of luck you might even make the Irish Aga Khan team this year – and your mother . . . she's going to fucking ruin all of it.' I can feel his anger with every step he takes, and I know that he's frustrated for me, but also for himself. He has put so much time and effort into training me, and everyone knows I'm working with him. He wants to prove himself as a world-class trainer as well as a world-class competitor. I know it's his back-up plan for when he is too old to compete.

'I know.' I'm furious, but I still don't really want to join in with the verbal bashing of my mother.

'But none of that means anything to her, because she's a gold-digging, bitter whore who can't stand the idea of her daughter being successful.' I flinch as Edward slams his hand down on the granite kitchen counter. He's silent for a moment and I feel myself fill with anxiety. If Edward can't fix this, I don't know what I'm going to do.

'How much money does your mother want for Wildfire?' he asks suddenly.

'I don't know,' I say. 'I don't think she cares about the money. I just think she wants Wildfire gone.' Edward sits down, facing me, and grabs my hands.

'What if I bought Wildfire for you?' he says.

'What?'

'I could buy Wildfire and you could continue to compete on her, just like we planned.' His voice is soft, as if he were speaking to a child, but I can't believe what he is saying.

'My mother would never sell her to you.' That's all I can get out of my mouth.

'She wouldn't know it was me. I'll get one of my friends to approach her and your father. They won't know I'm the true buyer until everything is over.' Edward speaks with such certainty I know that, in his mind, he is going to do this, no matter what. I think of my mother and what she would do when she found out that Edward and I had tricked her. I don't think she'd ever speak to me again. But the thought of losing Wildfire completely is too terrifying. She's my dream, she's my everything, and I will do anything to keep her.

'You'd do that for me?' I ask, realizing that this is what I have been praying for. I wanted Edward to fix this, and now he's going to.

'Of course. When will you realize, Elizabeth, that I'd do anything for you?' As the relief hits me, irrationally, I start crying. Edward looks at me, panicked.

'What's wrong?'

'Nothing,' I say, in between floods of tears. 'I just love you so much.' He laughs, relieved, and wraps his arms around me.

We stay like that for a little while. I feel so tiny engulfed by him. I close my eyes and enjoy every moment of it. I think of everything that has happened today. I can't take it all in. I think of my mother and wonder what she's doing at this moment. I feel a pang of regret when I remember all the horrible things I said to her, but I push those feelings aside. She deserved it, I tell myself. Edward's right: she just can't stand the thought of me being successful.

After a while, Edward stirs, interrupting my thoughts.

'I need to go back to the yard,' he declares. 'I've a lot of work to do – but don't worry . . . by the end of the day I will own Wildfire.' He speaks with such conviction and determination I don't doubt him for a moment.

'Thank you,' I say.

'Don't even mention it. Why don't you go take a shower and you can meet me at the yard later?'

I kiss him appreciatively, and he holds my head still with his hands. It's only a few moments before I hear the familiar sound of his phone. He jumps up and snaps it open.

'Hello . . . Yes . . . No . . . How much . . .? What's the real price?' He leaves the room, and I know that's our conversation over. In the time I've known Edward, I've realized that his phone never stops. It's like his own head: he's constantly thinking of the next competition, the next horse, the next deal – it's never-ending. But I guess that's what this world is all about.

I make my way up to the bathroom and strip. The water stings my red face, but it feels cleansing. As I stand in the boiling-hot shower I think of the dream I had this morning. I don't know why it comes back to me now, but I'm surprised how clear it still is in my mind. I try to push it away, but I can still see Matt's face and feel him kissing my neck. I'm very glad I'm alone. The images and thoughts disappear only when I step out of the shower and see what's in front of me: curling tongs, blush, mascara, foundation, and many more things which undoubtedly belong to Katherine. In my rush to get into the shower I hadn't noticed any of this, but now it's all in front of me, making me feel like an intruder.

I stand quietly for a moment, trying to hear if Edward is still here, but there is nothing but silence. I'm not used to seeing Katherine's things, and again it hits me how much more she'll be around if she gets that job in Dublin. I want to talk to Edward about it. I want to ask him what our future together will be. Is he going to leave Katherine? *People are bound to find out eventually* – what does that mean, exactly? I want to ask him so much, but I know now is not the right time. He's buying Wildfire for me; he's giving me my dream back. It's too much to ask him to leave Katherine as well. I just have to keep reminding myself that he doesn't love her; he's just being kind to her, protecting her from embarrassment. I look away from her things and begin to get dressed. *He doesn't love her, he loves me.*

9

Down But Not Out

'I DON'T CARE IF YOU'RE CRIPPLED, MATT, WE HAVE THIRTY stables to do and you're seriously holding me up. For fuck's sake, we're going to be stuck here till midnight if you don't move faster!'

It's been three days since the show, but the stabbing pain in my ankle has remained. I've iced it every night and the swelling is slowly going down, but I'm still pretty lame. I can't argue, though: Nick is only telling it how it is. It's taking me twice as long to do my work. I'm not normally finished before dark even on a good day, but these last few days have left me working later and later into the night. Nick was sympathetic at first, offering to do some of my work for me but, as soon as he realizes how slow I am, his patience becomes strained.

'I'm sorry, Nick, I'm trying!'

He grunts at me and walks on ahead, fed up waiting for me. My hips seize up with every step I take, and whenever my foot touches the ground, a roaring pain shoots up my leg. I can't carry anything either; Nick has to do that for me. Usually, he's the guy I go to when I need cheering up. Usually, we'd go back to our little bungalow, owned by Shane and in his yard, and order chips and beer for dinner and watch trashy TV. The last few days, though, Nick's locked himself in his room the second we get home: after a day at work, he's – understandably – sick of dealing with me.

I can't really talk to the other grooms either. It's like a hierarchy and Nick and I are ranked above them; mostly, they seem too afraid even to speak to me. When I try to joke with them, they just stare at me, terrified, as if I'm trying to trick them into doing or saying something wrong. Most of them don't last that long anyway – a couple of months possibly – before they get bored and leave, or they mess up and Shane sends them packing.

I try not to but I whimper as I walk up the steps. The pain is no longer just in my ankle; my hips, my ribs are badly bruised too. I take deep breaths, waiting for it to pass, and I think of Edward, the smug face he had on him when he was talking about Liz. He spoke about her as if she was an object, something precious he owned. Well, if there's anything I know for certain about Edward, it's that he doesn't like to share. And I have the bruises to prove it.

When I reach the top of the stone steps I see Shane. He's talking to Nick, his arms crossed. Nick looks frustrated and is throwing his hands about as if he's explaining something. They both turn to look at me, and Nick's face goes bright red, guilty. I know then what they're talking about.

'Matt, come here for a second, would you?'

I walk over, trying not to limp, but I know it's not going to fool anyone.

'Nick tells me you hurt yourself at the show?'

Nick is staring at his feet, ashamed. I nod, knowing there's no point in lying.

'Yeah, I fell from the lorry roof . . . someone moved the box we use to get up and down.' I feel like I'm in school again and I'm being punished for something that someone else did.

'Who moved the box?' Shane asks, looking at Nick sceptically.

'I don't know,' I answer quickly. 'Nick was in the stables and I was busy tying the hay to the roof, so neither of us saw.' There's no point in telling Shane it was Edward Dawson. He already dislikes the man plenty, though I'm not sure why.

He stares at us both, unsure of what to say next.

'Matt, have you been able to do your work? To the same standard you would have before?'

I hesitate. Nick is still staring down at the floor. I really want his help, but I know I'm not going to get it.

'No – I'm a little slower than normal, and I can't carry the heavy stuff . . .' It's only luck that Shane hasn't asked me to ride any of the horses over the past few days. I wouldn't have been able to do it.

'Do you think you've done any real damage?'

'No, no. Just aches and pains. I'll be fine in a few days.' An injured groom is useless. Shane is kind, most of the time, but he wouldn't hesitate to get rid of me if he thought I was no longer able to work at the level he wants me to.

'OK, take a few days off. Head home, recover, and come back to me on Monday ready to work.'

I sigh with relief. I hear Nick do the same.

'Thanks, Shane.' I realize I've been holding my breath. I'm just starting to relax when he speaks again.

'Matt, next time, just tell me if something like this happens. I don't like things being kept from me. And that goes for you too, Nick.'

We both nod without saying a word, worried that speaking might ruin our good fortune.

Once Shane is out of sight, I turn on Nick.

'For fuck's sake, what was that about? Ratting me out to Shane like that! I know I've been pretty useless the last few days, but I could've lost my job.' Now that my panic has passed I feel the full sting of Nick's betrayal.

'I was trying to help you—' I can tell Nick is beginning to get angry himself.

'How is that helping me?' I'm shouting now, and I know that the other grooms can hear, but I don't care.

'Shane has three new three-year-olds coming in tomorrow. He told me that he wanted you to break them, and when I said that I thought I should do it instead he got suspicious . . . he thought you'd lost your nerve. I had to tell him you were injured . . . If one of those three-year-olds had dumped you the way you are now, you'd have been broken and you'd have definitely lost your job.'

My anger subsides. Of course, he's right: there's no way I could break a horse the way I am now. I would have seriously hurt myself.

'I'm sorry,' I say, swallowing my pride. He looks at me in silence for a moment, trying to figure out if I mean it, before he replies.

'It's OK . . . and Matt, I'm sorry too. I didn't want to snitch on you but I just didn't see any other way . . .'

I shrug. I would have done the same thing.

'Why didn't you tell Shane it was Dawson who moved the box?'

I look at Nick for a moment before I answer. 'I don't know . . .' I say truthfully. 'I didn't think it would make a difference . . . It's not like Shane could do anything.'

'True,' Nick agrees. 'Those two hate each other enough already.'

'Why?'

'Because of FireCracker.' FireCracker was the horse that

made Shane's career. With that horse, Shane proved himself one of the best riders in the world. 'FireCracker went to Edward first and he said that the horse was useless and would never compete for anyone. And then when he started performing so well for Shane, Edward was humiliated . . .' Nick tells me this casually, obviously surprised I didn't know before.

'Wow! Shit one for Edward – he missed out on a serious horse!' I say.

'Yeah, he did . . . And the two have been in serious competition with each other since then.'

We both fall silent, wondering what it would be like to have competed on a horse like FireCracker. I think back to all the scathing and passive-aggressive remarks I've heard pass between Edward and Shane, and it all makes a lot more sense. Shane is a humble man who loves the sport because he loves great horses. Edward loves the competition, the glory. The two couldn't be more opposite.

I do as much as I can to help Nick that day. I know I have the time off now, but I don't want to leave him with the rest of a full day's work. One of the other grooms can help him to-morrow. But by six o'clock he's sick of me limping around behind him like an injured puppy.

'For God's sake, Matt, would you just go? The sight of you is making me depressed!' I laugh, trying to lift one of the bags of feed into the wheelbarrow. 'You're making me think that you don't want to go home?' Nick asks. There's a note of suspicion in his voice.

'Well, I kind of don't,' I say, in all honesty. 'I always get grief when I go home – they don't really get why I'm still working here . . . They don't see it as a viable career.'

'At least you *can* go home . . .' Nick's tone has changed, and I stop what I'm doing and look at him.

'You OK?' I ask. His expression changes in a second and he is back to the carefree, joking Nick he was a few moments ago.

'Fine . . . why?' he says nonchalantly.

'Just you said about going home—'

'Ah, don't get all "Let's talk about our feelings and shit". Otherwise I'm going to think you have started batting for my team.' I laugh.

'Don't worry, Nick, I'm still straight.'

'Good, because even if you go gay, you still don't have a chance with me.' Nick laughs at his own joke and I join in. I decide to forget about his earlier comment, assuming that it must have been a slip of the tongue. 'They're right, though – your parents. It's not like you and me are climbing the corporate ladder,' he goes on, adding another bag of feed to the wheelbarrow. 'Why don't you give that Liz girl a call? I'm sure she'll make you feel better.' Nick makes kissing noises and I move to hit him.

'No,' I say, more to myself than him. 'I haven't seen the family in a while. I should probably visit them.' The temptation to call Liz is there but the pain in my leg is a reminder why I shouldn't. I like her, but she made it clear that I don't have a chance, and I really don't want the drama.

I'm making my way to our bungalow when I hear someone call my name. I turn around to see Adam, one of the temporary grooms. He looks panicked and worried. I stop and he rushes up to me.

'Matt, I need help. I can't get Cedric in from the field. I've been trying to catch him for an hour now and he keeps galloping away whenever I get near him.' He's practically begging me for help.

'No bother,' I say, and he seems to relax.

'Thank you so much. I know you have your own work to do,

but it's nearly dark and I know Shane will kill me if that horse spends the night out in the field . . .'

'It's OK, honestly,' I say, trying to reassure Adam. He's seventeen and has only been working here for two weeks. He hasn't learnt the tricks and personalities of all the horses here yet. I grab a bucket and some feed before making my way towards the field. 'If he knows you have food, then he'll come straight away,' I say.

True to my words, Cedric comes trotting over immediately as soon as he sees the bucket in my hand.

'I should've thought of that,' Adam says, in a slightly defeated tone.

'Sure, you know now,' I say, and this makes him smile.

I walk with him back to the stables to make sure he gets Cedric there all right. A loose horse running around the yard is the last thing we need.

'So, how have you been finding it here?' I ask, just to make conversation.

'Good,' Adam replies, but he sounds unsure. 'I find it hard to keep up sometimes, though . . . Everything has to be done in such an exact way. I didn't expect it to be like this.'

'The yard is like a business,' I explain, trying to do it kindly. 'And the horses and riders are our clients. We have to do things in an exact way because we have to please the client. It's not always easy, or even logical, but it's the way we have to do it to keep the business going.' Adam nods along as I speak, but he doesn't seem at all comforted. 'It gets easier,' I reassure him. 'And if you're ever really stuck with something, just ask me or Nick. We don't bite.'

'Have you known Nick for long?' he asks.

'Um . . . yeah, about four years . . . Why?' I reply, curious.

'Is he . . . um . . . I mean, is he . . . you know?' Adam stutters.

'Is he what?' I ask angrily, knowing where this is going. It's not the first time one of the grooms has had a problem with Nick being gay. Adam starts to panic.

'No, it's not like that . . . I was just wondering . . . but I guess it doesn't matter . . .'

'Yes, he is gay. Do you have a problem with that?'

'No . . . no . . . not at all. I like Nick . . . it's just—'

'It's just what?'

'My da goes to the same church as his da.'

'So?' I ask, missing the point.

'It's just surprising, that's all . . . I have nothing against Nick, I swear.'

I look at Adam for a moment, and I can see he's more embarrassed than anything else. We've reached Cedric's stable now.

'Are you OK from here?' I ask.

'Yes, thanks,' Adam replies. 'And sorry about what I said about Nick. I swear I didn't mean any offence.' I look again at Adam's face and decide I believe him.

I think about what Adam said as I pack my bags for home: 'It's just surprising, that's all . . .' I can't figure out what he meant by it. I'm tempted to ask Nick, but I don't want him to think that Adam has something against him. I decide it's better just to leave it. Nick doesn't like talking about his family – he's made that clear over the years – and who am I to force it out of him just because I'm curious? We all have family dramas and now I need to deal with mine.

10

A New Home

'THANK YOU AGAIN,' I ANNOUNCE FOR WHAT MUST BE THE hundredth time. 'You have no idea how grateful I am.' I carry the last box into Orla's apartment, and she closes the door behind me.

'Oh, would you shut up, Liz! I'm thrilled to have you. I hate living alone.' After Edward had sorted everything out with Wildfire, I realized I needed to find somewhere to live. Edward suggested I take one of the grooms' apartments in his yard. As much as I like the grooms in Edward's yard, I know I couldn't be around them 24/7; between Edward and all the grooms, I have become desperate for some female company. I contacted Orla with the intention of asking her could I stay for a few nights while I figured things out, but once she heard about everything that had happened she insisted I move in with her.

Orla's apartment is in Dublin city centre so she's close to Rotunda Hospital. It's a beautiful and modern place, with two separate bedrooms, and it's only a twenty-minute drive from Edward's yard. Thankfully, with my winnings, I'm able to help out with rent and bills, but I know Orla would let me stay here even if I couldn't. The last few days have been beyond stressful. Edward put me up in a hotel until I got my living situation sorted, but I felt so guilty that he was spending so much money to keep me happy.

Every time my phone rings I know it's my mother. She's tried every tactic under the sun to convince me to come home. She's screamed at me, cried – she's even threatened to go to the press and tell them that I'm having an affair with Edward. For an awful moment I thought she'd do it and that my relationship with him would be ruined. But as the days went on I realized she was only bluffing. The one thing she hasn't tried is compassion. I may not have always been the best daughter but I do wish we could understand each other more. I'll never be as beautiful or elegant as her but I really think I could be a great showjumper. I just wish she would try to understand why I left and why I'm so desperate to keep Wildfire. If she tried to understand that, I might consider going home. But it's clear she'll never get it.

Moving into Orla's apartment should've only taken a day, but because I've continued to train and compete every day, it's nearly a full week after everything happened that I'm finally here.

'So, what do you want to do tonight?' Orla asks excitedly.

'Truthfully, I want to sleep. I'm exhausted.'

'Don't be a boring old sod! Anyway, we have to celebrate your victory!' Today I competed in the Balmoral Equestrian Centre and won the Premier Grand Prix. The fences were massive, but Wildfire jumped everything with such ease. Edward wasn't there today, he was off in Hickstead competing on the Irish Nations Cup team, but I had a message of congratulations from him, on my phone, as soon as I got off the horse.

'You must be thrilled!'

'I am,' I say, lying down on the couch. My whole body is exhausted but I can't stop smiling. Orla wasn't there today either − she had to work − but I gave her a detailed play-by-play of my whole round the second I arrived here.

'There must be something going on? There's always a party after a big show like that.'

'Well … Dom did say that Sally Murphy is having a blowout,' I answer, giving in to her excitement.

'Perfect,' Orla sings, practically dancing on the spot. 'Sally Murphy's parties are always wild. It's exactly what we need.' Sally Murphy is the daughter of a hotel tycoon and she spends her father's money excessively on both horses and parties. 'So shall we get into our slut disguises and have a wild one?' Orla is already pulling the vodka out of the fridge.

'Fuck it!' I announce, letting myself forget about all the drama that's gone on this week. 'Let's have a great one.'

Within minutes Orla has me feeling happy and excited. She's the type of person who is never in a bad mood, and she can make anyone feel at ease. My clothes are still packed away in boxes, but with some frantic help I manage to find some skinny jeans, a silky white top and black heels. Orla wears a summery dress and her red hair is set in perfect curls. I can't help but be envious of how pretty she looks: her red lips and pale skin make her look like a Fifties pin-up girl. I tower over her in my heels, and I do my best to hide my bony shoulders with a black blazer.

We leave the apartment and, as Orla hails us a taxi, I take out my phone to ring Edward. No answer. He jumps for Ireland tomorrow, so he'll be having an early night, but I want to wish him luck. I try to call again, but it goes straight to voicemail. As Orla and I clamber into the taxi, I get a text message: 'In a meeting with Taidgh Bourke.'

Taidgh Bourke is the Irish team's chef d'équipe, which basically means he is the trainer and captain. He must be having a last-minute meeting with the team to finalize their game plan for tomorrow. I write my reply quickly, hoping that Edward won't mind me disturbing him.

'Just wanted to wish you the best of luck tomorrow. I love you x.' I've barely put my phone back in my pocket when I get his reply: 'Thanks. You too.' I want to send another message, I want to keep the conversation going somehow, but I know I can't. Tomorrow is so important for him. I can't annoy or distract him. I put my phone away, pushing away any feelings of hurt. He needs to concentrate. I need to support him as he always does me, even if that means keeping my distance.

I've been to a few of Sally Murphy's parties before, but tonight surpasses any of them. She has rented out the Pembroke Suite at the Four Seasons Hotel. As Orla and I walk in the door, our senses are ambushed by loud dance music and flashing lights. All the girls are done up, with hair styled perfectly and scantily clad in small, tight dresses, while all the boys wear polo shirts with Ralph Lauren V-necked jumpers. Flutes of champagne are put into our hands by a waiter, and Orla and I clink our glasses together before knocking it back.

'How is Sally getting away with this? Surely the other guests must be going nuts!' Orla shouts over the music.

'I don't know!' I watch one of the girls dance on the expensive wooden table while pouring the contents of a whole champagne bottle into her mouth and down her now see-through white dress. 'Sure, who cares? It's not our problem.' I grab a half-empty, abandoned bottle of champagne from the counter and refill our glasses.

As Orla and I make our way further into the vast suite, people stop and congratulate me. At first I'm flattered and chuffed but, as it happens more and more, I become slightly embarrassed. I know some people here but, in all honesty, most of them are strangers to me. How on earth do they all know me?

'You're famous!' Orla cries, giggling.

'My horse is famous.'

'Don't sell yourself short. You're talented – everyone can see that.' I'm about to reply when I feel someone grab me around the waist.

'Hello, beautiful ladies. How are you tonight?' I recognize Dom's voice and turn around just as he leans in to kiss me on both cheeks.

'We're good – enjoying the champagne!' Orla declares, moving in to hug him. With heels on, both Orla and I tower over Dom, but he exudes such confidence and charisma no one notices how short he is.

'How are you?' I ask, topping up his glass from another discarded bottle I've found.

'I'm good. I'm riding Lady Gregory's horses now.' Dom finishes his glass in one go and refills it without any encourage-ment from me. Lady Gregory owns a string of incredibly talented showjumping horses, but she is known to be difficult and is always falling out with various riders.

'How's that going?' Orla asks.

'Grand,' Dom replies unenthusiastically. 'She's bat-shit insane, but the woman owns great horses . . . Sally really threw some party here, didn't she?' he goes on, clearly wanting to change the subject.

'Yeah,' I agree. 'This is seriously excessive, even for her.'

'Have you looked around?' I shake my head. 'Oh, it's insane. Massive dining room – and the bathroom is unreal. Though I wouldn't go in there now. Paul's in the jacuzzi with some French groom.' Dom gives Orla and me an impish look.

'I thought Paul and Sally were dating?' Orla asks, puzzled.

'They are,' Dom says coolly. 'Sally is out on the balcony scoring Francis. His wife is in Spain for the week.'

'Each to their own,' I say, shaking my head, now well used to

the incestuous whirlpool that is the Irish showjumping world.
'Is Edwin here?' I ask Dom cheekily, remembering how the two
of them couldn't keep their hands off each other at the last party.

'Edwin has decided he's straight,' Dom says, a hint of bitterness creeping into his voice.

'How can you just *decide* you're straight?' Orla asks. She's
slurring her words, and I realize I'm feeling quite drunk myself.
Even so, I pour myself another glass. This is the happiest I have
felt all week, and I don't want to come down from it.

'You can't!' Dom exclaims angrily. 'He'll shag a few girls and
then realize it's shit – but I'm not waiting around for him to
figure that out.'

'Onwards and upwards!' I cheer, and it seems to make Dom
smile.

The three of us stay there in that same spot for the next hour
or so. We gossip and laugh about the people around us and I
continue to guzzle the champagne.

'Elizabeth!' I turn around to see Sally stumbling towards me.
Her short dress barely covers her bum and her make-up is
smeared. I smile at her as she practically crawls over to us.

'Cokehead.' Dom coughs, and I turn around to give him a
filthy look, but Sally doesn't seem to have noticed.

'Elizabeth, you were amazing today! You must be thrilled!'
Sally grabs me in a bear hug and, in my slightly intoxicated
state, I fall backwards with Sally on top of me. The whole room
cheers, and I can hear both Dom and Orla laughing. I try to
struggle to my feet: I really am drunk now. After I fail a few
times to get up, Dom pulls me upright, still laughing away. A girl
I don't recognize seems to have helped Sally up.

'I'm so sorry.' Sally looks as if she might burst into tears.

'It's fine.' I'm slurring now, and leaning up against the wall for
support. The dark-haired girl who helped Sally is staring at me,

a grumpy look on her face, and I begin to feel paranoid. What's her problem?

'This is Tiffany!' Sally exclaims, all of a sudden upbeat and happy again. 'She's from America and . . . Does anyone know where Paul is?' she asks, her train of thought shifting.

'Bathroom,' Dom says. He's unable to hide the smile on his face when Sally starts heading in that direction.

I'm about to turn back towards Orla and Dom when I hear Tiffany speak.

'So you won the Premier Grand Prix today?' she asks in an American twang.

'Yeah, I did,' I say cheerfully, thinking that she's about to congratulate me.

'You ride an American horse, don't you?'

'Yeah, I do . . .'

She smiles at me snobbishly.

'Who trains you?' she asks rudely.

'Edward Dawson.'

'I know him. My sister is a friend of his wife.' She just stares at me, waiting for a reaction.

'I don't really know his wife,' I say, but knots start forming in my stomach at even the thought of Katherine.

'No . . . I don't suppose you do . . .'

An awkward silence follows and I'm wondering how I can get away when Tiffany speaks again. 'Is he still fucking about?'

'What?' I ask, dumbfounded.

'Edward? Is he still fucking other girls? I heard he was fucking one of his grooms before, and Katherine found out and now she'll only let him have male grooms.' Her words take a few minutes to sink in. Edward's grooms are all male, but I'd never thought anything of it.

'That's not true,' I say, as assertively as I can, but I can feel my voice beginning to shake.

'Yeah, it is. My sister said that Katherine caught him red-handed. Apparently, he fucked the groom in Katherine's bed and everything.' Tiffany smiles as she says this, as if it's all one funny joke, but I can feel myself filling up with anger.

'Fuck off! You have no idea what you're talking about.' I feel someone grip my arm, and I assume it's Orla or Dom, but I don't turn around to check.

'What's wrong with you? Are *you* fucking him or something?' Tiffany asks, still smiling and now almost cackling. Without thinking, I pick up my glass and throw the full contents into her face. I know people are watching us, and we both just stand there for a moment, shocked at what I've just done. The smile fades from Tiffany's face and she dives at me. Orla pulls me out of the way and Dom grabs a now-hysterical Tiffany.

'Fucking bitch!' she screams, fighting against Dom, and I'm suddenly very glad that he's holding her back. Orla drags me out of the suite and into the hallway, which is practically deserted. I can't keep up with her in my drunken state and I stumble to the ground and burst into tears.

'Oh God, Liz, it's OK. Calm down – she's not going to get past Dom.' Orla stares at me, worried, but every time I look at her I just break out into another round of hysterics. 'What is it?' she asks.

'The things she said about Edward . . .' I gasp, between racking sobs.

'She doesn't know anything about Edward. Those are just silly rumours—'

'But what if they're true?

Orla stares back at me. It's obvious she doesn't know what to say. Instead, she picks me up and takes me home.

I wake up the next morning feeling sicker than I ever have before. My mouth is dry, and my head feels as if someone has thrown a brick at it. I want to go back to sleep, but Marshall is licking my cheek, dying for attention. I groan as I roll over in bed and open my eyes. I look down at myself to see that I'm still wearing my jeans and white top. Marshall is now licking the back of my neck.

'Go away!' I moan, trying to push my furry friend out of the way, but he's having none of it.

'Do I hear life in there?' Orla calls from the kitchen. But the only reply I can manage is a louder moan. I look up and see her standing at the bedroom door with a cup of tea in her hand. She can't help the smile growing on her face.

'You look pretty,' she says sarcastically.

'I think I may die,' I groan, my voice sounding as though I've just smoked a pack of cigarettes.

'Well, I was going to let you sleep, but I didn't think you wanted to miss Edward's round.'

'What time is it?' I say, jumping out of bed as quickly as my hung-over body will let me. Marshall follows me excitedly, hoping he'll get a walk.

'One o'clock,' Orla says, walking back into the living room, me following her.

'One? Fuck! Thank God I didn't have to train today.' I pick up the TV remote and try frantically to find Sky Sports. I only relax when I see the green arenas of Hickstead come up on the TV screen.

'I know. I only woke up an hour ago myself. So glad I have the day off work.' Orla and I sit in silence as we watch the Nations Cup unfold. Edward jumps brilliantly, with a clear in the first round and a mere four faults in the second, but the rest of the Irish team does terribly, getting cricket scores of faults and leaving Ireland nearly at the bottom of the leader board.

'Well, at least Edward will be happy,' I mumble, as we watch a supermodel hand the trophy to the German team, whose rounds were practically flawless.

'Yeah, I'd say he will! But that Irish team is definitely going to have to be changed before Dublin Horse Show.'

'They'll put Shane Walker on the team for Dublin. He's been unstoppable this season,' I say to myself, wondering who else the selection committee will have to choose from.

'Yeah, probably . . . but that still leave two spots . . . and possibly a reserve.' Orla smiles at me, and I know what she is thinking, but I can't even allow myself to imagine it. I want to be on that Dublin team so badly, but I'm afraid to speak my desires out loud in case I jinx it.

In the excitement of watching the Nations Cup, I'd managed to forget about the events of last night. But sitting here now, hung over and exhausted, the image of Tiffany's champagne-soaked face comes rushing back to me. I look over at Orla. I feel humiliated.

'I'm sorry,' I mutter, out of the blue. Orla looks at me, bewildered. 'I'm sorry for getting so drunk last night. I must have been such a mess to take care of . . . I didn't ruin your night, did I?'

'Of course you didn't, Liz. We all had a great night until I had to drag you away from the crazy American . . . I'm still shocked you threw a drink at her, though. I didn't think you had it in you . . . I just don't like to see you so upset,' she finishes.

I look down at my feet and try to forget how vulnerable and hurt I felt last night, but I can't.

'That was just the drink talking . . . I don't know why I got so upset,' I say. I don't want to think about it any more.

'Are you sure?' Orla asks, concerned.

I think again of everything that Tiffany said, and I can't stand it. The idea of Edward sleeping with someone else is unbearable, but I reason that it must have been before me. Then I think of all the things he has said to me over the last few months: he loves me, he cares about me. I never really thought about if Edward has had another relationship, while still married to Katherine, before. Logically, it's probably true and even though the idea of it makes me feel ill, I can't say anything. What right have I to judge how he acted before he met me?

'Edward would never do something like that, not since he met me. I'm sure of it,' I say, certain of myself. This seems to satisfy Orla, and she doesn't say another word about it.

'Can we have a girly night tonight?' I ask. 'No parties, no drama — just pyjamas, ice cream, rubbishy TV and a bit of unpacking? I have some photos I want to put up, if you don't mind?'

'Sounds great.'

11

Family

I KNOCK ON THE DOOR TIMIDLY. I DON'T KNOW WHY I'M nervous – it's only my family. I warned them I was coming, and they sounded excited. I'm excited too. I haven't seen them in over a month and, as much as I hate to admit it, I miss them. I miss my mum's overbearing kindness, my dad's infectious laugh and my sister's cheekiness. When I come home, I feel like I can get grounded again, that I can escape from my work, my life, even if it's only for a short while. And yet I'm nervous. As much as I joke about it to Nick, I *do* care what my family thinks, and I'm dying for them to approve of my life and my choices.

My mum hugs me hard as soon as she opens the door; my ribs cry out, but I try not to let it show.

'Oh, Matt, it feels like so long since you were last home. I'm so glad you finally have a few days off.'

She's squeezing even harder now, but I stay close to her and reply. 'I've missed you guys too. How've you all been?'

Mum pulls away and looks me up and down. 'Oh, same old, same old . . .' I start to feel embarrassed as her eyes examine me. 'You look very thin and pale. Have you been eating properly?'

I nod, knowing it's pointless to say anything: she'll never believe me.

'Is that Matt?' I hear Dad shouting from the kitchen.

I walk into the house, hoping that Mum doesn't notice me limping. But she cringes, watching me shuffle along.

Dad's sitting by the dinner table, reading the newspaper. He puts his glasses on his forehead and squints at me. My dad is blind as a bat, but yet he refuses to use his glasses unless he is forced to by my mother.

'Matt!'

'Hi, Dad.' I stop as soon as he turns in my direction. Dad is never one to avoid a sensitive topic. Mum might remain silent, but he certainly won't.

'How are you keeping? How's work?' He's now standing opposite me. I've always found his tall, broad figure intimidating. Even now, I feel like a child next to him.

'Work is good, very busy . . . I'm breaking some three-year-olds next week.'

'Breaking?'

'It means the horses are being ridden for the first time in their lives,' I explain. 'We school them on a lunge rope for a while, then put on their tack and eventually get up on their backs ourselves.'

'Do the horses go a bit wild when you first sit on them?' Mum asks.

'Sometimes,' I admit. 'But don't worry – I'll have all the safety gear on, and Nick is always there to help if I need it.'

'That's tough stuff,' Dad comments.

'It's not too bad,' I say, trying to shrug it off. My dad knows very little about what goes on in a showjumping yard and I prefer to keep him in the dark.

'Well, it's good to have you back.' Dad raises his right hand and, before I realize what he's doing, pats me hard on the back. Before I can stop myself, I let out a whimper of pain.

'Are you OK?' he asks, worried.

'Fine,' I mumble, trying to keep in the tears of pain prickling behind my eyes. 'Just had a tumble at the show last week.'

He stares at me for a long time. It's impossible to tell what he's thinking: there's no emotion, no expression on his face. After a moment, Mum breaks the silence.

'Shall we all sit down for dinner then? Where's Ann? John, will you go get Ann?'

Dad jumps a little when he hears his name. He looks as if we've jolted him out of his thoughts.

'What?' he asks, turning towards Mum.

'Will you go get Ann, please?' He nods and walks upstairs, leaving Mum and me alone. She looks me up and down again: I feel like an animal in a zoo, like people are constantly staring at me. 'Do you need anything? An anti-inflammatory? A painkiller?' I shake my head.

'No, I'm fine, honestly. I'm a lot better than I was.' This is true: the morning after my fall I was barely able to get out of bed, and the next day it was so bad Nick had to help me shower and get dressed, which made me feel humiliated and incredibly embarrassed, especially when he began to make inappropriate comments. Mum doesn't look any more comforted by this, but she drops the subject.

'I'm a little worried about Ann,' she says abruptly. She's no longer staring at me; she's turned towards the stove and is mixing whatever's in the pot. It smells like potato and leek soup. She used to always make it for me when I was a kid.

'Why?'

'She has started seeing this boy from her class, and he is all she ever talks about now – "Christopher says this, Christopher likes that." I just don't want her to get too dependent on this boy. She's too young for that.' I can hear the muffled voices of Dad and Ann upstairs, but it's impossible to work out what they are saying.

'She's fifteen, Mum,' I say, not thinking it's too big a deal. 'This is probably the first time she's dated anyone. She's just excited . . . She'll grow out of it.' I know very little about teenage girls. I avoided them completely when I was younger; even now, I prefer the company of slightly older women – a fact that often earns me a lot of teasing from Nick.

'I just don't want her to get hurt,' Mum says, getting the bowls out. 'I wish she wasn't so keen on him.'

'Honestly, Mum, I wouldn't worry so much. Ann has always been able to take care of herself.'

She gives me a grateful smile, but I know she doesn't agree with me. I guess it's understandable: Ann has always been Mum and Dad's sweet little girl. It was never going to be easy for them to see her grow up and start dating.

Ann walks cheerfully into the room. 'Sorry we took so long. I was on the phone to Christopher. He was telling me the funniest story about his little brother, David, and I just had to hear the end of it.'

Dad seems mildly frustrated as he comes in behind her. I smile and step over in her direction. She grabs me in a hug and again I try not to show that it hurts. My sister has always been a pretty girl; she always keeps herself looking very well, wearing fitted clothes that flatter her slender frame. Her hair is perfectly blow-dried and her make-up is done skilfully. She's extremely popular in school with both girls and boys – it drove me nuts that all my classmates fancied her, even though she was so much younger than us.

'So, how are you?' I ask, genuinely happy to see her.

'I'm great,' she replies brightly. 'Was Mum telling you about my boyfriend, Christopher?'

'Briefly,' I admit.

'Oh my God, Matt, he is so amazing and cute and sweet, and all the girls are jealous because he only wants to be with me.' I suddenly understand Mum's concern. Ann has always had tons of pursuers but she never seemed that interested in any of them. It was weird to see her so keen on this Christopher.

'You'll have to meet him, Matt. You'll love him!'

'Sure,' I reply, knowing it'll probably never happen.

We all sit down and Mum ladles out the soup. Ann is barely in her chair before she starts recounting the story Christopher has just told her. I stare at her. I'm shocked how grown-up she looks. Her fat baby cheeks are gone and her sweet eyes are coated heavily in eyeliner. It hits me that I really am missing a lot living away from home.

'So Dad, how's work going?' I ask, trying to move the conversation away from Christopher. Dad perks up straight away, clearly happy about the change of topic.

'It's going well. Weather was good this year, so the crops did well. We sold more livestock before Christmas than we have in the last five years, so that was a nice end to the year. Your mother is growing cooking apples out in the back and we have been selling them to the local grocer, so that has left us with some nice extra cash . . . But, sure, you have no interest in any of this, Matt, so I won't bore you any more.'

Dad is skilled at little digs like this one. He doesn't come right out and insult me but instead resents me for not wanting to be a farmer like him.

'Matt, why don't you tell us what's going on at Shane's? Are you getting to ride much?' Mum's voice is strained, as she serves our main dinner, shepherds pie. I know she feels the same way I do – panicked. Dad's face has settled back into the expressionless stare he had earlier. It worries me that I have no idea what he's thinking.

'It's going really well' – I try to sound as positive as possible –

'Shane's horses are performing seriously well and I'm riding the young ones a good bit . . . which I'm really enjoying.' It's a lie. I'm bored senseless with all the young horses. It's the same thing every day. I'm desperate to jump bigger, but there's no point telling my parents this. 'And we're going to Scotland in a few weeks. There's a big show over there . . . it should be fun.' Mum nods politely, but then Dad speaks up.

'What happened to you?' He speaks louder than I think he had planned to; Mum and I both jump at the sound of his voice.

'I had a fall,' I say. 'I told you that.'

'But how?' He speaks more quietly this time, but his voice is still intimidating.

'John, please . . . not now.' It's clear Mum hasn't got any better with conflict.

'It's just a question . . . For God's sake! Our son comes home beaten to a pulp – practically crippled! – I think I have the right to know what happened to him.'

The anger boils up inside of me. I take a deep breath and try to control it. 'I fell off the roof of the lorry . . . That's it, OK?' I want to shout at him, but I do my best to keep my voice under control.

'Why on earth were you on the roof of a lorry?' His face is turning red and I can see that, like myself, he's doing his best to keep his anger under control. For the first time all night, Ann is no longer smiling. I know she's wondering what's going to happen next.

'I was attaching hay to the top of Shane's lorry. It's how we transport it.'

'So it was Shane's lorry you fell off?' my dad asks, trying to get things clear in his head.

'Yes,' I reply, wondering where he is going with this.

'And you fell while doing a task he asked you to do?'

'Yes.'

'Well, surely his insurance should cover this? Have you seen a doctor?' My dad knows that is not how my job works, but he's trying to make a point.

'I don't need to see a doctor. I'll be fine in a few days,' I say, no longer angry but frustrated that he wants to bring up the same old argument.

'But surely—' he starts.

'Just drop it, John, please,' Mum says sternly.

He opens his mouth as if to argue but changes his mind. Mum is Dad's weakness: he hates upsetting her and he'll do anything to avoid it, even if it means he has to swallow his pride sometimes. I smile at her in gratitude and she gives me a quick grin back to let me know she understands.

'You know, Christopher said the funniest thing earlier . . .'

It's Ann who breaks the silence; the tension between my father and me slowly dissolves.

'Are you sure you don't want to stay here tonight?' Mum asks as I stand at the door.

'I'm sure,' I say, trying to reassure her. I'd been planning to stay, but after the tension during dinner I decide it's better to leave on a good note. I don't want a blowout with my father and I feel that, if I stay, it'll happen.

'You know, he doesn't mean to be so judgemental and sharp,' Mum whispers, gesturing behind her to my father, who's in the kitchen cleaning dishes with Ann. 'He just worries about you. We both do.'

'I know,' I say gently, trying to not sound defeated.

'Please remember you can always come home . . . no matter what . . .' I know she's trying to be kind, but her words cut into me. Coming home means admitting defeat. Coming home means I've been wrong and naïve all along.

I leave feeling confused and a bit disheartened. I don't feel grounded, like I'd hoped; I feel . . . more . . . lost. I've always known what I wanted and what I had to do to achieve it. But it's been four years now, and I have nothing to show for myself. I start to wonder, am I still doing this because it's my dream or am I only doing it because I want to prove my parents wrong?

I stand in the freezing-cold air at the bottom of the lane. I'm looking through the contacts on my phone, trying to work out what to do. I don't want to go back to the yard; there would be too many questions from Nick and Shane, questions I don't want to answer. I have very few friends other than Nick, and most of them live hours away. I'm starting to feel hopeless when I hear someone's footsteps behind me. I turn around to see Ann, her big brown eyes staring at me, full of worry.

'Are you OK?' she asks, pushing that perfectly groomed hair out of her face.

'Yeah, I'm fine,' I reply. I can't believe how much older she looks than she did just a few weeks ago, when I saw her at Christmas.

'Why don't you stay here tonight? Mum'll keep Dad from saying anything stupid.'

'You know as well as I do that no one can stop Dad when he gets on one of his rants,' I say, trying to lighten the mood.

'You shouldn't let him bother you so much. You're doing what you love, and that's all that matters. As long as you're happy, then who cares what he thinks?' Ann has always supported me. I don't think I ever really appreciated that support until now. 'You *are* happy, aren't you?'

I think about it for a moment. Sometimes I *do* doubt that showjumping is what I really want, sometimes I *do* think would I have been better off just staying in school and becoming a farmer like my dad. But then I think about the past four years. True, I don't have anything much to show for them: I'm not famous, I'm not rich. But I have my memories, and when I think back on all the people I've met, the horses I've ridden, the fun I've had and all the places I've got to travel to and see, I realize that those last four years have been the best years of my life and I wouldn't give them up for anything.

'Yeah, I'm happy,' I say, and it's the truth.

'Then that's all that matters.'

'When did you get so smart?'

'I've always been smart. You're just never around to see it.' I know Ann means this in a joking way, but there is truth to it and I suddenly feel guilty that I'm no longer much of a part of her life.

'You should come to the yard some time – I could show you around.'

Ann smiles at me. 'Great. I will,' she says, clearly chuffed at my offer. 'Goodnight, Matt.'

'Goodnight, Ann.' She disappears back into the house, part of me wishing I could go with her. I'm now left alone with the same question I had before Ann came out: where am I going to sleep tonight?

I must be sitting there for thirty minutes before it comes to me. At first I shove it out of my mind, knowing that it's insanity. But as the minutes roll on, I realize it's too tempting to resist. Even so, I'm afraid I'll lose my nerve at the last second and hang up, but I don't.

'Hello?' Her voice sounds quiet and frail. Fuck! I think to myself. Was she asleep?

'Hi, Liz, it's Matthew.'

There's an uncomfortable silence before she speaks again. 'Matthew, are you OK?' I'd rehearsed in my head what I was going to say before I called. I'd planned to stay calm and relaxed, keep it vague and politely ask her could I sleep on her couch for one short night. But that's not what happens. Instead, I panic, the words pour out of me and I find myself telling her every detail of my night. She stays silent the whole way through my story and now that I'm finished I'm almost certain she'll tell me to get lost. It's a shock when, instead, she gives me directions to her apartment.

The apartment is exactly like Liz: beautiful, sophisticated, modern but surprisingly warm and friendly. It's decorated in mad, eclectic colours. Her dog starts yapping as I walk in the door, making me feel unwelcome and out of place.

'Be quiet, Marshall,' Liz says sternly, picking up the small dog and patting him gently. 'Sorry. He's not good with new people.'

'It's OK . . .' I stand awkwardly in the middle of the sitting room, afraid to move or put my bag down. Everything is spotless, and I feel very grubby in comparison. Liz leaves the room to take Marshall away and I notice the pictures on the wall. Lots of her jumping, mostly ponies. She looks very young in most of them. The pictures have dates and the names of the places below them: Hickstead, Olympia, Spain, Turkey, California – Liz has jumped all over the world. It's not until I look at them more closely that I realize she's alone in all these photos. She stands with her horse and her rosette, but there's never anyone else there. Where's her family? Where are her friends? I look round when I hear someone walk back into the room. I'm expecting it to be Liz, so I'm startled when I see someone I don't know standing in front of me.

'Hello,' she says. Her tone of voice tells me that she hadn't expected me either.

'Hi,' I say gingerly. 'I'm Matt. I'm a friend of Liz's.'

'I'm Orla,' she says. 'I'm Liz's room-mate.'

Orla is a petite girl, at least a head smaller than myself. She has fiery red hair and her face is warm and relaxed. I take her hand awkwardly to shake it, and she laughs.

'This is very formal of you,' she says. She's in her pyjamas.

'Would you like a glass of wine?' Liz asks, walking back in. She stops when she sees Orla. 'Oh . . . have you guys already met?'

I nod.

'Yeah, Matt's been introducing himself,' Orla says with a wink.

'I just shook your hand. It wasn't like I bowed and kissed it,' I say, deciding to get in on the joke. Orla giggles again and makes herself comfortable on the couch. Liz sits down next to her.

'So, do you mind Matthew staying?' Liz asks her.

'Not at all. As long as it's not my bed that he wants to stay in.' Orla winks at me again, and I feel myself go a little red. Liz looks at her friend in surprise, and I feel like I've missed something, but she recovers quickly.

'So, *would* you like some wine?' she asks again. I nod, still stuck to the same spot. 'You can sit down, Matthew,' she goes on, smiling.

'Sorry.' I can feel the heat rising in my face. I feel like such an incoherent fool around her. I sit down on the couch. It's black and squishy, big enough to sit six people comfortably, and it faces a big but old TV. Liz hands me a large glass of red wine, and one to Orla, and then sits back, pulling her bare feet under her. Orla's sitting between Liz and me. I take a large gulp of my wine before I even try to speak.

'Thanks for letting me stay here. I promise I'll be gone in the morning.' The wine is warming my stomach; I must have been colder than I'd realized.

'It's OK, honestly. I know what it's like to have domestics with the family.' Liz smiles at me compassionately and I'm thankful she doesn't say any more in front of Orla. I take another swig, still trying to calm myself. 'It's not as if we had any plans. We were just going to curl up and watch a film . . . it's too cold to go anywhere tonight.'

When I first walked in I knew Liz must have been planning on staying in; she's in a baggy T-shirt and navy running shorts. Her hair is loose around her shoulders and she has no make-up on.

'I hope I'm not disturbing your night in?'

'Not at all, it's nice to have some company,' Orla says, giving me a friendly pat on the knee. I shiver slightly as she touches me and I notice how cute she is. I've finished my glass of wine already, and Liz pours me another one without even asking.

'So, how do you guys know each other?' I ask, just for something to say. Orla and Liz look at each other for a moment and laugh. Liz speaks first.

'Orla and I dated the same guy for a while . . .'

Orla goes slightly red at this.

'Seriously?' I ask, surprised.

'Oh, yeah,' Liz continues. 'Do you know Ben Wallace?'

I nod. Ben Wallace used to showjump at a fairly high level. He had a bad fall two years ago and broke his arm and a couple of ribs. No one has really seen him on a horse since but he is still involved in the horsey world as an owner. In fact, he owns some of the horses that Edward rides.

'You guys dated Ben Wallace?' I ask, surprised. Orla speaks up.

'Well, I never officially dated him, I was just seeing him casually . . . But what I didn't realize was that he was casually seeing at least four other people – Elizabeth one of them.' Orla hides her face in embarrassment, but both girls are laughing.

'We figured it out when we got talking by chance at a show . . . Weirdly, we have been friends ever since.' It's Liz who finishes the story.

'That's mad!' I say. 'So are you a showjumper too?' I ask Orla.

'I have an amateur horse and I do a few shows a year

for fun, but I'm not nearly as serious about it as Elizabeth.'

I look at Liz and realize she's staring at me. She blushes and takes a large mouthful of her wine. She fills up my glass again, but not Orla's. Orla has barely touched her drink.

'So, go on, Matt,' she says. 'It's your turn to tell us an embarrassing story now. I'm sure you have plenty of them?'

'Oh, I do.' I can feel the wine going to my head but I keep drinking, just so I have something to do with my hands. Liz is plenty intimidating on her own but I feel completely out of my depth with Orla here too. 'But I think I will keep those stories to myself.'

'I've certainly heard some rumours about you,' Liz says. I look at her, nervous, and search my brain for what she could've heard.

Orla looks at Liz, excited. 'Ah, go on, Liz, do tell.'

'A little birdie told me that you have a thing for the older ladies,' she says. Orla gasps in shock and I feel myself go purple with embarrassment.

'No way! So you have a thing for the cougars, do you?'

I think for a moment before answering, slightly braver with half a bottle of red wine in me. 'Well, it depends what you mean by cougars . . .'

All three of us jump when Marshall barks from Liz's room.

'That bloody dog gives me a fright every time,' Orla says, holding her free hand up to her chest.

'So sorry,' Liz says. She stands up and makes her way to her bedroom. 'My phone is probably vibrating — it always makes him bark. Just give me a few minutes. I'll try to make him go to sleep.' She closes her door behind her and I'm left alone with Orla.

'It's probably her man. He checks up on her most nights,' Orla says casually, taking a sip of her wine.

'Her boyfriend, you mean?'

Orla shrugs her shoulders. 'I guess you could call him

that . . .' She studies me for a moment before continuing. 'Did Elizabeth tell you about him?'

'Not really. I've just heard things . . . gossip . . .'

'It's not Edward Dawson,' Orla says quickly. She seems to have surprised herself with this, and rushes to explain. 'Sorry . . . it's just, I know that's what some people are saying . . . and it upsets Elizabeth . . . because it's not true.'

'I never thought it was true.' When I say it aloud, I know I really didn't.

'Good,' she says. We're quiet for a moment. There's a certain tension between Orla and me, and I have a feeling it has nothing to do with Liz.

'Thanks again for letting me stay,' I say.

'It's no problem. We have a nice big couch just waiting for someone to crash on it.' I smile at her. 'Actually, I knew who you were before I met you tonight,' Orla blurts out, sounding slightly embarrassed for the first time.

'Oh,' I say, surprised. I don't recognize her at all.

'Don't worry – I don't stalk you or anything. I've just seen you at the odd show, and the guy you work with . . . Nick, is it?' I nod. 'Yeah, he hooked up with my brother once so . . . small world . . . I'm sure you must have seen me once or twice before, but you probably don't remember.'

'I have definitely never seen you before,' I say, sure of myself.

'How can you be so certain?'

'Because I would have remembered you.' The words are out of my mouth before I can stop them and I'm worried she'll think they're cheesy.

'Thanks,' she says, astonished. She looks down for a moment before she speaks again. 'I know this is a weird thing to ask, but what did you think of me when you first saw me?'

'I thought you were really cute,' I say, my heart rate beginning to quicken.

Orla smiles and blushes some more. 'That's funny, I thought the same thing about you,' she says.

Without meaning to, I look down at her lips. They're full and pink and, in my slightly intoxicated state, I'm finding it hard to look away.

'Are you single, Matt?'

'Yeah, I am.' But as soon as I say it I'm drawing back. I know where this conversation is going. I know Orla is flirting with me and I'm flirting back. Part of me really wants to kiss her, and I think she wants me to kiss her. It's not every day I have a pretty girl like Orla attracted to me and I can feel myself getting more excited with every moment that passes alone between us. But I can't get Liz out of my head. If something happened, she'd know about it. Another part of me is saying, Why do I care? Liz has told me she is not available – but I do care.

'Do you want to kiss me, Matt?'

'I—' My mind is screaming at me. I want to kiss her, but something's holding me back. What is it? Without realizing it, I glance at Liz's door. Orla looks at me quizzically then lowers her head and lets out a small laugh.

'Fuck! How did I miss that?'

'Miss what?' But Orla just shakes her head.

'Nothing . . . Here, look, I was only joking. I'm a bit tipsy from the wine and I'm just acting silly.' Orla is back to her casual, confident self and I find myself almost disappointed that I've lost my opportunity. I want to apologize, make a joke, do something, but she speaks before I get the chance. 'I think I'm going to go to bed,' she says.

'Are you sure?' I ask, feeling bad all of a sudden, but I don't know why.

'Yeah, I'm sure. I have to get up early for work, so I really should get some sleep.'

'Well, it was nice to meet you,' I say pathetically.

'It was great to meet you too, Matt. You seem like a lovely guy. I'm glad you and Elizabeth are friends.' She gives me a quick peck on the cheek and I feel that electricity which was there earlier. As she gets up I hear Liz's bedroom door open.

'Finally, Marshall is asleep. I had to rub his belly for, like, twenty minutes before he drifted off.' She notices that Orla is standing. 'You going to bed?'

'Yeah,' Orla answers. 'I need to get up fairly early so I think I'll say goodnight.' I expect Liz to try to convince her to stay up with us, but she doesn't.

'OK . . . Well, goodnight then.' Liz leans in and gives Orla a kiss on the cheek. Orla gives me one last smile before disappearing into her room.

'So what were you guys talking about?' Liz asks, sitting down and picking up her glass.

'Nothing really.' I don't know why, but I feel guilty about flirting with Orla and I really don't want Liz to find out. But she smiles warmly at me and I find myself relaxing.

'So how's it going with Wildfire?' I ask, trying to sound nonchalant. Does Liz have any idea how lucky she is to have a horse like her?

'She's amazing. She's everything I've ever dreamed of.' Liz speaks like she's in love and I guess, in a way, she is.

'So what's the aim then?' I ask boldly.

'What do you mean?'

'Come on. All competitors have an aim . . . a certain title or competition they want to win above all else. What's yours?'

'I don't have one,' she answers, but I know she's lying. I cock my head to the side and look her up and down. 'OK, fine, I do have an aim . . .'

'Tell me.'

'I want to jump on the Irish Nations Cup team at Dublin Horse Show,' she says tentatively.

'That's some aim.' I'm impressed.

Liz turns the question on me.

'What about you?'

'Well, my aims are pointless,' I reply. 'I'll never reach them because I don't have the horse.' This slips out without me thinking and I instantly regret it. Liz lowers her eyes and I feel like scolding myself. I wish I wasn't jealous of her, but I am. I'm jealous of the money and the opportunities she has. I can't get over that. 'I think showjumping is a dangerous topic,' I mumble, embarrassed now.

There's a tricky silence which we both fill in by finishing off the second bottle of wine. I had passed tipsy a while ago and it is safe to say that now I'm drunk. I know I'm sitting still, but the room is spinning around me, my head feels heavy and my face numb. I concentrate hard on staring at the same spot on the floor, but I can't stop my eyes wandering over to Liz. She's drunk too, there's no doubt about that, but she doesn't seem as bad as me. I can't understand it: she's drunk the same amount, if not more, and she sits there looking as clear-eyed and elegant as ever.

I let myself stare at her; she's looking at her phone. It's been buzzing the whole time I've been here. I haven't asked who it is and she hasn't offered to tell me. She starts texting, her petite fingers working furiously, her brow set in concentration. She's biting her lip as well. She doesn't seem to know that she's doing it and it's the sexiest thing I've ever seen. I want to kiss her. My body slowly starts to lean in to her, but she looks up and smiles at me, making me jump back into my place.

'You fancy another one?' She gestures towards the empty bottle. I shake my head. Any more would make me violently ill. 'You're probably right. Don't want to get too drunk – we might end up doing something we shouldn't?' She smiles and winks at me, and I suddenly wish I'd said yes to another bottle. 'So, how's the love life?' she asks brashly. I sink back in the couch, trying to act casually, but my hand slips on the fabric, and I nearly keel to one side. Liz holds her hand up to her mouth to hide her laughter.

'Umm . . . pretty shit, to be honest,' I say, pretending that the last few seconds didn't happen. I sit on my hands to stop them from fidgeting. I hate it when people ask me about girls.

'What? Don't tell me a gorgeous guy like you finds it hard to get laid?' I can tell she's enjoying making me feel uncomfortable.

'What about you? Didn't you say you have a boyfriend?' I want to be cool, but my curiosity is eating away at me.

'Well, he's not a boyfriend per se . . .' For the first time tonight she looks uncomfortable. 'He's . . . he's just a guy.' It's obvious she doesn't want to say any more and I'm not brave enough to ask. I'm worried things will get awkward again, but she jumps in: 'I think showjumping is a safer topic . . .' and the two of us break into a fit of drunken laughter.

I wake up stiff, but the stabbing pain in my leg and back has started to fade. It takes me a minute to realize where I am, and slowly the memory of the night before drifts back. I sit up too quickly and my head starts to pound. I fell asleep in the clothes I was wearing and feel desperate for a shower. I look around: no sign of Liz or Orla. Both bedroom doors are closed. I try to recall what happened last night and begin worrying that I said or did something stupid: large bits of it are completely blank. I walk across and gently knock on Liz's door. No answer. I knock again, a little louder this time. Still nothing. I decide it's best to leave her sleeping. I consider knocking on Orla's door but I reason that she's probably in work at this stage. I go back to the kitchen and pour myself a glass of water. In the morning light, the apartment looks completely different. Last night it seemed romantic and alluring, now it just seems messy.

I catch the smell of myself and decide I really do need a shower before anything else. It would be a lot better for Liz to wake up to a washed man rather than a smelly, unwashed one. My rucksack is still sitting by the couch where I left it. I don't own many clothes; I spend most of my money on riding gear and food. I pull out the only pair of respectable jeans that I do own (all my others have holes in them). I grab a towel as well, deciding it best not to use one of Liz's.

I walk over to the bathroom – I remember where it is from last night – and fling the door open, to find Liz standing there, naked. Her bare back is facing me and she has her leg up on the rim of the bathtub. Her hair is damp and water is dripping on to the floor. She must have been in the shower.

'Matthew, get out!' she screams when she sees me. I jump back and slam the door in shock.

'I'm sorry! I'm so, so sorry . . . I didn't hear the shower . . .' I'm rambling on the other side of the door. '. . . I just wanted to take a shower and I assumed you were asleep . . . I'm sorry, I'll leave . . . now.' I run over to my bag and start packing, but then I hear the bathroom door open.

'You don't have to leave, Matthew . . . But for God's sake – have you never heard of knocking?' I'm relieved to see that she's smiling. She's now wearing a light-blue robe, which highlights her slender figure.

'In my defence . . . most people lock the door.' I try to hide my face, knowing that it's bright red.

'I live with one other girl . . . I don't lock anything.' We both laugh, relief taking the place of shock. 'You can go take your shower now, if you want,' she says. I dash past her. I can't look at her without thinking of what I have just seen.

When I re-emerge, washed but still humiliated, I find Liz

standing in the kitchen fully dressed and drinking coffee. She smiles at me and gestures towards the coffee machine.

'Yeah . . . thanks,' I say.

She makes her way over to the expensive-looking device and starts to make another cup. 'Small or large?' she asks, holding up two different-sized mugs, neither of which look very big to me. At Shane's we drink coffee and tea by the bucketful. It's what keeps us going.

'Large, thanks.' I'm standing in the middle of the kitchen, not knowing whether to sit down.

'I'm going to have to run soon. I have a lesson with Edward in an hour and I'll probably end up being stuck there all day. Organizing the plan for the next show, you know.' She hands me my coffee. Her hands are shaking. I wonder if she's as hung over as I am.

'That's fine. I'll just get my stuff together and head back to Shane's,' I say, but Liz is shaking her head.

'Don't be silly, you should stay here. Those bruises on your ankle look pretty bad . . . you need to rest. Anyway, didn't you say you have the next few days off?'

'Yeah,' I reply, 'but how did you know I have bruises on my ankle?'

Liz giggles. 'You showed me . . . last night.' A horrid flashback pops into my head: I took off my trousers and shirt to show Liz my many war wounds. At the time I thought it was a brilliant idea. Nick and I both have the horrible habit of stripping once we have a few too many drinks in us; our inhibitions completely disappear. I panic, wondering what else I said or did.

'Don't worry, Matthew, it was really funny . . .' I smile, but it doesn't make me feel the least bit better.

'Why don't you just chill here for the day? Watch TV and stuff. I don't have much food, but there's an amazing Chinese takeaway just down the road. The number's on the fridge . . .'

I have to admit I'm tempted. 'Are you sure?' I ask, suddenly excited at the prospect of doing nothing all day.

'Of course . . . but I'll have to kick you out later on this evening, it's just . . . I have a thing — well, it's more a friend's thing . . . but I'm going to be out for the whole evening, so . . .' It's obvious Liz is nervous, but I can't understand why. I know she's seeing someone, she's already made that clear, so why lie about it?

'No problem at all,' I say. It isn't my place to ask any more about this guy. As she heads out of the door I think of something. 'Liz, wait . . .' She stops and stares at me, puzzled. 'I don't go back to work till Monday — you free tomorrow night?'

'Yes,' she says, more quickly than I'd expect, but she regains her cool fast enough. 'I'll text you tomorrow to make a plan?'

'Sounds good,' I say, smiling.

12

The Party

'DON'T BE SO NERVOUS. YOU LOOK BEAUTIFUL,' EDWARD whispers as I fidget with my dress. It's black lace, with a plunging V-neck. I didn't want to buy a new dress for tonight – I'm trying to keep hold of my money so I can help Orla out with the bills – and this dress is the only thing I own that is appropriate for this evening. My mother bought it for me, for my sweet-sixteen birthday, but I haven't worn it before tonight because it's so tight and uncomfortable. Orla tried to convince me to match it with heels, but I don't want to tower over everyone, including Edward. She basically dressed me this evening, as I'm so useless at looking girly while she's exceptionally skilled at it. By the time she was finished with my hair and make-up, I felt confident and pretty. Even Edward can't stop saying how amazing I look.

Matthew was gone by the time Orla or I got home. I was relieved, but I couldn't shake the feeling of disappointment either. He's just good company, I keep reminding myself. But I can't deny the fact that I was jealous of him flirting with Orla and then excited when the two of us were left alone. Edward was texting me constantly and that's what stopped me from doing anything. I get so confused around Matthew. I fancy him – I've accepted that – but I'm still in love with Edward. Is it OK to be attracted to someone when you're involved with someone else? Yes, just don't cross the line: that's what I keep telling myself. I am so excited about tonight but, if I'm honest, I'm just as excited about seeing Matthew tomorrow.

As we walk into Enda's beautiful home, my stomach does flips.

'There are so many people here,' I whisper to Edward. He only arrived home from England a few hours ago, but he's full of life after his exceptional performance. I'd barely said hello when he started kissing me, and it was only that I didn't want to ruin my hair and make-up that I didn't let it go any further than that. I scan Edward from head to toe as he looks about the room. He's wearing a fitted black tux that highlights his athletic figure. I subconsciously bite my lip, thinking how sexy he looks.

'I heard Enda invited over two hundred people – and you can guarantee they'll all turn up. She's a popular woman.' Edward grabs two champagne glasses from a passing waiter and hands one to me. The thought of champagne makes me feel ill after the other night, but I take a large mouthful in the hope that it will make me feel less nervous. 'Let's have an explore.' Enda's house is massive and very individual. Edward and I are standing in the entrance hall, which has a wooden spiral staircase, green walls and a ruby-red carpet. Theoretically, this room shouldn't work at all, but I find myself liking the colourful warmth it has to it.

'Does Enda have a room big enough to seat all these people?'

Edward shakes his head. 'There's a marquee outside,' he explains, looking at his watch. 'In fact, we should make our way out there – dinner will be soon.' I take another sip of my champagne, but my stomach protests after the red wine last night. I place it on a waiter's tray as he walks by. Luckily, Edward doesn't seem to notice. 'Shall we?' he asks, linking his arm through mine and kissing me affectionately on the forehead. I frown at him, surprised at how demonstrative he's being with so many people around, but he just smiles cheekily back at me.

Everyone seems to have decided to make their way into the marquee, and Edward and I get caught up in a swarm of people. We trudge along slowly and I'm suddenly glad that Edward has my arm, as I'm afraid I'll get lost in the crowd.

He's giving me a detailed play-by-play of his two rounds in Hickstead, speaking quickly and passionately. I often find in these conversations that he needs little to no encouragement from me. I listen to his words carefully, trying to learn as much as I can from his expertise, but something catches the corner of my eye. About twenty people ahead of us I glimpse the back of a dark-haired figure who seems to be limping slightly. I try to look more closely but as soon as I do my view is blocked. There are just too many people. Edward has noticed I'm no longer listening to him.

'What are you looking at?' he asks irritably.

'I thought I recognized someone,' I reply. It's the truth.

Edward scoffs. 'I say you'll recognize a lot of people here.'

When we finally make it to the marquee and go in I realize why everyone was moving so slowly. You can't help but stop and gaze at everything when you walk in. Twinkling silver lights are scattered across the roof. Each table has a black cloth on it, decorated with silver glitter and a centrepiece of white roses. There's a dance floor at the far end of the room and a small stage that looks set up for a band. I'm suddenly excited by the idea of a dance.

'This is amazing!' I'm so awestruck, Edward laughs.

'Yes, Enda certainly knows how to throw a good party.' We make our way over to our table and Edward introduces me to a couple of people. There are already two men and two women sitting there. The men look older than Edward and smile warmly at me as I sit. The women are both blonde and look in their early thirties. They lean into each other closely and seem to be talking in whispers. They don't even seem to notice when I join the table. They look so alike I begin to wonder are they sisters.

'Elizabeth, this is Adrian and Christoph,' says Edward. 'They were part of the winning German team the other day.' Both men shake my hand and kiss my cheek eagerly.

'It's so nice to meet you,' I say, feeling a little out of my depth. 'You must be thrilled with your win. It was amazing to watch.'

'Zank you,' Christoph says kindly, with a thick German accent. 'Edvard has told us so much about you, Elizabeth. Vee hear you are a certainty for zee next Irich Nations Cup team.'

I look away from Christoph because I know I must be blushing. 'Well, I'm not quite there yet,' I mumble, embarrassed by Christoph's intense gaze.

'You're not far off,' Edward says encouragingly, squeezing my shoulder. Once again I'm surprised that he's showing me affection in public.

'Vell, zat team of yours certainly needs some shakink up.' It's Adrian who speaks now.

'Don't even talk to me,' Edward says, vexed. 'But enough about that . . . Elizabeth won the Premier Grand Prix the other day, and she's only been riding the horse less than a year.'

'Fery impressive,' Adrian says humbly.

'So talented!' Christoph gushes. 'And incredibly beautivul – you must have zee men all over you.' I feel myself go even redder.

'Now, don't you get any ideas. I'm personally making sure Elizabeth is in bed by twelve this evening.' My jaw drops. He says it in a joking manner, but I can't help feeling there's a slight innuendo there. But Christoph and Adrian seem to think nothing of it. Both laugh innocently.

'Ah, Edvard, you alvays zink zee worst of me,' Christoph says.

'That's because I know you well,' Edward replies, joining in with the laughter.

Our starters are placed in front of us and we carry on chatting as we eat. Edward hasn't introduced me to anyone else at the table, but I soon realize it's because he doesn't know them, or, at least, he has no interest in talking to them even if he does. I want to ask Edward about the comment he made, but at no point is there a gap in his conversation with Christoph and Adrian. Occasionally during the meal Edward tries to include me, but I can't keep up. I don't know the people and places they're talking about. I decline any wine or champagne offered to me, afraid that alcohol will only aggravate the irritation I'm feeling. I do my best to make polite conversation with the women across from me, but they still seem interested only in talking to each other. Instead, I listen in on the three men. Their topic seems to have moved on from horses.

'So, how's your new wife, Christoph?' Edward asks, finishing another glass of wine. His blue eyes are unfocused and I know he's getting drunk. Edward drunk is quite a rarity, and I never know what to expect from him.

'Young and beautivul. But she hates travellink. Never vill come vis me to the shows, no matter how hard I try,' Christoph complains.

'Do you really vant her there?' Adrian asks suggestively, and I suddenly wish I hadn't chosen to listen.

'Sometimes vould be nice. I miss zee company. You understand, Edward, I'm sure?'

'Well, Elizabeth is great company at the shows. I would be very lonely without her.' I nearly die of embarrassment when Edward says this and I bat away his hand as he goes to squeeze my knee under the table. He looks at me, bewildered by my reaction, but I don't have time to say anything before the lights go down.

A spotlight comes on and we all look up at the stage to see Enda Brown. I've only ever seen her on a horse before. Standing in front of me now, she looks quite glamorous.

'Hello, everyone,' she says shyly, her voice reverberating throughout the marquee. 'I'm flattered to have so many people here tonight to celebrate my birthday. I feel incredibly loved right now.' At this, many people raise their glass and cheer, so I pick up my water glass and join in. Edward continues to whisper away to Christoph and Adrian.

'When I meet people for the first time, the first thing they usually say to me is that I have had an amazing career, but I don't believe that. I believe that I've had an amazing *life*. Because showjumping is not just a job to me, it's my *life*. Most people come home from the office and they forget all about their work. Well, my office is my home and I never *can* forget about my work.' Enda speaks with such clarity and conviction that I find myself hanging on every word. 'Showjumping and horses are my life, and what I wonderful life I have! And I want to thank you all again for being here to celebrate it with me.' A huge cheer erupts and Enda looks close to tears.

She leaves the stage and a series of videos is projected on to one of the white walls of the marquee. They're videos of various competitions Enda has won over the years: Aachen, Paris, California, Hickstead, Millstreet and, of course, Dublin Horse Show. Music is playing in the background but everyone cheers as the videos of Enda show her jump clear round after clear round.

I look over at her table. She looks so embarrassed as people pat her on the back and kiss her cheek. Still so humble after all this time, I think to myself. The videos finish with one final cheer and this is quickly followed by the band starting to play. Within seconds the dance floor is virtually full, and Enda is dragged up by her husband. I look over at Edward. He's no longer talking to Christoph but finishing yet another glass of wine. I'm annoyed, and I can't hide it any more.

'Why did you say that earlier?' I whisper into his ear.

'What?'

'The thing about having me in bed by midnight and me keeping you *company* at the shows. Did you not think it was inappropriate?'

He frowns at me. 'You do keep me company at the shows,' he says, purposely playing dumb.

'I don't like what you were implying,' I say angrily.

'I was joking. You're being silly, Elizabeth,' he says, trying to brush me off.

'No, I'm not.' I'm starting to get angry. I look at Edward sternly, and his smile vanishes.

'Fine. Yes, I was implying, but it's because Christoph is an absolute pig and I didn't want him thinking he could chase after you all night,' he says in a harsh whisper.

'But *why* did you have to imply that we're *together*?' I'm finding it hard to keep my voice down.

'Because we *are* together, Elizabeth!'

'But people can't know we're together until . . .' The sentence hangs in the air.

'Until what?' Edward asks, frustrated, and now just as angry as I am.

'Until you divorce Katherine.' There it is. It's out. The one thing I desperately want from Edward but have been too afraid to say until now.

155

He stares at me for a moment. His expression is impossible to read. After a while he turns away, mumbling, 'I don't want to talk about this tonight.'

My heart sinks. All my fears about our relationship are finally out in the open, and he doesn't want to talk about it.

'Fine,' I spit out, standing up from the table and making my way outside. I hear Christoph laugh about something, but I don't dare look back to see if it's me he's laughing at.

I dive out of the marquee door, but I don't make my way to the house. Instead, I go round the back and find a deserted patio. It's dark, but I can hear running water. There must be a pond nearby. I can still hear the music playing and I'm surprised how sad I am that I won't get to dance tonight. The only light comes from the moon, but it's enough for me to find a small wall that's the perfect height to sit on. I don't cry, I'm too angry. I think about Edward's expression – or lack of it – when I mentioned him divorcing Katherine. He must think about the future, he must! my brain shouts. I just don't understand why he won't talk to me. But maybe he knows I won't like what he's thinking. I hear footsteps coming in my direction and look up to see a dark figure in a suit.

'Sorry to disturb you. I just came out for a cigarette.' I smile when I recognize his voice.

'Matthew?' I ask. He steps forward, and I see him properly. I breathe in, taking in his appearance properly. He looks great. His short hair is gelled back neatly and his face is freshly shaven. I'm no longer angry – I'm strangely exhilarated to see him.

'Hi,' he says, his smile broadening as he looks at me. 'So this was your thing?' He sucks on his cigarette.

'Well, yeah,' I say, slightly uncomfortable. 'You didn't say anything about going out tonight?'

'True, but I didn't know I was until a few hours ago,' he says, shuffling his feet. 'I'm really bad at checking my post. Usually because I don't get anything but bills . . . But I decided to sort through it today because I had some time for once, and while I was doing it I found my invite.' He's so relaxed about things.

'Do you want to sit?' I ask, patting the piece of wall next to me. He gently brushes against my arm as he sits down and I feel myself break out in goosebumps.

'You cold?' he asks.

'A little,' I lie. I'm shivering more with nerves than the night air. Matthew takes off his suit jacket and puts it around my shoulders. I can't believe how excited I feel when his arms reach around me. How does he do this to me? Is it just because he's so hot?

'You smell nice,' I say as the aroma from his jacket fills my nostrils.

'Thanks,' he says, laughing a little. 'It's Nick's cologne. I was afraid all the gay guys would hit on me if I wore it, but if you like the smell of it then I guess I'm not doing too bad.'

I'm glad it's dark because I know I must be blushing. 'Is Nick here?'

'No, he doesn't know Enda.'

'How do you know her?' I ask.

'I met her three years ago while I was on the sunshine tour with Shane. This awful storm came while we were in Portugal and they had put our horses in these horrific tent things. So, needless to say, they were all terrified at the sound of the wind and the rain. But one of Enda's horses was the worst – he was this big black stallion and he was going nuts, bucking and rearing . . . I thought the thing was going to kill itself. Enda was so calm, though . . . I swear that woman has nerves of steel . . . Anyway, no matter how hard she tried, she couldn't get close enough to the stallion to sedate it. Eventually, he turned himself over. I couldn't just watch her lose one of her animals, so while he was on his back I managed to pin him down long enough so that Enda could inject him . . .' He shakes his head at the memory. 'Ever since then Enda has been so nice to me. Always chatting to me when she sees me at shows and such . . . Still, I was surprised to get the invite.' I can't believe how laid-back he is at what he's done.

'That must have been terrifying,' I say. 'Did Enda not have grooms to help her?'

'Her grooms were more afraid than the horse was.' He laughs.

'Were you not afraid?' I ask in all seriousness.

Matthew thinks for a moment before answering. 'At the time, no. I knew the horse needed to be sedated and it was the only way I could think of to do it . . . Looking back at it now, I realize I'm lucky that thing didn't kick me to death.'

'You have no sense of self-preservation,' I say, giggling.

'I guess I don't . . . So are you having fun?'

'Not really,' I admit. 'Edward brought me . . . just to be nice' – I quickly correct myself – 'but I don't really know many people here.'

'Same,' Matthew replies, taking another puff on his cigarette. 'I was put at a table with Enda's granny.'

'No way. What was that like?'

'Hilarious. She's in her nineties, but she's still completely with it. She's one of these older people who are *so* politically in-correct you can't help but love them. She spent most of the dinner telling me about how she chased the Gardai out of her house with a shotgun because they had upset her Jack Russells.'

'Oh, that's brilliant,' I say, holding my hand over my mouth.

Neither of us seems to know what to say next. I try to think of something funny but I can't, and I'm afraid that, if I stay silent much longer, he'll get up and leave.

'I love this song,' I say as we listen to the band in the marquee play 'Dancing in the Moonlight'.

'Seems appropriate,' he says, standing up and stamping out his cigarette on the ground.

I look up at him.

'Dance with me,' he says confidently. How can he be so assured and relaxed when I'm so nervous?

'Are you serious?'

'Yes. I watch *Strictly Come Dancing* every Saturday night. I'm practically a pro.'

I take his hand without hesitation and he spins me unexpectedly, which makes me burst out into laughter. Matthew is laughing too, as the two of us attempt an assortment of lifts, dips and spins. I can feel my hair coming loose and I know my face is red, but I no longer care. I'm enjoying myself for the first time all night. Then the music slows and so does our dancing. He pulls me in close and I let him. He puts his hand on the small of my back and I wrap my arms around his neck. He looks directly at me. Neither of us is laughing. He leans in closer and rests his cheek against mine. He smells wonderful and sexy. My stomach is doing somersaults and my heart is pounding. Our bodies swing slowly together and I'm reminded of the dream I had about him. It's all too intense, and I pull away quickly.

'You're right. You're a great dancer,' I say kindly, trying to cover up my reaction. For a moment he looks crestfallen, I think, but he recovers so quickly I can't be sure.

'Thanks. You're not so bad yourself.' He steps towards me, but I move away.

'I'd better go,' I say, in a rush. 'I've got to get up early tomorrow . . .' I turn to leave, but Matthew follows me.

'Liz, wait!'

I stop and turn, wondering what on earth he is going to say.

'Um . . . do you mind if I get my jacket?' he asks, embarrassed.

'Oh yeah . . . Of course . . . Sorry . . .' I pull it from my shoulders and hand it to him. He smiles at me and I feel myself relax.

'Are you still on for tomorrow?' I ask, realizing that I really hope he says yes.

'Of course. I'll call you.'

I turn and walk back towards the party. I don't trust myself around Matthew, and yet I'm dying to see him again. When I think about him I feel so guilty and yet so excited. What's going on with me? I turn back towards the marquee and see Edward standing outside, looking frantic. He runs over to me.

'Where have you been?' He seems genuinely worried and my guilt just gets worse.

'I was only getting some air,' I say, my voice small.

'I'm so sorry.' He says it straight away, much to my surprise. 'You were right. I was being crude and unpleasant. It's just Christoph was looking at you as if you were some pretty thing he could play around with, and it was driving me crazy. You are so beautiful, smart and talented, and you have no idea how much I want to tell the world that I'm in love with you . . .' It's rare for Edward to apologize like this and I find myself falling for him again as I look into his blue eyes, now full of worry. 'And I do want to divorce Katherine,' he continues.

'You do?' I ask, shocked but thrilled.

'Of course I do. I want to be with you without feeling as if we're doing something wrong . . . But I don't want to be cruel to Katherine. I need to convince her that a divorce is the best thing for both of us and . . . that may take time. I'll understand if you're not willing to wait . . .' My heart breaks now I see how much this is hurting him.

'I'll wait,' I say, without hesitation.

'You will?' he asks, like an excited child.

'Of course.' I'm suddenly desperate for everything to be right between us again. Edward grabs me in an embrace and whispers in my ear.

'I love you.'

'I love you too.'

13

The Strip

I STAND ON ENDA'S PATIO FOR A FEW MOMENTS, ALMOST convinced that Liz is going to come back. My night feels so unsatisfactory. I want one more dance with her, one more joke. In truth, I need more of her. But she doesn't come back and, when I begin to shiver, I decide it's time to go home. It takes a couple of tries to get my beaten-up Toyota Starlet going. It seems the cold night has done it no good, but at last the engine gurgles into life and I'm able to make my way back to Shane's.

Nick is singing at the top of his voice when I walk in the door of our bungalow. I look down at my watch and see that it's only a little past midnight, which explains why he's still awake. He shouts my name as soon as he hears the door shut.

'Matt, you fucker, just the person I wanted to talk to!' I throw my bag on my unmade bed and make my way into our filthy kitchen. Nick is sitting on our torn-up couch with a beer in his hand, watching the latest episode of *Geordie Shore*.

'You not curious why I'm back early?' I ask, grabbing myself a beer from the fridge.

'Not really . . . pass me another one of those too, please,' he says. It's some label I don't recognize; it's cheap and we bought it by the trayful in Lidl. 'Do you want to tell me why you are home early?' he asks.

'No.'

'Good. Well, now that is settled, I have a . . . proposition . . . for you.' He's choosing his words carefully.

'What kind of proposition?' I ask, suspicious.

'Well, there's this kind of . . . talent competition being held in McGowan's tomorrow night . . . I'm thinking the two of us could enter. First prize is five hundred euro and free drinks all night . . .' McGowan's is our local, a small, dingy place that's usually home to wild hen parties and ridiculous karaoke nights. The guards never close it so it stays busy till about four in the morning. I've never heard of it having a talent competition before; it seems totally random for McGowan's.

'But we don't have a talent,' I say, taking a gulp of my beer.

'Well, that's not necessarily true . . .' I look at Nick, confused. 'The crowd votes for the best act . . . and you know the type of crowd in there . . . randy middle-aged women. So, what do you think they're going to want to see?' Light dawns.

'No fucking way!'

'You won't even consider it?'

'There is no fucking way that I'm going to strip at a talent competition—'

Nick starts talking over me. 'Oh, come on, Matt! D'you not remember we did it before in there, on the bar? The whole fucking place was cheering us on . . .'

'I was pissed and high . . . I fell off the bar before I even managed to get my trousers off . . .' It had been one of our messiest nights. If there hadn't been pictures, I wouldn't have believed I'd done it.

'And did you not get hit on by, like, every girl in the bar after that?'

'I have no idea!' I'm shouting now. 'I was so trolleyed I don't remember anything . . .'

'Well, you did . . . you even brought one home . . . I'm sure you remember that?' I did, unfortunately. She was very pretty, but at least ten years older than me; the following morning I woke up next to her naked body with absolutely no memory of the night before.

'Why me? Why not ask someone else to do it? Or do it on your own?' I suggest, trying to forget the awful memory of that one-night stand.

'I can't do it on my own – that's just sad. Also, you are my only attractive straight friend, and all the gay guys I know are way too . . . feminine . . .' I shake my head. There is no way we should do this. 'And I know you want the money just as much as I do . . . Come on, Matt, five hundred euro! We could replace that crappy TV, or we just treat ourselves . . .'

I think about it for a moment. It's been a long time since I had cash to burn. I'm so sick of being careful with money, buying cheap beer, filling my car with petrol ten euro at a time. Nick knows he's starting to crack me. I can see it.

'Fine, but I'm only going as far as my boxers. There is no need for a pub full of middle-aged women to see my ass.'

Nick claps his hands together. 'I knew you'd do it!' His laughter is contagious.

'So are we just going to get up there and strip?' I ask, a little terrified at what I've just agreed to do.

'No, no . . . We need a theme . . . I'm thinking we could wear our showjumping gear – you know, jodhpurs, boots and spurs? They'll love it, and we already have all the stuff . . .' It's clear that Nick has been thinking about this for a while.

'Fuck . . .' I try to imagine it.

Nick rubs my hair patronizingly. 'Don't worry – we'll get you pissed beforehand . . . You never mind taking off your clothes once you're plastered.'

That doesn't help, but we drop the subject and watch the end of *Geordie Shore*. But I'm not paying attention to the people on TV drinking way too much and shagging one another. Instead, I think about my night with Liz. She makes me so nervous, but excited at the same time. I can't understand how she can be so relaxed around me – she must have noticed my hands shaking when we danced. I was surprised when she ran off like that. I know I was chancing my arm a bit, but I thought she was enjoying herself as much as I was. At least, I suppose, she wants to see me again.

Then I realize. We'd planned to meet tomorrow night. If Liz was ever going to see me naked, this was the last way I would've hoped it would happen.

'You fucking sly dog . . . here I am feeling sorry for you because I think your sex life is non-existent and then I find out that you spent the night at Elizabeth O'Brien's house! I'm gay, and even I find that girl attractive!' Nick's voice is full of disbelief. I held off telling him about Liz until I had to, but I couldn't avoid it any longer as I knew she'd be here soon.

'I told you, nothing happened . . . My dad was being his usual disapproving self and I needed somewhere to crash for the night. Anyway, she's dating someone already. She kicked me out pretty promptly the next day.' It's impossible to hide the dis-appointment in my voice. Nick gives me a knowing look. I don't bother telling him that I saw her at Enda's party; it'll only add fuel to the fire, and I want him to know as little as possible about what is going on with Liz. Especially since I don't know what's going on myself.

'But that's not going to stop you from trying something, is it?'

I say nothing. It's stupid to deny that I fancy Liz; everyone who knows her fancies her. Her personality, her looks, the way she speaks – everything about her is impossible to resist. The thought of her being with someone else makes me feel uncontrollably jealous.

'I have one question for you, Matt . . .' I look up. We've finished work for the day and Nick's making dinner, some sort of Irish stew that doesn't smell too appetizing. I'm so hungry, though, I'll eat anything, as long as it at least *resembles* food. 'If you fancy this girl, why on earth did you invite her tonight?'

'I didn't want to cancel on her.' I sigh. 'And I really could use the money from this stupid thing . . .' Nick is smiling again, but it isn't a sympathetic smile, it's more a 'You are seriously fucked' smile. 'Ah, fuck, it's fine. She doesn't fancy me anyway. What damage can I do?'

Nick hands me a bowl of the mystery Irish stew. 'You're stripping for a bunch of middle-aged women – I'd say a lot!'

Liz arrives on time, which of course means that Nick and I are not even close to being ready. I hear the knock on the door while I'm in the shower and yell at Nick to let her in.

'Sorry, mate . . . I can't!'

'For fuck's sake, Nick, it's freezing outside. Let the girl in!' Shampoo is pouring down my face and into my eyes.

'I'm not dressed. Don't get me wrong, Matt, I'm perfectly happy to answer the door naked. I have done it many times before. But I think it's slightly inappropriate for your date to see my dick, especially since you say she's not even seen yours yet.'

Liz rings the doorbell again and I wrap a towel around myself and head towards the door, shampoo still dripping down my face.

'You're a shit friend!' I shout as I pass Nick's door.

'I know.'

I open the door to find Liz shivering. Her blonde hair is loose around her shoulders and her cheeks are pink from the cold. It's a harsh contrast to how she normally looks, collected and smart.

'I'm sorry . . . Am I early? I thought you said seven?' She looks at her watch to double-check.

'No, no . . . You're fine. Nick and I are running late . . . Come in.' I notice she's looking at my half-naked body. She isn't subtle about it, but it's impossible to tell what she's thinking. I show her into our living room. I've done my best to clean it and make it look respectable, but it's still a complete tip in comparison to her place.

'I'm just going to finish my shower and then I'll be ready to go.'

She nods and sits down. But as I turn to leave the room, she says, 'I hope you don't think this makes us even?'

'Sorry?'

'Just because you answered the door in a towel doesn't make us even. You saw me naked yesterday. You're going to have to reveal the full show to me one day . . .'

I laugh, mostly because I have no idea how to reply, but once I leave the room I smile to myself. I know it's just a joke, but the thought of her wanting to see me naked makes me feel good.

'So explain to me again why you guys are in your showjumping gear?' Liz asks as we briskly walk down to the pub. We're already late and I haven't properly explained to Liz that we're stripping – I want to hold off on the humiliation as long as possible.

'We need some cash and, well . . . there's a talent competition tonight that we're hoping to win . . .' Being vague no longer seems to be working. She's becoming suspicious.

'But what is your talent?'

I look at Nick for help.

'We're going to do a bit of a dance,' he says, lighting a cigarette.

'In your showjumping clothes?'

'Well, we won't have our clothes on for that long.' Nick winks at her. She clicks.

'No way! No fucking way! You guys are doing a striptease!'

'Oh, please don't say it like that,' I say, putting my head in my hands.

'I can't *wait* to see this!' she says excitedly, and she and Nick start laughing uncontrollably.

Just down the road from the pub, Nick pulls a large bottle of whiskey from his bag.

'I thought you might need some liquid assistance.' He hands me the bottle and I slug back a large mouthful before handing it to Nick, who does the same. The whiskey burns as it goes down my throat and into my stomach, leaving me with a warming sensation, which is nice, as I'm shivering with the cold. Liz hits my arm as I go to take another mouthful. At first I think she's going to give out to me for drinking too much even before we get to the pub, but I could not have been more wrong.

'Here! Are you two gentlemen not going offer me any?'

Nick looks as shocked as I feel.

'It's neat whiskey,' I say. Is she serious?

'So? I drank you under the table the other night, didn't I?'

I laugh and hand her the bottle. 'Very true,' I admit. She gulps back a huge mouthful then scrunches up her face. For a moment I think she might spit it all back out but instead she takes another swig before handing it back to me. Nick cheers her on, patting her on the back, treating her like she's one of the lads.

'I love this girl already. Come on – let's have a couple more mouthfuls and make our way in.'

By the time we walk into the packed bar I'm feeling light-headed and hyper. Liz has her arm around my waist and is giggling uncontrollably, though I can tell she is not nearly as drunk as Nick and me. I can't understand how she's able to do it – she's half my weight but she's able to drink just as much, if not more, than me. Nick disappears as soon as we go through the door. He tells us that he wants to go find the sign-up sheet and I say we'll meet him at the bar. I may be drunk now, but I know I'll need a lot more before I'll be able to strip.

People stare at me as we stumble in. I'm not sure if it's because I'm wearing white jodhpurs and a white shirt and tie or because I have my arm around Liz. She is way and above the most beautiful person in the room. When we sit down at the bar, she pulls off her jacket and scarf to reveal a black string top with dark skinny jeans and a gold necklace that looks expensive.

'I never seem to go to bars these days, only boring parties being held by people with more money than brains . . . I don't know why I've never gone out on a night like this before . . . this is so much fun. Nick is hilarious, he's like a walking comedy gig. Thanks for inviting me.' She looks delighted and I can't help but be drawn in by her good mood.

'Thanks for coming. We may need you later when the middle-aged women try to take us home. They can be seriously aggressive.' Liz laughs at what she thinks is my sarcasm but, in reality, I'm telling the truth.

'You think very highly of yourself, don't you, Matthew?' I give her an odd look. 'What?' she asks, puzzled.

'Sorry . . . you're just the first person to call me Matthew in a very long time. Not used to the sound of it.'

'Matthew suits you. You are more proper and gentleman-like than you think . . . And you're about the only person who calls me Liz. Everyone calls me Elizabeth, even my family.'

I think about my reply carefully before answering. 'I think Liz suits your personality better. You're more . . . fun than you think.' She doesn't say anything in reply, she just smiles, and it's an honest smile.

'How come you didn't invite Orla?' she asks suddenly.

'I don't want anyone else to see my humiliation,' I say jokingly. Liz laughs, but I can tell it's not the answer she wanted. I think for a moment before I speak again. 'Also, Orla didn't take me in the other night, you did . . . Thanks.' Liz blushes and looks like she's going to say something but then I half fall off my chair. Nick grabs hold of me.

'We're all signed up, mate. We're last to perform – they reckon we'll be on in an hour.' Liz squeals with delight, and I groan. 'Ah, man up. You'll be fine!' He waves at the bartender. 'Three shots of tequila, and keep 'em coming!'

By the time Nick and I get on to that bar I'm far too drunk to feel any sort of embarrassment. In fact, I quite enjoy it. The acts before us have been pretty pathetic, mostly old women singing depressing love songs out of tune. One guy tried to do magic tricks but he was so nervous he kept dropping the deck of cards and was booed off. Nick and I are met with great applause; McGowan's is our local, so nearly everyone knows us here. As I hear the opening chords of 'Sex Bomb', I turn to Nick and mouth, 'You bastard!' He laughs and starts doing the routine he tried to teach me earlier.

I find it impossible to remember what I'm supposed to be doing so I'm nearly always a step behind Nick. But no one seems to care; the cheers grow louder and louder as each layer of clothing is removed. The only detail I do remember is to keep my discarded clothes behind the bar rather than throwing them into the crowd. They're expensive, and I don't have many spares. I look down at Liz: she's holding her sides, she's laughing so hard.

It's obvious before our routine is even over that we have won. The crowd is supposed to vote for its favourite act and, going by the cheers and shouts, it can't be denied that we're the most popular choice. I grab my clothes and climb down from the bar clumsily once the music ends, still only in my boxers. I practically fall into Liz as people push and shove to congratulate us on our performance. Nick stays on the bar, enjoying every minute of the limelight. His lack of shame is impressive. Liz helps me pull my shirt and jodhpurs back on, giggling the whole time.

'That was . . . impressive . . .'

'Worth five hundred euro?' I ask, starting to feel more confident with her.

'Definitely. You should seriously consider it as a career.' She winks at me, and I feel so chuffed.

The bar owner doesn't hesitate to hand us the prize money. The rest of the night merges into a hazy blur, as the drinks keep coming. We stay in the bar until closing, but I have no idea what I'm doing or saying until we walk out into the night air.

'Fuck, that is cold!' says Nick.

'Yeah, it really is.' Liz is shivering uncontrollably; her light jacket doesn't seem to be giving her much warmth at all. Nick elbows me hard in the stomach and gestures at her, then runs away without a word. It takes me a minute to understand what he means.

'Here, let me warm you up,' I say when I realize, placing my hands on each of her arms and rubbing them up and down quickly to try to create some sort of heat. Liz laughs and copies my gesture with her own hands.

'Thanks. I really must start bringing a decent jacket out.' Her words remind me of last night, when she nearly ran off with my suit jacket. I smile.

'Sure, you don't need to bother . . . I mean, as long as I'm around anyway.'

For a moment I start to believe that something can happen between us. That if I lean in and kiss her right now she'll kiss me back. I'm about to take the leap when the atmosphere is broken by Nick shouting. He's run on ahead and is now screaming at us to catch up.

'What?' I ask, when we finally reach him. I'm very drunk, and now a little annoyed. I just want to go home. But I can also see that Nick is feeling mischievous and I want to stop him before he does anything stupid.

'Look!' He points at the local tack shop, which I pass nearly every day. It's where we buy most of our things for the yard and where we get most of our equipment repaired.

'Yeah, it's the tack shop . . . what about it?'

'Look what they have outside it.' There's a black plastic display horse standing outside the shop. 'It's Black Beauty!'

Liz and I laugh and follow Nick towards it. He strokes the plastic horse's fake mane.

'Isn't she beautiful? Matt! We're in our riding gear – it's a sign! We *have* to ride her!' Without a moment of hesitation, Nick jumps on to the horse's back. It wobbles for a moment but then Beauty seems to regain her balance. Liz gives me a playful look before following Nick's lead and hopping on behind him.

'Come on, Matthew . . . Don't pretend to be the responsible one,' she shouts. There's no way I'm going to argue with her. I crawl awkwardly on to Beauty's back and grab hold of Liz's waist for balance.

I don't know whether it's all the drink or because Nick is swinging about like a madman but the three of us are completely unstable. I lean forward and grab a plastic ear for balance, but it snaps straight off. Liz and Nick go into hysterics, and the horse topples over. I hit the ground hard, and feel Liz's form fall down next to me. She's still laughing. I roll over and reach for her in the dark.

'Are you OK?' I ask. She stares directly at me, not laughing now, and smiles.

'I'm perfect,' she whispers, leaning in a bit closer to me. Then Nick cries out in horror. Liz and I scramble up and search for him in the dark. He's staring down at the plastic mess that is Beauty.

'What's wrong?' I ask.

It takes him a few moments to reply. 'We killed Black Beauty . . .'

The night ends pretty promptly after that. Nick is devastated. In that extremely short space of time, it seems he'd grown quite attached to the plastic horse. Liz grabs a taxi and goes home. I'd wanted to ask her to stay, but I can't make myself do it. Every time I look at her, every time she makes me laugh, I have to remind myself that she isn't available. That some other lucky bastard already has her.

14

Trapped

'NO, FOR GOD'S SAKE, MAKE HER CANTER STRAIGHT! . . . HER head is all over the place! . . . Stop letting her lift her head like that – the horse is walking all over you!' Edward is shouting at me from the centre of his home arena. He's frustrated and agitated, and our schooling session today seems to be going nowhere. I try to do as he tells me and ask Wildfire to lower her head, but she's having none of it. She's fresh and over-excited today and my instincts are telling me that I shouldn't challenge her, but Edward is definitely thinking otherwise. I canter Wildfire in a circle but her head keeps rising, like Edward's temper.

'Elizabeth, what are you doing? Break that mare's fucking jaw if you have to!' Against my instincts I pull hard on Wildfire's mouth, and she comes to a sudden halt in protest.

'For fuck's sake!' Edward makes his way over.

'She's just a bit hyper,' I say, jumping to her defence. 'One of the grooms forgot to let her out yesterday.' Wildfire is a horse that needs to be out in a field most days. It keeps her relaxed and calm and makes her more biddable when I'm competing.

I'd been furious to discover that the groom had left her locked up in her box for over twenty-four hours.

'That shouldn't make a difference,' Edward replies stubbornly.

'Maybe we should leave it for today?' I suggest, praying that Edward will agree. 'We can start again tomorrow once she has had some time out in the field.'

'No. You can't let that horse get away with this – she'll remember it and take advantage of you next time.' Edward isn't even looking at me, he's staring at Wildfire, as if the horse is defying him in some way.

'I really don't want to do any more today,' I plead. He looks up at me then, and holds my gaze for a moment before replying.

'Fine.' I exhale with relief. 'Let me sit up on her,' he goes on. My body fills with tension.

'What?' I ask, not moving from my saddle.

'Let me up on her.'

'Why?'

'If you're not willing to make that horse work correctly, then I will.' Hesitantly, I slip down from the saddle. I don't know why, but I'm suddenly afraid for my little horse.

Edward sits heavy and hard on her back and Wildfire tenses underneath him. He pulls hard down on her mouth and the mare resists, much more aggressively than she had with me. Edward pulls harder and sweat starts to break out on her shoulders.

'You little bitch!' Edward mutters. I don't say anything but watch in horror as things escalate. Just do what he wants, I pray to Wildfire: just do what he's asking you to do. But Wildfire can't hear my desperate pleas and she begins to kick out as Edward saws on her mouth. Edward kicks her hard in the ribs and Wildfire retaliates by slamming his legs up against the wall.

'Stop!' I yell, no longer able to keep it in, but Edward

doesn't even acknowledge me. I can see bloody foam coming out of Wildfire's mouth as he continues to saw at her mouth. I yell again, but Edward ignores me still. Wildfire is rolling her eyes to the back of her head and I'm afraid that neither she nor Edward is going to back down. I run towards her, desperate to stop this, but I have to dash out of the way as Wildfire dives forward erratically then gallops around the ring. I stand in the middle, helpless, and watch as she gets faster and faster. Edward pulls heavily against her mouth, but it doesn't seem to be making a difference and, for the first time since I've known him, he looks afraid.

Wildfire continues to pick up speed and I'm dreading her turning herself over. Suddenly, she screeches to a halt. It's so abrupt that Edward comes flying over her head and lands with a hard thud on the ground. I see my opportunity and dive towards Wildfire. She's shivering with fear when I reach her and I almost want to cry when I see her bloody mouth. Edward stands up straight away and charges for Wildfire like a bull, but I stand between them, forcing him to come to a halt.

'No,' I say, my voice shaking, not wanting Edward anywhere near me, or Wildfire. But he's not looking at me, he's staring at Wildfire with pure hate and aggression.

'Get out of my way, Elizabeth!'

'No!' I say, with such anger and force it surprises even me. Edward stares at me. I know he is waiting for me to back down, but I won't. I'm shaking, but it's not because I'm afraid but because I'm angry. I know I'll take a swing at him if he dares come any closer.

I don't how long it is before Edward walks away. He doesn't say a word but storms off in the direction of his office. I listen, and after a few minutes I hear the sounds of an engine starting and a car speeding off. Once I'm sure Edward's gone, I walk Wildfire slowly back to her stable. She's exhausted, and her head hangs low. I remove her tack gently, carefully examining her body for any damage. Other than her mouth, she seems unharmed, but I still apologize every few seconds as I wash away the foaming sweat that covers her body. I don't get upset; I'm concentrating too hard on Wildfire, on taking care of her. She nuzzles into me, but I feel too guilty to enjoy her affection. I stare at her mouth for a long time. Once I clean away the blood, the cuts aren't as bad as I thought they'd be, but I know they must be stinging her.

'I don't know why he did that,' I whisper, my voice shaking. Wildfire's eyes are closing with fatigue. 'I'll never let him on you again, I promise.' I can't get the images out of my head. Edward is a tough, strong guy, I know that, but never before have I seen him so ruthless. For the first time, I think about leaving him and it doesn't hurt. Right now, I don't feel as if I love Edward; in fact, I think I hate him. I look at my exhausted horse and my stomach knots in anxiety. If I left, what would happen to her? Edward owns her; he could do anything he wanted with her.

The idea of not having her makes me want to curl up in a ball and cry. I don't have anyone but her. The realization of my situation hits me. I'm trapped: I can't leave without risking losing everything. I suddenly wish I had never met Edward, that I hadn't fallen in love with him, but then Wildfire nickers as if to say, If you had never met him, then you and I wouldn't be together. I wrap my arms around the horse and bury my head in her neck. It takes all my self-control not to burst into tears.

'It'll be worth it,' I whisper. 'It'll all be worth it. I won't leave you.'

After a while, I pull away from Wildfire, throw a cosy rug on her and give her some hay then make my way to the feed room. I don't normally bother coming into Edward's feed room, as his grooms organize all the meals for the horses, but I want to find some sort of cream or ointment to put on Wildfire's mouth. I look in random drawers and boxes, not sure where anything is. There are numerous jars of various foods and supplements I don't recognize but I continue to look, determined to find something. I see an old jar of manuka honey in the back of one the cupboards and I reach for it, but as I do so I knock over a large plastic bottle of white powder. I'm about to put it back without a second thought when I realize it contains steroids. I recognize the name on the bottle after years of lectures and talks about things you cannot give to a competing horse. I stare at it for a long time and it takes me a moment to grasp the magnitude of what I have just found.

I used to watch Edward on the TV when I was little, winning all the most prestigious competitions in the world. I look up to him, I idolize him. All those memories seem so silly now – Edward, the man I worshipped, admired and loved is nothing more than a cheat. Angrily, I put the steroids back and make my way over to Wildfire. I decide then and there that I'll give her all her meals from now on. I'm too afraid of what Edward's grooms may be giving to her. I put the question of whether to report him or not to the back of my mind for now. I hate cheaters but destroying Edward's career could also mean destroying mine.

Wildfire is practically snoring by the time I get back to her. She barely opens her eyes as I rub the honey into the raw cuts around her mouth. She wakes up slightly when I give her some food. She whickers thankfully and I pat her neck tenderly before I leave.

All the way back to Orla's, I can't shake the image of the pure hate and anger that was in Edward's eyes. What would have happened if I hadn't been there? How far would it have gone?

I don't even want to know the answer to these questions. But even though I can't get rid of the hate I felt for him this afternoon, I can't forget all the wonderful things he's done for me over the last few months either – all the places he's taken me, the way he kisses me with such passion, and, most importantly, the way he believes in me and my dreams. He's the only one. I've lost count of the numerous nights we've stayed up and just talked and talked about all the places we're going to see, all the competitions we're going to take part in together and how he's going to show me a life more exciting and full than I could ever imagine. It's these memories, and not the memory of this afternoon, that bring me to tears. Am I willing to lose this future just so I can stand on a higher moral ground? Or maybe I need to suck it up and realize that I won't reach the top without some hardship. But even as I tell myself this, I can't stop my whole body from shaking as I think of how terrified Wildfire had been earlier. I won't let Edward go anywhere near her again; that is something I won't settle on.

I open the door of the apartment, my face still soaking from my sobbing, unsure what I am going to tell Orla, and am overwhelmed by the sight and smell of red roses. Every countertop, every table – every seat, even – seems to be covered in the most beautiful red roses I have ever seen. The apartment is engulfed in them. I don't even spot Orla until she speaks.

'So, what did he do this time?' she asks light-heartedly. But then she sees my red face and her smile disappears. 'Oh God, Liz, what happened?' I can't answer her; I just stare at all the flowers around me, knowing that my mouth must be hanging open in shock.

'Where did these all come from?'

'There's a card on the counter . . . in Edward's handwriting.' I pick it up and open it.

Elizabeth,

You saw the worst side of me today and I am so ashamed of myself. My pride and anger took over but I can promise you that it will never happen again. You are my everything, Elizabeth, and I will do whatever it takes for you to forgive me.

I love you,

Edward

I read and reread the letter, but the words hurt more every time. Orla just stares at me, until, eventually, I have to speak.

'So are *all* these from him?' I ask.

'Yeah,' Orla answers carefully. 'A dozen bouquets of a dozen roses each.'

'Wow! That's quite sweet.' But Orla is not comforted by my words; in fact, she looks even more worried.

'Elizabeth, please tell me what happened.'

'We had a fight . . . it was silly, really . . .' My voice is a monotone, but I'm no longer crying. I can't bring everything up again, not when I've already decided what I'm going to do. My dreams and Wildfire are everything to me, and there's no point in denying the truth, if I want to keep them, I need to stay with Edward. I think I've known the truth of Edward's and my situation all along but this is the first time I've truly looked at it and accepted it for what it is: if I want to achieve my goal, I need him. But I can't talk about it, not even to Orla, it's too hard.

'Whose fault was it?' Orla asks, gently laying her arm on mine.

'His,' I say with certainty. 'It was his fault, but he's sorry—' Orla looks as if she's going to say something else but stops as we hear a knock on the door. I wipe my face before I answer, already knowing who it's going to be.

Edward stands there in front of me, looking sedate and guilty.

He lifts his head as I open the door and, shockingly, he looks as if he's been crying.

'Elizabeth!' he chokes out. I thought I would be angry when I saw him, but instead I just want to comfort him and tell him it's all going to be OK. Then memories of him sawing Wildfire's mouth come rushing back to me and stop me from reaching out to embrace him, even though that's what I want to do.

'We need to talk,' I say, letting him in. I turn around to see that Orla has disappeared, and I'm so relieved that no one else has to hear what I know I need to say.

'I'm sorry—' he starts, making his way to the couch, one of the few pieces of furniture that doesn't have roses on it.

'Why did you do it?' I ask, sitting down next to him.

'I don't know,' Edward says, hanging his head low. 'I'm used to horses that submit, and she just wouldn't . . .' He looks lost for words. 'But I will never sit on Wildfire again . . . I promise.' I feel relieved at his words and the tightness in my stomach loosens slightly, but I still don't know how to word what I want to say to him. 'Are we OK?' he asks, in an almost child-like voice.

'Where is our relationship going?' I ask, deciding to be blunt.

'I don't know what you mean—'

'You want to divorce Katherine?' He nods. 'And then what? I mean, what's the plan for us?'

He takes a deep breath before he answers. 'Well, then . . . if you are willing . . . I would marry you.'

'And what would happen after we got married?'

Edward can't hide his shock this time, but I no longer want vague promises. I need to know what his plans are, and I know he has one, because Edward Dawson always has a plan.

'I'd make your dreams come true . . . whatever it took.' All of a sudden I realize this is it: I can have the life I've always wanted as long as I continue to stay with the man sitting in front of me.

'Is that what you want?' Edward sounds nervous, and I can tell he has no idea what I'm going to say.

'It's what I want more than anything,' I say, my voice quivering.

He lets out a laugh of relief. He doesn't hesitate to lean into me, and he kisses me so eagerly I can't do anything but respond and kiss him back. I don't know how long we kiss for, but I pull away from him before it starts to go any further.

'You make me feel so alive, Elizabeth!'

'I love you,' I say. But I'm not entirely sure I truly mean it. 'I really believe you and I can have a happy life together.' Edward nods along, caressing my face.

'You are so beautiful, my girl.' He leans in to kiss me again, but I stop him. I take a deep breath. I haven't finished yet.

'I want to be with you, but . . . I don't think we should be *together* until you and Katherine are divorced. I understand that may take time . . . but I'm willing to wait . . .' He stares at me, crestfallen.

'I know that what you are saying is the right thing to do, but . . . Elizabeth, the idea of not being able to kiss you or be with you is torture.'

'It is for me too, but . . . I can't be the other woman any more.' Edward is silent for a moment.

'You must promise to wait for me,' he says sharply.

'Sorry?' I ask, not quite sure what he means.

'When I divorce Katherine, I need to know you'll be there, standing by my side.' His tone has changed. It almost feels as if he is discussing some sort of business deal.

'Of course,' I say, shaken that he could think I wouldn't be there for him. His expression softens and I begin to relax.

'I guess I'd better go home . . . alone,' he says, standing up.

'Thank you,' I say, wrapping my arms around him, but making a point not to kiss him. Edward seems stiff in his hug, but I try to ignore it.

★

I feel calm once he has left, clear in the decision I've made. I want Edward, but not in the way we were before. I need him, and in more ways than one. It's no longer about losing Edward; it's about losing my dreams, losing Wildfire. Everything I've ever wanted in my life now depends on one thing: making this man love me.

My phone buzzes in my pocket, breaking my train of thought. I look down at it and see a message from Matthew: 'Fancy a drink tonight?'

I stare at it for a long time before replying: 'Can't. But I'll cya in Scotland.'

It's time to end this strange fascination I have for Matthew. I want the life I can have with Edward, and that's more important than anything. Matthew is my friend, and it's about time I started treating him like a friend.

15

The Opportunity

PREPARATION FOR SCOTLAND HAS TAKEN UP NEARLY ALL MY time. Away shows are a common thing in Shane's yard and they need days upon days of work, but I'm still excited every time we drive on to that ferry. This time, I'm even more excited, because Liz will be there too. I'm astonished how much I'm dying to see her. I think of that moment in the dark again and again, and I wish I had kissed her.

'Matt! Why are you still on that one?' Nick shouts, gesturing at the horse I'm sitting on. I should be on Harvey by now. 'Will you put that horse away and come here? I need your help with something.' I give him a wave of apology, though I don't think he sees it. The three-year-old he's holding is bucking and hopping on the spot. Nick looks frustrated and exhausted. Adam is with him, but he's no help and just seems terrified. I make my way back to the stables, shaking away thoughts of Liz and what it would have been like to kiss her. The horses come first. The horses always come first.

I untack the horse I was on and run over to Nick, who has by now managed to get the three-year-old calm and in a stable.

Adam has disappeared off somewhere, and Nick is wiping the sweat from his forehead.

'What's up?' I ask.

'Shane's going bloody nuts,' Nick says, exasperated.

'Why?'

'He was supposed to be giving Kristine a lesson today, but she's fucking disappeared somewhere.' Kristine is the niece of Shane's fiancée, Justine. She's in her mid-twenties and is taking a year off between uni and work. Shane agreed, as a favour to Justine, to teach Kristine how to ride while she stays with them for a month, but Kristine is scatty and unfocused and Shane finds her incredibly frustrating. After every lesson you can find him ranting and raving to anyone who'll listen that he won't bother again. He only does it because, deep down, he adores Justine and he'll do anything for her.

'Where on earth could she have gone?' I ask, thinking of the miles upon miles of stables and fields she could be hiding in.

'I don't know,' Nick mumbles. 'Would you help me look for her? Shane was supposed to bring her home an hour ago and he's about ready to kill someone if he doesn't find her soon.'

'Yeah, sure,' I agree, imagining Shane running around the yard, his temper ablaze. 'You look in the bottom fields and I'll go look in the stables.' Nick nods and runs off.

I find the stables empty, as expected. I check in the tack room too. The only person there is Linda, having a cup of tea. I ask her if she's seen Kristine and she says she hasn't. I'm almost ready to give up when I see that the door to the hay barn is ajar. I'm about to disregard it, thinking that there's no way she could be in there; it's just an old barn where we keep extra hay and some equipment we don't use any more. But as I walk away I hear the faint sound of a giggle. I frown. Why on earth would anyone be in *there*? I go over to the door, and as I approach it I see Kristine at the far side of the barn, pressed up against the wall. Her arms are wrapped around Roger's neck.

I jump to the side, afraid they might see me. It takes me a few moments to take it in: Roger and Kristine are kissing. It hits me like a ton of bricks. I've always liked Roger – he's funny, generous and always stops for a chat. He dotes on Linda; he's constantly holding her hand and kissing her cheek. They've only been married for a few years but they have looked seamlessly happy the whole time. Part of me wishes I was wrong, that it isn't Roger kissing Kristine but someone else entirely. My mind goes into overdrive. What should I do?

I see Adam walking down into the stables I've just searched. I take a few, large steps towards him, then shout unnecessarily loudly, 'Hey, Adam! Have you seen Kristine? Shane is looking for her.' Adam looks at me, confused, and when he replies he speaks at a normal volume.

'Sorry, I haven't seen her,' he says. He leaves and I make my way over to the door of the stables and pretend to wash out some already clean buckets. Kristine leaves first. She has a quick look around before dashing in the direction of Shane's office, flattening her ice-blonde hair with her hands. I make sure to keep my head low.

About ten minutes pass before Roger slips out. My heart sinks when I see him, out of the corner of my eye. I'd really hoped I was wrong.

He spots me and walks over casually, a slight hop in his step.

'Matt, my man, how are you?' His voice is the same as ever.

'Good,' I say shortly, not looking up from the buckets.

'Have you seen Linda?' he asks.

'Tack room.'

'Are you OK?' I can sense he's getting suspicious. I look up and force myself to cop on.

'Yeah . . . sorry . . . It's just been a long day.' I force a grin, and Roger relaxes.

'Shane working you to the bone, like always?' I nod, not really wanting to talk to him. 'Well, don't forget to enjoy yourself a bit. You know what they say: Work hard, play hard.' He gives me a gentle nudge, and I attempt a chuckle, though the irony of what he is saying and what I have just seen is not lost on me.

'Thanks, Roger.' He skips off in the direction of the tack room. Watching him go, I think, God, I really don't know him at all. And it makes me wonder, do you ever really know anyone?

The night air hits me like a slap in the face. I napped on the ferry most of the way to Scotland. Nick and I were up until the early hours yesterday, getting everything ready for the journey. We've stayed down below with the lorry the whole trip, to be with the horses in case anything goes wrong. Young horses not used to long journeys can panic, and some of the stallions have been known to work themselves into a frenzy. Luckily, our journey has been smooth and uneventful, and Nick and I are able to catch up on some much needed sleep.

Shane is to travel to Scotland by plane and will meet us there tomorrow morning. Everything needs to be ready before his arrival or he'll be seriously angry. In the days leading up to this, Shane's been tense and quick to shout. The show in Scotland is a big deal: it's one of the biggest shows in Europe and most riders will want to prove themselves here for the upcoming season. I'd debated telling Shane about Roger and Kristine but he'd been in such a bad mood I decided against it. I didn't even consider telling Linda: I got along with her, and I considered her a friend, but I didn't think it was my place. In all honesty, I don't think she would believe me if I did tell her.

It's warm down below on the ferry and I drift back to sleep. I don't even notice when the ferry stops and Nick begins driving the lorry towards the Gleneagles Equestrian Centre, our venue for the week. He only wakes me when we arrive.

We've travelled all day, and it's dark and cold when we leave the comfort of the lorry. The horses are impatient and hungry when we unload them and place them in their temporary stables. It's only as we take down the last of our gear that I start to feel less drowsy. My excitement builds as I regain my energy. Nick and I have been clever with our packing this time: we have designated places in the lorry's compartments for every-thing we need. For once, everything's to hand. As soon as the horses are fed, rugged and watered, we can relax and do what we like for the evening.

'Pub?' Nick asks. I look at my watch and nod. It's only nine, and I'm full of beans after my day-long nap.

The pub is full of grooms – most riders and competitors won't be arriving until tomorrow morning. I recognize nearly all the Irish people, and some of the English grooms I've encountered over the years. But it's definitely a different vibe from the Irish shows. In Ireland, everyone knows everyone. You may have never spoken to a certain person before, but that didn't matter, you still knew who they were, who they worked for, what horses they rode, what height they jumped and who they were sleeping with. At the international shows there's a whole new group of people you don't recognize. You don't know anything about them and they don't know anything about you. I prefer it this way.

Nick and I find ourselves a comfortable place at the bar. The room is packed, and it's too difficult to try to move around and say hello to people.

I'm lost in my own thoughts when a male voice makes me jump.

'Can I buy you a drink?' A small, dark-haired guy I don't recognize slinks in next to Nick and me. Nick's face lights up with recognition.

'It's nice to see you again, Dom,' he says.

'It surely is,' Dom replies. 'It's been a long time.'

'You two know each other?' I ask.

'We jumped ponies together,' Nick says, stumbling over his words a little. Dom nods along politely.

As the two of them catch up, I notice that Liz is standing a few steps back from us, and staring at Dom.

'Liz! Hi!' I say.

She raises her hand at me shyly but doesn't make her way towards us. I stand up and make my way over to her.

'I didn't expect you until tomorrow,' I comment, amazed that she's standing in front of me. I wish I'd put on some nicer clothes before coming out.

'I came with Wildfire. Edward's grooms can be a bit . . . rough with her . . . and I wanted to have my own lorry to sleep in anyway. Dom travelled over on the same ferry as me.'

I look back at Dom and Nick, who are chatting away like old friends.

'You drove the lorry here yourself?' I ask, surprised and impressed. Liz's lorry is huge and looks very difficult to manoeuvre. I'd never imagined that Liz, who seems so little, would drive it herself.

'Yeah, of course. Who else would be driving it?' She looks smug and a smile breaks out on my face.

'Why don't you join us?' I ask, gesturing towards Dom and Nick.

'I . . . I don't know . . .' She's become so tense around me.

'One drink?' I tempt, giving her my best smile, and this seems to do the trick.

'OK.'

Now that Liz and Dom are with us, I don't even bother to try to talk to anyone else. Liz drinks with us, laughs at our stories and joins in with her own anecdotes. I find myself not saying much but staring at her. Watching the way she talks, the way she laughs – it's hypnotizing. Dom is extremely quiet and seems content to observe his surroundings, making the odd side-splitting remark. But I catch him sharing the occasional look with Nick. I wonder if there's a history between them?

'So you did a lot of pony-jumping too?' Liz and Nick are comparing stories from back in the day. Nick is a bit older than Liz, so they would never have crossed paths, but it sounds like their experiences were very similar.

'I did indeed. I'm not going to lie, but I was awesome. The old parents bought me a string of absolutely amazing ponies. It was class. For a while there I was practically unbeatable. I got placed at the Europeans three years in a row,' Nick boasts. I have heard this story a hundred times over. Nick was a very good pony jumper and he is definitely not humble about it. I stay silent and let him ramble on. He's drunk now and there's nothing I can say to stop him recalling his 'glory' days.

'That is class . . .' Liz says, impressed. 'So do your parents still come and watch you jump?'

'Definitely not.'

'Why?'

'Nobody wants to go down that road.' Nick answers rather bitterly.

'Anyone want another drink?' Dom's gesture is so un-expected that it takes us all a minute or two to realize what's going on. I seem to cop on first as to what Dom is trying to do.

'Um . . . yeah, I'd love one,' I say, over-enthusiastically. 'Do you want one, Liz?' Liz is staring at Nick, a little confused. It takes her a moment to answer.

'Yeah . . . Thanks, Matthew.' Nick still hasn't said anything and he's now gazing down at the floor. Dom rises from his seat and takes a step towards him. He places a hand on his arm and whispers something in his ear.

'You OK?' is all I can make out. Nick shakes himself and plasters a smile on his face.

'No drink for me,' he says. 'I think I'm going to head to bed . . . I'm pretty knackered. I will try going to bed alone . . .' He winks at me as he gets up to leave and I laugh and pat him on the back. Liz looks at me and Dom questioningly after Nick has left.

'Did I say something?' Liz asks. I don't know how to reply but, luckily, Dom gets there before me.

'No, I think he's just a bit drunk . . . He'll feel better once he sleeps it off a bit.' Liz nods as Dom speaks, but her expression is uncertain. I can tell she feels she's done something wrong.

'I'll get the drinks,' I announce, standing up.

Dom stands up too. 'I'll give you a hand.'

We squeeze our way to the front of the packed bar, waiting in silence for the first few minutes. It makes me slightly un-comfortable but Dom looks as content as he has all night.

'So you know Nick quite well?' I say.

He smiles knowingly at me. 'We've never dated, if that's what you're thinking.'

'I didn't mean that . . . sorry . . .' I stutter.

'But you thought it – at least for a moment, didn't you?' My instinct is to deny it and apologize again, but Dom doesn't seem annoyed, just mildly curious.

'Well . . . yeah . . .'

Dom smiles properly for the first time all night. He looks like he's just won a bet with himself. 'I shouldn't have assumed . . .' I mutter it under my breath, but Dom hears me.

'Ah, it's fine, don't worry . . . I'm gay, though, so you were half right . . . and I did know Nick very well, but he's never really felt that way about me . . .'

His smile falters for a moment. It's so quick I almost don't notice it, but it happens. I haven't met many people who knew Nick when he was younger. I think back to the conversation I had with Adam a few weeks ago and ask hesitantly, 'Do you know his parents?'

'I do,' he says. I can tell he's not going to elaborate unless I push it.

'What are they like?' I know I'm probably crossing some line here but I suddenly feel like I don't know anything about my best friend.

He thinks for a moment before answering. 'They're good people but . . . intense . . . they expected a lot from Nick, and I don't think he's lived up to what they hoped for.'

I can tell he doesn't want to say any more, but I feel unsatisfied by his answer. The bartender arrives and asks what we'd like. I order drinks for me and Liz and ask Dom what he'd like.

'I'm fine, actually,' he says unexpectedly. 'I think I might go to bed also. Will you tell Elizabeth for me?'

'Yeah, sure,' I say, a little worried that I've somehow offended him.

'Thanks, Matt.' He gives me a quick smile before diving out of the bar, and part of me wonders has he gone to find Nick.

Liz is sitting on her own at the table.

'Sorry I took so long,' I apologize.

'It's fine,' she says, putting away her phone. She's been texting. 'Where's Dom?'

'He went to bed.'

'Oh God, please don't tell me I offended him too?'

'Of course you didn't. I think the two of them are just tired.'

'I did upset Nick, though?' Liz raises her eyebrow at me and I know I can't lie to her.

'Nick's hammered, and he's always been a bit funny about his parents,' I say, trying to keep it vague.

'Do you know why?'

'No . . . Not really . . . He doesn't want to talk about it and I don't want to make him, so I just leave it. Some things are better left unsaid . . . Anyway, I think most people have dysfunctional relationships with their parents.'

'Yeah, that's true . . . I know my parents are whack jobs anyway . . .'

I smile and we both sip our drinks. Now that Nick and Dom are gone, the tension between us has returned. I don't know why, but I get the impression she doesn't want to be alone with me. I catch her looking at the door once or twice and I'm almost sure she's going to get up and leave. I don't know whether it's because she has a drink or it's her manners, but I'm so relieved that she stays.

She begins talking about Wildfire and the progress they have made. I can tell she really loves this life. When she talks about showjumping and competing it's as if her whole body lights up, and I'm happy to sit back and just observe her. The time flies by and I can see she is more at ease. I wish I could stay here all night with her. I become brave and reach out for her hand, but she pulls away and I know I've gone too far.

'I'm sorry,' I mutter, looking down at my feet.

'It's fine,' Liz replies, but she stands up. 'I'd better go to bed, though.'

Before I get a chance to say anything, she's gone. I feel deflated. I'd been so excited to see her and spend some time with her this weekend, and now I've ruined it in a matter of minutes. I drag myself from the stool and make my way to the lorry. I check my phone and see a number of missed calls and messages from Shane. I read the first message and sprint towards the lorry.

★

'Nick! Wake up!' I shout, turning on all the lights.

'What the fuck is wrong with you?' he says groggily.

'Shane has broken his leg!'

Nick is suddenly wide awake. 'What? How?'

'Car crash. Some idiot ran into him on the way home from the yard. He says he's fine, but his leg is broken in three places.'

'Fuck! Well, I guess all we can do is pack everything up in the morning . . . there's bound to be a ferry we can catch back to Ireland . . . But this is going to be a major blow for Shane . . .'

I shake my head. 'No, Nick . . . you don't understand. He wants us to compete in his place.'

16

Instincts

I HIDE BEHIND MY COFFEE, WATCHING EDWARD IN THE distance. He's talking to a petite blonde girl with a tiny waist and perfectly done make-up. I can't hear what either of them is saying but they seem to laugh every few seconds. Nobody is *that* funny, I say bitterly to myself. Dom is nattering away about something, but I'm not even listening. When he claps his hands in front of me I jump with fright.

'So, are you nervous about the Grand Prix today?' he asks, but I don't really hear. 'Earth to Elizabeth, are you there?'

'Sorry,' I say, looking away from Edward. 'Um . . . not really,' I admit. My confidence with Wildfire has grown drastically over the last few months. Every competition, we're getting better and better. The dream of being on the Irish team in Dublin is becoming more real every day.

'What were you staring at?'

'Nothing. It just looks as if Lindsey is flirting with Edward.' I try to sound as unconcerned as possible. Dom doesn't know about my relationship with Edward and, even though he's my friend, I have no idea how he'd react if he found out.

'Lindsey flirts with everyone,' Dom says dismissively.

I'm surprised how jealous I am when I see the two leave the canteen together. He's allowed to talk to other girls, I scold myself. Anyway, you're the one who wants to wait, not him. I push away these thoughts and concentrate on Dom. I can't obsess over a decision I've already made.

Dom's expression changes. He must have seen something behind me, and now he's the one who's hiding behind his coffee.

'You OK?' I ask, turning around. Nick and Matthew walk into the canteen, looking tired and stressed. They sit down without ordering anything and talk to each other in frantic whispers.

'You're really into him, aren't you?' I say.

'I don't want to be,' he groans.

'You can't help who you like,' I say reassuringly, but I surprise myself when I glance at Matthew.

'Nick has never been into me and I've always been into him,' Dom says, defeated.

'Have you ever told him?' I ask, but Dom shakes his head.

'There's no point in telling him. He's the ultimate gay player, but the annoying thing is, I know it's all an act.' I think of the few evenings I've spent with Nick: he's so full of life, you can't help but have fun with him. I find it hard to believe it's all an act.

'Really?' I ask disbelievingly, but Dom ignores me.

'If he was just open to the idea of a relationship, even a little bit, then I think he'd really like me.' Dom is staring openly at Nick now and I wonder how long he has felt this way. I grab his hand and he looks at me.

'If Nick doesn't like you, he's an idiot. So fuck him!' This makes Dom laugh and I'm happy to see him smiling again.

'Did you have fun with Matt last night?' he asks, changing the subject.

'Yeah, I did. But it ended kind of weirdly.'

'Why? What happened?'

'He tried to hold my hand,' I say quietly, in case someone overhears.

'And that's a bad thing because—?'

'I'm not into Matthew.' It comes out very abruptly.

'OK,' Dom replies, putting his hands up as if in defence. 'I just thought the two of you had a thing for each other.' He looks at me quizzically for a moment but I give him nothing in return. 'But I guess you don't. What did you do?'

'Well, I just left,' I reply, feeling embarrassed. Dom whistles through his teeth.

'That's a bit harsh.'

'You think?' I ask, starting to feel bad.

'Well, it's not like he tried to kiss you or anything. Holding your hand is fairly innocent.' I look back over at Matthew. Nick is no longer with him and Matthew is sitting with his face down on the table and his hands covering his head. I tried so much to keep my distance last night but it was so hard when Dom went up to Nick. Matthew is so charming and I don't really know how to be around him without being flirty. I don't want him to hate me.

'Doesn't look like he's having a good day.'

'I think I should go and apologize,' I say, feeling terrible and hoping I'm not the reason he looks so miserable. Dom gives me a smile of encouragement and I make my way over.

'Hi,' I say when I reach the table. He looks up slowly then lifts himself up properly when he sees it's me.

'I just wanted to apologize for last night. I completely over-reacted – what you did was pretty innocent, if you think about it . . . and it's probably partly my fault too. I may have been lead-ing you on without realizing it . . . Anyway, I just wanted to say sorry and I hope that we're still OK.' I'm rambling, getting more embarrassed by the second, but he just stares up at me, at a loss.

'Sorry, Liz, but . . . what are you on about?'

'Oh . . . um . . . I was just talking about when you . . . you know . . . tried to hold my hand.' The heat is rising to my face.

'Oh yeah, that . . .' he says, not really seeming to care. 'Yeah, I'm sorry too. Won't happen again.' I'm not used to Matthew being so dismissive and I'm surprised how hurt I feel as I go to walk away, but then he calls after me. 'Liz, stop. I'm sorry. I've just . . . I've got a lot on my mind.'

'It's fine,' I reply, trying to hide my disappointment. 'I'll just go.'

He calls after me again. 'I'd love to talk to you about something . . . if you have a minute?' He gives me a weak smile and I sit down next to him without hesitation.

'What's going on?' I ask.

'Shane's broken his leg.'

'Oh no! Does that mean you and Nick have to go home?' Again, I feel strangely disappointed. He shakes his head.

'Shane doesn't want the travel and entry fees to be a waste. He's asked me and Nick to compete instead.' Matthew sounds exhausted.

'He wants you to jump in the Grand Prix?' I ask, surprised. Matthew nods along.

'I'll ride Cedric. Nick's riding Gambler.'

'Have you ever jumped in a Grand Prix before?'

'No,' Matthew groans. 'I couldn't say no to Shane but I honestly think he's lost the plot. I've wanted to compete at a higher level for years, but this is insane. The Irish Horse Board is going to select the team for Aachen at the Grand Prix today. The fences are going to be fucking massive!' He looks on the verge of tears and I have the urge to grab his hand, but I stop myself.

'You'll be fine.'

'No, I won't – I'm screwed. At least Nick has some inter-national experience. I have nothing!'

'You have great instincts. I've seen you on young horses, and you ride better than half the people in the Grand Prix. Just trust your instincts in that ring and it'll go well.' I'm not sure if he believes me.

'Thanks,' he mumbles, a bit calmer in any case. 'I'd better go and get ready for this Grand Prix then . . . or execution, as I like to think of it.' He tries to sound perky but it feels forced.

'Doesn't Shane have a puissance horse as well?' I ask before he has a chance to leave. He nods, paling a little.

'So who's riding that?' I ask – but I already know the answer.

'I'm lighter,' Matthew says, and walks away.

'Up two!' I shout at one of Edward's grooms as Wildfire and I canter calmly around the warm-up. I rack my brain, trying to think of this groom's name, but my mind keeps coming up with blanks. I'm too embarrassed to ask, knowing that he has told me it before. Normally, Edward would help me prepare for a class but today he didn't offer, and I didn't ask. He and I have distanced ourselves from each other since that night we agreed to wait, but neither of us agreed what our professional relation-ship would be. Is he still my trainer? I don't know. I know I asked for time and space, but I'm surprised he hasn't approached me at all. Even though we aren't romantically involved at the moment, I thought we could still be friendly to one another, but it seems to be pretty black and white in Edward's mind: either we're together, or we're not. It hasn't been as hard as I thought it would be to stay away from him. I hate the fact that I can't talk to him when I see him at shows or at the yard, but most of the time I'm too busy to think about him.

I turn in to the fence the groom has built and pop it with ease. Wildfire relaxes into a walk and I pat her neck encouragingly.

'That's fine for now,' I shout, and the groom nods before dashing off. There's only Nick ahead of me now and I feel prepared and confident. I've walked the Grand Prix course – it was massive, but that doesn't bother me: I know today is going to go well. Wildfire is one of the most talented horses in the country. There is one bogey fence that is bound to catch people out – a massive parallel in the corner of the ring – but the striding to it is perfectly uneven. I feel thankful that Wildfire is so biddable, so easy to shorten and lengthen at a moment's notice.

A voice comes over the PA. 'Next, we have Nicholas Brown riding the Irish-bred gelding Gambler.' I rush over to the main ring to watch Nick's round. He canters into the ring slowly, looking cool and collected. You can see the concentration on his face; his hands are stiff. He's nervous. I hold my breath as he canters into the first fence. He rides well and with experience and his round is pure perfection – until he reaches the bogey fence, when he doesn't react quickly enough and is caught in an incorrect stride. The horse makes a huge effort to clear the fence but, unluckily, he clips the front pole and it thuds to the ground. Nick is beaming, though, as he trots out of the ring, clearly delighted that, other than that one mistake, he had a beautiful round. He should have ridden on, I tell myself, thinking that I mustn't make the same mistake. I want to go over and congratulate him, but my name is being called now. I'm on next.

Wildfire goes like a dream. She gives every fence miles of air and the bogey fence doesn't faze her in the least. I pat her hard on the neck as we trot out of the competition ring with the first clear of the day. I decide to stay on her, knowing that it won't be long before my jump-off. Neither do I want to miss watching anyone else's round.

After his round, Edward leaves the ring with an unexpected

eight faults. His horse looked tired as it struggled around the track. But even with his eight faults, Edward is lying third. Nick is second and I, as the only clear so far, am first. Everyone else seems to be building up cricket scores.

'Well done!' Dom exclaims from the ground, giving Wildfire an enthusiastic pat.

'Thanks,' I reply, still high after my clear. 'She was amazing.'

'You weren't so bad yourself!'

'Are you not riding in this?' I ask, confused by the fact that Dom is not on a horse: he's another of the riders who was expected to do well today.

'Damn horse cast itself last night.'

'Oh no!' I exclaim. Casting is when a horse gets stuck while lying down in its stable; when a horse casts itself it will usually panic and hurt itself struggling to get back up. 'Is he OK?'

'Nothing serious – he'll be fine in a few days. But I can't take the risk of jumping him when he's sore.' I can tell by Dom's voice that he's annoyed. He's a good rider and he would have probably done well. Unfortunately, horses are unpredictable and there's nothing you can do when they get injured.

'There's always the next show,' I say brightly, but Dom just grunts. I don't blame him for being so disappointed. I know I would be.

I catch sight of Matthew. He's sitting on Cedric, a beautiful grey stallion, and Shane's best horse, in my opinion. He looks comfortable but his face is as white as a sheet.

'Did you hear that Matthew is jumping in this?' I say, as casually as I can.

'Yeah, I did,' he replies, perking up. 'Everyone's talking about it. The poor fucker is terrified. I was in the bathrooms earlier and he was puking his ring up.' We watch Matthew approach a warm-up fence. I'm surprised how natural and fluid his riding is.

'I hope he does well.' I really mean it.

'If he rides like that, he'll be absolutely fine,' Dom replies, clearly as surprised as I am at how well Matthew looks on the horse.

Dom turns his attention back to the competition ring then gestures towards me.

'You have to watch this horse, Elizabeth,' he says excitedly. 'It's incredible.' I turn towards the competition ring and for a moment I think he's being sarcastic. In trots an absolute midget of a horse, no bigger than a pony. He's black and white, and his mane and tail are wild and unkempt. He looks like something you'd find tied up on the side of the motorway, next to the caravans.

'Are you serious?'

'Just watch!' A broad smile spreads across his face.

He's right. The guy riding looks no older than seventeen and he gallops the small horse at everything like a madman – yet the horse clears everything with ease. It goes like a motorbike, rallying around the corners at such speed that I think it's going to turn itself over, but it doesn't. In fact it comes out with the second clear of the day.

'That was superb!' I choke out. 'Who is he?'

'Stevie O'Leary – he's from Northern Ireland. He's been making his way up the rankings this year . . . like yourself, really.' I watch Stevie wrap his arms around his horse after leaving the ring. He then proceeds to feed it an excessive amount of sugar cubes, which the horse licks up eagerly.

'I don't think I can beat *him* in a jump-off,' I say. That was unbelievably fast. Dom laughs, and I know he's thinking the same.

I hear Matthew's name being announced, and he enters the ring. Oh God, *I'*m nervous, I think. He has gone past pale and now looks slightly green. The bell rings and he seems to be mumbling away to himself.

'What's he doing?' Dom asks. 'Praying?'

'No . . . I think he's talking to Cedric,' I say uncertainly. Matthew rubs the horse's neck affectionately before approaching the first fence. His round is pure perfection: every stride, every jump is textbook perfect and I almost find myself becoming jealous of his skill. And his round only gets better. When he finishes with a perfect clear, I realize I'm even more delighted than when I went clear.

The later stages of the competition, though, are really about Stevie and me. Matthew goes into the jump-off and does another beautiful clear, but it's slow, and it's obvious he's happy taking third place. Stevie goes even faster, and I find myself watching him in pure awe as he turns in the air and gallops at the last fence. He's a good five seconds faster than Matthew. I suddenly wish Edward were with me, giving me advice. To beat Stevie, I'm going to need to let the handbrake off and go for it. But is it too much of a risk? Am I going to scare Wildfire by going too fast? I'm standing, waiting to go into the ring, confused as to what to do, when Matthew pops up beside me. He's still sitting on Cedric but his face is no longer pale and he's beaming after his fantastic rounds.

'Good luck!' he says.

'Thanks,' I reply, realizing how nervous I am. 'And well done – you did brilliantly today.'

'I'm just happy I didn't die,' he jokes. I smile at him briefly, but I can feel my stomach starting to turn over. I don't know what to do.

'Are you OK?' he asks, sensing my nerves.

'I don't know what to do!' I blurt out. 'Do I try to beat Stevie or is it too much of a risk?' I jump with fright as the starter calls my name. Matthew looks at me seriously for a moment then breaks into another smile.

'We only live once, Liz. Go for it!' I don't have time to reply but give him a quick smile before I canter into the competition ring. The bell rings and I decide then and there to do what Matthew said. I go for it.

Wildfire seems confused at first as I kick her up into a near-gallop. I have trained her for months to go calmly and smoothly, but it only takes her a few moments to understand what's going on, and she rises to the challenge immediately. I've never gone this fast before and I have to rely on my instincts, as I don't have any time to fix anything. I forget all my training and go full pelt at the final fence. Wildfire takes off a stride early and rubs it hard, but it stays up, by pure luck.

Applause and whistles break out, and I look up at the clock to see that I've done it – I've won! I've beaten Stevie by a tenth of a second.

Wildfire won't stop dancing throughout the prize-giving and I decide it's best to take her away before the excitement gets too much for her. I say a rapid well done to Stevie and Matthew before I leave. Both of them look so happy you'd swear they had just won the lottery. Nick comes fourth and Edward only joint fifth, with another rider who received eight faults.

It's not until I get Wildfire back to the stables that she slowly begins to unwind. I can't blame her for being so wired after the speed round I've just done, but it's not long before she begins to yawn and become sleepy. I rug and feed her quickly before rushing back to my lorry, in desperate need of a shower.

As I change out of my dirty jodhpurs and into jeans and a string top, I get endless texts and calls of congratulations. Marshall is practically sprinting around the lorry as I put on my make-up. Soon, though, he's exhausted and conks out on the floor. I'm on a complete high from my round, and I can't wait to go out and enjoy myself this evening. The puissance doesn't start until eight o'clock. Every other class is finished by then, and the crowd can give the puissance its full attention.

My phone continues to buzz and I look down at it to see two new messages. The first one is from Dom: 'Get your ass down here! Celebration shots on me!'

The second one is from Edward: 'Well done today.'

It's the first time I've heard from him since we talked and I can't stop myself from feeling disappointed. His message seems cold and somewhat formal. In a way, I think he's punishing me, but I can't be sure. I suddenly have the desire to call him, worried that he may be going off me, but I don't have much time to debate it before I hear someone knocking on my lorry door.

'I'm coming, Dom!' I call, thinking he must have got bored waiting for me.

I open the door. It's not Dom. 'Matthew . . . Hi!' He's in a clean pair of jodhpurs and he looks nervous, but not nearly so bad as earlier.

'I didn't get the chance to say well done earlier,' he explains. 'God, Liz, you were brilliant!'

'Thanks,' I say, blushing. 'Do you want to come in for a drink?' I don't really know what else to say.

'Yeah, I'd love one. I think I need one before I tackle that massive wall.' He follows me into the lorry and sits down while I pour each of us a large glass of wine.

'Was Shane happy with you and Nick?' I ask, sitting down next to him but keeping a healthy distance.

'Thrilled. A third and a fourth . . . I don't think he expected us to do nearly as well as we did.' I can feel the energy coming off Matthew. It must be a combination of happiness, nerves and, perhaps, exhaustion.

'You excited to take on the puissance?' I take a large mouth-ful of my wine, very aware of the fact that I'm in my lorry with Matthew, alone.

'I don't know if excited is the word . . . The puissance isn't really about skill. It's more about bravery and . . . having balls, basically.'

'You have balls . . . Well, I hope you do, anyway,' I say, without thinking, feeling braver with some alcohol inside me. I'm mortified at my own joke so I'm thankful when Matthew laughs.

'Yes, I do have balls,' he says. 'I just hope I still have them when this competition is over . . . to tell you the truth, I'm fucking terrified.' Matthew is still smiling, but I can tell he means it. My body is shivering with so much tension that all of a sudden I want to get out of the lorry. I take another gulp of my wine before I speak.

'You need to take your own advice,' I say. 'Matthew, you just need to go for it!' Before I realize what's going on, his lips are on mine. At first I freeze, not sure how to react, and before I have time to work out what I want to do, he pulls away. I bite my lip. What I should say? I can't believe he just kissed me. He stares at me and I know he's waiting for me to say or do something. I don't know how long passes. It feels like an age and yet my mind can't seem to process any of it.

'Good luck,' is all I can manage.

Matthew smiles at me. 'Thank you.'

After he's left, I stare at the door. *I can't believe he just kissed me!* But what's more surprising is that I didn't pull away, and that I didn't want to pull away. I wanted him to kiss me.

17

The Moment

I TRY TO STAY CALM AS I MAKE MY WAY DOWN TO THE competition ring but I break into a sweat. Adrenaline is pulsing through my body and I feel like I could do anything. I kissed her! *I can't believe I just kissed her!* I keep repeating it to myself – but what's more shocking and exciting is that she kissed me back.

Nick is waiting for me in the puissance warm-up with Showstopper, the horse I'm doing the course on. He's cleaning and adjusting Showstopper's tack as the horse stands there, looking almost bored.

'Where've you been?' he asks frantically when he sees me.

'Nowhere,' I mutter, undecided whether to tell him that I kissed Liz.

'Did you puke again?'

'Not this time.'

I look into the competition ring and watch the stewards building the massive red wall I'm going to have to attempt. My excitement and happiness disappear, replaced by dread and fear. A large crowd has formed around the ring – much bigger than there was for the Grand Prix. All the competitors from earlier are now out of their jodhpurs and ready for a great night out. A lot of Scottish locals have also turned up. The puissance has always been a crowd-pleaser. It doesn't require as much skill as a Grand Prix; it's all about bravery, timing and, most importantly, luck. Luck has been on my side all day – I just have to hope that it continues.

'You shitting it?' Nick asks.

'No,' I lie. Nick raises his eyebrows. 'OK . . . Maybe a little.'

'You'll be fine.'

'Thanks.' Things have been slightly weird with Nick since I went clear in the Grand Prix. He hasn't said anything – in fact, he's been nothing but supportive – but I can't shake the feeling that he's a little off with me; that, in the manic situation we're in, he feels he should've done better than me. Maybe I'm wrong and he doesn't feel this way at all. But if he does, I wouldn't blame him, because, to be honest, I thought he'd do better than me as well.

'You feeling confident?' a male voice behind me asks. Nick and I turn around to see Stevie. He looks even younger off the horse and his pale face is covered in freckles.

'Not really,' I say with a nervous laugh. 'I've never competed in a puissance before.'

'When in doubt, just boot on. That's what I do.' I wish I had his confidence.

'Well done again!' I say. 'That horse of yours—'

'Dynamite,' he corrects politely.

'Well, Dynamite is some horse. What's his breeding?'

'He doesn't have any . . . Well, not that I know of, anyway. I picked him up in the sales for a couple of hundred; the poor thing was half starved and incredibly nervous. The fat man who owned him just wanted rid of him. But I liked the look of him, you know? I never thought he'd make a showjumper or anything like that. I just thought he'd be a nice horse to have around, go for a few hacks and that. But then one day he jumped the post and rails out of our paddock. They must be 1 metre 60 easy . . . I couldn't believe it! So I started jumping him at some small shows and he just got better and better. He'll do anything for you as long as you keep feeding him his sugar cubes. I forgot them one day and next thing I know he'd dumped me at the water fence . . . My da said it was just because Dynamite didn't like the look of the water, but I know it's because I forgot his sugar cubes. I haven't made that mistake since.'

I laugh, but I'm amazed. It's so rare to have a horse with no breeding competing at such a high standard.

'He sounds like a character,' Nick chimes in light-heartedly.

'He is!'

'Are you jumping in this?' I ask, gesturing to the now fully built wall.

'I was going to, but I pulled out. Dynamite is exhausted, more so than normal. I think he might be getting the flu.'

'It was a tough competition today.'

'It really was,' Nick agrees. 'The horse just needs rest – he'll be perfect in a few days.'

'You're probably right,' Stevie says, looking more cheerful. 'Anyway, I better go find my da, he's buying me a pint. Best of luck, Matt.'

I like him. There are so many egotistical competitors in showjumping, it's nice to meet someone so genuine.

'I can't believe he bought that horse for a few hundred. He'd sell it for fifty or sixty grand now, easy,' says Nick.

'I know,' I agree. 'But I don't think he'd ever sell him.'

'No, I don't think he would . . . and I don't blame him,' Nick murmurs. We're both quiet for a moment and I know we're both thinking about Dynamite and what it would be like to discover an incredible horse like him. We're pulled up by the voice of the commentator coming through the speakers:

'The puissance will begin in five minutes. Competitors, please begin warming up.' Nick and I stare at each other for a moment then burst out laughing. I don't know why I find this whole situation hilarious, but I do. Nick gives me a leg-up on to Showstopper's back, and I think to myself, I've been taking chances all night, no point in stopping now.

There are twelve people entered in the puissance and it's five rounds in all. The first four rounds go a lot more smoothly than I thought they would. Showstopper is like a machine. He turns himself on the second he enters that ring and he jumps that massive wall with all the strength and effort he can. The moment I trot back out of that ring, he switches off; he practically goes to sleep when I walk him around the warm-up. The standard of the competitors is high, and six of us make it into the final round. The judges and spectators aren't happy, they can't have more than five rounds, and yet they don't want six winners – it takes away from the drama. In the fourth round the red wall stood at 1 metre 90; for the final round the stewards have raised it to 2 metres 20.

'Thirty centimetres in one round – that's nuts!' Nick exclaims angrily. I can't say anything; all I can do is stare at that enormous red wall in fear, wishing I'd been knocked out in the last round. 'They're not supposed to raise it more than fifteen centimetres in each round.' I know he's annoyed on my behalf, but it's only making me feel worse. What I need right now is someone to tell me that it's easy, that 2 metres 20 isn't really that high if you think about it.

It's an unspoken rule that all the finalists in a puissance go to the bar together and have a shot before the final round. The other five riders are laughing and joking with each other, but I stand back silently, so tense I feel ill. There are three German competitors, a French rider, an American and me. The fact that

I'm the only Irish competitor who has made it to the final only makes my nerves worse.

'Here you go, Matt,' one of the Germans, Klaus, says, handing me a shot of whiskey. I throw it back and it burns my already raw throat. Klaus laughs. 'Matt, my boy, you're supposed to vait for us! . . . But it's OK. Vee vill get you anozer one.' He hands me another shot and, this time, I wait.

'On zree, everyone!' Klaus announces cheerfully. 'One, two zree . . .' I throw the second shot back, and it's not so awful this time, but I'm worried the two whiskeys won't sit well on my already uneasy stomach.

I'm about to make my way back down to Nick and Showstopper when I feel someone grasp my arm. I turn around to see Liz standing in front of me. I open my mouth to speak, but nothing comes out.

'I just wanted to wish you good luck,' she says in a rush, then leans forward and kisses my cheek. I don't have time to say anything before she runs away. It's all so quick I wonder did it even happen.

'What's that on your face?' Nick asks when I get back. I rub my cheek with my hand and look down to see red lipstick.

'Nothing,' I say, but I can tell from the look on his face that Nick knows.

The 30-centimetre increase in the height of the wall has made a huge difference. Four of the competitors so far have not only knocked the wall but spectacularly ploughed through it, with the French rider actually falling off. Klaus is the only one so far to clear it. The crowd whistles and screams with delight as he and his horse pop over the wall as if it was nothing more than a small fence. It's my turn next and it feels like my gut is twisting inside of me. The starter is calling for me to go in when I realize that I really do feel very unwell.

'I'm going to be sick,' I announce to Nick.

'You'll be fine,' he says, leading me and Showstopper towards the competition ring.

'No, really!' He turns to me. He looks more serious than I've ever seen him.

'Matt, you have to go in now. You'll always regret it if you don't . . .' He's being kind but stern, and I suddenly realize how much he wishes he was doing this instead of me. 'You can do this, Matt.'

These are the words I needed to hear. I kick Showstopper and canter into the ring as confidently as I can. Showstopper turns on instantly and the crowd shouts louder than it has all evening. I pat the horse on the neck without breaking my canter – I can't stop moving for fear that, if I do, I won't face the wall. I increase the canter slightly and Showstopper pulls me forward eagerly. I turn towards the huge red wall and my gut twinges. I think of what Stevie said earlier, and kick on.

I don't know if it's Showstopper's experience or pure luck, but I get a perfect stride. The horse soars into the air and lands on the other side, barely even rubbing the wall. I know I'm clear before I get the chance to turn around to look. The crowd is screaming and Showstopper has his ears forward, enjoying his moment. I leap off the horse and hug him.

'You're brilliant!' I say. Nick arrives and hands Showstopper a full pack of mints, which he licks up eagerly. People surround me, and I feel overwhelmed. I've won! I can't believe I've won! Klaus comes up and slaps me hard on the back.

'Fantastic performance, Matt, my man! I'm delighted to be sharink this vin vis you.' I smile at him and a smile beams out of his weathered face. There must be at least thirty people around me, congratulating me and Showstopper, now being fed even more treats by admirers. But I'm looking for one person only and, no matter where I look, I can't see her.

★

The celebrations go on into the early hours of the morning. Adrenaline keeps me going for a long time but, once I see the sun beginning to rise, I realize how exhausted I am. I crawl into bed at five o'clock and sleep for five hours solid, which is more than I have in the last few days combined. In my dreams I relive the evening: I jump that wall over and over, and every time I land I get the same feeling of excitement, relief and rush. It's addictive, and in my dream I want to do it again and again. I'm hooked.

I'd been disappointed when I discovered that Liz hadn't stayed out to celebrate. Dom found me and said that she was dog-tired and had gone to bed early, but she had seen my win and he knew she was delighted for me. I smiled at him and thanked him, but I couldn't shake the feeling of rejection. Did she regret that we kissed? Was this her way of saying she didn't want to see me any more? I'd felt so confident and daring yesterday, but now I'm worried that I'm starting to trespass on dangerous territory.

It's the slam of a door that wakes me. I open my eyes slowly to see Nick wandering around the lorry, pulling down various pots and pans.

'What are you looking for?' I ask sleepily. Nick turns to me, surprised I'm awake.

'A bowl. I want some cereal. Sleep well?' he asks, pouring some cornflakes into a questionably clean bowl.

'Yeah, great. The celebrations last night were full on!' Nick laughs. Like always, he was the life and soul of the party, shouting, singing and cheering until he became the centre of attention.

'Yes, it *was* great.' He's smiling, but his voice sounds unnatural. I let it pass.

'What time's the derby?' I ask instead. Shane wants Nick to

compete his derby horse and I know Nick's excited about it. He loves derbies and I want to support him today like he supported me yesterday.

'I don't know,' he murmurs. 'I don't know if it'll be on . . .' His smile fades and I know something must be wrong.

'What's going on?

Nick lets out a sigh. 'Stevie found Dynamite dead in his stable this morning . . . The vet reckoned he had a heart attack at some point in the night.' It takes a few moments for the news to sink in and when it does I'm lost for words. I pull myself out of bed.

'Oh God . . . That's awful . . . Poor Stevie . . .'

'I know. When Dom told me I almost didn't believe him . . . Like, the horse jumped so great yesterday and now . . .' Nick falters and I just stand there, still not able to believe it. I think of poor Stevie. He loved that horse, and Dynamite loved him. To Stevie, Dynamite dying must be like losing a brother.

'So what happens now?'

'Stevie's dad told the show officials that he wants the competition to continue . . . but I was talking to some of the competitors in the canteen and no one is really in the mood for it . . . I know I don't want to compete − it doesn't seem fair when Stevie can't . . . Dynamite was only seven, you know . . .'

'Seven? God, his life was only beginning.'

There's a knock on the door. I throw on a T-shirt before Nick opens it. A Scottish teenager wearing a yellow vest stands awkwardly outside.

'I'm here to inform you that the show officials have decided to cancel the rest of the competition out of respect to Stephen O'Leary.' It's obvious that this teenager has said these exact words a few times by now, but Nick and I nod along to let him know we understand. 'I was also told that I'd find a *Matthew* here,' he continues.

'That's me,' I answer, confused.

'You're wanted in the office in the next fifteen minutes.'

'Why?' It comes out more harshly than I mean it to.

'I don't know,' the teenager stutters before diving away.

'What's that about?' I ask Nick, but he's as much in the dark as I am. 'It's kind of shit that you can't compete,' I say cautiously, aware that Nick's opportunity has been taken away from him.

'It's fine,' he says. 'It wouldn't have felt right, not today.'

I dress in my only clean pair of jeans and a white polo shirt. I don't know why I'm being called to the office, but I know I should look as smart as I can. Nick has found some black bands in the back of one of the many cupboards in Shane's lorry and I put one around my left arm to show respect to Dynamite and Stevie. Walking to the office, I can tell the atmosphere has completely changed. Yesterday, the equestrian centre was buzzing, with people rushing about. Today, people are moving more slowly and everything is quieter. I start to wonder where Stevie is and what they've done with Dynamite's body.

I knock on the office door tentatively, but a voice shouts to me straight away. 'Come in! Come in!'

When I open it I see Liz, Edward Dawson, Captain Ben Sullivan, one of Ireland's highest ranked army riders, and Taidgh Bourke all standing in a circle. Taidgh comes over to me.

'Matthew! I don't think we've met, I'm Taidgh.' I shake his hand politely but of course I know who he is. Everyone in the Irish showjumping community does.

Taidgh is in his late fifties, but he has aged well and still looks fit and strong. I look past him and glance questioningly at Liz. She shrugs; she has no idea why we're all here either.

'Can we start?' Edward asks rather impatiently. 'I hope to catch tonight's ferry home since the rest of the competition has been cancelled.'

'Of course,' Taidgh says cheerfully. 'Sit everyone, please.' Edward and Ben sit next to each other and Liz and I across from them. I suddenly find the age difference between the four of us rather funny and smile to myself.

'Right, so let's get straight to it then,' Taidgh says, pacing. 'I have called you all here because you have been selected to represent Ireland in the upcoming Nations Cup competition in Aachen.'

'Are you serious?' I blurt out. This makes everyone else in the room laugh, apart from Edward, and I feel myself blush.

Taidgh smiles kindly at me. 'I certainly am. I talked to Shane on the phone this morning and he is allowing you to compete on Cedric.' I want to shake my head in disbelief but I make an effort to keep control, not wanting to embarrass myself again. 'Now, since our unfortunate performance at the last Nations Cup, it has been agreed that we need a new team.' He turns towards Liz and me. 'Now, Elizabeth and Matthew, I won't lie. You two weren't originally on the team we selected. Elizabeth, we chose you after Shane Walker had his accident, and Matthew . . . we chose you after Stevie's awful tragedy this morning.' At once the excitement and happiness I felt a moment ago is replaced by guilt. 'But even though the two of you are considered somewhat of a gamble . . . I have full faith that you will both compete well.'

'I think it's a great choice,' Edward chimes in. 'Elizabeth is one of the most competitive riders in the country and Matthew impressed all of us yesterday with his performance.' I look at him, taken by surprise.

'This is a strong team,' Ben agrees. 'We'll do well in Aachen.'

'Thanks,' I mumble, and so does Liz.

'Well, I'm glad everyone is so confident . . . I'm confident as well, but I want us to be prepared. Shane said he would, in his own words, "whip you into shape", Matthew. And I assume you would like to continue to work with Edward, Elizabeth?' Liz doesn't say anything but looks at Edward.

'Of course,' he says casually and I see Liz relax.

'Lastly, I want to say that I'm very sorry about what has happened to Stevie today. It's a true tragedy and he doesn't deserve it. But I think it will teach us all to take the opportunities that are given to us; it'll teach us to be brave and take risks, because, if you think about it, that's the only way you will succeed in this competitive world.' I'd never realized what a great speaker Taidgh is, and I find myself hooked into every word he says. 'So when we get to Aachen, give it all you have.' I look around me and see that everyone is nodding, so I join in enthusiastically, hoping I don't look silly.

'Great. Well, that's everything, and I look forward to seeing you all in Aachen.' Edward and Ben stand up and leave the moment Taidgh is finished. Liz and I stay in our seats. 'You two will be great,' Taidgh says encouragingly, and leaves too.

We sit there in silence for a short while. When I look up, she's staring at me. I don't know why, but we both break into hysterical laughter.

'I can't believe this!' I exclaim, breathless.

'I know!' Liz is smiling from ear to ear. Another few moments of laughter go by, and I still feel like I can't take any of this in. Liz grabs my hand.

'I need to do something. Will you come with me?' I agree without a second thought.

Liz won't tell me what it is she needs to do as we're walking across the equestrian centre and towards the parked lorries. At first, it doesn't really bother me, but now I'm starting to worry what it's all about. She stops at a small blue lorry. It's older, and has a number of dents and scratches on it.

'That's seen better days,' I comment. 'Who owns it?'

'Stevie,' Liz says quietly. Before I can ask anything else, she knocks on the door. Stevie's dad opens it. He looks tired, and much older than he did yesterday.

'Hi,' Liz says gently. 'Is Stevie here?'

'It's Elizabeth, isn't it?'

She nods. 'And this is Matthew.'

'I remember. You won the puissance last night?' I nod too.

'We just wanted to tell Stevie how sorry we are. Dynamite was a one-in-a-million horse.' Liz's voice wobbles.

'He was,' Stevie's dad agrees. 'But Stevie is quite upset at the moment and he's not really up to seeing anyone.'

'That's completely understandable,' I say, hoping Liz won't push it any further.

'Can you give him something for me?' she asks, pulling a red rosette and an envelope out of her jacket pocket. Stevie's dad looks in the envelope and shakes his head.

'Oh, you're a sweet girl, but we can't accept this. You won fair and square.' I realize the envelope contains Liz's winnings from the Grand Prix yesterday.

'Of course you can. Stevie deserves them.'

'No, I don't.' Liz and I jump when we see Stevie appear at the door. His eyes are swollen and red and his face is pale. It's clear he's been crying for hours.

'But you do,' Liz continues. 'I absolutely rattled that last fence. It was only luck that it didn't fall; it deserved to fall, but your round . . . Your round was perfect. So please take the winnings. You and Dynamite deserve them.' Stevie stares at Liz with a blank expression; I can't tell what he's thinking.

'I don't know what to do with it,' he mutters eventually.

'I thought you could maybe use it to transport Dynamite home . . . if that's what you want?' Stevie is holding his hand up to his face, and I know it's because he's holding the tears back. But his dad is smiling.

'Thank you, Elizabeth. That is very kind of you.' Elizabeth smiles once more before we walk away, in silence.

I think about everything I've witnessed so far today and how quickly everything has changed. I think about what Taidgh said as well, and I realize how right he is: we have to seize the opportunity when it comes and not be afraid of failing. I stop between some parked lorries and Liz stops too.

'You're really special, you know that,' I say.

Liz shakes her head.

'It was the right thing to do . . . and he did deserve to win—'

'No. I mean I think you're really special . . .' Her eyes widen as she looks at me. 'I like you.'

'I like you too, but . . . things are complicated.'

'But you like me?' I ask, trying to sound confident.

Liz smiles at me. 'Yes, I do like you.'

'And you liked kissing me?' I ask, smiling myself now.

'Yes, I liked kissing you, but—'

'Do you want to kiss me again?'

She pauses a moment before answering. 'Yes,' she breathes.

I don't hesitate. I lean in and kiss her, putting my hands on either side of her face. She wraps her arms around my waist. When I pull away, I feel breathless.

'Go out on a date with me?'

'Oh, Matthew, I want to, but . . .'

'But what?'

'Things are complicated,' she says again.

'I like complicated, it makes life interesting.' I gently stroke her face and ask again. 'One date, Liz, that's all I'm asking.'

She stays silent for what feels like an eternity. I stand there, not moving. After a moment she pulls herself a little closer to me.

'OK,' she agrees. 'One date.'

18

Decisions

'WHERE ARE YOU TAKING ME?' I ASK NERVOUSLY AS MATTHEW and I clatter on in his old, battered car.

'It's a surprise,' he answers.

I haven't seen Matthew since Scotland, which was over a week ago. Since then I've been a bundle of nerves. I don't know how I got myself into this situation, and I have no idea how to get out of it either. Edward can offer me so much, but I don't want to lose Matthew completely. I know I'm playing a dangerous game here but I'm not prepared to disregard whatever it is I have with Matthew. I look over at him while he drives. His dark hair has grown a bit since I first met him and now looks a bit scruffy; his skin is pale but soft-looking and his face has this slight boyish quality to it that I hope he never loses. Every time I catch sight of his lips, I have this overwhelming desire to kiss him, but then my stomach goes into knots with dread and guilt. *What about Edward? He wants to marry you!* It's as if my subconscious is glaring at me. I think about poor Stevie and how he's lost everything with Dynamite. I've chosen Edward and I know we could have a successful future together.

But what if I lost Wildfire: would Edward be enough to keep me happy? I shake away those thoughts before they engulf me and remind myself that, technically, Edward and I aren't together at the moment.

In fact, things between Edward and myself have never been stranger. True to his word, he is training me for the upcoming Nations Cup in Aachen, but he's no longer relaxed and there's no warmth there. Instead he's cold and formal and, as soon as our sessions are over, he leaves promptly, without giving me a single word of praise or affection. I can't help but be a little hurt by it, but I have to remind myself that this is what I asked for, what I wanted — or at least what I thought I wanted.

'A penny for them?' Matthew says brightly.

'What?'

'Your thoughts?'

'Oh right . . . well, I'm just wondering, are you planning to murder me and bury me out here or something?' I joke. We're no longer on a road, it's more of a dirt track, and I'm not sure if Matthew's Toyota Starlet can survive much longer.

'Don't worry — if I had planned to murder you, I wouldn't have taken you here. Too many walkers about . . . If I was going to kill you, I'd use pigs to get rid of your body.'

'Pigs?'

'Yep. Pigs'll eat anything. Including bodies.'

'It worries me that you know that,' I say, but I'm unable to hold back a smile.

'I grew up on a farm,' he says defensively.

'You're so strange.'

'Well, you're the one who agreed to go on a date with me. So I guess that makes you strange too.'

'I guess I am,' I say, and we catch each other's eye for a moment.

Matthew slows down, causing his brakes to screech loudly,

and pulls over to the side. There's barely enough room for another car to pass.

'We're nearly there.' He hops out. 'But we need to walk the rest of the way.' I get out, and he pulls a small rucksack from the boot.

'Where are we?' I ask, not really expecting him to give me an answer.

'On one of the Wicklow mountains,' he says, and starts to walk briskly up the hill. I have to jog after him to catch up.

'You're taking me up a mountain?'

'Well, we drove most of the way. It should only take us about twenty minutes to reach the top.' He can't stop smiling, and I can tell he's enjoying my surprise.

'Fine,' I say, motoring on past him, glad that I wore jeans and flat shoes. Matthew keeps up with me easily. It's a dry day, but cloudy, and it's not long before we're so high we're in the clouds, making it hard to see where exactly we're going.

I stumble over a rock and Matthew grabs my waist before I hit the ground.

'Can't be hurting yourself before Aachen. Taidgh would kill me if I knocked out a team member,' he says, holding on to my hips a little longer than he needs to.

'Ah, so that's your plan. Injure me, so you can have all the glory to yourself!'

'Definitely not! If I can get through Aachen without embarrassing myself, then I'll be the happiest person in the world.' I know he's joking but I can't ignore the hint of worry in his voice.

'You'll be great in Aachen.'

'No, *you* will be great. I'm just aiming for satisfactory . . . In all fairness, it's a complete fluke that I made it on to the team.'

I grab his arm and force him to face me, though his expression is not completely clear through the cloud. 'Matthew, you deserve to be on this team. You have more raw ability than anyone I've ever seen. Your natural instincts are better than mine,' I say, although it stings me a little to admit it. It took me years of training to be able to ride in sync with any horse; Matthew seems to be able to do it instantly, and with ease. He stares at me for a moment, but in the mist I can't quite figure out what he's thinking. He leans forward and kisses my forehead.

'Thank you,' is all he says. We turn and continue to walk up the mountain, but I stumble again. This time, Matthew isn't quite quick enough to catch me and I do fall to the ground.

'Fuck!' I'm not hurt, but I'm embarrassed by my clumsiness.

'I think you have better balance on a horse than you have on your own two feet,' Matthew says kindly as he pulls me up.

'You're certainly right about that.' I'm glad the fog is hiding my red face. Matthew doesn't let go of my hand once I'm standing, and I can't bring myself to draw it away.

'I think we're nearly through the clouds anyway,' he says, and we walk forward, holding each other's hand tightly.

When we reach the peak I realize why Matthew brought me up here.

'Wow!' We're clear of the clouds now and can see nothing below us but white mist. I look around. There are other mountain peaks scattered across the clouds, like little islands.

'It's like being on the edge of the world,' I say, looking around in every direction.

'Most people like walking up here when it's bright and sunny, because there's a great view,' Matthew explains. 'But I like it when the clouds are thick and below the peaks . . . It kind of feels as if you're in another universe when it's like this.'

I smile at him. 'It's great. Thank you for bringing me.'

He rummages through his rucksack.

'Would you like a blanket? It gets quite cold.'

I nod, only noticing now that I'm shivering in the strong wind. I wrap it around my shoulders and Matthew pulls out another and does the same. 'I also have tea and sandwiches?' he offers.

'I'd love some tea.'

We sit, making ourselves comfortable against the large, standing rock which identifies the peak. The longer we stay still, the gladder I am that Matthew brought blankets and hot tea. The wind is harsh up here – but the view more than makes up for it.

'Do you come here a lot?' I ask.

'A bit,' Matthew answers. 'Nick and I run up here sometimes, to stay fit. I rarely get the chance to stop and enjoy the view though.'

'You and Nick are really close,' I say, only realizing now that all Matthew's stories involve Nick in some way.

'Yeah . . . I guess . . .' he says hesitantly, frowning at me.

'Has he ever—' I start, but I can't finish because I'm afraid that I'm crossing some line.

'Has he ever what? Hit on me?'

'Well, yeah,' I say, ashamed to bring it up. Matthew looks at me for a moment before he answers. Is he deciding whether he wants to tell me the truth?

'Once,' he mutters eventually. 'We'd only been living together a couple of weeks and one night while we were watching TV he placed his hand on my . . . well, on my manhood . . .'

I clasp my hands over my mouth. 'What did you do?'

'Nothing . . . I just sat there in shock. Nick knew straight away I wasn't into it, but he wasn't the slightest bit embarrassed. He said, "Just thought I'd check," and then we carried on watching TV as if nothing had happened.'

I'm relieved to see that Matthew is smiling as he speaks. I smile too. 'Has he ever brought it up again?'

'He jokes about "turning me" all the time, but I know he's only messing. He's my best mate, nothing else . . . You're not worried I'm gay?' he asks, trying to lighten the mood.

'Definitely not,' I say reassuringly.

I expect Matthew to laugh, but he doesn't. Instead he tilts his head towards me and looks at my lips. I sit there, frozen to the spot, wishing my brain would tell me what to do, but I can't seem to think at all. All I feel is my heart quickening as he fully leans into me. I expect his kiss this time so I let my lips move in sync with his. He's slower, not so eager and rushed. His kiss is different from the way Edward kisses me. When Edward kisses me, I stay passive and follow his lead, but with Matthew we respond to each other, almost teasing until we realize that we want the same thing. I'm all sensation; my brain has turned to nothing but mush. It's not until Matthew pulls me forward on to his lap that I realize the seriousness of what I'm doing. I pull away and he stares at me, bewildered. I jump up and start pacing back and forth, my head in my hands.

'What's wrong?' Matthew asks, worried. 'Did I do something?'

'No!' I exclaim, feeling like a fool. 'It's just . . . I shouldn't be kissing you.'

'Why not?' Matthew asks, standing up himself. 'Is that guy you were dating before still around?' he asks, sounding deflated.

'No, not really,' I say, trying to be as truthful as I can. My mind is going into overdrive. Part of me wants to tell Matt everything, but I know that's a stupid thing to do. He won't understand the relationship that Edward and I have – or had; I'm not sure which it is any more. No one understands it . . . and maybe there's a reason for that.

'I thought I was in love with someone else, but then I met you, and now . . . I'm not sure,' I say. I hope he'll understand. His face is unreadable, and once again it surprises me how afraid I am that he won't want anything to do with me.

'Is this guy in love with you?'

'I think so,' I say, my voice starting to crack.

'And you're not in a relationship with him?' I shake my head. 'But you want to be?'

'I did, but then you came along,' I say, wishing we weren't standing so far apart.

'I came along,' Matthew repeats, his voice calm. 'So when you said "complicated" the other day, you really did mean "complicated".' He laughs, but sadly. I look at him pleadingly, but I don't know what I'm pleading for. 'Look, Liz,' he goes on, 'I like you, and I don't know what this other guy has offered you, but I think I could make you really happy . . . If you have a decision to make, then you need to make it, but . . . I really do hope it all comes out in my favour.' My heart melts as he speaks and I wish I hadn't said anything. I wish I was still sitting by the rock kissing him.

'Why couldn't you be a massive jerk?' I say, and I'm thankful when he laughs at the joke.

'I'm sorry I'm so perfect,' he says. He has no idea how dead on he is. 'Do you want me to take you home?' he asks, and I nod.

We walk back down the mountain in silence and my hands begin to shake with anxiety. I wish I could say or do something to break the tension, but everything I think of feels so silly. It's not until we've done the forty-five-minute drive back to Orla's apartment that I know what I really want to say.

'I wish I had met you eight months ago.'

'Why eight months?' he asks. I want to say, 'Because it was before I met Edward,' but instead I say, 'It was before everything got so complicated.'

Matthew smiles, but it doesn't reach his eyes. As I let myself out of the car, he says one last thing. 'I hope I hear from you before Aachen.'

I know what he means, but knowing it doesn't make things any easier.

When I let myself into the apartment, Orla is sitting on the couch reading a newspaper. She looks up and knows straight away that something has happened.

'What's going on?' she asks.

I don't cry, I don't run; instead, I calmly sit down next to her and tell her everything. I tell her about my fight with Edward after he turned on Wildfire, about everything he's promised me; I tell her that I kissed Matthew and that I think I might be falling in love with him.

'Oh God, Elizabeth. That's a right mess you've got yourself into!'

'I know,' I say, relieved that I've talked to someone at last but still as confused as ever.

'I knew Matt liked you when he stayed here that night . . . I just didn't know you felt the same way,' Orla says, taking my hand compassionately.

'I didn't . . . Well, at least, I convinced myself I didn't, until he kissed me.'

Marshall jumps up from the ground and on to the couch. He curls up next to me and starts dozing off. I appreciate his affection and it makes me feel a little better. 'Edward's offering me this amazing life, the life I've always wanted. I'd be a fool to give that up, wouldn't I?' Orla frowns at me; I'm sure she must hear the uncertainty in my voice.

'Let me ask you something . . .' she starts, squeezing my hand. 'Are you in love with Edward, or are you in love with the life he's offering you?'

'With him!' I say, but so defensively that Orla knows she has hit a nerve. I change tack immediately, trying to cover up my outburst. 'The problem is, I think I'm in love with two people . . . Do you think that's possible?'

'I don't know,' she answers gently. 'But I think you need to choose one, because someone is going to get really hurt otherwise . . .'

'I know,' I mutter. 'If I give up Edward for Matthew, then . . . then I'm giving up so much, but if I give up Matthew, then . . . I don't know what I'm giving up. And I'm scared that I'll spend the rest of my life wondering, What if—?'

Orla looks confused, and I know that she doesn't know what I should do either. 'I think we both need a drink,' she says eventually.

'Oh God, yes,' I say, relieved that she's the one to suggest it. She pours us each a large glass of red wine and we finish them and refill the glasses before going back to the topic.

'I think I have an idea,' Orla says gingerly as she pours a third glass.

'I'm all ears.'

'You said that you and Edward aren't planning to get back together until his divorce is final, right?' I nod, wondering where she might be going with this. 'Well, then, until that happens, you are, technically, single and uncommitted. Maybe you should use that time to get to know Matt better so you can figure out how strong your feelings are for him.'

I think about it for a moment. 'Would that not just be me using Matthew?' I ask. I feel guilty about it already.

'Maybe,' she admits. 'Or maybe it's just giving Matt a fighting chance . . . Think about it – you know what it's like to be in a relationship with Edward, but what's making this decision so hard is that you don't know what it's like to be in a relationship with Matt . . .'

'That's true,' I say. 'But if I do date Matthew for a while and I realize what I want is Edward, won't Matthew hate me?'

Orla grabs my hand again, and I know she's going to tell me something I don't want to hear.

'Elizabeth, you need to accept that, whichever way this works out, whether you choose Edward or Matt, only one of them is going to be in your life – you can't have them both.' I squeeze her hand back in gratitude. I'm so lucky to have a friend like her.

'You're right.' But I don't think I'd been willing to accept that fact until now, and it makes everything that bit harder.

19

Twenty-One

I FEEL THE SUN TRYING TO BREAK THROUGH MY CLOSED EYES, but I pretend it's not there. I curl up in a foetal position, cocooning myself in my duvet. I hide my head under the pillow, but the sunlight still sneaks into the corner of my eye. I don't close my curtains at night; I find the sun rising is better than any alarm. I've got up at the same time every morning for the last four years yet I still find it a struggle to crawl out of bed. My mind knows it's time to get up, but my exhausted body is screaming at me to stay, even if just for a few moments. I can hear my bedroom door creeping open, but I keep my eyes shut, pointlessly hoping that if Nick sees I'm asleep he'll leave me alone.

'Is that the birthday boy I see hiding under all those covers?' He tiptoes towards me and I close my eyes even tighter, trying to prepare myself for whatever it is he's going to do. He tries to pull my duvet off but I grip on to it as tightly as I can. 'I knew you were awake!' he cries.

'Go away,' I moan, finally opening my eyes. The sun is really bright now, and my eyes sting at the sudden change.

'Time to get up, birthday boy.' Nick stands on my bed over me and jumps up and down, as if he were a kid.

'Fine . . . fine! I'll get up. Just stop jumping!' I say, laughing and accepting that there's no way I'll get back to sleep now. Nick leaps off the bed and grabs my duvet too – leaving me there in my boxers, freezing.

'You dick!' I call after him, and my duvet. He shrugs.

'Happy birthday, Matt!'

My birthday snuck up on me quickly this year. Between everything that's been going on with Liz and the horses, I haven't had time to stop and think about it. It's been over two weeks since I last saw Liz, and I do my best not to think about her, but I can't help myself. Aachen crawls closer and closer every day, and I know if I don't hear from her before then, it's all done, she's picked the other guy – whoever the son of a bitch is.

Over the last few days I've caught myself thinking about this mysterious guy. Who is he? Does he showjump? Does he know about me? As I sit up, I do my best to push all these thoughts to the back of my mind. I'm twenty-one today, and in less than two weeks I will be representing Ireland on a Nations Cup team. For once, I really feel like things are going my way. Most people in the yard know it's my birthday, so I'm surrounded by well-wishers all day, which puts me a good mood. Nick bought me twenty-one bottles of Corona. I discovered them on the kitchen table, a big bow around one of them. The sight of them makes me laugh, and I appreciate the gift greatly. Nick is low on cash most of the time, like me, and even though it's not a big present, it's unexpected, and makes me instantly glad to be twenty-one.

Shane finds me around lunchtime and gives me a new pair of white jodhpurs. I'm chuffed to bits. Jodhpurs are expensive, and

I'm in desperate need of a new pair for Aachen. Some of the others got me small presents, too: Linda and Roger gave me some cash, and Adam got me a card. My mum rings briefly in the morning to wish me a happy birthday and suggests that I go over for dinner this weekend. Part of me is surprised she doesn't ask if I'm free this evening, but I guess she assumes I have plans with my friends. Most people just wish me a happy birthday, though, and ask do I have any plans for the evening. The answer to which is no, I don't have any plans whatsoever. Originally, I hadn't wanted to do anything but, as the work day goes on and I talk to more people, I get more and more excited by the idea of celebrating and going a little wild.

That evening, I ask Nick, 'So what are we doing tonight?' The sun is setting and Nick is filling buckets of feed so we can give the horses their dinners and be done for the day.

'What do you mean?'

'It's my birthday . . . are we not going to go out?' Normally, Nick's the one dragging *me* out.

'You said you didn't want to do anything,' he says off-handedly, passing me a couple of buckets.

'I know,' I say, feeling a bit disheartened now. 'But maybe we could go out for a drink or something?'

'McGowan's is probably open?' he suggests, half-heartedly. I feel a bit let down – I had hoped that Nick and I could go into the city centre and maybe hit a few bars and nightclubs. We go to McGowan's every week, and it's never that busy, unless they have a special night on. Part of me wonders is Nick a little bitter about me being selected for the Nations Cup team in Aachen, but I push that thought aside. He's shown me nothing but support since I told him.

'How about Dublin?' I ask hopefully, but Nick just gives me a face.

'It's such a trek to get into the city centre, and it's so fucking expensive too!' He doesn't even look at me, just continues sorting out the feed.

'I guess McGowan's will be fun . . .' I can see from Nick's body language and tone of voice that he really doesn't want to go into Dublin city centre. He's right in a way: it's difficult to get in there at night and drinks are much more expensive than they would be in McGowan's – but I still can't help but feel a little hurt; I'd thought he'd be more enthusiastic about celebrating my birthday. He's always so keen on everything, but at the moment he couldn't seem to care less. He must notice the look of disappointment on my face, because he tries to reassure me.

'Oh, don't look like such a sour puppy. I didn't plan anything because you told me not to . . . Look, we'll have a bit of craic tonight, OK?'

I suddenly feel bad for making him feel guilty. He's right: it's my own fault for saying I didn't want to do anything. I should be thankful he wants to go out at all.

'Yeah, it'll be really good,' I say, doing my best to put some eagerness in my voice.

Just as we finish up our work for the evening, the rain starts. The day had been a warm spring one but now the sun has set, the sky has turned cold and wet. Nick offers to pay for our takeaway that evening since it's my birthday, and I take him up on it, glad he's getting into it, even if it's just a little bit. I shower and change after we've eaten, throwing on an old pair of jeans and a work hoodie, not wanting to get any of my good clothes wet. I walk out into our living room and see that Nick is all ready to go. In one hand he has one of my twenty-one beers; he's texting away on his phone with the other. When I come into the room he puts it away, looks me up and down and frowns.

'What the fuck are you wearing?'

'What?' I'm not dressed particularly well, but it's not like I'm wearing a sack.

'You look like a homeless person.' I look at Nick and realize he has made a decent effort. He's wearing a blue-and-white pinstriped shirt, dark jeans and his best dress shoes.

'I don't look that bad,' I say, wishing I'd at least given my filthy runners a wipe.

'You don't look good.'

'Why are you all dressed up? Is fucking Dom coming tonight or something?' Nick goes red, and I feel bad for putting him on the spot.

'I don't fancy Dom, I've told you that . . . We just used to be close once.' I want to kick myself. I don't know why, but Nick always gets tense when I ask about Dom or how Nick and he know each other. I know it annoys him when I imply he fancies Dom, and what I said just now was a low blow.

'I'm sorry. I know you don't fancy him.'

'It's your twenty-first, Matt. I thought I would dress nice because you seemed so put out earlier when I wasn't making a big deal.' Nick finishes his beer and opens another one, not even looking at me.

'I'm a twat,' I say. I see the corner of Nick's mouth twitch.

'Yes, you're a twat.'

'A massive twat.'

'Yes, you're a massive twat.' Nick is smiling now, and I feel better.

'Sorry,' I say, glad he no longer seems cross.

'It's OK – it's your birthday. You're allowed to be a twat.' He takes a swig of his beer then hands me a bottle.

'Thanks,' I say, taking it and slurping a large mouthful.

'You're allowed to be a twat on your birthday, but you're not allowed to look like shit. Get changed.' I laugh, and I'm happy to see that Nick's laughing too. I leave the room with my beer and go to choose which one out of the few shirts I own I should wear.

We run down to McGowan's, as the rain has only got worse. Both of us are wearing heavy jackets but I still feel like the water is soaking through. I keep my head down while I run, following Nick's lead. When we're across the road from McGowan's, I lift my head. The lights are on but there isn't a sound coming from it. Crossing the road, I'm afraid that Nick and I will be the only ones in the place. Nick slows down as we reach the door for some reason, but I don't stop to question him. I shove past, wanting to get out of the rain, and dive into the bar. I nearly fall backwards as a huge group of people starts cheering. Everyone shouts, 'Surprise!' and it takes me a few moments to realize they are here for me. I look behind me to see Nick laughing away and I realize that his grumpy, distant attitude all day must have been an act. McGowan's is decorated from floor to ceiling in banners and balloons and it's packed from corner to corner with people I know. A huge gold poster hangs above the bar with the words 'Happy 21st Birthday, Matt!!!' painted on it.

'Am I the greatest friend or what?' Nick asks, giving my shoulder a hard squeeze.

'You did all this?'

'Your family and Elizabeth helped me out a bit, but I was the genius behind it all.' He looks smug.

'Elizabeth helped?' Nick nods, knowing how delighted that would make me. 'So she's here?'

'She is indeed . . . somewhere, anyway!'

The next twenty minutes or so are filled with people hugging me and kissing my cheek. There are at least forty people here and the small pub feels incredibly full. Most people from the yard are here, including the other grooms. Adam tells me that he'd been in charge of making sure that no one spoke about it over the past few days. Even some of the people I know from competing had managed to come – a girl called Sally Murphy practically falls on top of me when she goes to hug me. She stinks of tequila when she screams 'Happy birthday!' in my ear, but I'm so happy I don't care. Shane and Justine are sticking in the corner with Roger and Linda, not wanting to join in too much with the younger people and their excessive drinking. I also think Shane might be worried some drunken idiot will bump into him on his crutches. Since his injury, his temper and tolerance have been rather short. He wishes me a polite 'Happy birthday', like he did earlier, and I thank him again for the jodhpurs. Eventually I make my way to the back of the room and see my family sitting together. They don't really know anyone else. Dad is the first one to stand up, and he gives me a hard pat on the back.

'Happy birthday, son, and congratulations!' This is the first time my family has seen me since I told them about Aachen. They were all thrilled for me, but what surprised me most is how excited and proud Dad is. Ann told me that he's organized a big group of people to come over to the house on the day of the Nations Cup and watch the competition live on TV.

Mum stands up next and gives me a peck on the cheek. 'I can't believe you're twenty-one,' she gushes. 'Only seems like yesterday I brought you home from the hospital.'

Ann grabs me in a hug the second she can. 'It's so great to see you,' she whispers in my ear.

'It's great to see you too,' I whisper back. As she pulls away, I see she's wearing a white dress and seriously high heels. She looks great, like she always does, but once again I'm blown away by how grown up she looks. Sometimes I wish she could be that cute eleven-year-old again, not this sexy teenager.

'Where's Christopher?' I ask.

'No longer around,' she says brightly. I'm glad to see she's back to her confident, cheeky self.

My dad grabs a box from behind him and hands it to me.

'This is from all of us,' he says. The box is white and decorated with a black ribbon. I open it carefully, not sure what could be inside. There's a wooden box with the word 'Citizen' carved into the top. I open the lid to find a silver, square watch. Its face is black and the hands are a dark, night blue. I look up at my family, speechless, and my dad begins to chuckle.

'I'm guessing you like it then?' he asks, clearly chuffed with himself.

'It's really nice . . . Thank you,' I say, to all of them.

'You're welcome,' Mum says happily. 'Twenty-one is a big deal, so we wanted to get you something special.' I take the watch out of its wooden box and try it on. The strap will need adjusting, but other than that it looks great. It's by far the most special thing I own.

'I've been watching some of those big international competitions on TV lately, and the one thing I noticed is that all the riders have a fancy watch. So maybe you could wear this in Aachen?' I stare at Dad, overwhelmed.

'Thank you – really,' I say, putting the watch back carefully in the box. 'I won't wear it tonight – I'm too worried I'd damage it.' Ann gives me a wink and I realize she was the one to pick it. I look around the room and see that Nick is waving me over.

'I'll introduce you guys to Shane,' I say suddenly, not wanting my family to be left alone in the corner. Dad looks hesitant, but I encourage him. 'He's just over here . . . I'm sure he'll be thrilled to see you again,' I say to Mum, and she smiles gratefully at me.

I make my way over to Nick afterwards. He has a drink in his hand for me.

'What is that?' I exclaim, looking at the dark-red concoction.

'I don't know, but Elizabeth and Orla are handing them out to everyone,' he says cheerily. He's already slurring his words.

'It's rocket fuel!' I hear a female voice say behind me. I turn around to see Liz and Orla behind the bar. Orla is pouring Jägermeister into a large bowl while Liz mixes with a spoon.

'And what's in this rocket fuel?' I ask, my heart racing at the sight of her.

'It's a secret but, if you drink it, you are guaranteed to have a good night.' Liz gestures to the glass in my hand, and I laugh before taking a swig. It tastes like cough syrup, but I like it and drink a second mouthful.

'So, are you having a good night?' Orla asks.

'I really am,' I say, unable to take my eyes off Liz. Her blonde hair is loose and curly, and she's wearing a black mini-skirt that makes her look even taller than usual.

'So why are you guys bartending?' I ask, surprised that Benny, the owner of McGowan's, is letting anyone but himself serve drinks.

'Benny seemed a bit overloaded earlier, so we offered him our help for the night,' Liz says.

'The whole night?' I ask, a little disappointed that I won't be able to get her alone for a moment.

'Don't worry – we'll join you guys later, when things die down a bit,' Orla says, but I don't move. Now that Liz is here, I have no interest in talking to anybody else.

'Go!' Liz announces, as if she knows what I'm thinking. 'It's your party, you have to socialize. I'll find you later, I promise.'

'So you're not going anywhere?'

Liz blushes.

'No, I'm not going anywhere.'

The night seems to fly by. Every time I start chatting to someone, someone else grabs me to say 'Happy birthday'. Most people have insisted that they buy me a drink, but I can't keep up with it and I'm also determined to remember this night, so I hand most of them to Nick, and he is more than delighted to help me out. The owner of McGowan's is delighted too: the pub is much busier than on an average Thursday. Nick tells me that Benny let him rent the place for free as long as Nick could guarantee more than fifteen people. He's practically dancing with glee as he struggles to keep up with the endless drink orders.

Any chance I get, I look over at Liz. She and Orla are laughing away, filling people's glasses with their dangerous cocktail. I get a boost every time I catch her looking back at me.

Some of the younger grooms are getting a bit rowdy and I can see Shane keeping a bit of an eye on them. I'm about to dive off to the bathroom when Adam grabs hold of my arm.

'S'Matt . . .' he slurs, trying to stand up straight.

'Are you OK?' I ask. He's hammered; his eyes can't focus.

'Fine . . . D'you . . . d'you know that girl . . . ?' He gestures towards Ann, who is talking to Linda.

'Yes . . .' I say, wondering where he's going with this.

'She's . . . She's real pretty . . .' He's now leaning on me for support.

'She's also my little sister.' I don't say it in a nasty way. I know Adam doesn't mean any harm. He just has no control over what he's saying.

'Fuck . . . S—sorry . . . no-go area. Sisters are a no-go area . . .' He waves his arms in front of me to make sure I know exactly what he means, but it makes him wobble violently and he grabs hold of me for support again. 'S—sorry . . .'

'It's OK,' I reply, laughing openly now. I catch Shane looking at us and I decide it's time Adam went home. I lift his head so that he's looking at me and speak slowly.

'Adam, you need to get a pint of water and then a taxi. Do

you understand?' He gives me a thumbs-up. 'Water and then taxi,' I repeat.

'Got it,' he says, smiling. As he stumbles off, I hear him mumbling to himself. 'Water . . . taxi . . . water . . . taxi . . .'

It's not long after Adam's departure that the older people start to leave. It's nearly one in the morning and most have work the next day. My family are among the first to go, and I thank them all again for coming. Ann doesn't look like she wants to leave, but my parents are insisting. Shane, Justine, Roger and Linda are next; Shane says a curt goodnight as Justine falters a little next to him, clearly having enjoyed her night. The younger crowd has no intention of leaving, and I'm encouraged to do a round of shots with everyone.

At some point, I go to look for Nick. I find him in the corner having what looks like a very serious conversation with Dom. Dom looks angry and seems to be doing most of the talking; Nick looks exasperated and frustrated. I still have no idea what's going on between the two of them and I don't think Nick is going to tell me any time soon. I decide it's best to leave them to it.

'So what do you think it is between them?' Liz asks, suddenly appearing at my side. Like me, she's staring at Dom and Nick.

'I don't know . . . Nick doesn't like talking about it.'

'Dom's the same, but I know he's mad about Nick . . . I think, for Dom, Nick is the one person he's just never been able to get over,' she says. We sit down together and she takes a small sip out of her glass.

'So you finally got away from bar duties?' Liz stops looking at Dom and Nick and smiles at me.

'I decided that everyone has had enough rocket fuel for one evening.'

'Where's Orla?' Liz jerks her head, and I turn to see Orla and Stevie O'Leary kissing in the corner.

'I didn't see that one coming!'

'I know! He's seventeen! I can't wait to tease her about it tomorrow.'

I stare at her for a moment, not quite able to believe she's here. 'You came.' I sound nervous.

'I did,' Liz replies, equally timid. She gazes at her glass for a moment. 'I like you, Matthew, and I know I would really regret it if I didn't give whatever this is a chance.'

I want to jump and scream with delight when she says these words. I was hoping for this as soon as I saw her here tonight but I wouldn't let myself believe it until I heard her say it.

'I knew you fancied me,' I say cockily, to break the tension.

'God knows why!'

We stare at each other for a moment and I have the strongest urge to kiss her, but before I get the chance she starts talking again.

'I do want to take things slow, though . . . if that's OK with you?' She's nervous again.

'That's fine,' I reply, glad I didn't lunge for her.

I look around for Nick, but there is no sight of him now. I'm about to ask Liz if she saw where he went when Benny taps me on the shoulder.

'Happy birthday, Matt.' He says it kindly, but he looks a bit stressed.

'Thanks, Benny, and thanks for letting us have the party here. It's really generous of you.'

'Ah, it's not a bother . . . not a bother . . .' He's looking around nervously. I follow his gaze and see Sally Murphy Irish dancing on a tiny table that shakes with every extravagant kick she makes. A small circle of people have gathered around her, cheering her on.

'If you don't mind, Matt, I might close the bar, just because people are getting a bit boisterous . . . You can all stay as long as you like, but . . . I'm not keen on serving any more drinks . . . If that's OK with you?'

'Of course,' I reply. I feel a bit embarrassed about Sally's behaviour. 'I can tell her to get down if you want,' I say, standing up, about to make my way over, but he shakes his head.

'Ah no, no need for that, Matt . . . Sure, the girl is only having a bit of fun. I hope you are too?' I sit back down, relieved I don't have to be the responsible one at my own party. Benny makes his way back to the bar and pulls the shutters down. People moan in disappointment.

'I feel a bit guilty,' Liz says, once Benny's out of earshot.

'Why?'

'Well, I gave Sally about eight glasses of that rocket fuel . . .'

'Fuck it! Sally is good entertainment when she's drunk!'

Liz and I keep to ourselves for the next hour or so, mostly talking about Aachen. Every day, my excitement grows, but so do my nerves. I feel like I got this opportunity by chance and I'm desperate to prove to everyone that I really do deserve it. People come up every few minutes to say goodnight, but I barely acknowledge them. It's not until much later that I realize Liz and I are the only ones left.

'Orla must have gone home with Stevie!' Liz exclaims, scandalized. I laugh at her shock and she grins at me.

'Come back to mine,' I say boldly.

'I don't know . . .'

'What if I promise no funny business?' I ask, trying to keep the mood light. Liz smiles at me, but says nothing. I let out a sigh and reach for her hand; I'm relieved when she lets me hold it.

'Look, I get that it's a bit too soon for *that*,' I say, being as obvious as possible. 'I'm just really enjoying spending time with you, and I don't want it to end.'

'OK,' Liz replies quickly. 'Let's go.'

We laugh and giggle as we make our back to the bungalow. It's pitch black out and there's not a soul in sight. Once we're inside, I can't decide if we should stay in the living room or if I should take her to my bedroom. I meant what I said earlier − I don't expect Liz to sleep with me tonight − but I can't stop myself from hoping that it might still happen. Eventually, I decide to take her to my bedroom, afraid that Nick might walk in on us if we stay on the couch. I still have no idea where he is. Liz sits awkwardly on the edge of my bed, and I show her my watch to ease the tension.

'It's beautiful!'

'Thanks. My da said he bought it so I could wear it in Aachen.' I place my hands firmly under my legs, afraid of what they might do in my intoxicated state.

'He's obviously really excited for you.'

'He is − he really is.'

'You sound surprised.'

'Well, I am, a bit . . . For years he just didn't get it, didn't understand, but now . . . he's so happy for me. Ann said he's been staying up at night, studying the world rankings and watching old Nations Cup competitions . . .'

'He's proud of you,' she says, gripping my hand.

'Yeah . . . I guess he is.'

'Are they going to Aachen?'

'No . . . It would be a really expensive journey for them and my dad can't take that many days off . . . But they'll be watching on TV − he's making a day of it. What about your family?'

'No, they won't be there.' For the first time all evening, Liz looks uncomfortable. 'My father is busy with work, and my mother . . . Well, I don't really talk to my mother any more . . .' Her voice goes quiet at the last bit.

'What happened?' I ask, hoping I'm not being too nosy.

'She . . . she just doesn't like the way I live my life . . . She never really wanted me to be a showjumper . . .'

'But you're so talented, she must see that . . . especially now.'

'It's not whether I'm talented enough that concerns her . . . She just doesn't like the showjumping world. She's quite private and conservative and, when she hears about the stuff that goes on, it shocks her.'

'Yeah, some of the riders are a bit dodgy, but she must know you're not like that?'

'You don't know me that well, Matthew. I don't always make the best decisions.' I don't quite know what she means – and I don't want to know. She doesn't look at me for a moment; she looks lost in thought, but I have no idea what about. Then she stands up and reaches for her handbag.

'I forgot to give you your birthday present,' she says, bright and perky again. She hands me a tiny bag and I open it to discover a pair of red checked socks, with 'Lucky Socks' stitched into the bottom of them. 'Nick said you didn't really have any lucky charms or anything so I thought you might like these . . . You can wear them in Aachen.'

'I love them!' Without knowing how it happens, I kiss her.

We talk for a little while after that, but it's not long before both of us drift off to sleep. When I wake up I see Liz's form lying on the bed next to me, fully clothed and fast asleep. I watch her for a moment; her blonde hair covers half her face and her chest rises and lowers slowly. The early morning sun is sinking in through my curtains and I'm filled with an overwhelming feeling of happiness. I want to stay where I am, enjoying this moment of peace – but my full bladder protests and I force myself to get up.

I feel groggy as I make my way to the bathroom, and I nearly miss the toilet as I go to pee.

'Shit,' I mumble to myself. I wash my hands and am tiptoe-ing my way back to my bedroom when I see Dom in the hallway. He freezes, standing there in nothing but his boxers, when he sees me.

'Hi,' I mumble awkwardly.

'Hi,' Dom mumbles back, equally embarrassed.

'Who you talking to, Dom?' Nick stops as soon as he sees me, but he doesn't look at all embarrassed.

'I'm just going to use the bathroom.' Dom dashes past me and closes the door. Nick stands there, looking as if this is all com-pletely normal; in fact, he's smiling.

'I thought you two were fighting earlier?' I ask, suddenly more awake.

'What can I say?' he says. 'I like angry sex.'

20

Aachen

I FEEL SICK, UNSTABLE. MY BODY SEEMS TO BE INVOLUNTARILY swaying from side to side and I can't seem to find my balance. I'm confused, disoriented. I think I'm asleep – no, I *am* asleep – but I would like to wake up now. I'm aware of someone talking to me, but I can't seem to open my eyes.

'Elizabeth, are you awake?' Yes . . . no . . . I think so. I feel groggy and unwell. I think I may need to be sick. I really don't want to get sick.

'Elizabeth, we're here. We're in Germany.' I open my eyes to see Nick leaning over me. He squeezes my arm gently and I know I'm finally fully awake. It's been an awful ferry ride, hour upon hour of nausea and throwing up. I knew I didn't have a great stomach, but this journey is by far the worst thing I have ever experienced.

'How you feeling?' Nick asks kindly.

'Awful,' I groan, sitting up. We are all down below in the lorries with the horses, but I can't help thinking that being down here has made the journey much worse.

'Are you OK to drive? They're going to unload us soon.'

'I'm fine,' I say, giving myself a shake. I appreciate his concern, but I hate the idea of anyone thinking I'm weak or incapable. 'Where's Matthew?'

'He's with the horses. Cedric panicked a few hours ago and tried to lie down in the lorry. Matt managed to calm him down, but he didn't want to leave him alone for the rest of the journey.' I feel guilty: if anything had happened to Wildfire, I'd have been in no state to look after her.

'I should check on Wildfire.' I stand up quickly, making myself feel even dizzier.

'Don't worry – she's fine. I've been keeping an eye on her.'

'Thanks,' I say, touched.

'It's not a bother. Sure, we're all on the same team, we've got to look out for each other.' He winks cheekily before disappearing. After he's gone I check out my appearance in the mirror. My face looks a bit green and my eyes are slightly glazed. No wonder Nick looked concerned, I think to myself. I look in on Wildfire. She's as relaxed as ever. By the time I make my way into the driver's seat, people are beginning to disembark.

Dom told me what happened between him and Nick, and how, even though it had been a great night, it seems to have changed nothing between them. In a way, I wish I could hate Nick for the way he's treating Dom, but I just can't bring myself to. Now that I'm spending so much time with Matthew, I see Nick a lot, and I've started to understand why Dom just can't get over him. Nick's loud, in your face and sometimes a bit of an asshole, but every now and again he'll do something really kind and considerate and you can't help but like him. I wish he'd fall for Dom, but part of me thinks that will never happen, though I'm not quite sure why.

The drive to Aachen gives my stomach time to settle and by the time I arrive, park and put Wildfire away in her stable, I'm feeling quite bright. We've been travelling all day and I'm looking forward to a shower and bed. As soon as I pull up, though, I see Taidgh, Edward, Matthew and Ben standing together.

Taidgh waves me over, and I go, although seeing Edward and Matthew next to each other makes me want to run away and hide. What am I doing? What if they find out about each other? What will happen then? It's been so easy to spend time with Matthew and not feel guilty about it, as I haven't really been talking to Edward. But seeing the two of them together now, I realize the situation I've put myself in.

'Are you feeling OK, Elizabeth? You look a bit pale,' Taidgh enquires kindly.

'Fine,' I mumble. 'I just found the journey a bit tough.' I do my best to look at Taidgh and no one else.

'You'll feel better after a good night's sleep,' he says warmly. I nod, wanting to get away as quickly as possible.

'So,' he goes on, 'the Nations Cup team event is the day after tomorrow and the individual event is on Friday. I suggest that you give your horses only a light exercise tomorrow, as they'll be tired after their journey. I expect you all to be in bed by ten the next three nights – I will personally check on each one of you. I also expect you to go to bed *alone* . . .'

'For God's sake, Taidgh, I'm not a child,' Ben says angrily.

'No, you're certainly not. But I'm in charge this week and I'm not letting you ruin Ireland's chances of a win by acting like a horny teenager.' Ben looks as if he wants to retaliate, but he holds his tongue. I brave a glance at both Matthew and Edward. Matthew looks rather tired and gaunt but seems to be listening intently. Edward looks as relaxed and calm as ever, almost a little bored.

'Tomorrow we'll all have dinner together to relax and talk tactics for the next day,' continues Taidgh. 'Tomorrow day, you're free to do as you like, but I strongly suggest that none of you does anything that strenuous . . . The last thing we need is for someone to injure themselves.' Taidgh looks at all of us individually, and we all nod our agreement.

'Good,' he says smartly. 'Sleep well – and, as I say, I'll be checking up on you later.' Ben turns on his heels and strides off in a huff. Edward grabs Taidgh's attention and starts walking him off towards the stables.

'Taidgh, I've been looking at this horse and I would really love your opinion,' I hear him say. Matthew and I are alone.

'Well, that ruins my plans for tonight,' he says cheerfully.

'What plans?'

'I was thinking of sneaking into your lorry later,' he says suggestively.

'Were you now?' I say, unable to resist flirting back.

'Oh, yes . . . Well, as long as your devious guard dog Marshall didn't try to attack me.' Matthew takes a step towards me.

'Actually, I left Marshall at home with Orla . . . I thought the journey would be too much for him,' I say, glad that no one is around to hear our conversation.

'Damn it . . . so my plan would have worked – if it weren't for Taidgh,' he says, shaking his head melodramatically.

'I guess it would have,' I agree. I can never resist it when Matthew flirts with me like this. We've never done anything more than kiss, but when we banter like this I start not to trust myself.

'What are you doing tomorrow?' he asks.

'Nothing.'

'I saw them setting up a small fair for the spectators. Do you want to go?'

'I'd love to!' I have a quick look around before kissing him on the cheek. 'Goodnight, Matthew,' I say, starting to walk away.

'Goodnight, Liz!' he calls after me, looking ecstatic.

★

In bed, I toss and turn for a few hours with nerves and anxiety but, when I sleep, I sleep heavily. I wake up rested and feeling like a new person. I do as Taidgh told us to and give Wildfire only a light ride. She's as agile as ever but I can feel her tiredness after the journey. She nips at my pockets affectionately when I feed her some Polo mints.

'How is she?'

I lift my head up, unable to hide my surprise. Edward is standing outside the stable in a white polo shirt and a pair of designer sunglasses. He looks immaculate, sexy. I suddenly feel shy.

'She's good, a little tired. But I reckon she'll be raring to go by tomorrow.'

'I've no doubt,' he replies, smiling and showing me his full set of perfect white teeth. 'How have you been?' he asks, his tone different now.

'OK . . .' I mutter, not really knowing how I've been. Yes, I've missed him, but at the same time it's not as if I've been miserable the past few weeks – in fact, I've had a lot of fun.

'I haven't given up on us, Elizabeth. Have you?' he asks, his smile gone. He seems vulnerable.

'No,' I answer, but I can't bring myself to say any more than that. I'm afraid if I start talking about this with him I'll tell him about Matthew, and then I have no idea what will happen.

He takes a deep breath before continuing. 'Look, I want to talk to you about all this, but now isn't the right time. We all need to be focused for tomorrow.' I nod, avoiding his interrogative gaze. He doesn't say anything, just watches me as I finish up with Wildfire. I feel as if he's examining me, that every lie I've told and mistake I've made is written somewhere on my body and he's reading them all, one by one, until I'm nothing but a collection of bad choices. He leaves without saying anything more and, when I'm sure he's gone, I let out a massive sigh. I feel I can breathe again.

★

The fair is packed with people. Young kids run past my knees every few minutes and I'm afraid I'm going to knock one of them over. Matthew is acting like a kid himself, dragging me on to every ride, forcing me to take part in every carnival game. He buys me endless sweets and chocolates, and by the end of the day I feel a bit hyper.

'Thank you for suggesting this today,' I say as we head towards the exit. 'I didn't think anything could distract me from the competition tomorrow, but you managed it.'

'Not a bother,' he says casually.

I feel a gentle tug on my arm and turn around to see a little girl of about ten standing nervously in front of us.

'I'm sorry to disturb you . . .' She's speaking so quietly I almost can't hear her. 'But are you Elizabeth O'Brien who rides Wildfire?'

'Yes, I am.' The girl turns and shouts to an older man and a girl a little older than her who are standing a few feet away.

'Dad! Jen! It's her – I told you!' Both promptly make their way over to us, the father blushing a little.

'I hope you don't mind,' he begins, embarrassed, 'but Abi and Jen are mad into their horses. We're originally from Ireland, you see, so we follow all the Irish teams.'

'It's fine,' I just about manage, dumbstruck.

'Can I get a picture with you?' Abi asks, suddenly much braver.

'Of course,' I stutter.

'I can take the picture if you like,' Matthew offers. The man stares at him for a moment.

'You're Matthew, the team underdog,' he exclaims, not think- ing what's he's saying.

'The team underdog?' Matthew repeats, unable to hold in his laughter.

The man backtracks immediately. 'I'm so sorry, I didn't mean to offend you . . . It's just that's what the newspapers call you . . .'

'I'm not offended at all. In fact, I'm flattered . . . I quite like the idea of being the underdog,' he says, beaming.

'Will you come in the photo too?' Abi asks, dragging at his sleeve.

'Sure, no bother.' Matthew and I lean down next to the two little girls, who smile brightly as their father takes the picture. This whole moment feels completely surreal. I knew there had been some press about us; there always is when someone is selected for a Nations Cup team. But never in a million years did I think anyone would recognize who I was and want a picture with me.

'Thanks so much,' the man says, shaking my and Matthew's hands. 'You have made their day.'

'It's no hassle,' I reply, feeling a little shy.

'Is it true you're dating Nadal?' Abi asks.

'The tennis player?' Matthew asks, gobsmacked.

'Um . . . no . . . I've never met him. Why do you think that?'

'I read it in a magazine,' says Abi unapologetically.

'I told you it wasn't true,' Jen snaps.

'Come on, girls. I'm sure Elizabeth and Matthew have a lot to do . . . Thanks again.'

As soon as they're out of earshot, Matthew says, 'So, apparently, you're dating Nadal?'

'And, apparently, you're the underdog?' And the two of us burst into giddy laughter.

Matthew and I go our separate ways once we get back to the showgrounds. We laughed and joked the whole way but now I am alone I can feel my stomach beginning to knot with anxiety about the dinner tonight. A whole evening with Matthew and Edward on the same table – it feels as if I'm walking a tightrope, and one I'm going to fall off some time or other. I do my best to look as girly as possible and take a taxi to the restaurant, which is only a couple of minutes away; the others will probably walk but I don't want to in my high heels, which are an unusual accessory for me. I arrive a few minutes early and I'm momentarily relieved when I see Taidgh sitting at the table alone. He stands up when he sees me.

'Elizabeth, delighted to have you here.' He kisses my cheeks formally and squeezes my hand. 'Sit, sit . . . I've come directly from an FEI committee meeting and I'm famished. I was looking at the menu. A lot of meat and cheese – but everything sounds delicious. You're not a vegetarian, are you?'

The restaurant is dark and cosy – some may even call it romantic – and Taidgh has found us a table in the corner away from the other guests.

'No, I'm a carnivore,' I say brightly, glad that he is so friendly.

'Great, just thought I'd check. You never know these days, and I get the impression the Germans don't even know what a vegetarian is.' I pick up my menu and see that he's right. Every dish seems to contain some sort of dead animal. I raise my eyebrows when I see the prices. Taidgh notices.

'Don't worry, dinner's on me. So go wild if you like.' I smile gratefully at him.

'Thanks, I'm famished,' I say, feeling a bit more relaxed. Just then, we spot Ben.

'Ben,' Taidgh says, rather sternly. Ben just makes noises, and his eyes seem slightly unfocused as he pulls out the chair next to me. I can feel the tension between the two of them: something must have happened earlier. Ben orders a few double whiskeys in the short time that we are waiting for everyone else and doesn't say a word to Taidgh or to me, as we chat about horses. Matthew arrives next, looking slightly uncomfortable in slacks and a shirt. I'm suddenly glad that Ben has placed himself next to me, even if he is downing the whiskey if it were water. At least I'm spared having to choose whether to sit next to Edward or Matthew. Matthew sits on the other side of Taidgh, and the two of them begin to discuss the menu. It's a good twenty minutes before Edward arrives. We all hear him before we see him.

'I'm sorry – I'm so terribly sorry, everyone! I know I'm late, but we had a bit of a scare with Minnie . . .' Minnie is the mare that Edward has decided to compete on this week.

'Is everything all right?' Taidgh asks. He doesn't want anything to happen to the strongest member of his team.

'Oh, it's fine,' Edward says, sitting down on the one free chair at the table. 'My groom came running in to me in a blind panic saying that she was colicking. So I, of course, ran out to the stables to check on her. The poor mare was in a muck sweat, but not because she was colicking but because my idiot groom put the wrong bloody rug on her. The horse was just way too hot . . . Anyway, it's all sorted now . . .'

He picks up his menu. I feel sorry for whatever groom made that mistake: I know Edward, and he's far from tolerant with his grooms. I've no doubt that one will work this week and then be gone.

'Well, I'm glad Minnie is OK,' Taidgh says.

We all look at the menu now, and when we've chosen, Taidgh calls a waitress over. She's young, blonde and pretty, and her attention is completely centred on Edward. It's Edward she asks if he would like any wine for the table, even though Taidgh was the one who summoned her.

'I'll have a glass of white – but maybe we should get a bottle for the table?' he suggests.

Taidgh shakes his head, and Matthew and I decline politely. It's unlikely we'll stop at one bottle, and the last thing I want tomorrow is a hangover.

'Just one glass for me then,' Edward says, giving her a warm smile.

She blushes and giggles and I feel a pang of jealousy.

'I'll have another double,' Ben shouts after her rudely. 'Bloody hell, Edward, it's hard to get any female attention with you about,' he adds. Edward ignores him. I can tell Ben is getting on his nerves.

Our food arrives promptly and, as we eat, Taidgh tells us what the plan is for the next day.

'You all have to jump two rounds, so the team will have eight rounds in total, but only six of them are counted. So we disregard the weakest first round and the weakest second. Ben is going to jump first, Elizabeth second, Matthew third and Edward, as our most experienced rider, will take the pressure-filled last spot.' Taidgh goes on, speaking as if he were laying out a battle strategy, but I guess, in a way, he is.

'How many teams are there?' Matthew asks. I look at his plate and see that, like me, he has barely touched his food.

'Eight – Ireland, Belgium, France, Great Britain, Germany, Netherlands, Switzerland and the USA. Now, if you ask me, the Germans are the ones to beat. They're on their home turf, and Christoph has been practically unbeatable these last few weeks. But I wouldn't underestimate the Americans either, they've been consistently getting stronger at each event and I think they're about to peak.' Edward nods along politely, but Ben looks as if he is barely listening. Taidgh stares at him crossly. 'Now, if two teams are left on equal score then I will select one person to jump off in a speed round—'

'Who will you choose to jump off?' Ben interrupts.

'Certainly not you, if you keep pounding those whiskeys,' Taidgh snaps, rather unexpectedly. Ben looks as if he wants to say something, but holds back.

'If a jump-off situation arises, I will choose whoever seems to be performing best on the day . . . Anyway, we have a strong team here and I think we'll do well. So let's just enjoy each other's company this evening.' His voice becomes more upbeat and his smile reappears.

'Oh, so we're actually allowed to have fun?' Ben says sarcastically and now unmistakably drunk.

'Yes, you're allowed to have fun, but acting like a drunken idiot is not allowed.' Taidgh practically spits this at him.

'Well, since you say it's OK . . .' Ben elbows me, making it obvious. 'Let's get out of here, Elizabeth, and have some *fun.*'

'Here, mate, back off, would you?' Matthew says loudly.

'Calm down, kid. Elizabeth is no angel, are you?' Ben squeezes my shoulder, but I push him away, disgusted. Matthew and Edward stand at the same time, but Edward reaches Ben first. He grabs him by the collar of his dinner jacket and lifts him up. Their faces are only an inch apart.

'You apologize now!' Edward is not shouting; it's a controlled anger which I find even more terrifying.

'Edward, it was only a joke—'

'*Now!*'

'I'm . . . I'm sorry, Elizabeth.' But Ben isn't even looking at me; he's still staring directly at Edward.

'It's OK . . .' I mumble, afraid to move from my seat. Edward calmly lets go of Ben and fixes the creases in his dinner jacket.

'Go get a taxi, Ben. It's time for you to leave.' Ben does what Edward says without an instant's hesitation.

Edward picks up his jacket from the back of his chair. 'I'm going to make sure that idiot goes straight to bed and not to another bar,' he says, putting it on.

'Edward!' Taidgh says sharply. 'Don't do anything stupid.' The two men look at each other for a moment, as if each knows what the other is thinking. After a moment Edward looks away and follows Ben out of the restaurant.

After they've left, Taidgh is the one to break the silence.

'I'm really sorry about that, Elizabeth.'

'It's OK.' I just want to go home now.

'No, it's not OK. Ben is an arrogant pig who drinks too much and sleeps with anything that will let him. Truth be told, I have wanted to kick him off teams on numerous occasions, but I can't. Not when he's performing so well.' Taidgh shakes his head. He looks tired. 'The drinking won't affect his riding tomorrow . . . It never does . . .' he finishes, as if to reassure us.

'Edward's not going to beat up Ben or anything, is he?' Matthew asks, out of the blue. I stare at him, surprised he would even think something like that, let alone say it aloud. Taidgh takes a moment to answer.

'No . . . Not when he's jumping tomorrow.'

I leave shortly after this. Matthew offers to come home in the taxi with me, but I refuse. Matthew doesn't push, obviously happy to stay in Taidgh's company and I'm glad of that. I want to be alone and, more importantly, I don't want to think of anything except the competition tomorrow.

Wildfire is practically shaking with excitement when I tack her up the next morning. It's as if she knows this is a big day for me – for us. The showgrounds are electric with excitement; everybody has been up for hours preparing for and setting up the Nations Cup. I don't see anyone from the team until we go into the warm-up. Ben looks stern, Edward relaxed and Matthew so green I'm afraid he may be sick. Nick stands to the side and lets Shane warm up Matthew. Shane is wobbling on his crutches, but he's still able to bark orders at Matthew as they prepare. Taidgh seems to be having another argument with Ben and Edward has one of his grooms warming him up. I suddenly wish Orla were here – not because I need someone to tell me what to do but because I want some company, some support, even just someone to make me laugh.

I trot Wildfire on a loose rein, letting her relax and loosen out. Nobody has put on their green jackets yet. I guess it's because, when we do, it's real: we're riding for Ireland. It's so surreal to be in this warm-up: I'm surrounded by riders I've admired since I was child and they all look as nervous and anxious as I do. It's strange to be on equal footing with the people I've always wanted to be, but now I want more: I want to beat them.

We all walked the course together with Taidgh. It's the biggest thing I have ever seen. Every fence looks impossible and there's not a moment's rest anywhere. I desperately try to remember everything he said, but there was so much detail that it's all muddled together in my mind.

'Well, hello there, darling,' Nick says chirpily. 'How are you?'

'OK . . . Scared . . . But I think I can do this. I just have to trust Wildfire.'

'You're going to be great, Elizabeth. Don't doubt yourself,' he says, being more genuine than I have ever known him.

'Thanks,' I say, really appreciating his kindness. 'Do you wish you were jumping today?'

'I did,' he admits, 'until this morning, when I saw how nervous Matt is. I don't envy him.'

'How's he doing?' I chance a glance in his direction: he has Cedric working in a very relaxed way, but he looks as pale as ever.

'Well, he's only been sick once so far . . . But the funny thing is that the nerves don't affect his riding. He's dying on the inside and he looks like shit, but I know he's going to go on in there and do a beautiful round, even if he doesn't know it himself.' I think back to Matthew's previous performances and I realize Nick is probably right. If I didn't know how lovely Matt is, I'd be jealous of him.

'Would you mind warming me up, Nick?' I ask. He looks up at me, surprised.

'Of course . . . but I thought you'd get one of the officials to help you.'

'I was going to . . . but right now, I really want a friend helping me.'

He hops into the warm-up without hesitating a second.

'I'd be honoured, Elizabeth.'

The course rides just as difficult as it walks and by the time Ben goes in to jump not a single person has gone clear. Taidgh is no longer his happy, kind self; he's focused, and he watches Ben canter into the competition ring with a strong intensity. Taidgh is right about Ben: his excessive drinking last night has in no way affected his riding ability. He jumps each fence with such precision and correctness he does the army proud. He's clear until he reaches the three-metre-long water. He gallops at it from over five strides out and ends up taking off too early, not only clipping the edge of the water but also knocking the tall fence that comes directly after it. Taidgh turns to Edward, Matthew and myself.

'You three! Don't make the same mistake – he kicked on too early for that stride. Wait and *then* kick.' Ben finishes with eight faults, but as the other first riders jump and build up cricket scores, his round is quite strong. The only person to do better is the German rider, who finishes his first round with four faults.

The second riders for each team begin and, for the first time ever before a round, I feel as if I might be sick. By the time my turn comes, there are still no clears. Nick warms me up well and I'm so glad I asked him to do it. He smiles at me encouragingly and joins in with the rest of the team as they cheer me on into the ring. The sound from the crowd is deafening and I feel so small. Wildfire flattens her ears back, put off by the loud noise, but I pat her neck and she relaxes.

She jumps the first half of the course beautifully, and as I clear each fence my confidence grows. I turn for the long water and wait, just like Taidgh told me to, but I don't see the correct stride and, before I know it, I've reached it and my canter is too slow. Wildfire does her best, but she can't quite reach the other side and I clip the end of the water. I finish on four faults. It's one of the strongest rounds so far, but I can't help but feel slightly disappointed. I canter out of the ring to massive cheers. I can't believe how much support I'm getting from the crowd.

'Great round, Elizabeth! Small mistake at the water, but I know you won't do it again next time.'

'Thanks,' I reply, feeling slightly happier. Edward pats me on the back as I pass him.

'Well done, Elizabeth! Really – well done.' I don't want to, but I melt at his praise.

By the time it's Matthew's turn, Germany is in the lead, Ireland second and America third, just as Taidgh predicted. Every other nation seems to be having disasters and the crowd is getting excited at the thought of a home win. Shane is giving Matthew instructions until the very last moment. Matthew himself is silent and looks as if he may be sick on the horse's back.

He's startled by the cheer that greets him as he enters the ring, but Cedric, who's used to competitions like this, doesn't flicker an ear. Matthew canters into the first fence and Cedric balloons over it as if it were a puissance wall.

'This is going to be a great round,' I hear Taidgh mutter to himself. He's right: Matthew rides perfectly and Cedric makes the course look easy. He doesn't make the same mistake Ben or I made at the water but clears it with ease and leaves the ring with the first clear round of the day.

The crowd explodes, and I scream out, '*Yes!*' as Matthew can-ters across the finish line. He enjoys the moment and does a lap of the competition ring as the crowd continues to scream with delight. The Irish underdog has shown everyone else how to do it. When he leaves the ring and comes back out to us, I forget everything. I forget all the drama that's going on and I forget everyone around us. I run towards him and grab him in a bear hug the second he's off the horse. He grabs me back and, for a moment, it feels as if it's just the two of us.

'You are amazing!' I whisper into his ear.

'So are you!' he whispers back. I let go of him then, remem-bering where we are and who is around but, luckily, in the excitement, no one's thought anything of our embrace. Taidgh is nearly in tears he's so happy.

'I knew I was right to pick you! I knew it!'

After Matthew's round, other riders go clear. It's almost as if Matthew proved it was possible and, after that, others could pull it off too. Just before Edward goes in, he becomes agitated and snappy with his groom. I know it's his nerves, but when he shouts and gives out like that, it makes everyone else uncomfortable.

Edward, as always, is met with great cheers. He's popular and loved in this sport, and I know that popularity is important to him. He rides incredibly well and I'm almost convinced he's going to be another clear, but as he takes off for the final element Minnie clips the pole with her back leg – just enough to knock it to the ground, giving Edward four faults.

'You must have put on her bloody back boots wrong!' he shouts at his groom as he leaves the ring, and I know it's best to stay out of his way.

The second round sees a lot more clears, and I could almost cry with happiness when I'm among them. Wildfire bucks with delight as she leaves the ring. Ben, unfortunately, has four faults, and he leaves in a huff, not interested in how the rest of his team does. Matthew repeats the perfect clear he did earlier and, for the first time in a while, I see Shane smile. Edward continues to bark at everyone, but he relaxes a little when he too manages to go clear in the second round. After every nation has jumped, we are lying joint first with Germany and America. There'll have to be a jump-off.

'OK, everybody, come here!' Taidgh announces. Ben has reappeared, but he stands there with his arms crossed and his face in a frown. I'm almost sure he would rather be anywhere else than here right now. 'So, we have a jump-off situation. Now, I've already heard that the Americans are going to use Jessica Ryan. Jessica is a demon against the clock, but she's jumping first and I think she's going to overdo it and possibly cost herself a pole. The Germans have picked Christoph, which is no surprise. Now, Christoph won't be as fast as Jessica, but you can guarantee he'll go clear. So what we need more than anything right now is another clear . . . That's why I want Matthew to jump off.'

I know I shouldn't but I gasp. I know Matthew has done a double clear today, but he and Cedric would be a lot slower than Minnie or Wildfire.

'You want me to jump off?' Matthew asks, just as shocked as I am.

'You're the only one, other than Christoph himself, who hasn't touched a pole today. Do that once more and I think we could win this thing.' Taidgh is talking just to Matthew now, but Edward clears his throat, getting everyone's attention.

'Now, Taidgh, I'm not trying to question your judgement. I wholeheartedly agree with you that Matthew has jumped wonderfully today, but . . . he has no experience at handling the pressure of a jump-off . . . and I don't think it's fair to put it all on him, when so much is at stake.' He says all this calmly, but I can hear the hint of aggression in his voice. He's angry about this decision, but he can't show it. Taidgh doesn't even look at him; instead he stares at Matthew.

'Matt, if you say you can't do this, then I won't judge you . . . but I really believe you can, and I think you do too.' Matthew doesn't say anything for what feels like ages. I'm filled with conflicting emotions. I want to be happy for him, but I can't stop myself feeling that it's a bit unfair. *I* can jump off. I can *win* this. I know I can.

'I can do it,' Matthew eventually mutters. Taidgh claps him hard on the back.

'Brilliant! Now go get Cedric and tell Shane to warm you up.'

Matthew and Taidgh head back towards the warm-up ring together, leaving Edward and me alone.

'It's not fair,' Edward announces, once they're gone. 'It's not fair on you and me, and it's not fair on Matthew either. He's just a kid. He's done so well up until now, but Taidgh is expecting too much from him.' I don't say anything, not completely sure how I feel about the whole situation. 'I need to talk to you, Elizabeth,' he goes on. 'I've been holding back so much because of this competition, but now that it's over, I can't hold it in any more.' He stares at me and, once again, I feel incredibly vulnerable.

'We should watch the jump-off,' I say, wanting to avoid this conversation just a little longer.

'We can watch from the riders' box, but we're going to talk. It's been too long, and I need to hear the truth about some things.' He leads me there, and I know I can't escape.

The riders' box is rather full now that the jump-off is the only thing that remains, but Edward finds us a place in the corner where no one can hear us.

'You were great today,' he starts. I'm surprised.

'Thank you. So were you.'

'I shouldn't have had that last fence down in the first round. Stupid mistake. It won't happen again,' he says smartly. Below, Jessica Ryan comes into the arena at a roaring pace and does exactly what Taidgh said she would. She screams around with an amazing time, but she kicks out the final fence.

'Do you still love me, Elizabeth?'

'Of course,' I answer instinctively.

'Do you love Matthew?' I go silent at Edward's question, partly because I don't know the answer and partly because I'm so shocked that Edward knows. 'There are rumours going around that you two are dating.'

'We went on one date,' I admit, unable to look at him.

'Are you sleeping with him?'

'No! I wouldn't do that to you!' Edward's expression is unreadable. Matthew comes in to the competition ring and does another beautiful clear but, as Edward predicted, it's not that fast. Our only hope is that Christoph knocks a pole.

'I don't understand you, Elizabeth. Do you want to be with me?' Edward asks coldly.

'I . . . do . . . but . . . I'm so confused,' I choke out, near tears.

'I've helped you achieve your dreams, Elizabeth, and I want to keep doing that – but not if you're just going to run off with some kid.' I don't recognize this harsh Edward, and I'm worried about what he's implying.

'What do you mean?' I ask, afraid of the answer.

'You know exactly what I mean.' He's no longer looking at me. An image of Wildfire passes through my mind and I get a sharp pain in my stomach. 'I love you, Elizabeth,' he starts, his voice softer again. 'And I will give you everything you want – a marriage and a career. But I need you to promise that you will stand by my side from now on and that you will never leave it.

I want everyone to know that you are mine.' A million things rush through my mind, and my body is so full of anxiety I feel I might faint. Christoph canters into the ring and jumps. He does amazingly, cutting every corner, clearing every pole. His time is incredibly fast and he has zero faults.

'Second,' I mutter to myself. I know Edward is staring at me, but I don't know what answer to give him. *I* don't know what I want, *who* I want.

'Take a few days, Elizabeth. If you come back to me, I want you to be sure.'

He stands up, clearly to make his way into the ring for the prize-giving. 'For what it's worth, you would have won this competition. I know that. Second isn't good enough for you. It'll never be good enough for you.' He leaves without another word.

I sit there for a moment, feeling numb. I can't process it. It feels like too much. Eventually, I pull myself out of my seat, knowing the others will be waiting for me. As I make my way over to them, I murmur to myself, 'I *would* have won it.'

21

The Fall

MY EARS ARE RINGING WITH THE SOUND OF CHEERS AND clapping. I canter out of the competition ring, surrounded by people, and even though they're all talking directly to me, I have no idea what they're saying. Some of the faces around me are familiar, others aren't, and I can't really distinguish any of them. I slide off Cedric and someone grabs him from me. I spot Taidgh and suddenly everything comes into focus. I can understand the praise from people around me and I know exactly what's going on. We've come second. Ireland has come second. Not looking at anyone else, I head straight for Taidgh.

'I'm sorry I didn't win,' I say.

Taidgh's smile disappears momentarily. 'Matt, you did brilliantly. You have nothing to be sorry about.'

'I went too slowly. I should've gone faster, taken more of a risk.' Taidgh pulls me aside, and the others let me go with him.

'You did three perfect clears today! Do you know how amazing that is?' Taidgh whispers, so no one else can hear. 'Yes, Christoph came in and went faster, but it was only luck that he didn't knock a pole and, if he had knocked one, everybody would be saying how talented you are to have got your clear. You were smart and clever today, and you are the reason we have come in second. You were the best choice for this jump-off and I stand by that decision.' I nod along, starting to feel happy, rather than disappointed.

'I can't believe I just jumped off for Ireland!'

Taidgh's smile comes back. 'Get back up on that horse and enjoy that prize-giving. You deserve it!'

I run back towards Cedric to find Nick already there, feeding the horse endless Polos.

'Don't spoil him!' Shane barks, but he's unable to hide his smile when he sees me. 'That was a great round, Matt. I dare say I wouldn't've been able to do better myself.'

'Thanks,' I mumble. Nick grabs me in an unexpected hug.

'That was fantastic,' he says.

'But I didn't win.'

'Matt, no one expected you to even get around! And instead you did three perfect clears in one of the toughest competitions in the world. Stop criticizing yourself and bloody enjoy it!' He throws me up on to Cedric, and I have to laugh. Sometimes I love his bluntness. The others are already on their horses by the time I get myself fully sorted and am ready to go in. Ben is as grumpy as ever. He doesn't even look at me when I join them in line. Edward is smiling kindly, though.

'Well done, Matt. Great round,' he says.

'It was brilliant!' Liz joins in, smiling, but her voice sounds strained. I'm about to ask if she's OK when the music starts and we all march in to the German national anthem. The German team is in front and is met by roaring cheers; the crowd is delighted with their home win. We walk in second and the cheers for us are, surprisingly, nearly as loud as they were for the Germans. Cedric begins to act up a bit with all the noise. He dances on the spot and makes the marching-band members a little nervous, but I don't care. I rub him on the neck, taking Nick's advice and enjoying every moment.

After the prize-giving, Taidgh takes us to the bar and buys champagne to celebrate. Ben and Edward don't stay long, both claiming they need to get horses ready for the individual competition tomorrow.

'Will you jump Cedric in the individuals tomorrow?' Taidgh asks me.

'He certainly will not.' Shane's answer comes out a little more harshly than he means it to. 'I just mean,' he says, controlling his tone of voice, 'that Matt and Cedric both did very well today. I think they deserve a day off. No point in competing a tired horse, especially at this level.' I nod, not daring to argue with him.

'Good idea – save him for the next Nations Cup,' Taidgh says, smiling, and my heart jumps at the idea that I might be selected to compete in Dublin.

'What about you, Elizabeth?' Taidgh asks, turning his attention away from me.

'I'll give tomorrow a go. See if I can get Ireland another placing,' she says, rather cockily I think. She downs the last of her champagne. 'I'd better go. Get some rest before tomorrow.' She leaves without another word, but I can't stop myself from running after her. I catch up with her just outside the bar and she turns around when I grab her elbow.

'Hey, what's going on?'

'What do you mean?'

'You're acting weird. You mad at me or something?'

'No, not at all,' she answers, but the words come out in a tumble. 'It's just been a mad day, so exciting and nerve-racking. I think I need to lie down for a while.' Liz barely looks at me, and I get a bad feeling in my gut.

'OK . . . well, I can come over and check on you later, if you want?'

'Ah, don't bother. I'll probably just be asleep. Anyway, you should enjoy yourself tonight. You really did great.' Liz kisses me on the cheek, and lingers there for a moment before turning around and trotting away. As I walk back towards the others, I ignore the feeling in my gut. I'm just being paranoid.

Taidgh doesn't stay long. His phone doesn't stop buzzing, and he eventually gives in and picks it up.

'Business as usual,' he mutters, and wanders off. Nick and Shane both stay, and we get slightly tipsy. Shane's relaxed, but I watch myself, knowing how dangerous it is to get drunk with the boss. Nick has no such inhibitions and continues to guzzle back the fizz, with Shane not too far behind him.

'I have to say, Matt' – Shane is slurring slightly – 'after my accident, I thought this season was going to be an absolute write-off, but between you and Nick, you guys are making it probably my most exciting season yet . . . I've always seen myself as a competitor, but now . . . I don't know . . . Maybe my future is in coaching.' He's swaying on his stool.

'Wouldn't you miss the competing?' Nick asks.

'Oh, I would still compete,' Shane says quickly. 'I meant I could do coaching on the side.' Of course: Shane would never give up his horses. It's a bittersweet thought that, once he's recovered, Nick and I could be back to square one. That's why we have to take risks and make an impact when we have the chance, in the hope that an important owner will like the look of us. It's our only hope of moving forward.

'You excited for tomorrow?' I ask Nick, wanting to take my mind off things.

'Excited . . . terrified . . . All of the above, I guess.' He goes to take another mouthful out of his glass but Shane snatches it from him.

'You're done for the evening,' he says, once more the

professional and curt Shane we all know. Nick isn't annoyed; in fact, he laughs.

'You're right,' he says. 'I'll need all my wits about me if I'm going to do well tomorrow.'

'You have a strong chance of getting placed,' Shane says matter-of-factly.

Nick snorts. 'I could never beat Elizabeth in a jump-off,' but Shane's already shaking his head.

'Wildfire will be tired after today, and tomorrow is going to be tough . . . Elizabeth is naïve, and it's a bad decision for her to jump tomorrow. She's doing it for pride, not the wellbeing of her horse. I'm surprised Edward didn't advise her against it, but he also can be pig-headed about these things.' I take another sip of my champagne, afraid that if I say anything I'll let the cat out of the bag.

'Careful what you say in front of Matt,' Nick says cheekily. I could kill him.

'Ah, don't tell me you still have a thing for her, Matt? I thought you were over that?' My mouth opens and closes, but I have nothing to say.

'It's more than a thing – they're dating,' Nick says, enjoying my discomfort. Shane looks at me.

'Really?'

'Um . . . Yeah . . .' I answer, feeling incredibly embarrassed. Shane's facial expression changes. I don't know what he's think-ing. 'We're keeping it quiet, though,' I finish, glaring at Nick, who has a look of pure innocence on his face. Shane chews the corner of his mouth, like he's unsure whether to say something.

'I was very like Elizabeth when I was her age,' he starts, com-pletely surprising me. 'She has a lot of the same traits I had: she's ambitious, talented and extremely competitive . . .' Nick and I stare at Shane, neither of us having any idea where he's going with this '. . . but ruthless and selfish as well. I did a lot of things in my early career that I wish I hadn't, but at the time I felt like I had to, because, to me, succeeding was the most important thing. I know better now, but it took years of hurting people and losing people that I cared about to realize how far wrong I had gone. I see that in Elizabeth, that desperation to succeed. It's a dangerous thing.' Shane looks down at his feet, embarrassed at how much he's revealing. 'All I'm saying is keep your eyes wide open when it comes to Elizabeth. I think if you look a bit closer, you'll see a lot more than you expect to see.'

My mind is galloping. I understand what Shane is saying, but it can't be true, I don't want it to be true. Then again, I can't ignore the feeling now growing in my gut.

Shane stands up, leaning unsteadily on his crutches.

'I should go,' he announces. 'Justine has booked us a table for dinner and, if I want to have a fiancée tomorrow, then I'd best not be late. Nick, I suggest you get some food in you then head straight to bed. Tomorrow is important.' Nick nods, not daring to argue with him. Neither of us says anything until he's gone.

'Well, that was a bit intense.' I'm trying to make a joke of it.

'Yeah, it was . . . I can't imagine Shane being anything but fair and playing by the rules . . . but I guess we all push the boundaries of what's right when we want to succeed,' Nick replies.

'I don't know,' I disagree. 'I think you can reach the top without hurting people along the way.' Nick smiles patronizingly at me.

'That's a nice thought, but a bit naïve. It's not realistic – not in this world, anyway.'

I smile weakly back at him, but I don't want to admit he's right. I change the subject. 'Food?'

'There're some frozen pizzas in the lorry. Let's have them and hit the hay,' Nick offers.

'Who says I'm going to bed?' I say. 'I'm not competing tomorrow.'

'Yes, but tomorrow the roles are reversed and you are my groom, aka my slave, and I need my slave to be well rested.' I laugh at Nick's pretend evil voice.

'Fair point,' I say, standing up. 'Let's go.'

I part company with Nick when we leave the bar, telling him I want to check on Cedric. I pass Liz's lorry on the way down to the stables, but I don't go in, partly because she told me not to, and partly because I need a few moments alone to think. I try to understand what Shane was talking about earlier, but I can't see in what way Liz could be using me. There's nothing I can do to help her succeed and, if there was, I'd happily help her. Part of my brain tells me to ignore what he said, that Shane doesn't know Liz like I do. But then I think about all the times she's been vague and guarded and all the times I feel she isn't telling me something. Maybe Nick is right – maybe I *am* being naïve?

Cedric whinnies affectionately at me when I reach his stable.

'Well, hello there, friend,' I say, happy to see him. He roots in my pockets for treats. 'No Polos on me, sorry,' I say.

He loses interest in me then and goes back to the corner of his stable so he can sleep in peace. I put my hand under his rug to see if he's warm enough and check his water and feed.

As I'm walking back to the lorry, I pass a horse weaving erratically in its stable. I stop to have a closer look. It's Minnie, Edward's horse. She's damp with sweat and she's shaking her head back and forth – she's stressed and upset. I open the door to her stable, and she eyes me suspiciously.

'It's all right,' I mumble, taking a step towards her. Minnie doesn't move, but I can tell she's nervous of me. She has only a thin rug on but she seems far too warm. I look into the corner and see that her water and feed are completely untouched.

'Strange . . .' The horse seems really stressed, but I can't figure out why. I stay with her a little while, rubbing her face and neck softly. She calms down in the end, but I still think something's wrong with her. Not knowing what else to do, I make my way to Edward's lorry.

I knock on the door nervously, wondering will anyone even be in there. Edward himself always stays at hotels and his grooms are known to stay out late and party. There's no answer the first time, but I knock again and nearly jump with fright when I hear Edward's voice from the window.

'Who is it?' he asks, sounding mildly irritated.

'It's Matt.'

'Ah, Matt, my man, come in, come in!' I pull the handle on the cab door and it swings open. Edward turns on the lights and I see him standing in front of me in boxers and a T-shirt.

'Oh, I hope I didn't wake you?' I say, embarrassed.

'Not at all.' He walks into the living area and I follow him. There's a blonde girl lying in the bed, the blankets wrapped around her.

'Oh my God, I'm sorry! I didn't realize you had company.' I look away from Edward and the girl, and I begin to wish I was anywhere but here.

'Ah, don't worry, Lindsey doesn't mind, do you, hun?' I don't dare look in the blonde's direction, but I hear her snort, letting me know that she does mind quite a bit. 'So what can I do for you, Matt?' I do my best to look just at Edward but it's hard to ignore the fact that Lindsey is in the room, and it's safe to say she isn't wearing anything underneath those sheets.

'I was just checking on Cedric and I noticed Minnie looked distressed—'

'Oh, don't worry – I know, and I've already had the vet check on her. The poor thing is a bundle of nerves after all the travelling, so the vet gave her something to relax. I've pulled her out of the individual competition for tomorrow. She'll be perfect once I get her back in Ireland. But thanks for letting me know . . . It's nice to know you have my back.'

'No problem,' I reply, even more embarrassed now it seems I've come for nothing. 'Well, sorry for disturbing you guys,' I say, and turn to leave.

'Wait!' says Lindsey. 'Your name's Matt, right?' I force myself to turn around, doing my best not to go red as I look at her.

'Um . . . yeah . . .'

'Can I ask your opinion on something?' she asks rather sharply.

'Sure,' I say, keeping my eyes focused on her face. She pulls down the blankets and reveals her enormous breasts.

'Do you think my boobs look fake?' I shoot my eyes up to the ceiling, but the image of her breasts is clear in my mind. I hear Edward chuckle away to himself behind me.

'Um . . . they seem fine,' I announce, now looking anywhere but at her.

'So you think they look real?'

'Yeah . . . I guess . . .' I answer, wondering whether it's best to run for the door at this point.

'Told you,' Lindsey spits out at Edward. This makes him laugh again.

'Darling, I love your breasts. I just find it hard to believe they're natural.' He makes his way towards her and I decide it's time for me to go.

Edward shouts after me. 'Thanks for telling me about Minnie. I appreciate it.'

'No problem,' I say, diving out of the truck. I can hear them laughing as I close the door behind me.

I walk back to Shane's lorry in a bit of a daze. I've heard rumours about Edward cheating on his wife, and it's common enough for riders to sleep around, but I'm surprised how open he is about it. It's like he knows he's untouchable and he's flaunting it in front of my face. I can't get the image of Lindsey's massive breasts out of my head. What was she doing showing them to me? Was she trying to make Edward jealous, or just showing off? Either way, I'd say the two of them are having a good giggle at my expense. I climb into Shane's lorry to find two large pizzas ready to eat. Nick has the TV on and is watching some documentary about whales. He barely acknowledges I'm back. I stare at the TV for a moment before saying, 'You won't believe what just happened to me.'

'I can't believe Edward didn't even react when Lindsey showed you her boobs – like, she was in bed with him!' Nick says for the hundredth time as he walks around the warm-up ring on Gambler the next day. Gambler has his head high and his ears perked, excited about his upcoming round.

'He just laughed,' I say, not able to understand it myself.

'You don't think they were like . . . inviting you to join them or something?' Nick says.

'No! Well, at least, I don't think so . . .' The thought hadn't crossed my mind until then. 'She couldn't have been suggesting that, could she?'

'I don't know. Edward is fairly ancient . . . Maybe she wanted something young in bed to balance it all out.' I shiver at the thought of being in bed with Edward.

'Not a fucking chance.'

'How are you guys this morning?' We both jump at the sound of Shane's voice. He looks at us suspiciously. 'Everything OK?'

'Fine,' I blurt, knowing that Nick is on the verge of laughter.

'Good. Come on, Nick, the course is open to walk. Matt can hold Gambler.'

The competition is massive, with over sixty competitors, and the course is possibly even bigger than it was yesterday. I know Nick's nervous because as every rider comes in and then leaves with a cricket score he gets quieter and quieter, and silence is something that has never suited Nick.

Shane warms him up and I keep out of the way, only stepping in when Shane asks me for something. I've always admired the way Nick rides. I rely on instinct and luck, while he is very polished and rides with flawlessness and such experience. Everything he does is so effective and yet, if you weren't watching closely, you wouldn't think he was doing anything at all. I catch a glimpse of orange out of the corner of my eye and turn around to see Liz warming up Wildfire at the far end of the ring. She's on her own and looks really nervous. I walk over, but she doesn't spot me at first.

'Hi!' She looks up, and I see that her eyes look very tired.

'Oh, hi,' she says. It's barely a whisper.

'How are you?' I ask, worried about her.

'Fine,' she says, a little sharply.

'You don't look fine. What's wrong?'

'Nothing,' she says, turning Wildfire away from me, but I follow her.

'Liz, I know something is up, so you might as well tell me.'

She stops, and so do I. She looks at me for a moment before she says anything. 'I . . . I . . . I'm about to jump a round . . . So I don't really have time for your neediness at the moment.' Her words are harsh and I almost can't believe they came out of her mouth.

'Fine,' I say, shaking my head. 'Fine.' I walk away before I lose my temper, though I'm already shaking with anger.

I force myself to brighten up when I reach Shane and Nick, knowing that Nick needs my support today. When he's called in for his round, he doesn't say a word. I wish him luck as he canters past but part of me knows he can't hear me. Shane and I find ourselves a perfect viewing spot.

'He's riding great today. He just needs to trust himself.' Shane sounds like he's talking more to himself than to me. Nick does ride great and leaves the ring with a mere four faults.

'That puts him into the lead,' I say. The person in second place has twelve faults.

'That could win it for him,' Shane starts excitedly. 'That course is so tough, I don't think there'll be any clears.' Gambler bucks and squeals with delight as he leaves the ring, and Nick hangs on, letting the horse enjoy his moment. As he approaches us, I think I've never seen him look so happy.

'That was fucking class!' I say.

'It was very good all right,' Shane says, trying to be composed, but he can't conceal his smile either.

As the class continues, more and more competitors leave the round with massive faults. Nick and I curse all the riders into knocking, and as the remaining riders get fewer and fewer, I begin to think that Nick really could win this thing. Liz is the last competitor and, even though I'd like to wish her good luck, I don't. I still feel hurt from her comment earlier. Luckily, Nick doesn't notice and he cheers her on as she canters into the ring.

My body tenses as she picks up canter and approaches the first fence. Wildfire is damp with sweat and there's foam forming at her mouth: she looks unsettled and unhappy. Liz jumps the first four fences without a problem. Wildfire looks strong but she's taking the fences on. Liz takes her time, giving the horse the longest and best approaches she can. The rhythm is broken when Liz jumps fence five – it's a tall straight and very tight off the corner. She gets a bad approach and ends up taking off far too early. Wildfire throws in an enormous jump, though, and is able to clear the fence without a pole hitting the ground, but the two are both put off by Liz's mistake and the next fence is the treble.

I hold my breath as she approaches it. Liz sits quiet; it looks like she is going to wait for an extra stride. It's the right thing to do. Wildfire has a big jump but is physically small, and Liz can't ask for another enormous jump after her mistake, it's too risky. Three strides from the fence and it looks like Liz is going to have the perfect shot at it, but then she panics. She drops her reins and kicks on, asking Wildfire to leave out that final stride she had set her up for. Wildfire comes to an abrupt halt; she knows she can't make it over the fence even if she tries and she's lost trust in her rider after Liz's mistake. Liz comes loose and flies over the fence herself, crop and reins still in her hands. Her head hits the ground first, then her neck, then the rest of her body flops to the ground, limp.

Wildfire stands on the other side of the fence, shaking, clearly frightened by what's just happened. I let out a gasp and grab the railings in front of me. I'm about to haul myself over and run to help her when I feel someone pull me back. I turn around to see Nick holding on to my shirt.

'What are you doing?' I ask angrily, trying to get away. 'She could be hurt—'

'The paramedics are already with her, Matt. Too many people standing over her will just make her panic . . .' He doesn't let go of me as he speaks.

I turn back around to see that he's right. Three paramedics are kneeling down next to Liz. She's still lying down but she seems to be conscious. After what feels like ages, the paramedics allow her to stand and she's able to walk out of the arena by herself. She's limping slightly but, other than that, she seems fine. Everyone claps once they realize she's OK. I watch her carefully as she leaves the ring but she is still surrounded by paramedics, who seem to be insisting that she go in an ambulance to the hospital.

'I can' t . . . I can't . . .' she says, on the brink of tears. 'I need to take care of Wildfire. There's no one else—'

'I can do it,' I say, stepping in. Liz and the paramedics look at me.

'Are you sure?' she asks, the tears now freely falling down her face.

'Of course,' I say, no longer angry with her. The paramedics rush her into the back of the ambulance.

I hear her say 'Thank you' as they close the doors.

I walk Wildfire around the warm-up ring for a few minutes, allowing the mare some time to relax after her round. It also means I can watch as Nick accepts his prize for first place. My emotions are all over the place: I'm over the moon for Nick – he's worked so hard for so long, and there's no one who deserves this win more than him; but I'm devastated for Liz – that fall is such a major step backwards, and I know she'll be heartbroken.

Once I get Wildfire happy and settled in her stable, I try to call Liz, but her phone seems to be switched off. I don't think she'll be back in her lorry yet, but I check anyway. No one's there. Eventually, desperation gets the better of me and I ask Shane if he knows anything.

'I think Edward said he was going to put her up in a hotel for tonight. I guess he thought she might be more comfortable in a proper bed after her fall and everything.' Shane's angry. 'That guy is supposed to be her *trainer*, but where is he when she's jumping? Everyone knew from the state of Elizabeth and her horse that that round wasn't going to go well, and it's his job to tell her that.' He's shaking his head as he walks away.

I go to the bar that night with Nick and do my best to celebrate with him, but my heart's not in it. I stay away from the drink, knowing that it would be a bad idea to get drunk tonight. Liz is fine, I know that, but I dislike the fact that she's cut off all communication with everyone. It makes me nervous, and I know if I drink it'll only make my nerves worse, and I'll become irrational, and then I know I'll do something stupid, something idiotic that I know I'll regret.

Nick is, as always, the life and soul, and a small crowd grows around us in the riders' bar. It's like Nick has become instantly famous – and he's making sure to enjoy every moment of it. As he flirts with one of the French riders, I check my phone. Still no word from Liz. I don't understand why she's doing this; all I want is to hear from her own mouth that she's fine. I start to wonder if I should ask Edward what hotel he has put her in, but then I think of what she said earlier: 'needy'. The last thing I want is to be needy. Begrudgingly, I put my phone away and try to enjoy Nick's moment.

It's early enough in the night when I decide to head to bed. Nick's full attention is on the French rider, so he's not the slightest bit bothered when I say I'm going to leave. The night air is warm, and I take out my phone and look again. *Nothing.* Why is she doing this to me? Is it a really obvious message that I'm just not getting? When I get back to the lorry, I turn on the TV, to find some mid-week American movie about two teenagers. The plot is non-existent but it's easy watching, so I leave it on. I soon realize how tired I am. My eyelids are heavy and I find myself drifting off.

I wake with a start when I hear my mobile ringing. Confused and disoriented, I start searching under duvets and dirty clothes for it. The TV is still on in the background: the film ended hours ago and there's a man on the screen talking about the weather. When I finally find my phone the number on the screen is unfamiliar. I answer it, not knowing who it could be.

'Hello, is zis Matthew?' There's a voice with a German accent on the other end of the line, sounding stern and impatient.

'Um . . . yes, it is . . .' I answer, confused.

'Hello, Matthew. My name is Officer Adler and I vork with zee Aachen Police Department. Your sister has been arrested for zeft, beink drunk and disorderly and resistink arrest. No charges vill be pressed but vee need you to come and pick her up.' I rub the sleep out of my eyes, uncomprehending.

'My sister?' I'm beginning to think this guy has called the wrong person. Ann is in Ireland, at home with my parents.

'Yes, sir, your sister Elizabeth.' I understand and start panicking.

'Yes, yes, that's my sister. I'll come and get her now . . . Where are you? Is she OK? What happened?' So many thoughts are going through my head at once. I pull on the first pair of trousers I can find.

'I vill text you the address now, sir. She vas caught shtealing a bottle of gin from a hotel bar. When she vas caught she caused a bvit of a . . . scene. The hotel doesn't vant to press sharges, so vee can release her, but in her intoxicated shtate vee vanted a family member to come and take her. She gave us your number.'

'I'm on my way . . .' I run out of the door, throwing on a jacket.

I don't have a car with me in Aachen so I have to take a taxi to the police station. When I get there the officer looks me up and down. He must know that there's no way Liz could be my sister. We look nothing like each other. I just pray he won't question it. I soon realize he's just happy to see her go. I hear her before I see her. She's screaming at a female officer who's standing outside her cell.

'Fine . . . Keep me fucking here! But you need to sort out someone to feed my horse in the morning. A scoop of oats and half a scoop of beetpulp. Do you fucking hear me? A scoop of oats and half a scoop of beetpulp!' Liz's eyes are unfocused and she's slurring. Her hair is a mess and she's still in her jodhpurs from earlier. It looks like she's been drinking since early afternoon. She jumps with happiness when she sees me.

'Matt! Thank God you're here. Can you tell these retards that I have to leave? I have shit to be doing!' I try to give her a smile, but it's hard. I'm so flabbergasted by the state she's in.

'You're zee brother?' the female officer asks. I nod; she looks even more annoyed than Officer Adler did. 'Pleaze take her now, then . . .'

I asked the taxi to wait. He doesn't seem keen on taking Liz, but I promise him she won't cause any problems. I sit in the back seat with her, and she cuddles up tight to me and whispers drunkenly in my ear. At first it's apologies but then she makes no sense at all. I'm thankful when she falls asleep; it gives me a moment to get my head together. Looking down at her, I feel so disappointed. I see Liz as this beautiful, well-mannered, together girl. I'd never have thought she'd be capable of acting like this. It suddenly hits me that I don't know her at all.

When we get back to the equestrian centre, I lift her out of the taxi, hoping she won't wake up. Unfortunately, her eyes snap open as soon as we're out in the night air. She struggles against me as I carry her up towards her lorry.

'Put me down, Matt! I can walk just fine!' I do as she tells me but keep a firm grip on her waist, as, despite what she says, she's unsteady on her feet. Luckily, we don't meet anyone, but I'm worried people can hear us. Liz is shouting at the top of her voice.

'It was so fucking ridiculous . . . Yes, I took the bottle of gin, but they completely overreacted . . . I tried to tell them to put it on my hotel bill, but they started freaking out for no reason . . . And then they called the fucking police! Seriously!'

I let go of her as she stumbles into her lorry. I follow her and stand awkwardly in the corner, not sure what to do. I don't know if it's safe to leave her alone in this state but, at the same time, I don't know how I'm supposed to help. I'd wanted to get into her lorry for weeks, to spend a night with her. But right now, I'd rather be anywhere else.

'You're very quiet,' she says, staring up at me and giggling.

'Sorry . . . I guess I'm just tired . . .'

She runs to the fridge. 'You need a drink!' she says, pulling out a bottle of wine.

'No, I'm fine,' I say, shaking my head.

'OK . . . All for me then!' She begins to undo it but I take the bottle away from her.

'I think you've had enough,' I say, putting it back in the fridge.

She pouts like a spoilt child. 'You're no fun!'

I don't say anything, just gaze at her. She looks so vulnerable and fragile. I can't leave her. I desperately want to, but I can't. She collapses on to the bed and pats the spot next to her. 'Come lie down with me, Matt,' she says. I sit tentatively next to her but she grabs my shoulders and pulls me down so that I'm lying parallel with her. She's giggling uncontrollably again and, despite everything, it makes me smile.

'Are you mad at me?' she asks. There's fear in her voice.

'No,' I say. 'No, I'm not mad—'

'I knew I could call you, I knew you would come and get me . . .' She turns her body sideways, towards me.

'You shouldn't drink like this,' I say nervously.

'Why not?'

'It's not good for you. I'm sure you wouldn't want your parents to see you this way.'

She gives me an odd look. 'My parents?' She laughs. 'Matt, who do you think taught me to drink like this?'

'I don't like it,' I say, and Liz stops laughing. 'You're better than this.' I'm looking her straight in the eyes now, and I can't make myself look away.

'You're so kind, Matt . . .' she's edging closer so that our faces are only an inch apart '. . . you're so sweet to me . . .' I can feel the warmth of her breath. I don't move, I don't breathe. She places her hand on my cheek and glides her fingers over my lips. 'You're great . . . You're really great.' My heart is thumping hard and I can feel my body quiver.

I close my eyes in the hope that I can regain some control but instead I just enjoy the feeling of her touch as she traces the outlines of my face. She begins to kiss me. I don't kiss her back, but I don't push her away either. She rolls over on top of me and places her hands behind my neck, her kisses becoming faster and more eager. My mind is screaming at me to stop this, but I can't. My lips have taken on a life of their own and they now move in sync with hers. I try to speak when she breaks away from me to pull off my top.

'Liz, I—' She grabs my face and continues to kiss me. It's almost aggressive. I feel light-headed and dizzy. Our bodies are getting warm and I'm shaking with excitement. She stops kissing me for a moment and starts to undo my jeans. I realize then that if I'm going to stop this, it has to be now. And I have to stop this.

'I can't do this!' I don't sound very convincing and Liz begins to laugh.

'Of course you can, Matt. I'm the one who's been drinking, not you. I'm sure you are well "up" for the challenge.' She tries to kiss me again, but I push her away. The smell of alcohol on her breath is potent and I know I couldn't forgive myself if I went through with this.

'That's not what I mean . . . We can't do this. You're not thinking straight.'

Liz makes fun of me. 'I'm not thinking at all, I'm just doing! Come on, stop being so noble. I know you want to—' I push her away and stand up. As I dress I can see she's getting angry. 'What the fuck is your problem, Matt? Sex is just something people do . . . Why are you making it into this huge thing?'

As she speaks, I realize something. 'Why are you calling me Matt?'

She seems taken aback. 'Because that's your name . . .'

'But you've always called me Matthew before . . . Why are you calling me Matt now?'

'I don't know . . . Everyone calls you Matt. That's just who you are . . . You're Matt, Shane's groom.'

I feel the anger boiling up inside me. 'So that's what I am, is it? Some groom you can fuck to make yourself feel better?'

She hesitates a moment before answering.

'Maybe . . . So what if it is? People fuck each other all the time to make themselves feel better . . . I know you've wanted to sleep with me since the moment you met me . . . Well, here you go – I'm giving it to you. Take it!' I look down at her sitting on the bed, drunk and dishevelled, and I begin to hate her a little. I have to get away from her.

'Trust me, Liz, there's no one I want to fuck less right now than you.'

She stares at me, silenced, and I walk away.

Rain is pounding on the lorry roof. It feels like only a little while ago that I closed my eyes and tried to forget the events of the night. I check my watch: it's 6.30 a.m. There's little point in trying to get back to sleep now. I wipe my eyes and drag myself out of bed. I can hear Nick snoring loudly and decide to leave him be. The morning sky is a dull grey and when I look out of the window I see people sprinting for cover from the rain. Most are soaked within seconds. I groan with tiredness and put on my jacket, readying myself to face the elements.

The horses whinny loudly when they see me. Some kick hard against their stable doors, impatient for their breakfast.

'Wait a minute, would you?' I ask pointlessly. Their eyes widen when they see me scoop oats into their empty feed dishes. Each meal is individual to each horse and I list them to myself as I go along to make sure I don't mix them up.

'Talking to yourself? You must be cracking up.' I turn around at the sound of a familiar voice and, for the first time ever, I'm disappointed to see her. Liz makes her way towards me. I can tell she's nervous.

'I'm surprised to see you awake,' I mutter.

She looks awful. Her hair is a mess and her face is pale and blotchy, and I have no doubt she's suffering from a mighty headache.

'I knew you would be up feeding, and I want to talk to you.'

'Are you sober?' I ask harshly.

'Yes . . . Just hung over . . .'

'I want the truth.'

'It's complicated—' she starts, but this time I interrupt her angrily.

'I don't care!' I shout, unable to hold back any longer. 'I want the truth and I bloody deserve it too.'

Liz closes her eyes and starts breathing heavily, and she keeps her eyes closed when she speaks. 'When we first met I was dating Edward Dawson.' The words come out level and controlled, but they hit me like a ton of bricks. I put down the feed buckets and lean against the stable door.

'Are you dating him now?' I ask, my voice small.

'We've been on a break,' she replies.

'But there's still something there? It's not over, is it?' Liz shakes her head and opens her eyes. I look at her and realize that she's a completely different person to who I thought she was. 'He's married.'

'He's leaving her,' she says defensively.

'For you?' I snap.

'Yes,' she replies. It's her voice that's small now.

'So what was I?' I ask, angry again. 'Something on the side to keep you entertained until Edward got his act together? Or were you just using me to make him jealous?'

'Neither,' she says, taking a step forward. 'I liked you. I still like you.'

'But you're going back to him?'

Liz looks directly at me for a moment before answering. 'Yes.'

My hands are shaking I'm so furious. I have the urge to throw something, break something. I feel like such a naïve fool, and I've no one but myself to blame. I was warned by everyone – even Liz – and still I went for it, ignoring all sense. And more than anything else, I'm tired, I'm just so tired of all of it.

'Well, good luck to you both,' I say bitterly, turning my back on her, not wanting to hear another word of what she has to say.

'Matthew, I'm sorry,' she calls after me, but I keep walking away until I know she's no longer there.

22

Mother

'LIZ, WILL YOU PASS THE WATER?'

'Liz, the water?

'Liz!'

I jump at the sound of Orla's voice and scramble to grab the jug of water on the table. We're both home at our apartment and Orla has ordered takeaway to welcome me home.

'Sorry,' I mutter, feeling slightly frazzled.

'You OK?'

'Fine,' I say, picking at my untouched Chinese.

'You thinking about Aachen?'

'Yeah,' I admit.

'What part?' Orla asks. I told her the full story the moment I got home last night.

'All of it.' I wish I could forget it – forget the fall, forget the ultimatum with Edward, forget being arrested, and forget the look of hurt and disappointment on Matthew's face when I said I was with Edward. Orla was kind when I told her but I knew from the look on her face that she's surprised at me. I'm surprised at myself – I've fucked it up. I've really fucked it up.

'Edward's coming here tonight . . . I hope you don't mind,' I say, trying to sound as nonchalant as possible. Orla can't help but raise her eyebrows.

'So you've decided?'

'Yeah . . . no one will ever be able to offer me as much as he can. I'd be an idiot to give that up.' Orla nods along, but makes no comment, and I can't tell anything from her facial expression. I wish I could ask her what she thinks, but I know I have to make this decision on my own, and I choose Edward.

'He'll be thrilled,' Orla says kindly, giving me a warm smile.

'Thanks,' I mumble back, feeling more anxious by the minute.

When the doorbell finally does ring, my stomach is in absolute knots. I can't push the thought out of my mind that, after all this, Edward might not want to be with me and then I'll have lost everything. I take a deep breath to calm myself and open the door. Edward stands in front of me, looking perfectly groomed and wearing a beautifully tailored grey pinstriped suit.

'Hello, beautiful,' he says confidently, and leans in to kiss me on the cheek.

'Hi,' I reply. Why's he so dressed up?

'I thought I'd treat you to dinner at the Dylan Hotel,' he says.

'Oh . . . I . . . I didn't know. I've just had takeaway with Orla.'

Orla had disappeared to her room as soon as the doorbell rang but the remains of our takeaway are evident on the kitchen table.

'That's no problem,' he says brightly. 'We'll just get dessert — it's the best part of a meal anyway.'

'I'm not dressed!' I had put on a bit of make-up earlier, but I'm wearing jeans and a T-shirt.

'Don't worry, you have time to change. That dress you wore to Enda's birthday would be perfect. You really looked wonderful that night . . .' His voice softens at the last bit and I know I must be blushing. My anxiety about seeing him has waned and now I can appreciate how great he looks.

I do as he tells me and change quickly into my lacy black dress. I leave my hair loose, deciding I don't want to waste any time doing it. As we drive to the Dylan Hotel, Edward chats cheerfully of horses and Dublin, and I'm drawn into his infectious happiness. He talks as if the last few months hadn't even happened, and somehow we slide back into being together.

'Dessert and champagne,' he says to the waiter when we sit down at our table, before I have a chance to say anything.

'Any dessert in particular?' the waiter asks, looking mildly surprised.

'We'll have a taste of them all. A bit of a mix-and-share situation, if that's OK?' He smiles broadly, and the waiter smiles back at him.

'No problem, sir.' Once the waiter has left, I examine our surroundings. Everything looks so extravagant and expensive, and I wish I had done something with my hair. I push it behind my ears, not knowing what else to do with my hands. Edward watches my every move.

'God, you look beautiful,' he says in awe. I stop fidgeting and look directly at him. I'm about to say something when the champagne arrives. The waiter goes to pour my glass first, but I shake my head.

'No, thank you,' I say politely. 'I'll have water instead.' Edward looks at me quizzically. 'I'm quitting,' I explain. 'Until Dublin is over at least.' He smiles again.

'That's what I love about you, Elizabeth. You're so driven and self-disciplined. You're incredibly mature for your age.' Edward takes a large mouthful of his champagne before continuing. 'Taidgh hasn't released the team for Dublin yet, but he will soon. You'll be on it, I'm sure.'

'I'm not so sure,' I say, embarrassed. 'After my fall and everything.'

'That was a mistake, and you won't repeat it. Taidgh knows that.' He's dismissed the subject and I know it's best not to bring it up again.

'I want to talk to you about Matthew,' I say bravely, and Edward's smile vanishes. 'First of all, I'm sorry and—' Edward raises his hand to silence me.

'Elizabeth, I've asked a lot from you in this relationship and you have been incredibly patient with me. I understand that you slipped up and sometimes we need to get these sorts of things out of our system. I just hope that that fling is over with and that you're ready to be with me.' He's being so calm and under-standing, I'm confused.

'I am,' I reassure him. I don't know what else to say.

'Good.' His smile returns. 'Then let's forget the past and focus on us.' He raises his glass, and I do the same.

'To us,' he says, clinking my glass.

'To us,' I repeat.

I spend the night with Edward and, even though I'm nervous at first, we both find our way and I'm reminded how well he knows my body and how intense and comforting it is to be with him. I don't ask where Katherine is and he doesn't say. I don't want to know; the less I know about her the better. Edward falls asleep soon after, and it's one of those heavy sleeps I know he won't wake from for a long time. I try to sleep too, but my body is full of tension and I'm unable to settle.

After a few hours of lying awake, I get up from Edward's bed. I didn't bring any spare clothes, so I throw on my underwear and Edward's shirt. I walk down slowly to his kitchen. It doesn't matter how loud I am – I won't wake him. I run my hand along the cool marble of his kitchen counter. Edward's house is always so clean. I wonder if he cleans it himself or does he hire someone. I stare at the oven and try to imagine myself cooking him dinner. It's a strange thought.

I don't know why, but I feel uncharacteristically nosy and I decide to explore the house in a way I've never been brave enough to do before. Every room I go into, I somehow associate it with our future together. This will be the study from where we'll run the yard; this will be the dining room where I host dinner parties for all of our married friends; this will be the bedroom that we'll turn into a nursery when I get pregnant . . . But these thoughts don't make me happy, they scare me. I go on and on through Edward's house, I can't seem to stop, and as I enter each room my anxiety gets worse and worse until I'm almost at the point where I'm running around the house like a madwoman.

I pause for a moment when I come to Edward's sitting room. The walls, carpet and couches are all the same perfect cream, flawless and beautiful. This is the room where I will spend every birthday, Christmas and holiday with Edward. My legs suddenly feel heavy and I let myself slowly collapse on to Edward's pristine carpet. I lie face down on the soft fabric and I know I can't get up. I begin to cry, hard and irrationally. I lie there for hours and cry.

It doesn't take long for Edward and me to get back to where we were before. I do my best to forget that night in Edward's house, reasoning that it was nothing more than exhaustion. Edward begins to train me again and soon my days and mind are full of nothing but preparing myself and Wildfire for Dublin Horse Show. Exactly two weeks before the Dublin Nations Cup, Taidgh announces the team. It's the same one we had in Aachen – with one small difference. Nick is the reserve.

'Why do we have a reserve this time?' I ask as we leave the

yard for the evening. It's nearly dark and the place is practically deserted. As Dublin approaches, our workday gets longer and longer.

'Taidgh is probably worried Ben will get hammered and be unable to compete . . . He's getting worse – I couldn't believe how he behaved in Aachen. Nick might need to step in at the last second.'

Since we got back together, neither of us has mentioned Matthew. Even when the teams were first announced, I didn't dare bring up his name, but now I feel as if we're dangerously close to talking about him. I decide it best to change the subject, but what I want to talk about is just as tricky.

'How's Katherine?' I ask, trying to keep my voice calm.

Edward tenses a little. 'Difficult,' he mutters, clearly annoyed at me for bringing her up. 'She refuses to accept this divorce. She insists that we haven't tried hard enough, even though I keep telling her that I don't want to try any more . . .' He bangs the front gates closed before locking up.

'Does she know about me?' I ask, trying to not sound so afraid.

'No,' Edward says briskly. 'No, that would make everything a lot worse. If she knew, I wouldn't put it past her to go to the papers . . . She can be quite hysterical at times.' I'm annoyed now too, but I'm not sure who with. Edward, perhaps, because this divorce is taking so long; Katherine, because she keeps stalling and trying to prevent the inevitable; or myself – though I'm not quite sure why.

'I've something to tell you. Katherine is coming to Dublin Horse Show.'

I'm not really sure how I feel about this. The thought of meeting her is so surreal. 'Why?' I ask, more angrily than I mean to.

'I think it's her last attempt – at salvaging something that is already dead, to my mind at least . . . But, in a way, I think it might be a good thing. She'll see that she doesn't fit in my life any more and then maybe she can let this whole thing move forward.' We've reached my car at this point and Edward squeezes my shoulder affectionately.

'I hate this,' I say, wishing that everything could be easier.

'I know. So do I,' he says, his blue eyes soft. 'But it won't be for much longer, I promise.' He leans down and kisses me. His kiss is tender and I can't help but respond.

'Let me take you out. We can go and have a beautiful dinner – or let's have a stroll around Dublin and I can buy you some new clothes? You deserve to be spoilt, Elizabeth.' I smile at the offer but shake my head.

'I can't,' I reply. 'I promised Orla I'd have dinner with her . . . I feel as if I've been neglecting her lately.' Since Edward and I got back together, we've spent nearly every evening together, and it's been intense and exciting, but I'm kind of looking forward to an evening without him.

'Oh, if you must.' He groans like a spoilt child who isn't getting his way. As I drive home, I try to push Katherine to the back of my mind, reminding myself that it's only a matter of time until that part of it's all over. One thing I can't ignore, though, is the dread in my stomach at the thought of seeing Matthew again. I've been thinking about it non-stop since I found out we'd be competing together in Dublin. How do I act around him? Do I ignore him? Am I to be friendly? Does he hate me? The image of his face when I told him about Edward and me is clear in my mind. Yes, he does hate me.

I can hear Marshall barking loudly before I even reach the door of the apartment. I frown, wondering what on earth would have him so excited. I open the door to see the dog jumping up and down while a nervous-looking middle-aged woman stands over him, trying to shush him.

'Mum!' I can't believe my eyes. I startle her, and my eyes shoot to Orla, who is sitting at the kitchen table. 'Why is she here?' I ask. Orla also looks nervous.

'She just wants to talk to you,' she pleads, but with a hint of sternness in her voice. She's the perfect balance between sensitivity and tough love; I suppose that's what makes her such a good nurse. I stare at her for a moment before sitting down at the table and crossing my arms.

'Fine. What do you want?' I ask rudely. My mother continues to stand, looking more flustered than I've ever seen her.

'I wanted us to talk, to work things out,' she says cautiously.

'Did you bring more college letters with you? Or are you just going to call me a slut again?' I snap.

'Don't be a bitch,' Orla scolds me. I look at her, surprised, but I don't say anything else.

'I admit that I came on too *forceful* last time we talked, but you must understand it was only because I'm *worried* about you . . .' My mother makes her way to the table and sits down timidly. 'I don't like the choices you have made, Elizabeth, I'm not going to pretend otherwise, but . . . after your fall in Aachen, I realized that *anything* can happen and life is so *short*. So I want to be part of your life, no matter *what* way you choose to live it . . . I don't expect you to come home or to give *anything* up, but . . . I'd like us to have . . . some sort of *relation-ship* . . .' She is staring down at her hands as she speaks, clearly embarrassed at being so honest and open with me. I take a moment to understand what she's trying to say.

'You watched me in Aachen?' I ask, unable to hide the surprise in my voice. She looks shocked I'd even ask.

'Of course I watched you. You were amazing, Elizabeth . . . I wanted to fly over to watch you, but I . . . I thought I might upset you if I came.' She pulls her rings on and off as she speaks. I can see where my anxiety comes from. 'I've missed you and I'm . . . *trying* . . .' We all sit there in silence for a moment and I try to digest what my mother has said. She watched me compete in Aachen, she cares. Orla stares at me for a moment and I know she wants me to say something. This is a big step for my mother and I know I need to meet her halfway.

'Would you like to come to Dublin?' I ask. Both Orla and my mother look at me open-mouthed. They weren't expecting my reaction; I'm surprising myself to be honest.

'I would love to . . . but do you really want me there?' My mother asks, looking straight at me. I think about her question for a moment and of all the times she has been hard on me, critical of me; but then I think of the past few months without her and how lonely I've felt and, if I'm truthful with myself, I've really missed her. I need someone and I'm glad it's her.

'Yes, I want you there.'

23

Death

'HELLO THERE, BUDDY,' I WHISPER TO CEDRIC AS HE NUDGES HIS nose against my hands. He lowers his head and begins to sniff and nibble at my pockets, looking for food, as always. He's so greedy. 'No treats for you today, unfortunately,' I tell him.

The sun has arrived and, with it, a relaxed attitude has entered the yard. It's a Monday, so most people haven't come in to ride their horses, either because they've work or because they've decided to go off somewhere to enjoy this beautiful day. Shane's off today too, which means I have a break from the intensive training he's been putting me through before Dublin. Nick's been a victim of Shane's scrutiny also. He was so thrilled to be selected as a reserve for the team, but now I think he almost regrets it, as Shane's worked us both to the bone. Shane's patience is short these days, but I don't mind because I know he's only trying to get the absolute best performance out of us, even if it makes us hate him. Even so, I'm glad to have this day of rest, a day without Shane barking at me every minute.

As I push Cedric's head away I notice his stable hasn't been cleaned out. Odd, I think. Today it's Nick's turn to muck out and he'd normally have it done by now. I go to the stable next to Cedric's and notice that it hasn't been mucked out either. I haven't seen Nick today, but that isn't so unusual. He often gets up extra early to get a head start on the day. He likes getting things done so he can have some time to himself later.

I start searching the yard for him, but I can't find him anywhere. He can't still be in bed, and if he's ill or injured and unable to work he'd have let me know when he heard me getting up this morning. I'm about to walk back to the bungalow to check when someone calls my name. I turn around to see Shane walking towards me. He looks angry, and I immediately feel tense.

'Hi, Shane, how are you?' I say, hoping he won't notice the stables aren't done. He won't care who's supposed to do it – he'll kill both of us.

'Fine,' he says curtly. 'Will you come to my office, Matt? I need to chat to you about something.' I nod and follow him, feeling more and more anxious. He only calls us into his office when it's something serious. Last time, it was because he caught me smoking in his yard. I was out in the open space, nowhere near any horses or anything that might catch fire, but that mattered little to Shane. He pulled me into his office and screamed at me for an hour straight, docked me two days' pay and told me that if he caught me doing it again I'd be out. Now, he closes the door to his office, and I know it can only be bad.

'Sit.' I do as I'm told. 'Have you been talking to Nick today?'

I try to think of ways to cover for him; if Shane is on a rampage, then I don't want Nick to get caught up in it.

'No, I haven't . . . but I'm sure he's out in the yard doing his work. I can run and get him for you if you like?' I offer, hoping I can find him quickly and warn him something's up.

'I guess you haven't heard yet then?' He no longer looks angry, but sad.

'Heard what?'

'Nick's dad died three days ago from a heart attack. His funeral is tomorrow. I've arranged people to cover for you here so you two can go.'

'Nick's dad is dead?' Shane nods. 'And he died three days ago? Why didn't Nick tell me? He seemed perfectly fine yesterday . . .' None of it makes any sense. Shane hesitates.

'I doubt Nick knew until it was announced in the newspaper this morning. His dad was highly involved in the Church and local charities. There's a small article about him and his life's work.'

'Would no one have told him before now? His family? What about his mum?'

'Nick doesn't get along with his family, Matt. You know that.'

'I know but . . . his dad is dead. Surely that's more important than some stupid argument?' I imagine how I'd feel if my family didn't tell me about something like this. I'd be furious, and so hurt.

'There's so much you don't know about Nick,' Shane says quietly. 'Don't be fooled — being cut off from his family has affected him a lot. He just hides it well.'

I nod: he's right, of course. Outside of the horse world, there's very little I know about Nick.

'Obviously, he won't be working today, so I need you to take over.'

'No problem,' I say. Nick's often helped me in the past. As I go to leave, Shane calls me back.

'Matt! Make sure he's OK when you go home later. His dad's death . . . It will have hit him hard.' I nod. Shane and I are all Nick has right now.

Work is slow without Nick's help, and it's well past dark before I'm back in our bungalow. At first it's silent when I walk in and

I begin to wonder is he even here. I call his name, and there's no answer. I call it a second time, louder this time, and I hear him grumble something from his room. I don't normally knock before going in to Nick's room – the bungalow is so small and it's hard to hide anything from each other – but today I'm worried what'll be on the other side of that door. So I knock.

'Come in . . . Come in . . .' I hear him mumble. He's sitting on his bed with a half-full bottle of Jack Daniel's on his lap and the local newspaper in his right hand. He stares at me with unsteady eyes. 'Sorry about today, Matt . . . Didn't feel well . . .' I sit gingerly at the end of his bed.

'It's fine,' I reply uncertainly. Nick raises an eyebrow at me and smiles, but it's not his usual warm, joyful smile; his expression seems malevolent somehow.

'Shane told you then?' he asks. I nod, deciding it's easier than lying. 'It's not that big of a deal . . . not really. I haven't spoken to the bastard in six years . . . It's not really going to affect my life in any way.' He sounds like he's trying to convince himself more than me. He takes a swig from his Jack Daniel's before going on. 'They really talked him up in this thing.' He gestures towards the newspaper, which is open at the article about his dad. How many times has Nick read it today? ' "Huge loss to the community" . . . "Will be greatly missed" . . . "Loyal and faithful husband" . . . didn't mention me at all in this, did they? They wouldn't, though, would they? Those nut-job priests think of me as dirt . . .' I know he's no longer talking to me, but I also know I can't leave him alone, not when he's like this.

'Shane gave us both the day off tomorrow . . . so we can go to the funeral.' Nick's shaking his head before I even finish speaking. He's not looking at me but staring at the newspaper article.

'I'm not going to that thing,' he says bluntly. He hands me the bottle then. 'Drink with me?' When I hesitate, he adds a desperate 'Please?' The two of us drink in silence for a long time. My head gets heavy and I begin to feel very drunk.

I think what it would be like if my dad died. We have our differences, my dad and me, but I still couldn't imagine my life without him. His death would be like this massive hole in my chest that just wouldn't heal. And I would feel that hole every day, no matter where I was, who I was with or what I was doing. Saying goodbye would be everything, and I would fight against anyone who told me that I couldn't say goodbye to him.

'You should go to the funeral. You'll regret it if you don't,' I say. I know I have to get Nick to that funeral somehow, however hard it may be.

'I appreciate the concern, Matt, but honestly . . . I'm not wanted at that thing.'

'He's your dad. You have every right to be there. I know you and your family have had your arguments, but I bet they want you there – even if they're too stubborn to say it.' Nick looks up from the newspaper for the first time since I came. He takes another large mouthful of whiskey then stares at me.

'You're so fucking naïve, Matt.'

'I'm just trying to make you realize how big a mistake it is not to go.'

'I called my mum today,' he says. I stay silent and let him speak, not sure where he's going with this. 'I haven't spoken to her in years either, but when I saw that newspaper article I just had to call. I didn't think . . . I just needed to hear from her what had happened.' His voice is low and emotionless, his eyes still out of focus.

'What did she say?'

'At first she didn't know who I was . . . she didn't recognize my voice . . . When I told her it was me, she went quiet. I kept asking questions: how did it happen? Where? Had he been having problems with his heart, or was it unexpected? She didn't answer any of them . . . Eventually, when I stopped talking, she spoke. She told me that she was tired and busy and that she didn't want to have to deal with my drama . . .' Nick's voice begins to crack, but he manages to hold back the tears. 'I pleaded with her, begging her to help me understand, and then she blamed me . . . She said that the stress I had caused the two of them over the years was what weakened his heart. She said it was my fault that he's dead and I should be ashamed of myself . . .' He traces the label of the Jack Daniel's bottle, his whole body shaking. I sit there stunned, unable to speak. 'Do you still think my mum will welcome me at the funeral, Matt?'

I open and close my mouth silently for a moment, but I get the words out at last. 'You know it's not true, though. Don't you? It's not your fault your dad is dead. Your mum is blind with grief – she doesn't know what she's saying . . .' My words sound so pathetic after what he's just told me, but I speak slowly and hope it will sink in.

'That's what I tell myself,' he says. 'That she's just a spiteful bitch and there's nothing I could have done to stop my dad from dying, but . . . but in a way she's right. When I left, it destroyed both of them . . . But I had to . . . They fucking forced me to leave . . .' I start to understand what must have gone on between him and his family. 'Fuck! It would have all been so much easier if I wasn't gay. I gave up everything to be gay, and for what?' He throws his head into his hands.

'It's not your fault . . . They . . . they just didn't understand,' I say, trying to stop him from falling off the edge.

'No. I fought for my right to be gay, and what have I gained from it? I don't have a boyfriend; I don't have someone who loves me . . . I'm all alone . . .' His voice is shaking and I'm afraid he's going to burst into tears. I place my hand awkwardly on his shoulder, wondering what I can say to comfort him. 'What's wrong with me?' He almost chokes on the words.

'Nothing,' I say. 'Finding someone is hard . . . It's so fucking hard . . .' Images of Liz come into my head; I try to force them away, but I can't. 'But you'll meet someone one day and they'll just be . . . right . . .' I struggle to get the words out but I get there. Nick stares at me. I don't know what he's thinking. Suddenly, he jumps forward and places his lips harshly on mine. The taste of whiskey on his is strong, and it makes me feel dizzy. For a moment I consider it, how easy it would be to be with Nick – we know each other better than anyone else and I know he'll always be there for me. I can take care of him, protect him, like you're supposed to for the one you love. But that's just the thing, I don't love Nick in that way. The sound of his voice doesn't fill me with warmth and his touch doesn't fill me with excitement. It only takes a moment for this to go through my head and for me to gently push him away. I want to help him, but I can't kiss him back. It's not fair or true to either of us.

'I'm sorry,' I whisper. 'I don't . . .' Nothing more needs to be said. Nick knows. He probably knew before he even tried to kiss me, but he's so distraught and confused with grief. The tears that have been threatening to come out all evening finally fall from his eyes.

'Shit . . . What the fuck is wrong with me?' I try to tell him that it's OK, but he shouts over me. 'I know you're not like me, Matt. I've known that for a long time . . . I just feel so alone, and you're here . . . you're always here for me and . . . Fuck! I've ruined it with my stupid gay self . . . Fuck, fuck, fuck!' He buries his head back in his hands and won't look at me.

'Stop!' I yell over him, and he slowly lifts his head. His face looks vulnerable and scared. 'It's OK, Nick. It's OK . . .' I'm not sure if he believes me, but he seems to be calming down. 'I'm still here for you.' He smiles in gratitude, and now the tears fall silently down his face.

'I'm sorry,' he mumbles. We sit in silence for a while. My head feels like it weighs a ton, and the last fifteen minutes seem like a weird dream. Tiredness catches up on me and I decide I need to get some sleep. I get up to leave, but I know I need to say one last thing to him.

'You have to go to the funeral tomorrow. You know it.'

Nick nods. 'Yeah, I know . . . I have to go.'

By morning Nick has convinced himself that he isn't attending the funeral. I feel frustrated and hung-over and end up giving out to him like he's a bold, disobedient child. It seems to work, though, because by the time we need to leave he's dressed in a suit and ready to go. He's incredibly nervous, and his whole body trembles as we get closer to where the funeral is being held. Neither of us owns a nice suit. We look scruffy in our second-hand clothes, and the suits don't fit us properly. Mine used to belong to my dad and Nick bought his in a charity shop.

'This is a mistake,' Nick mumbles to himself.

'It's going to be fine,' I say. I've been trying, unsuccessfully, to reassure him the whole way. 'We'll stand at the back . . . People probably won't even see us, and then, when it's all over and everybody is gone, you can go up to him and say . . . whatever you need to say . . .' Again, Nick's not even looking at me, and part of me thinks he's not listening either.

There's uncomfortable silence the rest of the way. The funeral is over an hour away; it's in the church of Nick's hometown, just outside Kildare town. Shane generously gave me money for petrol: Nick would have been in no state to drive today and so he is begrudgingly directing me where to go. Nick's nerves are catching and I find myself feeling tense and unsettled as we get closer. We're nearly there when Nick speaks.

'I never told you what happened between my parents and me, did I?'

'No,' I reply, 'but it's OK, you don't have to . . .'

'You deserve to know,' he says with a shrug. 'No point keeping it a secret any more.' I stay silent and continue to look at the road but give him a slight nod to let him know that I'm listening.

'I was sixteen years old when I figured out I was gay,' he begins. 'I'd had my suspicions before then, of course. I didn't have much interest in girls and I always seemed to be happier when I was surrounded by guys. But it was my sixteenth birthday when I realized I *fancied* guys. My friends and I had gone to the local under-18s' disco. We'd been binge drinking in a field previous to that, so we were all pretty hammered by the time we got there. My friend James and I had managed to sneak some drink in. James was a pony jumper, like me; we'd been friends for years. We went to the bathroom and started knocking back the vodka we'd snuck in in Coke bottles. We were both so drunk . . . James started making jokes about how I should go out to the dance floor and find myself a girl. He said I had to get a birthday score . . . I told him I had no interest in the girls out there. That's what I always said about girls, and it was true. And then . . . then James kissed me. I had kissed girls before, but never like James kissed me. I realized then that I really liked kissing him . . . much more than I ever thought I would. I pulled away after a while; I didn't really understand what was happening. James was smiling. He put his fingers to his lips and whispered, "Our secret, yeah?" I smiled back and said, "Yeah". . .' Nick pauses for a moment.

'Where's James now?' I ask. I'd met most of Nick's friends and I'm surprised I've never heard of him before.

'He got married last year; his wife is pregnant too . . . He stopped talking to me when I came out. I guess he was worried I would out him too.' Nick smiles, but it's a sad smile.

'What did you do when you realized you were gay?' I ask,

hoping I'm not being too nosy. Nick is so tight-lipped when it comes to his personal life, and now he's telling me everything. At last, I'm starting to see who he really is.

'I wasn't really that surprised. I grew up surrounded by showjumpers, most of whom had . . . alternative lifestyles. My parents had been at many shows with me and they at least knew some of the stuff that went on. I made the mistake of thinking that they'd be OK with it. I waited a few months before telling them. I dated some guys – I wanted to be sure. But as time went on it became clearer and clearer to me that I didn't really have a choice. It's just the way I am . . .' Nick scrunches up his face. It's obvious this is a painful memory. 'I told my parents straight out, I just said it – "I am gay" . . . My mum looked shocked and my dad just confused.

'My mum hugged me and I thought for a moment that this was her accepting it all. I was so relieved and happy, and then she said, "My poor boy . . . My poor little sick boy . . ." I pulled away from her. I started to panic . . . I didn't know what she meant . . . My dad stepped in. He told me that it was OK, they would help me. He could send me to a place that would fix me. I asked him what he meant and he said there were institutions set up to help people like me . . .' Nick stops. He's shaking, and for a second I think he's going to leave it at that, that it's just too hard to continue. When he speaks again his voice is cracking.

'I couldn't believe it; they wanted to send me away to some place that would force me to be straight. I tried to defend myself. I told them there was nothing wrong with the way I am, but it only seemed to make things worse. My mum started crying and my dad starting quoting sections of the Bible at me. It was all so overwhelming. I ran to my room and locked the door. I started freaking out then, I was so afraid he was going to send me to one of those institutions against my will.' Nick stares at his hands and squeezes each individual finger until it is red. When he's done with the ten, he starts again.

'What did you do?'

'I ran away. At first I thought I had nowhere to go – all my friends' parents were friendly with mine, they were sure to find me . . . I turned up on Dom's doorstep. His parents were complete hippies and I knew they were the last people my parents would ask for help from. I was distraught and I told Dom everything . . . He didn't even hesitate when I asked could I stay the night. He's never told a soul what I told him that night . . . I don't think the fucker knows how much that means to me . . . how thankful I am . . .' Nick buries his face in his hands. He doesn't cry but takes deep, long breaths. When he speaks again it's in a more calm and measured tone.

'Staying at Dom's wasn't a long-term solution. His parents were relaxed but I couldn't live there without them realizing something was up . . . I got desperate. I was so afraid what my parents might do. Dom tried to convince me to go home; he was sure I could talk my parents around. Maybe he was right, but I was too afraid to take that chance . . . I needed a new place to live, and . . . then I remembered a conversation I once had with Shane. We'd met at a show; he'd complimented me on my riding ability and said that I should go work for him when I finished school. I hadn't thought much of it at the time but just then it seemed like the perfect way to escape.

'I arrived at his door the evening after I'd run away from home. I had a rucksack of clothes and very little money. He must have been so shocked when he saw me, just turning up out of nowhere. I told him I was ready to work for him; he laughed and said I should come back when I was finished with school. I broke down then – he was my only hope. I told him what had happened with my parents . . . God, I was such a mess, and I landed it all on him. He barely even knew me. He took me on and said I could live in the bungalow with the other four grooms . . .'

'Four?' Only Nick and I live in that bungalow now, and it feels small between the two of us.

'Yeah, it was pretty hectic, but at least I had somewhere to stay. Shane got rid of a lot of them when the recession hit and he needed to start saving money. I was so relieved he took me on . . . He told me, though, that he wouldn't stop my parents if they came to get me. For months I was terrified they'd turn up and drag me away. They didn't, though. They called me constantly for the first few weeks, then, slowly, they stopped trying to convince me they were helping me. Instead they began to use hateful and scornful words. Eventually my dad told me I was a disgrace and that he never wanted to see me again. A few weeks later I heard that he'd sold all my ponies. I knew then that I'd never be welcome at home again . . . I dropped out of school – my parents didn't even try to make me finish – and I've been working for Shane ever since.' He seems out of breath when he finishes. I feel I should comfort him but anything I think of sounds so pathetic and unhelpful when I rehearse it in my head. But the silence gets painful and I know I need to say something.

'D'you really think they would have forced you to go to that institute if you had stayed?'

'I guess we'll never know now.'

People are gathering together at the funeral. It's a cloudy day, but dry. My heart sinks when I realize there's only a small crowd so our presence will definitely be noticed. Everyone is walking slowly down a hill; a priest waits at the bottom. In front of him there's a casket and around it a number of seats. A petite, elderly woman is standing next to the priest. I can't see her face, because she's wearing a large black hat and her head is lowered, but I imagine she must be Nick's mother. Nick suddenly halts halfway down. He places a hand on my arm, making me stop abruptly.

'Can we stay here?' he asks desperately. 'Just until the service is over and everybody else is gone . . . Please?' We're the last to arrive, so nobody is behind us, and we're in clear view of everybody. I realize it's not about hiding for Nick; he needs the distance to feel safe.

'OK,' I say. I take a step back up the hill so that I'm standing next to him, and then we both turn so that we're facing his father.

The priest starts the service. The wind carries his voice, and Nick and I are able to hear every word. He says very similar things to what was in the newspaper article; talks about Nick's dad's charity work, says that he was a loving husband. Nick isn't mentioned. It makes me so angry I almost want to start shouting at the crowd, telling them that this dead man's son is standing right here. About ten minutes into the service I notice that Nick is trembling and quiet, and gasping noises are coming from his mouth. I panic that he's about to break down. I grab his hand in mine and whisper in his ear.

'You're OK . . . I'm here . . .' I relax when his breathing slows and he seems to pull himself together. He even cracks a joke.

'Please, Matt . . . I just don't feel that way about you,' he says, gesturing at our intertwined hands. Even so, he doesn't let go, and neither do I.

The priest seems to be the only one speaking at the funeral, and I think that's a good thing. Nick's mother has undoubtedly seen us by now and I have no idea how Nick would handle hearing her speak about his deceased father. I hear footsteps behind me. I don't bother looking, assuming it's someone who works in the church or a late guest. I nearly fall over in shock when I see who appears at Nick's side.

'Liz!' She's wearing a black shirt and black jeans, her hair is loose and messy and her face is clean of any make-up. I think it is the most dishevelled I've ever seen her, except for that night in Aachen.

'I'm sorry I'm late,' she murmurs, looking directly at Nick and gripping his free hand.

'Thank you for coming,' he whispers back.

The service ends after about an hour, but people hang about, thanking the priest, expressing their sadness to Nick's mum. The three of us wait in the same spot, while the guests leave around us. Nick breaks the silence. He lifts both my and Liz's hands into the air, saying, 'This is really going to confuse everybody!'

We burst out laughing. For a moment it feels like it did when we were all friends.

Nick's mother is the last to leave; she walks away slowly in the opposite direction, not once looking over at us. A man throws dirt into the grave, and it's only then that Nick lets go of our hands and walks closer. Liz and I follow. I glance at her when she's not looking. I'm so amazed she's here. It's only been a few weeks since Aachen, but she looks different, sterner and more stressed. Nick stops a few yards away from the grave and stares in. The man had stopped shovelling the dirt in when he saw us coming.

'What am I supposed to say?' Nick asks.

I have no idea. I've never thought about what you should say to a grave.

'You should forgive him,' a voice behind us says. The three of us turn to see Dom standing there in a black suit. His hands are in his pockets and he's staring directly at Nick. 'It's the only way you can move on. It's the only way any of us can move on . . .'

'I didn't know if you would come,' Nick says.

'I didn't plan to, but . . . I wanted to make sure you were OK. I'm sorry I'm so late.' Dom seems embarrassed but Nick smiles at him.

'Thank you.' He gives us all one last smile before walking down the final part of the hill.

'You should go with him,' Liz says suddenly, and I realize she's talking to Dom. He hesitates and looks at me. I don't know what the right thing to do is, but I do know that Dom really cares for Nick and that's got to help.

'Go,' I say. Dom doesn't hesitate again; he jogs down the hill after Nick. Liz jerks her head at me and I realize she's trying to say we should leave the two of them alone. Silently, we walk up towards the church.

'Thanks for coming . . . I think Nick really appreciated it,' I say to her. 'Did you see it in the newspaper?'

She nods. 'I haven't known Nick that long, but I still consider him a friend . . . I felt that I should come.' She stares at her feet. It's so strange to act this way in front of her, so formal and impersonal.

'Look, I know it's awkward, but—'

'Today isn't about you, Matthew. It isn't about us. It's about Nick . . . I came for Nick.' Her words are harsh, but I accept them. I know her turning up today hasn't changed anything. 'I have missed you, though.'

'I've . . . I've missed you too . . .'

'You know, I think Dom and Nick are made for each other, but the two of them get so caught up in other things . . . in life really, that they just can't . . . see it . . .' She's blushing.

'I think you're right,' I reply, equally embarrassed.

'I'd better go . . . Tell Nick I'm just a call away if he needs me.' Her voice takes on the formal tone it had earlier.

'I will.' I'm about to walk towards Nick and Dom when I realize Liz hasn't finished speaking.

'You were there for me, Matthew . . . When I really needed someone, in Aachen, you were there. I just wanted to be able to do that for someone else. I wanted to do it for Nick.' Her voice is breaking up and I think she might burst into tears.

'You did,' I say simply. She smiles at me, then leaves. Looking after her, I understand something I didn't expect, something that makes everything more painful and complicated. I understand that I'm hopelessly in love with her.

24

Dublin Horse Show

ORLA AND I PUSH AND SHOVE OUR WAY THROUGH THE EVER-growing crowds that have formed in the RDS arena. It's Friday, Nations Cup day, and thousands of people have arrived to watch one of the most highly anticipated showjumping competitions of the year. It's early August now, and the heat has risen to the point where most are hiding in the shade for comfort.

'This is madness!' Orla exclaims, gripping tight on to my arm so that we don't lose each other.

'Yeah, I know . . . I think the crowds are way bigger this year,' I agree, trying to ram my way to the riders' bar.

'No, not that!' Orla corrects me. 'I mean it's crazy how every second person is staring at you. You're a celebrity!'

'Shut up!' I say, giving her a nudge, though I can't hide the smile on my face. We squeeze our way into the riders' bar, but it's fairly packed also, full of all the competitors for the Nations Cup Aga Khan and their family and friends.

'Where's your mum?' Orla asks, as we find ourselves a seat at the bar.

'She's on one of the corporate tables with her friends. She'll be able to watch the Aga Khan from there,' I say, happy she's here but also happy I don't have her stuck with me all day.

'I'm glad you guys are talking again,' Orla says cheerfully, ordering herself a drink and me a glass of water.

'Me too,' I say, and I mean it. 'She still makes the odd snide comment, but I can tell she's really trying.'

'Have you talked to her about Edward?'

I shake my head. 'We're avoiding it. I know we'll have to talk about it at some point, but we're both dreading it.' I notice Orla's concentration fading and turn around to follow her gaze. Stevie has just walked into the bar with a young blonde girl who looks awestruck at her surroundings. The two are holding hands.

'What is he doing with her?' Orla asks bitchily. 'They couldn't be, like, together – she's a child.'

'So is he,' I say, laughing at her jealousy. It's so obvious. 'I thought you were the one who told Stevie that nothing could happen again between the two of you?'

'Yeah, I was, but still . . . just because I don't want to be with him doesn't mean he shouldn't want to be with me,' she says like a grumpy child.

'That's a mature way to look at it,' I reply, laughing, but Orla is barely listening to me.

'I'm going to go say hi,' she says, standing up. I don't bother trying to stop her, knowing I couldn't even if I tried.

I take a sip from my glass, enjoying the cold water in the heat. My jodhpurs feel a little baggy and I wish I'd bought another pair. I've been training and stressing so much about this day I've managed to lose half a stone. I thought I would like being skinnier, but in fact it only makes my hips and shoulder bones look more pronounced and I'm now rather shy whenever I undress in front of Edward. I've punched a few new holes in my belt so I know my jodhpurs won't slip down, but the fear of something embarrassing like that happening is still there. A slightly older man takes the seat that Orla has left empty. I'm about to tell him the seat is taken when he holds his hand out to me.

'Hello, my name is Oscar Gillman, and I'm guessing that you are Elizabeth O'Brien?' I take his hand hesitantly, wondering if I should know who he is.

'I am,' I reply politely.

'It's pleasure to meet you, Elizabeth. I'm a big fan.'

'Thank you,' I say, reddening.

'How are you feeling about today?'

'Nervous, but prepared.' It's the answer I give everyone.

'Brilliant. Well, I'll be rooting for you,' he says, clapping his hands together excitedly. 'Elizabeth, may I ask you, are you being sponsored by anyone at this point?'

'Oh . . . um . . . no,' I answer.

'Great! Well, I run a company that designs and distributes fashionable riding attire and I would love if you could be the face of it?' He sounds eager, but also a little nervous, as if he has no idea how I might react.

'You want to be my sponsor?'

'Well, yes. You see, Elizabeth, you would be perfect for my company – you're young, fashionable and very successful. That's exactly the image I want to portray.'

'What would I have to do?' I ask, more than interested.

'Not much . . . A few ad campaigns, and I'd ask you to wear our clothes while competing – that's about it.' He seems more relaxed now that he sees I'm keen.

'I would love to!'

Oscar laughs. 'Well, look, let's not get into detail today but, now I know you are interested, I'll have my assistant send you a formal offer on Monday.' I can't stop smiling I'm so excited.

Sponsorship means that I'll be paid to compete, that I'll be able to make a living out of showjumping. 'It was nice to meet you, Elizabeth,' he says. 'We'll talk more on Monday. Best of luck today.'

'Thank you,' I say once again. I'm dying to tell Orla.

Then I spot Matthew sitting across the bar with his family, and my spirits droop. He looks nervous, but not as bad as he was in Aachen. Seeing him at the funeral last week was so much harder than I expected. The last few weeks with Edward have been intense, but I really did think I'd done the right thing. But seeing Matthew then and now just makes me question everything.

~

'So, all these people are competitors?' Ann asks, looking around.

'Competitors and friends,' I answer, not really able to concentrate on anything she's saying. My stomach feels like it's on a roller coaster and my mind is going over and over the course we walked earlier. I haven't been sick yet though, so I tell myself that's progress.

'Nick!' Dad calls. He and Dom are walking over. I can tell they're still a little awkward in public. My dad knows Nick's gay – most people figure it out fairly quickly if they know him at all – but wouldn't even think of treating him differently because of it. I'm only now appreciating how great that is. Dom introduces himself to everyone and my family welcomes him politely.

'How you feeling?' Dad asks Nick, patting him hard on the back.

'I'm fine. I'm only a reserve, so I've nothing to be too nervous about.'

'Still, that's some accomplishment, to be chosen as reserve. You should be very proud.' I smile gratefully at him. I told my family that Nick's dad had died last week and that the two weren't on great terms, but I didn't tell them any more than that.

'Thanks,' says Nick, and the conversation begins to flow.

Nick hasn't been quite himself the last week, but in the light of everything that's happened he's been coping really well. I think Shane's intensive training has been helping – in the last week, Nick and I've been too busy to think about anything else: something I've been glad of, because, if I think, I think of Liz. Dom has stayed most nights in the last week and I know something more serious is going on between them. But I don't ask Nick about it; he needs time to sort things out in his head, to start feeling like himself again. I just have to hope that Dom is giving him that time too.

Our group conversation is broken by the arrival of Taidgh. He looks flustered and stressed. I'm about to introduce him to my family, but he talks over me.

'Nick, Matt, I need to talk to both of you now. Sorry, everyone.' He turns around without another word and Nick and I rush after him. Taidgh runs to the far side of the bar, then stops.

'Where's Elizabeth? I swear I saw her here a moment ago.' I look around but I can't spot her either. 'Oh, never mind, I'll tell her later . . . OK, so we have had some unfortunate complications this morning.' Taidgh tries to sound calm but I'm getting more anxious by the second. 'Edward's horse, Minnie, colicked this morning. She's going to be fine but, obviously, she can't compete today. So, Nick, you're going to have to step in. Ben's already agreed to it and Shane assures me that you've been preparing for this, so I have no doubt that you'll do great.'

The colour drains from Nick's face. I know exactly how he feels: it's the feeling I had before I jumped in Aachen, the feeling I have today even, that I'm in way over my head.

'OK . . .'

'Now, I know Edward dropping out is unexpected, but that's why I selected you as a reserve – in case something like this happened. I'm going to rearrange the running order of the team. Edward was due to jump last, but I now want Elizabeth to jump last. Ben will be first, like always; Nick, you'll jump second; and Matt, you'll be third. That OK with everyone?' Nick forces himself to nod.

'Great.' Taidgh is already walking away. 'I'd better go and find the others. I'll see you guys later.'

'I can't believe I'm jumping!' says Nick.

'Are you OK with it?'

'Are you kidding me? I'm jumping for Ireland. I'm fucking great!' He's grinning from ear to ear and, for the first time all week, he seems like himself.

'Matt' – Nick points at me dramatically – 'you and I are going to win this fucking thing!'

'Yeah! Yeah, we fucking are!'

~

I can hear Edward screaming before I see him. I'd been sitting in the bar, still gobsmacked by Oscar's offer, when I received his text: 'Please come to the stables now!'

Even compared to most of his texts, this one is pretty blunt; I could tell that something had gone terribly wrong. Before a competition like this, he can be snappy and a bit grouchy but, at the same time, he is always calm and prepared. Now, he is definitely not calm.

'This is bloody ridiculous! You're going to replace me with some amateur?'

'Your horse is unable to compete!' Taidgh is clearly at the end of his tether.

'I have numerous Grand Prix horses sitting at home. One of my grooms could have one here in less than thirty minutes . . .'

As I round the corner, I see the men are standing dangerously close to each other.

'None of your horses have competed at this level. Gambler has. Nick is jumping in your place – that is my decision.' Taidgh is more aggressive than I have ever seen him and I'm starting to think I should go when Edward sees me.

'Elizabeth!' he says, ushering me over. He turns his attention back to Taidgh. 'I can overrule you if the team doesn't agree, right?' Taidgh says nothing, but purses his lips. 'Elizabeth, don't you agree that this is a ridiculous idea?' Edward squeezes my shoulder a bit harder than I would like him to.

'It doesn't matter what Elizabeth thinks. Ben, Matt and Nick have all already agreed, so you're outnumbered. Elizabeth, the competition starts in hour. I'll see you then.' Edward gives Taidgh daggers as he walks away.

'This is crazy!' He doesn't even wait until Taidgh is out of earshot.

'What's happened, Edward?'

'Minnie's colicked. She's in the equine hospital now. Vet said she'll be fine, but she can't bloody compete!' He's pacing back and forth. 'Maybe I should go to the organizers, complain that Taidgh is unfit to make this decision . . .' I'm not really listening. I just think of poor Minnie. That mare is so sensitive; she won't like vets poking and prodding at her.

'There's always next year,' I say, trying to help, but it only seems to make Edward worse.

'Next year? *Next year?* Elizabeth, do you realize that I have been on the Irish Aga Khan team for the last five years running? I'm not breaking that record now.' He practically spits the words out at me and I stand there in silence, not sure how to take them.

'Everything OK?' a voice asks. Edward and I turn around to see a dark woman in a beautiful cream dress and a matching wide-brimmed cream hat. I look at Edward. His expression has changed completely: he almost looks afraid.

'It's fine,' he says, his voice muted. As the woman gets closer, she looks vaguely familiar, but I can't work out how I know her.

'Are you sure? Some people are saying you're not jumping today.' Her voice is patronizing, and I wonder why Edward doesn't snap at her, like he just did with me.

'I'm getting it sorted,' he says, looking right at her and ignoring me.

'I do hope so. I was so looking forward to seeing you compete.' She smiles brightly and suddenly I know exactly who it is. My stomach drops to my knees and I break out in a sweat. It's Katherine.

'Excuse me,' I say, and try to walk away, but she turns after me.

'I'm so sorry – I interrupted you two,' she says, beaming from ear to ear. 'I don't think we've met before. I'm Katherine.' I can smell Chanel no. 5.

'Elizabeth,' I mumble, unable to look her in the eye.

'Oh, Elizabeth. Edward has told me all about you – it's lovely finally to meet you.'

'You too,' I say. I'm terrified of saying the wrong thing. I glance at Edward. He looks frozen to the spot.

'I need to talk to Taidgh,' he mutters, and dashes off. Katherine and I watch him go. The magnitude of what Edward and I are doing strikes me with full force. I'm destroying this woman's marriage. I'm the home-wrecker, the whore. She's the innocent woman who's trying to reconnect with her husband, and I'm the slut who keeps getting in the way. What have I been doing? What is wrong with me? Standing here with her is too much, I can't cope with it.

'Excuse me, I really must go,' I say. I rush off and find the nearest ladies' and am violently ill.

I'm not quite sure how long I'm in there, but my stomach now feels empty. I do my best to pull myself together, telling myself that Edward will fix things, Edward will fix everything. I nearly fall over when I open the loo door to see Katherine standing there, as calm and composed as earlier.

'Hi,' I splutter.

'Hello, Elizabeth. Are you OK?'

'I'm fine . . . just nervous . . . about the competition.' I walk over to the sink and start washing my hands. Katherine reapplies her already perfect make-up.

'I can imagine . . . I'm devastated Edward can't jump. I know how important all this is to him.' I nod. I can't speak. I'm about to leave when Katherine stops me.

'Stay for a moment, would you?' she asks. She's courteous, and I stop, wondering where she could be going with this. She takes her time finishing her make-up and, once she has put it away neatly in her designer handbag, she turns and looks directly at me. 'Elizabeth, how long *exactly* have you been having an affair with my husband?'

The moment feels so surreal and I'm so shaken it's as if she has slapped me in the face.

'I'm sorry?' I say, wishing I could dive for the door.

'I've been suspicious for a while. He talks about you a lot and I knew you were pretty from seeing your picture in magazines, but I wasn't sure until today . . . until I saw the guilt in your eyes . . . You two *are* having an affair, aren't you?' She talks so calmly you'd swear we were discussing the weather.

'Yes,' I answer. I know there's no point in lying. 'He's in love with me.'

'Is that what he told you?' Katherine asks, her smile faltering.
'Yes.'

'God, you're only a child.' She doesn't say this in a harsh way; her voice is sad and full of sympathy. I think these words hit me harder than anything else. She takes a moment before continuing. 'Edward is nothing more than a scared boy. He's afraid of growing old, and he will do absolutely anything to avoid facing that. You're nothing more than a distraction, Elizabeth, something to make him believe that his life and career are only beginning . . . He's not in love with you.' She places her hand on mine as if to comfort me, but I pull away.

'I don't believe you,' I reply, doing my best to hold back the tears.

'Elizabeth, I don't know what he's told you, but I can guarantee they're all empty promises, promises he has made to other young girls many times before.' For a moment I think she's going to cry, but she doesn't. Instead, she waits patiently to see what I'm going to say.

'If that's true,' I say hesitantly, 'why do you stay with him?' Katherine takes a deep breath before answering.

'Now, because I'm pregnant.'

~

The competition is due to start in twenty minutes and the sun is blazing down on all of us, causing tempers to fray. Taidgh and Edward won't stop arguing and Nick's confidence is disappearing with every word Edward utters.

'. . . I am this team's only chance of winning today. Take me off the team and it will all go to shit, I can guarantee you that.' He stamps like a spoilt toddler.

'My decision is final. You either support it, or you leave – that's it,' Taidgh says for what must be the hundredth time.

'You're putting a complete amateur in my place and he will *fuck up!*' Edward turns to Nick. 'You have no idea what it's like to canter into that ring and have thousands of Irish fans depending on you, putting pressure on you, expecting you to win for them. It's the most intense thing you will ever experience and you will *fuck* it *up!*'

'Our team has already decided,' Taidgh insists.

'I want Nick to jump,' Ben says smugly, obviously enjoying the fact that Edward is now the one in the dog house.

'Nick's going to be great,' I chime in, wishing that Edward would just leave.

'Oh, for God's sake. They're both idiots . . .'

I see Liz coming towards us at great speed.

'Here's Elizabeth, ask her!' he says. 'She's the only person on this team with any sort of sense.'

Edward turns to Liz, but before he gets the chance to say anything she smacks him hard across the face.

'How could you? How could you lie to me and string me along like that for so long?' She swings for him again, but he dodges her this time.

'Elizabeth, what is wrong with you?' he asks, flabbergasted by her behaviour.

'*You!*' she screams, beginning to cry. 'You manipulated me and made me into someone I hate.'

I stand back, shocked.

'Can we please talk about this later?' Edward says, gripping Liz's shoulders and trying to shush her, but she bats him off.

'She's pregnant, Edward.'

'You and I weren't seeing each other, and for all I know you were fucking Matt!' he says angrily.

I can feel everyone's eyes on me. Part of me desperately wants to step in; the other part doesn't know what to do.

'Admit it − you were never going to leave her,' Liz says accusingly.

'I'm *still* leaving her! I don't give a shit that she's pregnant!'

Liz gapes at him. Even Edward seems shocked at the words that have just come out of his mouth. She shakes her head at him and turns to me.

'I'm sorry,' she says, and sprints off.

Edward goes to follow her, but before he gets the chance I grab him by the collar and hit him as hard as I can. He falls to the ground, and I go for him again, but someone has grabbed my arms and is trying to pull me off him. I don't care that it's broad daylight and that I'm surrounded by people. I just see red and I want to cause as much pain to Edward as possible.

'Stop it, all of you!' I hear Taidgh scream. 'You're supposed to be on the same bloody team!' I realize it's Nick who's holding me back but I fight against him all the same.

'The bastard isn't worth it,' he says, at last managing to drag me away.

I pull away from him and run after Elizabeth.

'The competition starts in fifteen minutes!' Taidgh calls after me, but I no longer care.

I find Liz hiding under a small archway that was built to help support the stands. The sun's heat hasn't reached this hidden place yet and it's quiet except for the sounds of spectators far above. She's sitting on the ground and crying quietly, her head bowed. I sit down next to her. I don't say anything for a moment. She knows I'm here, but it's a few seconds before she can speak.

'I'm so sorry, Matthew.'

'For what?'

'For not picking you. I should've picked you.' She takes a few deep breaths. Slowly, she seems to be calming herself down.

'Why *didn't* you pick me?' I ask, needing to know.

'Because I was afraid Edward would take Wildfire away,' she says, looking me straight in the eye.

'What?'

'Edward owns Wildfire, and I knew that if I left him for

324

somebody else he would take her away, and I couldn't stand the idea of losing her . . . I kept trying to convince myself that I was staying because I loved Edward, but I don't. I was just afraid he would take away everything I've worked so hard to achieve, because he can . . . But I don't love him, I love you. I want to be with *you*.'

Before I have time to digest any of this, she kisses me. I don't pull away, because, even though this is so confusing and there's so much to take in, it's what I have desperately wanted for so long. I don't know how long we kiss, but it's not like any other kiss we've had before. It's full of need for one another. Eventually, she draws away.

'I've fucked up, Matt, I know I have, but I was so afraid of losing my dream. And now I know I'm so much more afraid of losing you.' Our faces are so close. 'Can you forgive me? Can you give me a second chance?'

'I couldn't say no if I wanted to.' I laugh. 'I love you, Liz, and I will give you a million chances if it means I get just one chance with you.'

She giggles, and I wipe away her last tears. I kiss her again, but this time it's less urgent. We take our time and enjoy each other. At last I pull away, knowing that the two of us have to face reality.

'Come on,' I say, standing up and offering my hand. 'We have an Aga Khan to win.'

~

'Where the fuck have you guys been?' Nick exclaims, seeing the two of us walking back towards the warm-up.

'Where's everyone else?' Matthew asks, ignoring Nick's question. I've managed to clean myself up as best I can. I'm embarrassed that I lost it in front of everyone, but when I look up at Matthew, I find it hard to care about anything else. I keep thinking: he loves me, he really loves me.

'Taidgh is looking for you two, Ben is about to jump, and Edward left after you decked him,' says Nick.

'You hit Edward?' I ask Matthew, shocked. He shrugs.

'I lost my temper . . .' He looks sheepish, and I can't help but smile at him.

'I think Edward's pride is bruised more than anything,' Nick says, a little calmer now that we're here and he knows that everything is OK. 'So what's going—'

Taidgh booms, 'Where the fuck have you two been?' He gives Matthew and me absolute death stares and I freeze inside.

'Matt, if you ever lay a finger on another competitor again I will personally make sure you never jump for Ireland for the rest of your career. Do you understand?' Matthew goes pale but nods. 'Good, now go get Cedric and Gambler; Ben has jumped clear, thank God. I never expected *him* to be the professional one on this team.' Matthew and Nick go off and do as they're told, leaving me alone with Taidgh.

'Taidgh, I'm so sorry—'

He holds up his hand. 'Elizabeth, I don't know what your relationship with Matthew or Edward is and I don't care. But when it starts dividing my team, that's when it becomes a problem.' I don't say anything because I know Taidgh doesn't want me to. 'I put you in the final jumping position because I thought you were professional and that you could handle the pressure. Right now, Elizabeth, I'm regretting my decision.'

'Don't,' I say, doing my best not to let my voice shake. 'I'll jump a great round for you today. I promise.'

'I hope so,' he says, and walks away.

I make it to the competition ring just in time to see Nick jump Gambler. The horse is fresh and unnerved by the massive crowds cheering when he enters the ring. To make matters worse, Nick is announced as Edward and the mistake is corrected only after numerous people scream up to the judge's box. Nick looks terrified and I can see that his nerves are getting to him as he canters into the first fence far too slow. Gambler does his best to jump, but he can't help but kick out the top two poles. Nick pulls Gambler to a halt, gives his neck a pat then starts for the second fence; he rides with much more confidence this time and clears the fence easily. The rest of his round is pure perfection and he leaves the ring with four faults and two time faults.

'That was amazing!' I exclaim when he comes barrelling out of the ring.

'I'm sorry about the first fence,' he says, cringing a little.

'Who cares about that?' I say, waving my hand, but I know that now Nick has had faults, the pressure is on Matthew and me to go clear. Nick runs to put Gambler in his stable and makes it back in time to see Matthew jump. For once, Matthew is not as white as a sheet. In fact, he looks positively perky and pops around the course with ease, making it look as if it's the simplest thing in the world. He finishes the round with a clear and I want to run over and congratulate him, but I don't have time: I need to get Wildfire warmed up.

Wildfire dances on the spot and I try to relax her. What with the heat, the crowds and my nerves, she knows today is important. I canter into the ring, aware that Matthew, Nick, Ben and Taidgh are all cheering me on. The noise of the crowd is like nothing I've ever experienced before. It was loud in Aachen, but this is at a whole new level. Showjumping is something that has never made me nervous, but here in this ring in Dublin, jumping for Ireland and knowing that, for my team, I need to go clear, I'm nervous.

Like a true partner, Wildfire gives me a little pull as if to say, This is no bother to us. I kick her on confidently and we soar around the course, her legs going higher and higher over each fence. I almost don't believe it when it's announced that I've jumped clear. The crowd explodes and Wildfire leaves the ring bucking for joy. On our way out, there's only one person I'm looking for. Taidgh stares up at me from the ground and says, 'One down, one to go.'

The course is riding well, and there are numerous riders who manage to pull off a clear, but Ireland, with Nick's score discarded, is the only country so far standing on zero faults, which means if we get three clear rounds in the second phase, we won't need to jump off, we'll win it clean. But Germany is right behind us, sitting on four faults, so there can be no mistakes.

Ben goes in first, annoyingly arrogant and confident as always, but he's too relaxed coming to the long water and has a foot in it. Christoph on the German team doesn't make the same mistake and comes out with a perfect clear. This means even more pressure on Nick, Matthew and me. If any one of us makes a mistake, we could lose this whole thing. Nick doesn't hesitate going into the first fence this time but instead canters around the course, confident that he's done it once now, he can do it again. Shane whoops when he goes clear, a sound I never expected to hear from him. Nick takes off his hat dramatically and throws it into the crowd when he crosses the finish line. Always the showman, I think to myself.

Matthew and Cedric start off their round as beautifully as always but, as he turns for the final distance, Cedric's back legs slip and he and Matthew stumble and almost fall to the ground. I can see in Matthew's face that he wants to pull up, comfort Cedric, circle and then attempt the final combination, but if he does that it will be four faults for our team and we'll lose our winning position. So, instead, Matthew picks Cedric up from the ground and kicks on. The horse is unbalanced but he makes a huge effort to jump the final two fences. Cedric hits both fences hard but by some sort of luck they manage to stay in their cups, leaving Matthew with zero faults. As he leaves the ring he hugs Cedric's neck as tightly as he can.

'Thank you,' I can see him mouth to the horse. 'Thank you.'

Then it's all down to me. If I go clear, there'll be no jump-off: we'll win. Ireland will win in Dublin Horse Show's most competitive and nerve-racking event. I know Taidgh is saying something to me, but I can't hear him; my ears are buzzing and everything is muffled. As I wait to go into the ring, I lean down to Wildfire.

'This is probably the last time you and I will compete together,' I say to her, trying to keep the tears from coming. 'Edward won't let me near you after all this is over, and . . . I don't think there is anything I can do to stop him . . .' Wildfire pricks up her ears, listening to my every word. It's as if she understands the importance of what I'm saying. 'But while we still have this one last round to jump, let's show everyone how great you are.' Wildfire pulls me forward into the ring and I'm met with the deafening cheers of the Irish crowd one last time.

~

Liz approaches the first fence at a strong pace and Wildfire leaps into the air like a young stag.

'She's jumping great,' Nick says, watching with fear and antici-pation, just like I am. Wildfire jumps bigger and better than I've ever seen her go before. She not only clears the fences easily, she leaves buckets of room between herself and each fence.

'Some jump,' I mutter to myself.

The crowd jumps every fence with Liz – in fact, it feels like everyone watching is too afraid to breathe until Wildfire and Liz have finished. The pair approach the last combination and I can't stop myself lifting my leg over each fence with Liz, will-ing Wildfire to keep jumping higher.

When Liz canters through that finish line, noise erupts all around. It doesn't even sound like cheers any more but like some sort of explosion. Taidgh is jumping up and down like a madman and Shane is swinging his crutches around dangerously, but no one cares: Ireland has won.

The press surround us instantly, wanting to get our first reactions. Ben stays cool but he can't hide the smile on his face, and Nick is near tears. I grab him in a bear hug. Reporters converge on Liz the second she leaves the arena.

'Elizabeth, you have just won the Aga Khan. How do you feel?' But Elizabeth doesn't answer any of them; she doesn't even acknowledge them. She leaps off Wildfire and runs over to me.

'Well d—' I start, but I don't get the chance to finish because she grabs my face and kisses me with full force. I hear the gasps of shock around us and then the many clicks of many cameras.

'About fucking time!' Nick screams at the top of his voice, and we laugh and pull away from each other.

'So I guess we're not keeping this a secret?' I ask, gesturing to the cameras around us.

'I guess not,' Liz replies, lost in laughter.

The prize-giving passes in a blur of excitement, cheering and champagne – a lot of champagne. It doesn't take long to get our horses settled in for the night, as they're exhausted and happy to be left alone with their food and bed. It's afterwards that we meet in the champagne bar, none of us bothering to change out of our showjumping gear. We're all hot, sticky and dirty, but none of us cares. My family joins us shortly and they grab Nick and me in hugs and kisses. My mum now dotes on Nick like he's one of her own.

'You were terrific, absolutely terrific,' she says, squeezing

Nick's shoulders like he's just won some football competition at school.

Ann leans in to me and says sneakily, 'There was free champagne in the riders' stand. Mum and Dad are locked.' I look at them and I see she's right. My mum is giggling girlishly and my dad is darting about like a maniac.

'Now, I haven't had the chance to meet this beautiful girl,' Dad announces, wrapping his arm around Liz and winking at me. I can feel my face going red but Liz laughs.

'I'm Elizabeth,' she says sweetly.

'Well, it's lovely to meet you, Elizabeth. And well done on your performance today. In fact, you all did brilliant.' Nick hands me another glass of champagne as everyone finds themselves a seat.

'I like your parents drunk,' he whispers in my ear. 'We'd better catch up.'

It's not long before Dom, Orla, Stevie and various other friends and colleagues join the celebrations. With the drink flowing freely, everyone is in high spirits. I've never seen Shane properly drunk before and, now that he is, he can't seem to keep his hands off Justine; the two are acting like teenagers. Orla and Stevie seem to be talking only to each other; Ben is nibbling some blonde groom's ear; and even though Nick and Dom aren't being quite as obvious as the others, I catch them holding hands under the table. I wrap my arm around Liz and keep it there for the rest of the evening, too intoxicated and happy to care what anyone thinks. She cuddles into me happily. The only time she pulls away is when an older blonde woman appears by her side.

'Mum!' she announces, surprised and a bit flustered.

'Hello, darling,' she says warmly to Liz. She ignores the rest of us. 'I just wanted to say *well done*. You were *great*.'

'Thanks,' Liz says, still knocked for six. 'Would you like to join us?'

'Oh no. I have dinner plans with the girls in the Four Seasons, but thank you for the offer . . . You were *wonderful* today, Elizabeth. I'm so proud.' She seems a little uncomfortable as she says the last bit, but still it makes Liz smile.

'Thanks, Mum.' She gives me a bit of a stern stare as she leaves and I wonder did she see us kiss after Liz had finished jumping.

'So that's your mum? She seems nice.'

'She's trying,' Liz says happily. 'She's really trying.'

The two of us turn our attention back to the group. It seems that Taidgh has now taken centre stage.

'Winning today was pure skill by everyone,' he says proudly. 'And to do it without a jump-off was even better, because facing Christoph in a jump-off is no easy thing.'

'That's true enough, but how does he do it?' Nick asks, slurring a little. 'Like, he's pretty unbeatable in a speed round.'

'Talented,' Taidgh says simply.

'Years of training,' chimes in Shane.

'He couldn't be cheating?' Orla asks innocently.

'He wouldn't do that, would he?' I ask, but Dom is shaking his head.

'He doesn't cheat. One of his grooms told me that all his horses were dope-tested in Aachen after they won. They didn't find a thing.'

'I told all of you, it's talent!' Taidgh shouts, rather drunk himself now. 'But he wasn't talented enough to beat us today.'

It's quite late by the time everyone starts to disperse. Ben's blonde groom disappears unexpectedly and he starts eyeing up Ann. At this point I suggest that my parents get a taxi, and I'm relieved when they agree. Orla and Stevie snuck out earlier without a word and Justine had to practically drag Shane into a taxi: it seems we got a taster of what the wild Shane is like. Nick makes up some excuse about needing to check on his horse and it's no surprise when Dom offers to go with him. I'm not going back to our lorry tonight, I think to myself. Soon it's only Taidgh, Liz and myself left, and I try to think of an excuse to leave, but Taidgh beats me to the punch.

'Would you two just go off and be together already. I know you're dying to.'

'Thanks,' I say, and we stand up to leave.

'No problem. Now go and have some fun. You two deserve it.'

Liz is virtually dancing as we walk along under the warm night sky.

'You're full of energy,' I say.

'I'm happy,' she replies, giving me a quiet peck on the lips that leaves me wanting so much more. As I grab her waist to dance with her, I notice her pocket is vibrating.

'Your phone is ringing,' I say, surprised she hasn't noticed it herself.

'I know. It's Edward.'

'What does he want?' I ask, not even trying to hide the bitterness in my voice.

'Wildfire . . . He says he's going to take her tomorrow and then sell her.'

I'm surprised at how casual she sounds when she says this. 'Liz, I'm so sorry . . .' I say, desperately trying to think of something to do or say that could help.

'I'm not,' she says cheekily. 'He's not getting her.' I stare at her. She's not telling me something.

'What's going on?'

'Edward might make around ninety thousand or maybe a hundred thousand out of selling Wildfire, but I know for a fact that he makes about a million a year through competitions and sponsorships . . . so what would he do if he couldn't compete at all for five years? It would be a major loss, right?' Liz says, teasing me.

'Yeah . . . but why wouldn't he compete for five years?'

'Five years is the standard ban from FEI if you're caught doping your horse.' I stop mid-walk when she says this.

'Edward dopes his horse?' I ask, astounded. Liz looks slightly sheepish for a moment.

'I've known for a while and I've wanted to reveal him for the cheat he is but I couldn't see a way of doing it without losing Wildfire. But when Dom said that thing about Christoph and how all his horses were dope-tested in Aachen, I realized this is exactly how I'm not going to lose Wildfire . . . So, tomorrow, when Edward comes to get Wildfire, I'm going to ask him to sell me her for exactly a thousand euro. If he doesn't take it, I'll threaten to report him to FEI . . . Edward is angry at me, but he won't be willing to ruin his career just to get back at me.'

'But won't that mean he'll still get away with the doping?' I ask, hating the idea of Edward being a cheat.

'I have to get Wildfire back, no matter what . . .' Liz says, brutally honest. 'But if he does agree to sell her to me, there's no reason why an anonymous tipster can't come forward about the doping in a few months from now.' Liz gives me a wink and I can't help but feel relieved.

'So you're not losing Wildfire!' I say, thrilled for her.

'I'm not losing her,' she says and then looks up at me nervously, 'and I'm not losing you?' Instantly I lean down and kiss her.

'No, you're not losing me.'

We take our time walking to Liz's lorry, enjoying each other's company. Even though it's late, I'm buzzing with energy. When we reach the lorry, I don't say anything. Instead I lean in and kiss her. Our kiss is hungry and passionate and I push her body up against the side of the lorry so that she's pinned under me. The more I kiss her, the more my need for her grows and I desperately want more. Eventually I move away. Our breath is heavy and ragged.

'Today has been a long day . . .' I start, my voice deep and panting, '. . . so if you don't want to . . . if you want me to go now, I will. We have all the time in the world to get to know each other. Tonight doesn't have to go any further.' Even as I say the words I'm scolding myself, but I know I can't push her; she needs to want this as much as I do. Liz smiles at me before replying.

'That's very kind and sweet of you, Matthew. But what if I said I can't resist you any longer?'

I don't need any more encouragement. I scoop her up as she breaks into laughter and carry her into the lorry. Once we're inside, we start exactly where we left off.

25

One Year Later

'HAVE YOU HEARD THE SCANDAL?' LIZ SAYS, SLIDING UP NEXT TO me and stealing a chip from my plate.

'Ah, here,' I complain, trying to defend my food, but she shoves my hands away, ignoring my outburst. Nick shoves his half-eaten plate of food towards her and she starts to eat eagerly.

'Thanks, Nick. I'm glad *someone* is a gentleman.'

'I don't share food,' I say. Liz rolls her eyes at me, but smiles when I kiss her forehead. Since Dublin, Nick and I have found ourselves sponsors. I'm sponsored by Fitz Horse Feeds, and Nick got himself a deal with Mills Horseware. We don't have it quite as good as Liz, but, because of our sponsorship, we've been able to pick up some nice horses each and are now both regular contenders on the Grand Prix scene, even though Shane has taken his own horses back. All three of us work out of Shane's yard now, but we pay livery.

Shane's teaching skills are highly in demand. He has an endless list of riders who want to be schooled by him; I guess they think he can get them to Dublin, like he did for us. Whatever the reason, business is booming and Shane's taken on more grooms to replace Nick and me. We've moved out of the bungalow also, and Nick and I rent an apartment about five miles down the road. It's small and a bit grotty, but at least it's our own and we're moving on.

'No bother. What's this scandal then?' Nick asks.

'Ah, I see what you're doing! You're trading food for gossip!'

Nick doesn't even try to defend himself.

'Maybe,' he says in a cutesy voice. 'Go on, Liz, you've started now. You have to tell us.' It doesn't take much convincing for Liz to spill. I've learnt in the last year that she's just as bad a gossip as Nick.

'Do you remember how Owen hooked up with that girl Sarah at the last show?'

'How could I forget?' I say, my mouth still half full of chips. We had all been in Spain a few weeks ago and nearly everyone who had been at the show had seen them getting together. It was very late in the night, in the local bar, and all the competitors were very merry. Owen had Sarah against the wall and she had her legs wrapped around his waist. They were impossible to miss.

'Well, Owen and Sarah started hanging out after that, went on a few dates and all,' Liz continues. 'But it turns out that Owen hooked up with Penelope as well that night, and he's been hanging out with her too . . .'

Nick and I look at each other. Have we missed something?

'That's not that bad. Owen wasn't officially dating either of them, so, really, he didn't do anything wrong,' Nick says – exactly what I'm thinking.

'Oh no,' Liz says, smiling. 'That's not the bad part. The bad part is that when the two girls figured it out they compared the text messages that he'd been sending them, and get this . . . they were exactly the same, word for word.'

'Amateur mistake,' Nick states. 'How did the girls figure it out anyway?'

'He forgot to change the name one time at the start of the text for Penelope—' Liz can no longer hold in her laughter, and Nick laughs too.

'Now that is pretty bad . . . but hysterical,' I admit.

Liz finishes off Nick's chips and I hand her the last of mine, knowing that she'll steal them from me anyway.

'You're whipped,' Nick states as Liz digs into my food.

'Here, she's strong. She'll beat me if I don't do as I'm told!'

Liz digs me in the arm.

'Damn right!' she exclaims. 'Matthew needs to know his place.'

I raise my eyebrows at Nick and he smiles.

'All right, lovebirds, I'm off. I have three more horses to ride before it gets dark. Don't forget, Matt – Billy wants to meet you in Wexford in less than an hour.' Nick taps his watch extravagantly, but I brush him away.

'I know, I know. I'll leave in a minute.' Billy is my main sponsor at Fitz Horse Feeds and he wants to buy me a horse. He claims he's found a great one, but he wants my approval before buying it. Nick almost skips as he walks away.

'He's in a good mood,' Liz says curiously.

'I think he's dating someone. He's out most evenings and he's pretty damn vague about where he's going.'

She pouts. 'I wish him and Dom had worked out. They were so good together.'

'Dom fucked off to America,' I say bitterly, remembering how heartbroken Nick was.

'He couldn't turn down that job!' Liz says in his defence. 'Anyway, Nick was the one who wasn't willing to try long distance.' The two of us have had this argument numerous times and we never settle anything. We've come to the conclusion that it's best just not to talk about it.

'So, how are you getting on today, gorgeous?' I ask, forgetting Nick and Dom. I wrap my arm around Liz and she nestles into me.

'Not bad at all. Wildfire was really good this morning, and I'm looking forward to the show this weekend. I'm knackered, though – Orla and Stevie were so loud last night.'

'Arguing or having sex?' I ask.

'First one and then the other,' Liz replies, a hint of annoyance in her voice. 'Look, I really like Stevie and I know the two of them are in love and all, but must they be so dramatic about it?'

'Well, you know, sometimes it's hard to avoid the dramatics,' I say, thinking of the many fights and make-ups we've had over the past year.

'True. At least I'm staying with you tonight.' She leans in and kisses me properly.

'You're not going to get any sleep with me,' I say suggestively, squeezing her hip and making her giggle.

'Well, when you keep me awake, it's different.' She kisses me for a moment but pulls away quickly, leaving me wanting more. After a year, I still can't get enough of her.

'I presume you heard about Edward?' I ask, on a less casual note.

'Yeah, I read it in the *Irish Field* this morning. Two-year ban for doping his horse. At least no one knows it was me who tipped them off...' There's always a hint of anger in Liz's voice when she talks about Edward. Her plan to keep Wildfire worked, but not without a serious fight from Edward. He had showed his true colours that day and called Liz a slut and a gold-digger. I'm glad I wasn't the one who destroyed the relationship between them; Edward did that all on his own. After Liz legally owned Wildfire, she went to FEI anonymously to tell them what Edward had been up to, but it hadn't been as easy to catch Edward out as we all thought. FEI had been hesitant to accuse Edward, one of Irish showjumping's best-known names, of cheating without any evidence. It was almost as if they were afraid Edward's guilt would damage the sport. But Liz had put doubt in the FEI committee's minds and eventually after months of indecisiveness they tested Edward's horses. But it didn't end there, even when Edward was caught red-handed, months of trials and appeals followed, Edward fighting his corner every step of the way. But now, a year later, it finally looked like he was going to pay the price.

'Sure, it's his own fault, the twat . . .' I agree.

When I heard about Edward's ban I felt no sympathy for him at all. He's a liar and a cheat and he got what was coming to him. I can't help but feel relieved that Liz feels the same.

'At least it means we'll have less competition.'

'Very true,' Liz agrees, smiling, and obviously not wanting to talk about it any more. 'You'd better go, you're going to be late for Billy.' I kiss her quickly before standing up.

'I'll pick you up at seven tonight. I have dinner booked in town.'

'Ooh, very fancy. See you later!'

As I set off for Wexford, I think about the last year. It would be easy to say that Liz and I have been nothing but perfect since Dublin, but that would be a lie. We haven't faced anything nearly as intense as what we had to deal with there, but we do still argue every now and again. But, with her, I'm happier and more content than I have ever been. Neither of us is afraid to say how we feel, and it does cause us to bicker like an old married couple, but it also means that I know she's never lying to me and she's always telling me what's going on with her.

I took Liz to see my family about a week after Dublin Horse Show. My dad smiled and I knew he would tease me relentlessly as soon as he got me alone. My mum was wary of her, but I'd expected that. Liz grew up very differently from the way I did and I sometimes worry that people can't see past her money. But Liz's charms eventually wore Mum down. Ann and she instantly hit it off; I didn't expect them to get on so well at all. I was worried that Ann might resent Liz a little because I spend so much time with her, but by the end of the dinner the two were inseparable. They even made plans to go shopping together. Now they talk to each other practically every week.

Liz and I are still learning how to be with each other. It's not easy and it's overwhelmingly frustrating at times, but when we do get it right, it's more than worth it. Liz still doesn't see much of her father – work seems to keep him away, but she is growing closer to her mother as time goes on. Barbara is still harsh towards her sometimes but I can tell that she's trying hard to watch what she says. I know Barbara doesn't like the idea of Liz dating another rider but, with every interaction I have with her, I think she's beginning to like me more. Time is all I need to prove that I'm the right person for Liz.

I pass the outdoor arena, driving out of Shane's yard, and spot Linda exercising her horse. She gives me a half-hearted smile before continuing her work. Last week she filed for divorce. I don't know how it got out, but it seems that everyone knows. The finer details of why they're breaking up changes depending on who you ask. Some people say she walked in on Roger sleeping with a twenty-year-old; others say she spotted him kissing a fellow co-worker on the street. I have no idea what the truth is and I daren't ask Linda herself, but it seems that he cheated on her and now their marriage is over. Linda has been up in the yard every afternoon after work the past week; it's obvious she's avoiding home. Roger hasn't come up at all in that time and there're rumours going about that he's now planning on selling his horse.

As I watch Linda work away I wonder if I should've said something all that time ago. Would it have made things any better? I don't know. But I'm relieved to see that her marriage breaking up doesn't seem to have destroyed her. She's still the kind, happy person I've got to know over the years. Roger is a dirtbag, and part of me wishes he would come up to Shane's yard just one last time so I could give him the punch he has deserved for so long.

I somehow arrive in Wexford on time and spot Billy waving me over to an outdoor arena. Billy looks slick in his white linen shirt and Ray-Ban sunglasses. I shake his hand politely but my attention has been hijacked by a massive black horse standing in front of me. A young lad with various cuts and bruises holds him and I begin to wonder how he got all those injuries.

'So, this is Satan,' Billy says excitedly.

'He's a monster!'

'He's 17.2 hands, but he's a complete gentleman,' the young lad says, patting the horse's neck.

'How'd he get the name?' I ask, dreading the thought of sitting on this thing.

'It's just a joke,' Billy assures me. 'You ready to get up?' He's dead serious, so I make my way over to the black monster.

Normally, I can hop up on any horse from the ground but Satan is so tall I need to stand on a block. But once I'm on him, I'm pleasantly surprised to discover that he *is* a gentleman. His trot is as light as air and his mouth is as soft as cotton wool. I ask Billy to put a fence up and Satan steps over it like it's a pole on the ground. Billy continues to put up fences, to a massive 1 metre 60 spread, and Satan makes it feel like it's nothing.

'I love him!'

'I knew you would,' Billy says smugly, proud that he was the one to find him.

'God, you really can't judge a book by its cover, can you? Looking at him, I thought he would be a monster, but he's as gentle as a lamb.'

'I think he might be good enough for you to ride him in the Dublin Aga Khan next year,' Billy says, already excited about it.

'You might be right. Taidgh always loves an underdog,' I say, unable to hide my own excitement.

'We should take his owner out to dinner tonight, get him a bit sloshed before we offer him a price,' Billy says, snapping into business mode.

'Good idea, but I can't do tonight. How about tomorrow?'

'Come on, Matt, this is important. I want to get the deal done on this horse quickly before anyone else realizes how good he is.'

'I agree, but I can't tonight. I'm proposing to my girlfriend.'

Billy breaks into a smile.

'You're proposing?'

I nod, enjoying being able to say it aloud. I haven't told anyone my plans yet, not even Nick. 'Yeah,' I say, loving the sound of it.

'Do you think she'll say yes?' Billy teases.

I smile. 'I don't know . . . but what's life without a few risks?'

Acknowledgements

First and foremost I would like to thank my literary agent and friend Marianne Gunn O'Connor. She's an incredibly inspiring and kind person and without her this story would never have been told. Thank you for always believing in me.

I'd like to thank everyone at Transworld Publishers, especially Cat Cobain, Sophie Wilson and Harriet Bourton who have all been so important in developing this story and I have truly enjoyed working with them all.

My family has been incredibly supportive of my writing career from day one and I feel extremely lucky to have them. Especially my older sister Lucy, who is my partner in crime in the Irish showjumping scene. Without them, I wouldn't have had the chance to have so many amazing experiences.

A special thanks to my close friends Miriam, Aoife and Feidhlim who were all great listeners, when things were going well and when things were going badly. They gave me invaluable advice throughout the whole conception of this story. I owe all of you drinks!

Finally, massive thanks to Showjumping Association Ireland, Cavan Equestrian Centre, Coilog Equestrian Centre, Millstreet Horse Show, Dublin Horse Show and the many more showjumping establishments in Ireland. Showjumping is such a huge and exciting part of my life and I'm thrilled to share this important and thrilling world with as many people as I can.

About the author

Emily Gillmor Murphy was born in 1990, in County Dublin, Ireland. Her first novel, *You and I*, was published in 2012 by Transworld Ireland. Also in 2012 she graduated with honours from her Arts Degree at University College Dublin, majoring in English and History. In 2013 she graduated from Trinity College Dublin with a masters in Fine Art. As a child she struggled with dyslexia but now has a great love for writing and literature. Emily lives in Enniskerry, County Wicklow, with her family. Emily loves animals and has an extended family of multiple dogs, cats and horses. She is also a competitive show-jumper, travelling across the country to events with her older sister, Lucy.